Night Sisters

Other books by Sara Rath

Fiction
Star Lake Saloon and Housekeeping Cottages

§

Poetry
Whatever Happened to Fats Domino

The Cosmic Virgin

Remembering the Wilderness

Dancing with a Cowboy

§

Nonfiction
Easy Going Guide to Madison & Dane County

Pioneer Photographer: Wisconsin's H. H. Bennett

About Cows

The Complete Cow

The Complete Pig

Night Sisters

A Novel

Sara Rath

Sara Rath (signature)

TERRACE BOOKS

A TRADE IMPRINT OF THE UNIVERSITY OF WISCONSIN PRESS

Terrace Books, a trade imprint of the University of Wisconsin Press,
takes its name from the Memorial Union Terrace, located at
the University of Wisconsin–Madison. Since its inception in 1907,
the Wisconsin Union has provided a venue for students, faculty, staff,
and alumni to debate art, music, politics, and the issues of the day.
It is a place where theater, music, drama, literature, dance, outdoor activities,
and major speakers are made available to the campus and the community.
To learn more about the Union, visit www.union.wisc.edu.

Terrace Books
A trade imprint of the University of Wisconsin Press
1930 Monroe Street, 3rd Floor
Madison, Wisconsin 53711-2059

www.wisc.edu/wisconsinpress/

3 Henrietta Street
London WC2E 8LU, England

1   3   5   ·   4   2

Printed in the United States of America

Library of Congress Cataloging-in-Publication Data
Rath, Sara.
Night sisters: a novel / Sara Rath.
      p.   cm.
ISBN 978-0-299-22870-5 (cloth: alk. paper)
  1. Channeling (Spiritualism)—Fiction.
    2. Wisconsin—Fiction.   I. Title.
      PS3568.A718N54   2008
        813′.54—dc22
        2008011970

For Del

The children's voices make their chanted rhyme,
Beautiful with evening and the dusk,
By evensong companioned, the musk
Of lilac leaf, and standing clear
Of where they are, I hear
The child's voice spectral still, I see
Lingering beyond the last, lost tree,
Lingering lost as time, forever,
The lost child and his childhood, never
From the mind's eye gone, moonbright,
Under light of stars, a ghost at night.

Starbright, moonbright,
First star I see tonight,
I wish to see a ghost tonight . . .

August Derleth, "Lost Child"

Part 1

1

"May I come to you?"

I was enrolled in Grace Waverly's beginning workshop called "Personal Development of Mediumship" when Grace taught us to begin delivering a spirit-message by addressing our subject and saying, "May I come to you?" Then we were to close our eyes and rub our hands together as though washing them in invisible water. After a moment or two, Spirit was supposed to speak through us to the person who had drawn our energy.

"In platform work," Grace explained, "we must always ask permission. When the subject has agreed, deliver the message exactly as you hear it. Take yourself completely out of it. Send the message out of your mouth as quickly as you see it, feel it, taste it, or sense it. Thinking about the message or trying to rationalize what you are getting may render it incorrect."

"May I come to you?"

After taking Grace's workshop at the Wocanaga Spiritualist Camp, where we experimented with other intriguing aspects of unfoldment (automatic writing, clairvoyance, reading auras), I rehearsed the permission phrase in my bathroom mirror at home. I tried squinting and zeroing in as I inquired, but that conveyed a seriously scary effect. Then I raised my eyebrows imploringly, which didn't exude much confidence. Finally I adopted Grace's approach, using a kindly smile and a "May I come to *you*?" as if to indicate that by selecting that one person from the crowd seated before me, I was ready to bestow an especially lovely gift.

Grace Waverly said right away that I was *clairsentient*. Some mediums are clairvoyant—they see pictures, visual images that reveal their messages. Some are clairaudient—they hear things. But clairsentience is a kind of thought-language. Clairsentience is soul sensing; a kind of "impressional" mediumship.

Apparently a lot of people receive impressions from the spirit world—artists and writers, musicians, and even doctors—although most of the time they're not aware they're even doing it. As Grace explained it, I'm supposed to be able to sense dangerous events that are about to happen and then take measures to avoid them. Well, it turned out Grace was wrong about that and a whole lot of other things, too.

∽⁊∾

I initially visited Wocanaga with the idea of writing an article for *Meanderings,* a travel magazine that features articles written in first person narrative (the "me" in *me*anderings). My stories naturally focus on areas of Wisconsin, because that's where I was born and I live in Madison. I grew up in a small north-central town called Little Wolf, which, looking back, seems like a fantasy world because we felt so safe. We had a population of one thousand but we had everything we might need—dentist, doctor, drug store, bank, library, dry goods, hardware, groceries. There was no lifeguard at the beach, we fished in the river, took our bikes everywhere, played Kick the Can outside after dark, and no one had to call home to tell their parents where they were.

Wisconsin is widely known as the "dairy state," of course, but we have other things to offer besides cheese and butter. For example, my editor loved the piece I did on Aztalan, a state park near Lake Mills believed to have been a ceremonial center for a vanished race of mound builders that became extinct around 1300 AD. Then I found an Amish farm family near Viroqua and lived with them for a week. I milked cows by hand, helped make bread and raspberry jam, and by lamplight laboriously wrote my story on lined paper.

After I wrote about Ceresco, a utopian settlement near Ripon founded in 1844 by followers of the nineteenth-century French socialist philosopher Charles Fourier, a reader wrote to my editor suggesting that I check out "Spook Hill." That's the name locals give to the Wocanaga Spiritualist Camp near Baraboo. I was surprised to learn that a relic of that curious religion was still thriving. At the entrance gate the welcome sign says those forty acres on a high bluff above the village have offered visitors a healing embrace since 1873.

Most of the Wocanaga Camp buildings *look* like they're over a hundred years old. An air of desolation quietly hovers around the periphery like an encroaching fringe of decay. The chapel, a wood frame auditorium that was once their glorious centerpiece, suffered greatly from a fallen tree. Now its caved-in walls prop up a sagging roof of blue plastic tarp.

Furry moss dapples the shingled roofs of forty-one rustic cabins that wind a vast warped circle through tall pines and ancient oaks. If you're ready to tolerate a few hardships you can rent one of those cabins for only ten dollars a night. Mediums who reside in the cabins during the summer months do private readings, forty dollars for thirty minutes. Séances are offered on Friday nights in Assembly Hall, where you can also witness table-tipping demonstrations and past-life regressions.

For the sake of authenticity, I opted for the whole shebang. My little white cabin with flowerbox (red geraniums) beneath the window and a birdhouse attached in front had a sign by the door that said "Rosebud." For one night it would be okay. The building reminded me of my childhood playhouse. The interior of bare studs and boards was whitewashed to give it a more finished feel. Lace curtains hung on the windows. A small table with two wooden chairs

5

stood against one wall and another lace curtain served as a divider between the main room and the bedroom, which was a step down—both physically and in charm (a framed print of a couple too-cute puppies frolicking with a ball), although everything seemed clean if one ignored the musty smell. I wondered if I'd have the courage to leave the exterior doors open and sleep with only the protection of screens.

I dropped my overnight bag next to the single bed and opened all three windows. A sign over the sink in the bedroom said the water was not safe to drink. I knew the restrooms were in the center of the campgrounds, it would be a long walk in the dark.

The bed sagged in the middle and had an annoying squeak whenever I moved. But the pillow was plump so I rested there for a moment, gathering courage for further explorations that lay ahead.

During my initial fact-finding visit I found the atmosphere of the Wocanaga Camp surprisingly serene. I claimed a picnic table, one of several nestled in a pleasant grove of tall pines, and unpacked a lunch I'd hastily packed before leaving the city.

Nearby, a handful of men and women chatted over coffee.

One woman was saying, "I sort of squint and try to take in the entire field. Usually there's a cloud of blue around the throat."

"That must be the throat chakra," a man added.

"What about silver in the elderly?" another woman wanted to know. "I've heard that's sometimes the case."

"When the red begins to disappear, it turns pink, and then it's almost white. At least that's what I've found."

"Mother Theresa's was white."

"And then it turns to silver, when they get to be seventy, eighty."

Their conversation was baffling. If I had a *throat chakra*, I hoped I'd be able to cough it up.

A voice at my shoulder inquired, "Not going to the service?"

He was young, balding, maybe in his mid-thirties—not much older than my own kids—with a neatly trimmed brown moustache and a closely cropped beard.

"Oh! I'm only visiting . . ."

I noticed the people at the next table were heading toward the building where the sign said "Dining Hall."

"I've heard the speaker before." The man placed his thermos mug of coffee on my table and sat across from me. "Do you mind? Hank Spencer. Everyone calls me Spence."

He was a contractor from Milwaukee, enrolled in a workshop to improve his psychic healing powers. His wife, Barbara, was taking the workshop, too, but she'd already gone indoors. They worked as a healing team.

I told him of my *Meanderings* research to the strains of "Bringing in the Sheaves" issuing from the dining hall. My foot was tapping in time to the tent-meeting tempo.

Sowing in the morning, sowing seeds of kindness . . .

"What's happening over there?"

"You can go inside and find out," he suggested. But I demurred, saying I didn't have time.

We shall come rejoicing, bringing in the sheaves.

"Today's speaker always talks on the same subject. I've heard her lecture before. She says Jesus was our first medium," he explained. "Even if you don't think of Christ as a savior, he's still one of the greatest mediums and healers and teachers that ever lived. Then she delivers messages from Spirit."

I scribbled a few notes. "And how does she do that?"

Spence took a sip of his coffee and patiently explained.

"It's pretty simple, really. All matter is spiritual energy at different rates of vibration. For example, prayer is the sending of thought vibrations to a higher source."

"Okay," I said, nodding, writing as fast as I could.

"When a medium delivers messages from Spirit, she tunes into vibrations from the spirit world when she raises her own vibrations to a higher level. Because their vibrations are higher than ours. At the same time, the spirit who happens to be communicating with her lowers his or her vibrations. So the two can meet somewhere in the middle. Does that make sense? Then the medium communicates the message to those of us who are still on this plane."

I nodded as if this did not sound peculiar to me at all.

"You can always find mediums on the grounds here this time of year," Spence said. "Last night I was given a message at Inspiration Point. That's a spot at the end of the path, a limestone shelf that's sort of an overlook. Grace Waverly always handles those sessions. She's the most famous, and probably the oldest medium we have here at Wocanaga. She lives just outside the gate."

I vaguely wondered if *Meanderings* would cover the cost of a medium's fee. But by then my thoughts were all over the place. I was reminded of my daughter Odessa's unhappy encounter with a carnival palm reader who relieved her of six weeks' allowance. And when I was a kid there had been a Ouija board that a girlfriend dragged from a closet at a birthday party, although we were never able to make it spell anything that wasn't hopelessly garbled . . . much like my teenaged attempts at reading fortunes from a deck of playing cards.

"You really ought to talk to Grace Waverly," Spence offered. "She's the head of the Medium's League, and she can tell you more about Wocanaga and Spiritualism than anyone else I can think of. If you want, she can read your aura and bring you a message, too."

It was research, I rationalized. Totally spontaneous. Serendipitous. Part of the adventure.

New Age philosophers insist there are no accidents and there is no such thing as coincidence. If you remain insightful and aware and trust your intuition, you will synchronistically connect with whatever is meant to be. What the hell.

Besides, for the meager payment I received from *Meanderings,* I doubted that I'd make an effort to drive all the way up there from Madison again. If she resembled her name, Grace would be gentle and understanding, so it was probably worth my while to get a bit of background color. I could ask her about chakras and auras and bringing in the sheaves.

"She doesn't take credit cards," Spence added.

"What for?"

"For her readings."

I didn't really want a reading; all I needed was some quotes. I hadn't come all that way to have my fortune told.

♔

According to the homework I'd done for my Spook Hill story, modern Spiritualism began in the United States in 1849 when two girls in Hydesville, New York, identified knocking sounds in their home as coming from the spirit of a murdered peddler buried in the cellar. They discovered they could communicate with his spirit by tapping out the alphabet. After that, the practice of conversing with spirits spread all the way to Wisconsin and beyond. Here, spirit circles were formed in Milwaukee, Madison, Janesville, Fond du Lac, and Appleton. The Morris Pratt Institute—the only spiritualist college in the nation—originated in Whitewater. Our ex-territorial governor, Nathaniel Tallmadge, was an ardent supporter of Spiritualism as was Lyman Copeland Draper, the secretary of the State Historical Society. Draper said he took up Spiritualism to contact his deceased daughter and to unravel historical mysteries by communicating with Indian fighters and deceased pioneers. One of Spiritualism's most famous "trance speakers," Cora Richmond, began her career in Lake Mills in 1851, at the tender age of eleven.

Wisconsin reputedly had 80,000 spiritualists by 1860.

The Wocanaga Camp opened in 1893 for immigrants who were adherents of Spiritualism. Campers came by railroad and stayed in tents that rented for three dollars per week. More than fifty years later, in July 1949, Madison's *Wisconsin State Journal* sent a reporter out to Wocanaga to observe one of the regular séances:

> Earl H. Williams, a slight young man from East St. Louis, Ill., was levitated without any visible means of support. While Williams was floating through space his "friend," Pansy, a small English girl dead for many years, told the crowd just what was going on. The reporter had watched Williams dress from the skin out to be sure there were no mechanical gadgets concealed on his person. The young medium had been strapped in a chair and placed behind a black curtain.

All the time Pansy was keeping the visitors informed, Williams had his mouth gagged with a rubber sponge and closed with tape.

The reporter drew no conclusions about the séance but allowed that the experience was "very dramatic."

I followed Spence as he walked toward the gate to point out Shadowlawn, Grace Waverly's home. Along the way I noticed some of the cabins had hand-lettered signs in their front windows with the resident medium's name and a note that said "Please Knock," or "Please Wait."

Shadowlawn clung to the crest of the bluff near the gate where I'd entered the campgrounds. Grace's cottage also disclosed signs of neglect: white paint on the exterior clapboards was peeling in large white curls, and a pair of battered pink shutters made gentle tappings in the breeze. In the window of the front door she had placed her own hand-printed notice:

Grace Waverly
The Medium is

and beneath that hung another sign in a little box that said, simply,

IN

Spence wished me well and gave my upper arm a meaningful squeeze before he went on down the hill with an amiable wave.

I was a little apprehensive when the front door opened, but there was a softness to Grace Waverly that made me yearn for a grandmotherly hug. She wore a pink organdy dress with a profusion of purple violets embroidered on her ample bodice. Above a benign smile her white hair was drawn into a gleaming coronet. With one hand she leaned on a cane made of gnarled wood polished to a soft gleam, and in her other hand she held what looked like an old-fashioned ear trumpet made of tin.

"Won't you come inside?"

10

Her voice was pleasant but commanding.

Because of the trumpet I assumed the elderly woman was deaf. "Thank you," I emphasized rather loudly.

After we were seated at her dining room table (lace tablecloth, pebbly milk glass vase embracing a bouquet of sunflowers and colorful zinnias), she did not hold the trumpet to her ear. Instead, she collapsed it inside itself and set it next to her chair.

"What *is* that," I asked.

She smiled. "Exactly what it looks like. It's a trumpet. Made of galvanized tin, as you can see." She handed it over.

"Oh," I said dumbly, pulling it back out again and telescoping it together as if I understood what she was talking about. "What's it for?"

"Trumpets like that were used in the old days of mediumship, to amplify spirit voices," she explained. "They are rarely used now. This one's an antique. Someone came across it in their attic and brought it by this morning. Our historian has several like it. Have you talked with our historian? I think she's home this afternoon."

Grace didn't wait for me to respond, but continued, "We had a medium who practiced trumpet mediumship many years ago. A trumpet exactly like this one would float all the way around the room in complete darkness, untouched by human hands. Levitated by unseen forces. And spirit voices, hushed, like little whispers, emanated from within. The spirit voices were intensified by the trumpet so they could be heard by those among the circle. The ectoplasm forms a kind of artificial larynx, you see."

I didn't see, but I was fascinated and began making notes as fast as I could scribble.

"Oh, it was a remarkable presentation," Grace Waverly assured me, smoothing a wrinkle from the tablecloth in front of her. "The spirit voices of the loved ones were thrown into and out of the trumpet and we were able to speak to them as if they were here on earth."

She was silent for a moment, recalling the good old days. It gave me time to catch up.

"Well, New Age spirituality . . . ," I began, and Grace perked up.

11

"The New Age," she sniffed. "There's nothing new about this so-called New Age. It's just a modern way of presenting old thoughts. Mediumship in the early days was far more evidential than it is today. We used to have psychometry, billet reading, apports, spirit photography, all that sort of thing."

"Billet?" I asked. "How do you spell that?"

"Just as it sounds," she said. "B-I-L-L-E-T. It's a little note. We had one man; he was a blindfold billet reader. Three blindfolds on, and he would wander through the audience and call out the answers to the questions people wrote on their billets. Mediumship like that has faded away. Now the mediums ask, 'Do you have a brother? Do you have a grandmother?' Today somebody gets a chill up their back, goes and hangs out a shingle, and claims they're a medium. But it's not the mediumship of the old days, I can assure you! In those days we had *real* psychic phenomena, and *real* spiritualism. There were visitors here all up and down the paths like a procession. But that kind of mediumship has worn itself out. Like this old trumpet. There's no one left who practices independent voice anymore, either, and that's a shame, too. The days of old-fashioned mediumship will never be seen again. It's truly a pity."

I hoped I could translate my mess of notes and condense Grace Waverly's eccentric information into a cohesive article.

"Well," Grace mused, "I have to admit I was never very adept at trumpet mediumship myself. I did practice *materialism* for a brief period, when I was younger. No more. As a matter of fact, for the past fifty or so years we've been forbidden to practice ectoplasmic séances at Wocanaga or anywhere else! That was the *ultimate,* you know, physical manifestation. It was the rarest and the most difficult of all the phases of mediumship because it involved the instrumentality of the medium plus spirit chemists and guides to assist us."

"And just how did that work?" I asked, feigning a cough to diminish my audacity. For someone who claimed to be a psychic, I thought, Grace seemed sublimely oblivious to my skepticism.

"First, the medium had to attain a deep, deep trance. Then eventually a white, vaporous substance would obliterate the face of the medium and imitate the appearance of the spirit entity with *ecto-plasm*. Once I saw it materialize as a tiny child and then gradually build up so the form was that of a grown woman!"

"And the ectoplasm comes from . . . where?" I asked.

"From the medium's body," she said, gesturing as if rolling the substance out of her bosom with both hands. "It's mostly etherealized protoplasm. But it renders Spirit remarkably visible to all who are present."

"Really?" I replied suddenly, too enthralled to be taking notes.

"Oh, yes! When they use ectoplasm for their manifestation, spirits can even converse, and they respond as actual sentient beings when they are touched."

"That's pretty incredible!"

"It is a wonderful phenomenon," Grace smiled. "It is also a very dangerous procedure, and my husband convinced me to abandon the practice even before it was outlawed. Our historian has photographs of ectoplasmic manifestations taken with a very low light—if you're interested in seeing some examples."

I wrote myself a reminder: *check ectoplasm photos.*

"You see, materialization like that is carried out in complete darkness because the ectoplasm has to be exuded from the living body of the medium and sometimes the sitters," Grace sighed. "I wasn't always very successful at materialization, either. Probably because back then I was slender, like you. Maybe I'd have more success nowadays!" She chuckled amiably.

"Usually the medium who practiced materialization was a stout woman. It was thought their bodies contained a superabundance of ectoplasm to produce the spectacle. And we had to have guards, more big, fleshy women, who were placed around the cabinet where she sat, to prevent disturbances.

"Why were only women involved?"

"I suppose it has to do with the fact that people who use visual perceptions such as these tend to be right-brained," Grace replied. "There happen to be more women mediums than men, because women are more right-brained than men are. It's been proven that spiritual and psychic activities are a function of the right side of the brain."

"And it was dangerous because . . . ?"

"Oh! Because the ectoplasm is only borrowed from the medium for the transfiguration and is obliged to return to her afterward.

"Some claimed the ectoplasm felt like cobwebs, but when I was in a trance I didn't remember what it felt like at all. One time I witnessed the sight of ectoplasm as a milky substance that flowed along the floor after another medium had ceased to use it. Then it was slowly reabsorbed into her body.

"The reason for concern is because if anyone stirs, or if a light is turned on too soon, that threatens to break the ectoplasmic cord or can cause it to recoil too rapidly. It can snap back inside her like a spring. The medium is powerless to protect herself."

"She'd get hurt?"

Grace nodded soberly. "The shock to her nervous system will kill her or at least make her an invalid for life."

"She'll die?"

"We think of it as passing over the threshold onto another plane, but, yes, friends of mine who were mediums were lost that way. It's just one more reason why these marvelous physical phenomena aren't utilized anymore. And it's also why we prefer that only the most serious sitters participate in our séances. A spirit-circle composed of those who are sending out thoughts of doubt is much harder on the mediumistic instrument than a group composed of those who are au fait with it and conveying constructive vibrations."

I made more quick annotations, then asked Grace to forgive my candor.

"I was advised to see you because I am interested in writing about the history of the Wocanaga Camp. And I'd really like to know what it is that mediums do here, and how they do it."

"My goodness, I naturally presumed you wanted a reading," she chuckled. "I must be losing my psychic intuition!"

From a stack of papers on a sideboard, she handed me a brochure with current Wocanaga Spiritualist Camp information. It listed resident mediums and healers with their biographies, the camp schedule, and membership fees.

"You can find more about how our camp was organized and history and so forth from the secretary in the camp office. But *how I learned to be a medium* is another story, Dear; *how I work*."

Grace gave me a charitable smile.

"Let me just say that you either are a medium or you are not. Some believe the best mediums were born that way, and psychic occurrences during their childhoods lead us to believe that such is the case. However, spirit teachers tell us that each and every individual has some latent mediumistic power. It's been my experience that, if you are a medium, you'll know. Sooner or later, you will find out. But Spirit cannot make a medium out of you if you're too lazy to respond!"

Okay. I told Grace I'd like to make an appointment for a reading. Some day.

I fished my appointment book from my handbag and riffled through the pages. I was thinking like, oh, next week? Or the week after that? I could always cancel.

"Is *now* convenient for you?"

I shrugged. "Um . . . I guess. Here? Right now? Okay. Sure."

"I do think *now* would be a good time," Grace laughed, a surprising laugh that was hearty and deep. I couldn't help but grin.

"Breathe deeply a few times. Center yourself. Try to relax," she suggested as she brushed back a wisp of white hair from her forehead and repositioned a hairpin.

"When you relax, it helps me enter your energy field. Close your eyes and envision yourself in a bubble of white light. You might think of it as a white satin cocoon filled with soft white light. Isn't that nice?"

I had my eyes closed and tried to imagine the cocoon.

"You haven't told me your name," Grace suddenly interrupted. "What is your name? Your first name is enough."

"Eleanora. Or Nell. That's what everybody calls me. Nell Grendon. That was my maiden name. Grendon was, I mean."

I thought she might pause, but Grace plunged right into my white space.

"I must tell you I am troubled by what I see, Eleanora," she told me.

Startled, I opened my eyes and found her investigating me with a fervor that was almost hypnotic.

"Let me take your hands in mine."

I reached over the lace tablecloth. My own hands were clammy, but her grasp was warm and dry.

"I am hearing music," Grace said. "Music has always been important to you, hasn't it?"

"Yes . . . ," I hedged.

"This sounds like a merry-go-round. No, like an accordion. Does that have any meaning for you?" Grace loosened her grasp on my hands and, her eyes closed again, tapped a peppy rhythm on the table. Her appearance expressed childlike pleasure as she nodded. "It sounds like a polka. This is jolly music! Yes, a polka. That's quite nice."

"Polka," I said, unamused.

"Someone is telling me that you played the accordion as a child," Grace frowned. "You were embarrassed. You thought it was unfashionable."

More like corny and dumb, I wanted to add, but I didn't. At least with her eyes shut, she could not see me blush. Then her expression became more serious.

"I am now being told by Spirit that you *do* have definite psychic gifts. You have been aware of these gifts since you were a little girl, although you will probably not agree. My source is *quite* insistent," Grace said sharply. "She tells me you have a definite talent but it frightens you. When is your birthday? What sign are you?" she asked, then, "No, don't tell me. You are a water sign!"

"Yes."

"Water signs are often afraid," Grace asserted. "Please. *Relax.*"

How could I relax?

Then she gazed sweetly at me, asking me to forgive her for reaching out if I was not yet ready to hear what she had to say, but she felt I was troubled. She could read that in my aura.

I found myself inexplicably close to tears and tried valiantly to cover my distress. There seemed to be a deep inner sorrow that Grace was touching upon, something I could not disguise.

I dug a Kleenex out of my handbag and blew my nose. Anyone might presume that a person my age, visiting a psychic or a medium or whatever she called herself, might have had marital problems or sorrows of some sort. By claiming I possessed psychic powers myself, well, wouldn't that assure that I'd come back here sometime, maybe enroll in a workshop, request another reading, slip my fifty bucks or whatever she charged (no credit cards!) under the table? This was fraud, pure and simple.

"I am getting *such* a powerful message, Eleanora. I need to mention it. I keep hearing the word 'Philistine'; does that sound familiar? No. No," she said quickly, off to one side as if speaking to someone else. "It has to do with the word itself. I am hearing it repeated, carefully, syllable by syllable." She paused, listening again. "The word is being pronounced for a spelling bee."

Grace Waverly had my full attention now.

"Phil-is-tine," she said. "Yes."

"Philistine," I replied softly. "Philistine, one of the people of ancient Philistia."

"That seems like an odd word for a spelling bee. Let me see if I can learn more. I don't know what this means, but it has something to do with a ring. I see a ring. A silver ring. A special ring."

"What about it?" My voice was trembling, weak.

"An extraordinary ring. Something written on it. What's written on this ring?" she asked, but again, not of me. "A prayer of some sort. Is it the Lord's Prayer?"

I was ready to answer, but she said, "Yes, it is the Lord's Prayer."

I thought she might appear victorious, having pried that nugget from my past. Instead, Grace stared across the table at me with what I could only interpret as deep regret.

"This ring does not rightly belong to you, does it, Eleanora? There is something very burdensome about this ring."

My eyes began to sting.

"Something about this ring is a problem for you. There is pain, a hurt, perhaps an association you have kept hidden deep inside your heart and have never before confessed to anyone."

At that moment Grace's expression changed to one of beneficent concern.

"I hope you will come to the healing service tonight. Seven o'clock, at Inspiration Point. You'll receive beautiful, channeled energy from our healers. It will help you, Eleanora; I know it will."

"That's not why I came here," I stated firmly. "I'm not here to be 'healed.' Actually, I need to run. Thank you very much, Mrs. Waverly. I have all the information that I need."

Grace insisted on grasping my hands again and held them resolutely in her warm, strong grip.

"It doesn't matter *why* you found your way here today, Eleanora, don't you see? Someone, *something,* guided you to this chair, this table, this message. Do you think for a moment our meeting happened purely by chance?"

2

My pieces for *Meanderings,* trivial as they may have been, were just about the only thing keeping me sane that summer. So many changes took place. My second divorce, for example—this time from Michael, for whom I'd worked as a legal secretary after my *first* divorce. We'd agreed long ago that our marriage wasn't working but stayed together because it was less arduous than moving apart. We traveled a lot. I had a cleaning lady twice a week. I ordered from one of those services where the chef comes in and cooks several weeks' worth of meals in your own kitchen. Except for the lack of sex, I'd have to have been stupid to give that up!

Now his law firm was opening a branch in Scottsdale where Michael was bedazzled by the Valley of the Sun and, I knew, another woman out there. We let go as friends but it was my idea. I quoted Elizabeth Kubler-Ross and said we needed to weed the garden of our relationship. Divorce was not necessarily *good-bye,* it was merely part of our history. Blah blah blah. He bought it and gave me a pretty nice settlement. As part of our agreement, I moved out of our home and into a house that his law firm had owned but that now became mine, in the same University Heights neighborhood. The historic house, designed by Frideswyde Quimby, is a story in itself—which I'll get to, eventually.

I read somewhere that when a couple divorces after forty, it's usually the woman who pulls the plug. Like when you hate your job, it's more demoralizing to be fired from it than to quit. So when you make the decision *yourself* to end a bad marriage, it's supposed to empower you to fight through the challenges that follow.

I moved into that faded pea-green mansion before the contractors had completed basic restorations (never a good idea). The astonishment of Grace identifying the silver ring was equaled by the fact I was actually able to find it amid the jumble of my clutter. While searching for it, I had a momentary attack of the "bag lady complex." All women over forty are haunted by a mental picture of ourselves wrapped in our bed of torn coats, pushing a wobbly shopping cart that's heaped with a pile of remnants, the leftovers that were our lives. Well, that was good for about thirty minutes of self-pity.

The ring was stuffed in a trunk beneath my prized childhood mementoes—scuffed go-go boots, school letters, a pink angora pullover from high school that had shrunk in the wash. Tied in a corner of a red bandana, the knot holding the ring was almost impossible to untie after all those years. Mother would secure my offering like that in an embroidered handkerchief when she sent me off to Sunday school.

❧

We had two Lutheran churches in Little Wolf, one Catholic church, and one Methodist church, which my family belonged to. The modest sanctuary had a high ceiling and walls of beige acoustical tile that were punctuated by several narrow stained-glass windows on two sides. There were few other adornments: a narrow brass cross above a rectangular wooden altar, two slender brass candlesticks with tall white candles, the brass collection plates cushioned with red velvet pillows, and a couple of large oil paintings, one of Jesus at the temple, the other of Jesus as a boy working as a carpenter. Each had ornate gold frames that seemed ostentatiously out of place.

A much smaller painting in front of the adjacent Sunday school room depicted Jesus swathed in a snow-white robe, seated upon a rock. "Suffer the little children," was engraved on a brass plaque on the bottom of the frame. That apparently explained the children gathered adoringly at his feet. For a long time I pondered the puzzle of Jesus and the suffering children. Perhaps they were crippled—it was hard to tell. I knew the actual Bible verse—"Suffer the little children to come unto me and forbid them not for such is the Kingdom of Heaven"—because one of the boys in my Sunday school class, Leonard Twyn, had recited it by heart when the painting was presented in memory of a stillborn baby.

I had put Leonard Twyn almost completely out of my mind, but the silver ring was linked to him in an inextricable way. So was Sharon Gallagher, a childhood friend whose memory I had endeavored, unsuccessfully, to abandon.

Sharon Gallagher's guardian angel flew over her right shoulder. Every Catholic child had a guardian angel, she claimed, and every morning she recited a prayer that began, "Angel of God, My Guardian Dear . . . ," but of course I've forgotten the rest of it by now.

Even before we were introduced, I knew Sharon was going to be a pain in the ass. Her aunt, Gloria Piekarski, lived next door to us in my hometown of Little Wolf. My dad claimed you could set your clock by the slam of Gloria's front door because every morning she left for Sacred Heart at 7:15, rain or shine. Mom once hinted that Gloria and Father O'Neil were having an affair, but then she giggled and said, "Joke!" as if we had no idea she was trying to be funny.

My mother was not a funny person. She was serious about almost everything, which probably contributed to her death from a perforated ulcer just after I'd given birth to my son, Sky. Mom fretted about Gloria Piekarski because she was a widow, so fresh batches of chocolate brownies were often delivered next door. Another of Mom's passions was the inclusion of fusty old bachelors around our holiday tables. Every Thanksgiving, Christmas, or Easter, the essence of mothballs seemed an ordinary part of the menu.

When Mother told me Gloria's niece was coming to Little Wolf for a visit during the summer between fourth and fifth grade, I was certain I'd be involved in some kind of compassionate act that I dreaded. I tried to explain the conventions of childhood; you couldn't bring a complete stranger along to swimming lessons or the school playground and expect that kid to fit in.

"You *will* introduce Gloria's little niece to your friends," Mother demanded. "Gloria Piekarski has always been a perfect neighbor."

That's why I was hiding behind the drapes in the dining room when a big Chevrolet station wagon pulled into the driveway we shared with Gloria. I figured I might be off the hook when the girl (obviously taller and probably older) got out of the car because Sharon walked with a distinct limp. She dragged a leg attached to an ugly black shoe that was harnessed with a clumsy metal and leather brace. Too bad, I thought. And I was embarrassed for her, too, because she had long hair twisted in ringlets like unfurled flypaper—a fussy, old-fashioned hairstyle that indicated a really uncool mother.

Only a half hour later, Mother and I were on brownie duty. Sharon was at least six inches taller than me; her mother was Polish but her father, John Gallagher, was Irish. Sharon lived in Stevens Point but was going to stay at her Aunt Gloria's for two weeks while she went to catechism classes at Sacred Heart and her parents went on a trip to the Corn Palace in Mitchell, South Dakota, and to see Mount Rushmore.

"You can call me 'Cookie,' Honey," Sharon's mom requested when I held out the plate of brownies. The heavy-set woman (as Dad would refer to her) had made a brave attempt to perk up her doughy appearance with black eyebrow pencil and cherry lipstick but it only made her look sad, despite her cheerful smile.

Mom intervened. "*Mrs. Gallagher* is fine . . ."

"Heck, even Sharon calls me Cookie, ain't that so, Sherrie?"

Sharon shrugged. "I guess."

"Why don't you show Sharon your tent, "Mother suggested. "Take a couple of brownies along."

I always pitched my tent near the asparagus patch. It was just a pink chenille bedspread that I stretched over clothesline rope between two trees, but it was my own private hideout, no boys allowed. That was especially aimed at Buddy, my little brother, who was Born to Annoy.

Sharon made her way inside my tent that afternoon and arranged her dress over the brace on her right leg. She sat on the flannel blanket I usually curled on to read my comics and flipped her curls back over her shoulders. Right away she wanted me to see her catechism booklets. They had pictures of Jesus stretching his robe open to show off a gory red heart, and close-ups of his face in agony with blood dribbling down his forehead beneath the prickly crown of thorns. She also had cards like those I got with Double Bubble, but hers were holy cards and I remember one had a man with dozens of arrows piercing his body.

"Listen to this," Sharon said, then began reading from the back of one of the cards: "O Gentlest Heart of Jesus, ever consumed with burning love for the poor captive souls in Purgatory, be not severe in Thy judgment but let some drops of Thy Precious Blood fall upon the devouring flames . . ."

She read "devouring flames" with special zeal. Where was *Purgatory*, I wondered, and why all the emphasis on blood?

We were both going into fifth grade, although Sharon was already eleven. When she was four, she'd had polio, which she called "infantile paralysis," and that was the reason for the brace. I couldn't help staring at the apparatus, which went all the way up to her thigh and was hinged at the knee. It squeaked when she walked.

"Did you have to be in an iron lung?" I asked.

"Sure," she replied archly. "When I was in the hospital I was in a room with about fifty iron lungs. I can still remember the sounds they made, like 'Swiish, hooo, swiish, hooo'; I thought it would never stop. It was so awful, everybody cried. Even the nurses cried! Cookie thought I was going to die and I was given extreme unction. But then I got the Sister Kenny Cure."

It nearly killed me to have to ask who Sister Kenny was. Sister Kenny, Sharon explained, was a nun from Australia who was a nurse and invented an unusual treatment for polio.

Sharon was seven when she was given her First Communion. This, I gathered, was a pretty big deal. I ate the rest of the brownies while she went back to Gloria's to return with snapshots of her dressed like a miniature bride with a filmy white dress, a crown of flowers with lacy veil, white stockings, and a white patent leather shoe on her one good foot.

"I was a Bride of Heaven," she said. "And I got lots of presents."

In the photographs she clutched a sparkling rosary, a prayer book, and a shiny white purse. That was when she told me about the priest drinking Jesus's blood and having him hand out "the host" made from Jesus's body. It looked like fish food and made her feel dizzy.

"Only the priest can touch the host," she announced, "because his fingers are consecrated. You have to stick out your tongue and he puts it there. And then you have Jesus inside you."

"Gross," I said.

"And you've *got* to swallow it right away," she went on. "Not bite it, just swallow it. Let it get soft on your tongue from the spit. Aunt Gloria told me that one Sunday she went to Mass and hid the host in her hankie instead of swallowing and then she took it to her room and hid it in her dresser drawer, but that night she couldn't sleep and when she opened her eyes there was a brilliant radiance coming from her dresser. So you have to swallow the host."

I tried not to show how impressed I was until she pulled the rosary out of her pocket and I was hooked. The circlet of pink crystal beads led to a crucifix on one side and clicked together in a most enticing manner. I had never seen a rosary or touched one, or closely inspected a crucifix. The tiny spikes!

"No," Sharon pulled it away when I attempted to admire the gleaming cross. "You can't touch my rosary; you're not Catholic! And you're not going to go to heaven like Catholics, neither. You'll be stuck in limbo for all eternity. That's next to purgatory, in case you didn't know."

I believe that was the moment when I began to develop my love/hate relationship with Sharon. The threat of not going to heaven was a real blow. I was steadfast in my Sunday school attendance and I thought about heaven a lot.

"Let me see that card again," I demanded. I wanted to learn more about the "poor captive souls in purgatory," just in case.

She refused.

But she explained that the rosary was for praying to Our Blessed Mother. "You say Hail Marys on the small beads and Our Fathers on the big ones. *Hail Mary, full of grace, the Lord is with thee; blessed art thou among women, and blessed is the fruit of thy womb, Jesus.*"

She spun the words rapidly and repeated them, an enigmatical string.

"Why do you have to repeat it over and over? Can't God hear you?"

Maybe it was a stupid question, but I was Methodist and our little church was so boring by comparison. Despite her detestable ringlets and her limp, Sharon obviously led a more fascinating life. After that day I occasionally called her a cripple behind her back and told myself Jesus really wanted her to suffer. I imitated Sharon's limp for my best friend Polly Cornbloom, but she said her mother told her not to make fun of a cripple or you might end up that way yourself. Warnings like that didn't stop me.

My favorite summertime activity was to curl up in a big wicker rocking chair on our front porch and get lost in a library book until Mother yelled, "Eleanora Grendon, get your nose out of that book and go outdoors!"

I got an allowance for mowing the lawn, which was a pain because it was a push mower. Polly and I had swimming lessons at Bear Lake most afternoons except during Dog Days, when they were cancelled because of polio, which meant most of July and all of August. Parents were still afraid about polio but swimmer's itch plagued us then, too. My mom wouldn't allow me to watch television during the day. We didn't receive much of a TV signal anyway and only got a couple Green Bay channels from the antenna on the roof.

I spent some of my allowance on movie magazines that I shared with Polly. The rest was spent on shows. Little Wolf had its own movie theater called "The Lenore." Nobody knew why—probably named after the wife of the first owner. Polly and I went to the Lenore every Saturday and Sunday afternoon for the matinees. When we got older we went to the Friday night double features, too. The tickets went up from fifteen to thirty-five cents when you turned twelve.

Entering the Lenore was like walking into a new mystery because you never knew what exciting thrills lay ahead. The air had a fresh chill and the darkness lent an enchantment to the cinderblock walls. Before the lights dimmed you could see the murals of Wisconsin's lumbermen painted there: bigger than life, loggers stood by pyramids of logs on sleds pulled by huge teams of horses. And there were scenes of Wisconsin's waterfalls, dense pine forests, and herds of deer peering out from stands of white birch.

During the week, cool summer evenings were spent playing Kick the Can and other games with our friends: "Red Rover, Red Rover, send Yellow right over," we called into the darkness, and "Ollie ollie, oxen free," or "You're IT," slapping someone on the arm and then sprinting away.

Older kids might have a pickup game of football in the village park across from our house, but Polly and I and our closest friends disappeared behind the elementary school where the playground, neglected for a month or more by now, was consequently plagued with sandburs. That's where we played Horses, our extremely secret game.

Herbie Bachelor lived out in the country. His dad raised Shetland ponies they took around to county fairs where kids paid to ride them in a circle. Herbie always wore high-heeled cowboy boots (for which I madly envied him because my mother said they were bad for my feet no matter how heartwrenchingly I pleaded) and a plaid cowboy shirt with pearl-covered snaps down the front. Herbie thought he was a cowboy and tried to act like one, too.

The thing was, Herbie had watched the ponies mate. He knew

how they "did it," how the pony stallion mounted the mare. So our game of Horses was simple and earthy. Boys ran around with rolled up newspapers stuck in the zippers of their pants and chased the girls—who endured the pursuit with glee, trying to outwit the boys who whinnied and bucked before selecting the girl they wanted to jump on—and we'd carry them around, bowing to their weight and their whooping, not realizing the true significance of this drama, for most of us we were not farm kids, nor had we seen cows or horses or any livestock copulating. Still, we knew we were playing a dangerous game.

Mother insisted I take Sharon along to play with my friends that first night she was at Gloria's. There was no way I could explain that we already had five girls and five boys and there had to be an even number. Or that this was a secret game we played, no outsiders allowed.

After supper Sharon came over and we headed downtown. My allowance covered double-dip ice-cream cones for each of us at Crandall's Drug Store after we looked at romance and movie magazines. Then we wandered around the neighborhood, making the ice cream last as long as possible in the heavy air. People sitting on their porches called out and waved, to say hello. "Who's that cute friend you got with you, Nellie?" they'd ask, and I'd have to explain.

We walked across the bridge and looked down at the river. We went past the old harness shop, the lumberyard, and down to the pickle factory, and by the time the cones were nibbled to the last runny morsel of liquid at the bottom tip we were passing the grade school where we could hear the whoops and the laughter.

"Who's back there?" Sharon asked. I said I didn't know and sped up, wishing I had been more vigilant. In a half hour it would be dark and the kids would be going home.

"Let's find out," she said. Even with her limp she reached the playground before I did.

Teddy Carter had always been my stallion, the one I allowed to catch me, and I wondered which of the girls he had been galloping after that night.

Polly Cornbloom noticed us first; she stopped running so Buck Springer ran into her and knocked her down. But Polly wasn't paying attention to Buck. She stood up, picked a sandbur out of her dirty knee, and looked over at Sharon. I could tell she was mad by the way she swung her black braids.

The whole game halted and my friends paused as if they were frozen. They looked at Sharon, and then over at me as if I had betrayed them by revealing our shared confidence, our forbidden and tantalizing game.

"Hey, Polly," I called. "C'mere a minute."

Polly trudged over to where we waited, glaring all the way.

"This is Sharon Gallagher," I said with feigned pleasure. "She's staying with her Aunt Gloria next door and my mom said I had to let her hang around with me tonight and she heard you guys yelling so she came back here and I couldn't stop her."

Polly gave Sharon a squinty-eyed inspection. I could tell she was angry but there was curiosity in her glance, just the same.

"Whatcha playing?" Sharon asked Polly.

"Horses." Polly swung her glance to me with a disapproving frown. "We're playing Horses," she said, returning to Sharon. "And all the partners have been chosen, even Teddy Carter," she added, pointedly. "He's been riding Carolina Sawyer."

Oh, great, Carolina Sawyer, the crybaby who said playing Horses always hurt her back but she wouldn't miss being there.

"Want to watch me on the monkey bars?" I asked Sharon. "I can twirl backwards a hundred times."

"I want to play Horses with these guys," Sharon said, ignoring my suggestion. "Tell me how." She was addressing Polly.

"There aren't enough boys," I told her, checking out Teddy and Carolina, who were standing apart now that I was watching.

"That don't matter," Sharon said. "Can't you and me be partners?"

"It doesn't work that way," I began to explain, but Polly said, "You can be my partner."

And that's what happened on the summer night Sharon played Horses for the very first time. I was paired up with Buck Springer and had to watch Carolina running ahead of Teddy, and Polly pretended to be one of the boys with a rolled-up newspaper tucked in the waistband of her shorts. She chased slowly and considerately after Sharon and everybody was happy except me because nobody talked to me, not even Buck, and I knew I was in deep trouble.

As it turned out, that was the last time we played Horses. Not because Sharon was in town, but Teddy and Duane Morris went away to Boy Scout Camp, Polly's family took a trip to Chicago to see her uncle, and instead of being The Summer We All Played Horses, it became the summer in which I was introduced to Catholicism and Sister Mary Alphonsine, who, of course, was friends with Gloria Piekarski since they'd all grown up in the same neighborhood in Stevens Point.

Sister Alphonsine, in her heavy black habit and starched wimple, her face smooshed together by the stiff white frame that squeezed her pale cheeks out like bubbles, often walked back from Sister School to Gloria Piekarski's in late afternoon with Sharon and stayed for a glass of lemonade on the wide front porch, which overlooked the shrine Gloria had made by setting a statue of the Virgin Mary in an upturned bathtub that her husband had painted light blue inside.

The reason Gloria left for Mass so early every morning, I found out, was because she played the organ at Sacred Heart. One rainy Saturday Sharon and I sat at Gloria's spinet piano playing "Heart and Soul" together. Naturally, Sharon chose the best part, the top, while I got the boring low notes. Sheet music for "Our Lady of Fatima" sat on top of the piano. The song was from a movie about a miracle: the Virgin Mary appeared to some peasant children in Portugal, Sharon explained. "The sun spun around, and these kids saw this mysterious lady in a cave wearing a white gown and a veil. It was on the thirteenth of May and she said if they came there on the thirteenth day every month then she'd tell them who she really was. When the time came and she did, she said she was Our Lady of the Rosary."

The rosary again. I sighed.

"And she said poor little peasant children should say the rosary every day and build a chapel in her honor. That's why we say the rosary every day. And in May we have a parade in church to honor her and one special girl gets to be May Queen. I got to be the May Queen last year, in Stevens Point."

Sharon showed me how the song went and asked me to play the melody, but I wasn't that good. So Aunt Gloria played it for us. It was a pretty tune. Sharon had a pleasant, clear soprano.

"Come on, Eleanora, sing along," Gloria suggested, beginning the introduction one more time.

I matched my voice to Sharon's, and we sang together:

Our Lady of Fatima, We come on bended knee . . .

Aunt Gloria had to play with one hand while she wiped her eyes.

"Could you and Sharon sing this for Sister Mary Alphonsine tomorrow afternoon? She's bringing Sister Mary Agnes over for dinner after Mass. It would give them such joy to hear your sweet voices."

I didn't know why not, so I agreed.

We pledge our love and offer you a rosary each day . . .

The nuns were impressed. I wore the sundress I'd worn to Sunday school in keeping with the religious solemnity of the occasion. I knew my parents were amused because I had never shown any enthusiasm for performing in public. There had been some discussion of signing me up for accordion lessons because my parents loved *The Lawrence Welk Show.* I said I thought the accordion was more suited for country bumpkins, at which my little brother, Buddy, began calling me "Nellanora Bumpkin." Thanks to my wisecrack, the matter was still up in the air.

After we sang for the nuns on Sunday, Gloria thought it would be nice to give them a ride and show them around since they didn't have a car. Sharon and I were invited to come along.

One stop was at Bear Lake. Sharon sat on the grass and slipped off her white sandal and unbuckled her brace so she could wade in the shallow water off the beach. I slid off my shoes, already copying her.

"You know how to swim?" Sharon asked.

"I take lessons," I said. "So does Polly. When you're at Sister School."

"I know you take lessons," she answered haughtily. "But can you *swim*? That's what I asked."

"Yes, I can swim," I answered. It might only be the dog paddle but I could get around okay. We were working on the sidestroke and by the end of the summer our Red Cross instructor promised we'd begin the Australian crawl.

"I learned to swim when I had infantile paralysis," Sharon said. "I spent every day at the Stevens Point High School swimming pool after I got out of the iron lung."

Gloria called us from the water then; she wanted to show the sisters the new church in Waupaca, fifteen miles away. I went along because I had nothing better to do and I had never been inside a Catholic church. But I still had not mentioned that I really should be sitting in the front seat because I always got carsick in the back. Suffering for Jesus, I hoped I would not throw up on a nun.

Waupaca's Blessed Sacrament Catholic Church was enormous.

"We need a chapel veil for Nell," Sharon informed the nuns. They asked Aunt Gloria for a handkerchief to spread on top of my hair. Sharon was given one too, because when you entered a Catholic church you had to cover your head.

"What else should I do?" I whispered to Sharon, thoroughly in awe and more than a little queasy from the ride.

"Follow me," she whispered back.

Imitating her actions, I dipped my fingers into the holy water and touched my forehead and my chest and each shoulder. I paraded after Aunt Gloria, the sisters, and Sharon, down the aisle into the serene darkness where our steps echoed in the sanctuary and we were watched over by life-size statues of saints and angels. Stained glass windows iridesced the vast interior and rainbow prisms fell across a gigantic crucifix that illuminated Jesus's grotesque pain.

I had never seen anyone genuflect before. The little carpeted kneelers were so very dear, so considerate, not like our hard, wooden Methodist pews.

Of course, I had no rosary. I had to make up what to say. As I recall, I repeated the Twenty-third Psalm several times, and then the Lord's Prayer.

After about an hour we lit some candles on one side of the room and we left the church to climb back into Aunt Gloria's stifling car.

"We'll make a Catholic of you yet," Sister Alphonsine threatened with a gentle smile and a tender pat on my knee as I slid next to her on the itchy back seat. I thought she must be joking but who knew for sure what Catholics meant and Sharon threw me what I felt was a sinister grin. Sister Alphonsine reached inside her voluminous black sleeve and handed me a holy card. It had a painting of Mary in a blue gown, standing on a white cloud, surrounded by a glorious starburst.

I wondered, later, why my parents let me go along with them that afternoon. Mother was already upset with my interest in Teddy Carter because he was Catholic and she didn't want me to have a crush on a Catholic boy. But she seemed to think it was perfectly all right for me to be friends with Sharon Gallagher, whom everyone assumed was perfect and devout and beautiful.

Polly and I never told anyone some of the things we did with Sharon, and afterward we seldom discussed what we knew or what we saw.

Sharon left at the end of the summer to return to Stevens Point and fifth grade. We wrote to each other with envelopes bearing cryptic messages like "SWAK" or "D-liver D-letter D-sooner D-better" on the back of the envelope after sealing it shut and sticking the stamp on upside down.

"I bought two pagan babies with my babysitting money," she wrote in October. "I named them Bridget Paradise and Cecilia Joy." She also said she had decided on her vocation: she would either become a Mouseketeer or go into a convent and become a Sister because that would ensure that everyone in her family had a special place in heaven reserved just for them.

I mentally added the pagan babies to her crystal rosary and the medals Sister Mary Alphonsine and Sister Mary Agnes handed out when Sister School was over, silver medals with saints' likenesses that Sharon was awarded because she was so pious, she said. Then there was her guardian angel, of course, and Sharon said Cookie sprinkled holy water on her bed every night so she never had bad dreams. So what?

I had no idea what "pagan" referred to, but it didn't make sense that you could buy a baby with babysitting money. And it didn't sound like Sharon's pagan babies were going to move in with her family, either. When I asked in my next letter, "How much were they?" in case I could buy one, too, she wrote back, "Five dollars each," but in a chastening P.S. she reminded me, "You can't buy one because you're not a Catholic."

I decided not to show Sharon my altar.

It was made from a small sewing table I brought down from the attic to place in my room. I polished it with Lemon Pledge and placed one of Mother's good white linen napkins on the top. Above the altar I hung the church calendar offered free from a table near the back door of our church. Every month featured a different scene from Jesus's life and a Bible message for every day of the week. I vowed to read the daily message first, and then began reading my mother's Bible cover to cover. I used the holy card given to me by Sister Mary Alphonsine as my bookmark. I studied the serene expression of the Virgin Mary cloaked in heavenly blue and tried to imitate her enigmatic smile, her aura of beatific gentility, as I struggled through the names and relationships of the characters in Genesis: I had no trouble with Abraham or Noah, but then I ran into Japheth and Magog, Tubal, Meshech, Nimrod, Jidlaph, Jahzeel, Guni, Jezer, Eliphaz, Esau, Omar, Zepho, Shammah, Mizzah, Shepho, Zibeon, and so forth. I was relieved when I finally reached Exodus.

I didn't show Sharon my altar, and I didn't show her the Lord's Prayer ring when she came to stay with her Aunt Gloria the next summer, partly because we had to help Gloria construct the rosary of bowling balls in June and excitement over that activity eclipsed everything else in Little Wolf. But there was another reason: by that time the ring had already been tied into the red bandana knot.

33

$\mathcal{E}$ach day that I prayed at my altar I sensed a calling to become a missionary so I could care for pagan babies in a foreign land. Then our new minister, Reverend Bennett, came up with what seemed to me to be a heaven-sent opportunity. Two special rings, one for a boy and another for a girl, would be awarded for correctly spelling and defining words they were asked from the Bible. Each ring would have the Lord's Prayer engraved on the top, which was flat and square, like this:

OUR FATHER
WHICH ART IN HEAVEN
HALLOWED BE THY NAME
THY KINGDOM COME THY
WILL BE DONE IN EARTH AS
IT IS IN HEAVEN GIVE US
THIS DAY OUR DAILY BREAD
AND FORGIVE US OUR DEBTS
AS WE FORGIVE OUR DEBTORS
AND LEAD US NOT INTO TEMP
TATION BUT DELIVER US FROM
EVIL FOR THINE IS THE
KINGDOM AND THE POWER
AND THE GLORY FOREVER
AMEN

The ring idea was particularly impressive since Sharon explained that Sister Mary Alphonsine and Sister Mary Agnes wore wedding rings as Brides of Christ. All nuns were married to Jesus, she said, and after that I noticed that every nun I saw wore a gold wedding band. Every nun was married to God.

Reverend Bennett, young and enthusiastic, had received his call to our church the previous spring. The Bible Bee, as he christened his brainstorm, was highly publicized in the church bulletin as well as in Sunday school, and the rings, already on order were spoken of as worthy of the most extreme spiritual and scholarly Christian endeavor.

I desperately needed a religious memento of my very own, something beyond my perfect attendance pin—a gold badge with bars added in a ladder, one step for each year of never missing a day of Sunday school. I had already garnered three bars.

As it was carefully explained, in lieu of a sermon on the Sunday after Thanksgiving, those of us competing in the Bible Bee would stand before the pulpit and face the congregation as Reverend Bennett called out the words to be spelled. There would be no special categories or age groups; the entire Sunday school would vie for the rings. For a fifth grader to beat someone in eighth grade, I knew I'd have to study hard. The Bee would include Old Testament as well as New, and from my self-directed Bible study, I was well aware of the tongue-twisting Nebuchadnezzar and Methuselah.

I discussed this problem with Polly one day after school when we were making a mess of her mother's kitchen by molding flour and salt maps of the United States. Polly did not comprehend my fervor about my Bible words. I knew Jews only used the Old Testament, but that was enough to help me practice.

"Can you spell *dreidel*?" she asked.

"Is it in the Bible?" I wanted to know.

She didn't think so. It was a toy like a top, with Hebrew letters on the sides—she'd shown one to me years ago. Then she asked if I could spell *Rosh Hashana,* or *Challah* or *Mazel Tov* or *Channukah.* Or *kanipshin.* Jews had more mysterious rituals than Methodists: special foods and holidays, enthusiastic music, a different language. They even had their own comedians! Exuberant dances! Methodists weren't ever supposed to dance. When my dad was little, he said, his Methodist grandparents disapproved of playing cards. And if his mother hadn't peeled the potatoes for Sunday dinner on Saturday, they went without potatoes for their Sunday meals.

Sometimes it seemed to me that the only fun thing Methodists were encouraged to do was sing. Vigorous hymn singing was heartily approved. And we could play "Sly Wink 'Em," the stupidest game for boys and girls ever devised.

If I won the Bible Bee, I promised God, I would wear the Lord's Prayer ring until the day I died.

35

As I turned from Exodus to Leviticus and began to recite daily calendar verses for November, Reverend Bennett's wife, who had been expected to deliver their first child well before Halloween, was at least two weeks overdue. When she finally labored in the Waupaca hospital, well-meaning women from the Priscilla Circle of the Ladies Aid launched their housecleaning of the parsonage. My mother, of course, stood at the head of the pack. Her personal fetish was dust.

To show my good faith and prove to God how sincerely I deserved the prize, I offered to help the Priscillas. I could vacuum and dust, I explained to Mom, while they tackled bigger tasks.

For weeks I had paged frantically through the Bible, making hasty, scribbled lists of every difficult word I came upon: Samaritan. Thessalonians. Gomorrah. Pharaoh. By the Saturday of the parsonage housecleaning there was only a week to go before the Bee and Mrs. Bennett, still in the hospital, had finally given birth to a son. The Priscillas went to work, removing the screens, then carrying storm windows up from the basement to be washed and dried before putting them up in place. Fortunately, for November in Little Wolf, that Saturday was unusually warm.

After I finished vacuuming and dusting downstairs I moved the heavy Hoover to the second floor, where I had never been before.

The Priscillas had painted the bedrooms, sewn and hung new curtains, and freshened up the house where, for two decades or more, our previous minister had lived with his elderly wife. Reverend Bennett's study overlooked the backyard, where the women were now occupied with garden hose, ammonia, and rags. I stood in front of Reverend Bennett's desk for a moment and watched them. Mother looked up and waved.

I vacuumed his study, dusted the bookshelf, and ran my dust rag over the spine of every book. I sprayed Pledge on Reverend Bennett's desk, careful not to disturb his papers, replacing everything I moved.

It was an accident, really, when I uncovered the sheet of notebook paper tucked beneath the green, ink-stained felt blotter. "Bible Bee" was clearly printed on top. I tried not to look.

Then, of course, I glanced toward the Priscillas in the backyard.

They were still washing storm windows. Mother's back was to the house.

I slid the blotter back in place, careful not to wrinkle the page beneath, sprayed more Pledge, and wiped the desk again with the dustcloth, to eradicate telltale fingerprints.

The kitchen door slammed. I jumped when my mother called, "Eleanora?"

"Up here," I said, making sure the blotter was exactly as it had been. Then I rushed to the top of the stairs. "You should see the dust bunnies under the baby's crib, Mom! They're everywhere in the nursery. It's really icky in there!"

The look of horror on Mother's face assured me I'd hit the mark.

She was telephoning my father to come over and help carry the storm windows up to the second floor. "As soon as he gets here I'll help you whip that nursery into shape!"

Panic rose in my throat and my heart beat even faster.

The spelling words were only steps away.

God saw everything. God knew everything. I felt him watching my every move. I scratched a mosquito bite on my ankle and heard God say to Himself, "Eleanora Grendon is scratching a mosquito bite."

I had never cheated at anything in my life.

It would be a sin to copy the Bible Bee words.

It was a sin even to read them!

What if God *wanted* me to find them? Maybe it was meant to be? I had accidentally caught sight of *Nazareth* and *Lazarus* before sliding the paper back under the blotter. They didn't count because I knew how to spell those anyway.

If I copied the words but didn't memorize them, simply kept them somewhere safe, that would give me more time to decide what to do. If they were as easy as Nazareth and Lazarus, it was possible there would be no surprises.

I heard Mother hang up the telephone and the back door slammed again as she went back outside.

Before I could stop myself, I had slipped the list from beneath the blotter, stuffed it under my undershirt, grabbed a pencil from Reverend Bennett's desk, and ducked into the bathroom, where I fastened the hook, sat on the toilet seat, and hastily transferred the list of spelling words from Reverend Bennett's list to a strip of toilet paper.

Nicodemus. Herod. Easy words. There were twenty-five. I knew, deep inside all that wild pounding in my chest, that this was cheating, despite whispered protests. To attain the necessary courage, I tried to imagine Sharon swinging her pink crystal rosary in front of me.

Pharaoh, I wrote, pressing the pencil as hard as I could against the toilet paper without tearing it. *Galilee. Damascus,* one I'd missed.

"Eleanora, are you in the bathroom? Do you have a stomachache?"

Mother was ready to tackle the nursery.

"I'll be out in a minute," I said, flushing the toilet for emphasis. The words had been copied. I folded the fragile squares of tissue into a tiny square and slid it into my sock. I could feel the lump every time I took a step. By mistake, I limped like Sharon.

"Eleanora, are you feeling all right?"

"Sure. I'm fine."

Mother stood in the hall with the vacuum cleaner handle in her hand like a lethal weapon. "If you've already vacuumed the Reverend's study," she said, "dust in there and then join me in the nursery."

She paused. "What's wrong with your leg?"

"I had a cramp in my calf," I fibbed, "but it's gone."

I nearly told her I was done with the study, but I needed time so I went ahead and dusted again. With my back to the door, I slid the official page of words back under the blotter. It was smudged only slightly from the sweat on my belly and my slippery hands. Despite yet another coat of Pledge and vigorous polishing, Reverend Bennett's desk reflected my guilty conscience.

*W*hen the Bible Bee rolled around, I was perfectly prepared. Every word and definition had been committed to memory, and my cheat sheet was flushed away. One of those rings was as good as mine. The guilt had not been that hard to rationalize. Surely I deserved a reward for sitting through all those tedious hours of Sunday school even when I had a sore throat or a stomachache so I would still have perfect attendance while some bored adult droned through the lesson and asked stupid questions like, "Where was Moses's basket hidden?" Who always came through with an answer to break the silence? Dependable Eleanora Grendon, that's who, because I couldn't stand the wait, the stupid looks on the faces of kids who were bored out of their wits and had dozed off or spent half an hour picking scabs on their knees.

Reverend Bennett took his time introducing the actual Bible Bee.

"There are ten Bible Bees," he said, and then he listed them. I thought he'd never get done.

"'Be Obedient,' from Second Corinthians, chapter 2, verse 9: 'For this is why I wrote, that I might test you and know whether you are obedient in everything.'

"Be Honest, from Psalm 139: 'Search me, O God, and know my heart. Try me and know my thoughts! And see if there be any wicked way in me, and lead me in the way everlasting.'"

I closed my eyes to block out all the rest (Be Kind, from Ephesians; Be Polite, from Isaiah; Be Loving, from Ephesians again; Be Content, Be Helpful, Be Gentle, Be Thankful, Be Faithful).

I was stuck on "Be Honest," because God must know I had been dishonest. Nevertheless, I won on the word *Philistine*. I tried to make it sound hard, taking my time, but I knew it very well. The only other person to spell it correctly was the boy who won a ring, too: Leonard Twyn.

A quiet, pasty-looking child, he was, like his name, plain and ordinary. Leonard Twyn was a year ahead of Polly and me in school and lived in a house trailer near the railroad tracks on the south edge of town. While I went home after Sunday school to read the funny papers, Leonard Twyn sat in church between his parents, who appeared to be very old. There was little else that I knew about him except that he often reeked of camphor.

Reverend Bennett presented us with our rings and then Leonard and I took our seats in the front pew. My parents were smiling proudly. I would have joined them, but the church was full; Reverend Bennett was going to baptize his new son after the sermon so all his family members were there. I found myself seated next to Leonard Twyn for the rest of the service, during which I had plenty of time to admire my ring and imagine flashing it in front of Sharon, elaborating upon my extreme competence in spelling Philistine and asking if she could spell all the words on the list. I was certain that she couldn't because Catholics weren't supposed to study the Bible. She wouldn't know what it meant, either: "One of the people of ancient Philistia," or a conceited, ignorant person who didn't know about cultural and artistic things.

I marveled at the miniature prayer imparted in its entirety, and slid the silver ring onto different fingers to find the right one, the finger that was most convenient for touching the cluster of magical words whenever they were required. The ring could serve in place of a rosary. It was the best that Methodists could do.

Only one thing was slightly disappointing. In our church we said "trespass" instead of "debts." The ring said debts, probably because debts took up less space. I preferred "Forgive us our trespasses as we forgive those who trespass against us," not "Forgive us our debts as we forgive our debtors."

I decided that each time I read the Lord's Prayer on the ring or brushed the words with the tip of my finger, I'd slide over "debts" and "debtors," and substitute "trespasses" and "trespassers." It was more poetic.

During most of the sermon I could feel Leonard Twyn watching me. I slid away, to increase the space between us.

Then, as Mrs. Bennett and her new baby and the baby's godparents were gathering in the front of the church, I saw Leonard stare at his own hand with the ring on it before slipping that hand inside the pocket of his cardigan.

"It's gold," he whispered. "It's gold. My ring is gold. Yours is only silver."

Sure enough, "sterling silver" was stamped into the band that ran beneath my finger and joined the flat circle of words surrounded by engraved hearts entwined.

I immediately suspected this was God's punishment. His way of giving me second place for cheating, making me suffer. And although I had never paid Leonard Twyn much attention before, I developed a sudden and profound dislike for his pale, translucent skin, his pouty lips that looked like they had been rubbed with lipstick, and the way he buttoned his shirts right up to his Adam's apple where his skinny neck stuck out like an ostrich. I was desperate to see his ring again, to compare it with my own.

After that morning, Leonard Twyn teased me unmercifully. He hid his ring from me whenever I was around. Even at grade school as the playground froze into wintry gloom, Leonard Twyn kept a watchful eye at recess so he could wave his mittened hand, then bite off his mitten and smirk as he waved the hand with the ring at me.

"He's probably a queer," Polly said, trying out a new bad word we'd recently learned.

"Gold," Leonard Twyn whispered, busting in line behind me at the bubbler in the hallway. "Your ring is only silver."

"Gold," he said, lurking at the door to the girls' room where I went to wash my hands before hot lunch.

"I don't know why you give a hoot," Polly said. "He's such a creep." She offered to tell him to get lost, but I said I'd take care of it.

After that, when I went to Sunday school I purposely sat behind Leonard Twyn and stared at the back of his ragged haircut until he could feel me staring and turned around to glare. One time when I did that he even licked his plump red lips with his wet tongue and silently formed the words, "Gold. Fourteen karat gold. Real gold."

"Lead me not into temptation," I whispered under my breath. I wanted to bop Leonard Twyn in his runny nose and if I didn't, Polly would do it for me. All I had to do was ask.

Mother said "suffer" in the Bible verse didn't really mean *suffer,* it meant "*Let* the little children come to me." And all of us were God's children because He was everybody's Father.

"The Lord's Prayer begins with 'Our Father,'" Buddy offered. "'Trespass' is in there, too, but it's not on Nellie's ring. Does that *trespass* mean the same as 'No Trespassing' signs?"

41

My parents thought it was adorable that Buddy wanted to know everything. It was because of Buddy that I was sometimes called Nell because when Buddy was little and tried to say Eleanora it came out *Nellanora,* and my mother thought that was so cute.

"If you see a 'No Trespassing' sign, that means KEEP OUT—THAT MEANS YOU," Dad said firmly. "Those signs are posted for a reason. So you don't go onto someone else's land without permission. I better not ever catch you doing that, Buddy."

"What about Nellie," Buddy whined.

"Eleanora is smart girl," Daddy told him. "She knows enough to obey a sign like that. Boys are sometimes, well, *tempted.*"

"Why?" Buddy asked.

"Because they're boys, for Pete's Sake." Dad was running out of patience. "You obey those 'No Trespassing' signs and see that you do!"

"Then what about 'Forgive us our trespasses'?'"

Buddy got into moods sometimes where he wouldn't quit no matter what. He reminded me of Polly.

"And how come 'trespass' isn't on Nellie's ring?"

"Oh, Buddy," Mom chuckled and gently ruffled Buddy's floppy bangs. She thought his persistence was so precious.

"That kind of trespassing has to do with sins. We ask God to forgive our sins and we forgive those who sin against us."

"Why?"

"Because that's what God wants us to do."

"So why does Nellie's ring say 'Forgive us our debts'?'"

"It's the same thing, Buddy. We are all, every single person on this earth, dependent on His forgiveness. A sin is—"

I interrupted, "Catholics believe there are two different kinds of sins, venial sins and mortal sins, but Methodists lump them all together. For us, a sin just has to be doing something bad, like lying."

Like saying your Lord's Prayer ring is gold when it's really silver, I thought.

"Or stealing," Buddy added helpfully.

"Stealing," I agreed. "Or cheating," I added, seeing myself in a cold sweat, hunched over the Bible Bee list on Reverend Bennett's toilet.

$\mathcal{D}$o you know Leonard Twyn?" Dad asked at supper one night near Easter.

I knew he was addressing me, but I casually poked a hole in the side of my mashed potatoes and watched the gravy river flood the slices of pot roast and rows of peas on my plate. I had recently attempted to put Leonard Twyn out of my life. He hadn't been around and I, for one, was glad.

"He passed away," Dad said when I didn't answer.

"Of leukemia," Mother added softly.

"Is it catching?"

"It's a disease of the bloodstream. Not contagious. Don't worry about it, someday I'll explain," Dad replied.

"He won a Lord's Prayer ring just like Nellie did," Buddy said.

"Mine is sterling silver," I said to Buddy, pulling it off so my family could see where "sterling silver" was imprinted in the band.

"I see," Dad said and went on to something else. He was already bored with the subject of Leonard Twyn and leukemia and the Lord's Prayer ring that seemed to me to have increased in size and importance already because now it was the only Lord's Prayer ring in the world and it would not matter if the other one had been gold or silver for Leonard Twyn would be buried with his stupid ring on his ugly, thin, pale, scrawny, dead finger.

Or would he?

"Eleanora?" Mom reached across the table to pat my arm. "You look a little peaked . . ."

The more I thought about it, Leonard Twyn's dying served him right. *Suffer the little children,* I could hear him reciting in a sanctimonious tone. I knew it was wrong but I hoped that Leonard Twyn really suffered on his way to meet Jesus.

Would he wear his ring in heaven, too?

"What about his funeral?" I asked, perhaps a bit too hastily. "Can I go?"

"No," Dad said. He spread the evening paper out before him on the table. "You're too young to go to funerals."

"Daddy and I think it would be best for you to remember your friend as he was in life." Mother pushed her chair back and began to carry dishes into the kitchen. "Not in death. We've already discussed it."

"He wasn't my friend," I said. "And ten isn't too young; Polly goes to funerals."

"Or to the wake," Mom added, clearing Dad's coffee cup.

"What's a wake?" I asked as my father gave my mother the "raised eyebrows" glance.

"Leonard's wake will be at Seger's funeral home," Mom said slowly, quietly, her back stiff against my father's watchful gaze. "It's a quiet time for friends and relatives to pay their respects."

"Respect for what?"

Dad's tone was impatient. "*Must* you ask so many questions, Eleanora? You're getting to be as bad as your brother."

"Paying one's respects means expressing sympathy, saying how sorry you are to the surviving family members." Mother picked up the empty milk pitcher. "And to view the body."

"Margery!" Dad's voice was harsh. He slapped the page of the newspaper on the tablecloth. "Really!"

"Leonard Twyn's body?" I was astonished at this revelation.

"Leonard Twyn's body?" Buddy echoed.

"Enough is enough," Dad said, and we all knew the subject was closed.

Later, I lay upstairs in the dark, imagining Leonard Twyn, dead. I thought of him in his coffin, envisioned the soft gold of his ring growing ever duller as the lid dropped slowly shut with a thudding echo and he was lowered into the damp earth to rot and turn to ashes, dust to dust.

Don't laugh next time the hearse goes by, for you may be the next to die, we chanted on the playground. *Your guts turn green like Vaseline, your pus runs out like whipping cream . . .*

Maybe Leonard Twyn had dared to laugh. It would have been like him.

They wrap you in a big white sheet and throw you down about sixty feet . . . The worms crawl in, the worms crawl out, the worms play pinochle on your snout. Your hair turns into sauerkraut.

I could not remember the rest. Poor Leonard Twyn.

3

*T*he subject of Sharon Gallagher came up unexpectedly when Polly visited me last summer. I had already been bedazzled by several visits to Wocanaga. My newfound fascination with Spiritualism had reached a crucial point where it could no longer be kept a secret, although I had not shared my "development" with Madison friends; I *sensed* (my clairsentient power in action?) their likely ridicule. When they asked why I wasn't golfing on Tuesdays or playing Bridge on Thursdays, I manufactured an excuse. Eventually, they stopped calling.

But I could share my enthusiasm with Polly. When you've spent almost every day going to school with someone from kindergarten through twelfth grade (and then add college to that), you've shared more formative time with them than you have with your own family. Polly had her own eccentricities and I loved her unconditionally. I admired her unique skills as an artist; I enjoyed her crazy quirks; I even grew to tolerate her tendency to act as my conscience once in a while. She'd always been reasonably forgiving about the nutty scrapes I'd gotten myself into.

So much had happened in our lives since the last time Polly and I enjoyed a leisurely break like this. After high school we'd both left Little Wolf to attend the university in Madison where we roomed together in the dorm. During the summer of our sophomore year I was working as a camp counselor near Minocqua in Wisconsin's Northwoods when I got a letter from Polly saying she was going off to study art in California and changing her name to Polly Blue. I cried for hours and all the little kids in my tent thought I was homesick. In a way, I was.

I hung around the UW campus for another year before I got pregnant with Sky (short for Schuyler); married Lee Wolf, a teaching assistant for Introduction to American Lit.; and dropped out of school. Odessa was born three years after Sky. It was the '70s. We lived in a communal house on Monroe Street, not far from campus. I was happy being a mother. Polly stayed with us when she was in town and laughed at my "Mother Earth" dresses, long Indian prints. I was writing poetry and belonged to a group that did weekly readings at coffee houses.

Lee and I outgrew the commune, but it took ten more years of marriage before I discovered that he and a grad student were having an affair. We divorced, and then I finished school. The kids coasted back and forth. Madison's always had a low unemployment rate but I didn't mind working for a temp agency and managed okay financially on my own.

Odessa and Sky attended the university and lived at home with me. My career path, such as it was, led to a job with Michael's law firm on the Capitol Square. After a year there I slept with the boss; two years later I married him.

Now the kids lived far away and my marriage to Michael was history, too.

Of course, visiting Madison that summer, Polly wanted to hang out on the Union Terrace, sail on Lake Mendota, and check out a few other favorite campus haunts. I deftly arranged our schedule so we were able to accomplish all that and attend our thirty-year high school class reunion in Little Wolf. But I really wanted to drive up through the Baraboo hills and introduce Polly to the Wocanaga Spiritualist Camp. She had been living in California for a long time and was exposed to all kinds of New Age experiences out there.

On the way to Wocanaga, I told Polly about my introduction to Grace Waverly and the article I wrote about the early days of Spiritualism that had just been published in *Meanderings*.

"Do you remember Leonard Twyn? He was a year ahead of us," I said. "He died . . ."

"He had one of those rings!" Polly interrupted, suddenly remembering, "From your Sunday school spelling bee."

"Bible Bee," I corrected her. "Guess what. Grace Waverly gave me a reading and she knew about the ring."

"No way!" Polly hit my shoulder with a dramatic punch.

"She did," I said, rubbing my shoulder, "and she knew other things about me, like my accordion lessons. She was incredible. Wait 'til you meet her."

"Will she help me decide about moving back?"

"Could be . . . but I think you've already made up your mind."

"Since when are *you* psychic, too?"

"You might be surprised," I replied enigmatically.

"Oh, God! Nell, don't tell me you're playing fortune-teller again!"

Polly's voice had an edge to it and I had to glance over to see if she was joking. She didn't seem to be. Crap.

I told myself to just concentrate on my driving but there wasn't any traffic on the country road and Polly's comment annoyed me.

"Okay, I won't *say* I'm telling fortunes. Because I'm *not* telling fortunes. Are you satisfied? Spiritualism is not about telling fortunes."

"I thought we were going to a place where mediums give messages to people," Polly argued.

"They do," I replied, exasperated, "but they're not fortunes. And you *might* be given a message by a medium at the message service, but I wouldn't count on it. You have to impart the right energy and the right attitude, which I don't think you're going to have."

"You're still such a worrier, Nellie!" Polly insisted on poking my shoulder again. "You're turning into your mother! I thought you said this would be fun."

"You've got to promise me you'll behave," I warned. "When people attend a message service at Wocanaga, it's a sacred thing for them."

But it *is* entertaining, I privately acknowledged, if you enjoy watching people who believe they're communicating with the dead.

*P*olly spotted a lazy tabby on the porch of one of the cottages as we walked the grassy trail to Inspiration Point.

"Grace says cats are very spiritual," I mentioned as Polly began to stroke the tabby's glossy head. "She says places like this are like *chakras* of the earth. Like the vortex at Sedona."

Polly laughed. "The last time I was in Sedona I bought something called 'Vortex in a can.' The label claimed it had been humanely gathered during the full lunar eclipse by nonsmoking vegetarians."

"Damn it, Polly—don't do something to embarrass me today, okay?"

I decided not to add that Grace also said we've each arrived in this plane from one of the other planes to experience and to learn, because Polly would have found some way to tease me for that statement, too.

The cat scratched Polly's wrist while leaping out of her arms before it scurried off into the ferns. I considered it a satisfying act of revenge.

On an ordinary summer day, Wocanaga's dense forest of old growth oak and pine can be majestic and awe inspiring. Whispers seem to come from far away, especially when there is a breeze. I am always reminded of the generations of Spiritualists who have sought solace and comfort in those woods.

"See the light on this little cottage?"

"You mean this lightbulb in front of cabin 13?"

"I call it the eternal lightbulb. Some call it the spirit light. That lightbulb hasn't been changed in thirty years."

"Oh, c'mon . . ."

"And, I've been told it changes colors all by itself."

"Wow, I'm impressed," Polly remarked wryly. "*The eternal lightbulb.* You sure know how to show a visitor a good time!"

*A*s we approached Inspiration Point we could hear voices raised in the old hymn, *"In the Sweet Bye and Bye, We shall meet on that beautiful shore . . ."*

Only a few seats remained by the time we reached the clearing.

As Spence had mentioned, Grace Waverly was always in charge of the message services at Inspiration Point—a narrow shelf of rock that projected precariously from the high bluff like a horizontal arrowhead. That afternoon she wore a hazy purple shawl that emphasized lavender shadows in her white hair. Royal purple is an auspicious aura for a medium. With her gnarled cane, Grace slowly paced between the crowd and a tall pine tree near the point that overlooked leafy treetops and the village far below.

"Curiouser and curiouser," Polly chuckled, a bit more loudly than I might have wished.

We squeezed onto one end of a sagging wooden bench toward the back.

"How will she see us way back here?"

"If you get a message, she'll find you. Calm down."

"Please!" a woman in the row ahead of us shushed a reprimand.

Had you not seen or heard her read Spirit before, you wouldn't wonder that Grace's voice was a little less imposing than when I'd met her a couple months ago. The venerable medium still evoked a powerful presence, even when she crowned her serpentine braids with a cap that advertised a bait shop on the Kickapoo River.

"May I come to you?"

Grace Waverly pointed to a twitchy woman I had often seen around the grounds.

"That woman's on the right track," I whispered to Polly. "Grace will say she hears a train."

"Show off," Polly whispered back.

"Shhhh," the woman ahead of us turned again and placed a warning finger on her lips.

"As I'm coming into your Spirit vibration I hear the sound of a locomotive," Grace told her subject, "very far away . . ."

The elderly medium cast an imploring gaze overhead as if a heavenly railroad bridged the verdant realm. She paused, eyes closed. "Yes. Yes," she nodded, "I am told you are being pressured to make a difficult decision. Spirit wants to assure you that you are on the right track."

Polly poked me in the ribs with her elbow but I was still feeling pretty smug. Then I heard Grace ask, "May I come to you? The woman with a bright blue streak in her long black hair?"

Grace was deliberately making her way toward Polly. Everyone craned around to watch.

"Me?" Polly asked. "Is she talking to me?"

"Yes," I prompted, grinning. "Tell her yes!"

"Yes, you," Grace echoed almost gruffly, facing Polly now. "May I come to you? Let me hear your voice."

"Say *yes*," I nudged Polly again.

Polly cleared her throat. "Yes?"

Grace tucked her cane under one arm, closed her eyes, and pressed her hands together in front of her royal purple bosom. She appeared to be musing over a difficult communication. Her voice softened and became more soothing as she spoke.

"As I enter your Spirit vibration I am hearing the name of 'Ada.' Does that name mean anything to you?"

Polly hesitated. I could hear her swallow.

It was her mother's name.

"I need to hear your voice," Grace prompted gently. "Speak up so Spirit can feel your vibrations."

"Y . . . yes," Polly replied.

"Ada passed over some time ago, is that right?"

"Right," Polly said.

"She comes to you in a motherly way and I see her ironing. Standing at an ironing board. And she wishes to say, to let you know, that things can be ironed out. 'Clear it up, Bubulah,' she says. 'Iron it out.' And you no longer need to worry about her love. She sends you her love."

Polly was silent.

"Thank you," I whispered in Polly's ear.

"Thank you," Polly said vacantly.

"You're welcome. I leave you that message with Spirit's blessing and may you go in peace." Grace leaned on her cane as she turned to move back up the aisle to the pine tree at the edge of the abyss.

"You told her about my mother," Polly accused harshly.

"I did not!"

"Quiet, you two," the woman in front of us warned again, this time with a venomous glance.

"May I come to you?"

Grace was now speaking to a man in a navy windbreaker.

"Your grandfather is standing beside you in Spirit. He wants you to check the left front wheel on your pickup. That wheel's out of alignment on that old Ford."

The man laughed comfortably and replied, "I wondered what was causing that shimmy."

Subdued chuckles trickled through the crowd as they shifted in their seats, more at ease.

Grace's bearing altered, too. Now she addressed the crowd in a conversational tone.

"Those of you who are regular visitors to our camp know that from time to time we allow mediums-in-training to read Spirit for us. However else would they be able to practice their natural gifts?"

The audience nodded in affirmation as Grace continued. "Since she is with us this afternoon, I invite you to welcome one of my private students who is currently undergoing her own spiritual development . . ."

52

"Way to go, Grace," I mumbled. My golden opportunity. Now Polly would really be speechless.

"Please join me in welcoming *Merrill Chase* to read Spirit."

I'd told Polly, truthfully, that I had found this place strangely appealing while I was writing my *Meanderings* article. I hadn't told her the rest of the story, *my* story, that I'd already taken a weekend workshop in mediumship development and under Grace's private tutelage I was practicing how to be one. For the purpose of doing readings I'd created a pseudonym from the maiden names of both of my grandmothers: *Merrill* and *Chase*.

The shushing woman's mouth hung open when I walked to the edge of the cliff. I could feel the warmth of the gathering increase. Turning, I was greeted with cordial applause and friendly smiles.

As I had been taught, I closed my eyes, rubbed my palms together, and savored the expectant hush. A few moments were necessary to clear my mind of the present and dismiss the knowledge that Polly had never witnessed me in this capacity and would probably mock me forever.

I wanted to forget everything and *feel*. "Enter into the Silence," Grace called it. *Enter the silence,* seek that place where I could allow my mind to become still and meditative. Even if I didn't come up with any actual spirit-contacts, the centering usually helped me deliver material that was persuasive enough.

"Tune into the power," Grace always advised, warning, "A shiver and a shake does not a medium make!"

Right away I actually did have an impression. I was aware of an area of agitation in the middle of a row to my right. But I was drawn, first, to a young man on my left and opened my eyes to sympathetically inquire, "May I come to you?"

I threw out the name "Paul," for no particular reason, and blurted the first thing that came into my mind. I told him that someone named Paul wished him to know he was happy at last. That was pretty easy. As Grace said, old-fashioned mediums may have had more to say, but modern-day mediums aren't expected to go much further. The young man expressed his gratitude.

I chalked up a win for Merrill Chase and closed my eyes again.

There was a queasy feeling in my stomach even before I asked a man in the second row, "May I come to you?"

You know how it is when you see a person who played a role in your life a very long time ago? There might be only a few vestiges left on the mask of their current countenance to identify, but enough to give you a clue.

No psychic gifts were necessary for me to recognize Karl Bittner; the discernable scent of his Old Spice cologne was a potent giveaway. He was a handsome man; his fair hair was now snow white but still sculpted precisely over his forehead as if an eternal wave had crested there. While he waited for me to deliver his message from Spirit he fingered a crystal pendant that dangled from a silver chain to nestle in the hairless V of his open shirt. His busy hands reminded me of the way his fingers would wander to his throat to nervously adjust the knot of his tie when he became impatient with his students.

Apparently (thankfully!) he did not recognize Eleanora Grendon.

Of course the woman who paced before the assembled believers was not the shy eighth grader he'd taught in Little Wolf. This was *Merrill Chase,* who was tan and toned from running. Her best feature, deep blue eyes she'd inherited from her mother, were hidden behind mirrored sunglasses that she had not bothered to remove. Instead of a brunette ponytail, the petite medium-to-be had striking gray hair (prematurely gray, I liked to think) worn in a short and wispy, boyish style.

Too many thoughts, too many extraneous issues. My concentration was blown. I hoped my furtive glance toward Polly resembled a heartfelt inquiry to Spirit for inspiration instead of despair.

Polly returned my gaze but she wore a puzzled frown. She was waiting, like Grace and everyone else, expecting me to respond.

I could feel the crowd hold its collective breath.

"Fake it 'til you make it," other beginning mediums had advised. Truthfully, I faked it most of the time. But absolutely *nothing* was there, that moment. Everything was blank.

I smiled weakly at Bittner in an attempt to soften dark furrows of apprehension on his face.

"As I come into your vibration . . . ," I began softly.

Knowing all I knew about this man, how could I pretend to deliver an unbiased message? I despised him!

An old aphorism came to me: "If three people call you an ass, buy a saddle." There was *no* way I could work that into a reasonable spirit-message no matter how badly I wanted to shout it. *Mr. Bittner, you are an ass!* Polly would agree with me about that. Okay, two of us thought so, but I knew Carolina Sawyer and Teddy Carter and Buck and Merry and most of our other eighth grade classmates would agree with me, too.

I coughed and cleared my throat.

"As I come into your vibration from the spirit side . . . ," I began, frantic for something fitting and safe to add. I was wringing my hands together so hard they began to ache.

Then I could sense, manifesting quite clearly now against the sun-sparkled foliage, a tall, hollow-eyed girl with long blond hair tangled over her shoulders in a careless manner. She stood closely behind Bittner as if she were claiming him.

I had been cautioned by Grace: "Even though you may see a spirit standing by someone, that *one* may not appreciate being apprised of the fact and if you force your message upon him you are 'casting your pearls before swine.' There is a proper time for all things. Choose it when giving your messages."

But I could not have spoken at that moment, even if I'd tried. The girl stared back at me with a dead, cold, defiant gaze. The sheer white dress she wore was torn, and it clung, dripping wet, to her ripening body. Her hair was wet, too.

I knew those icy eyes. I knew the insolent glance that was evolving into a sinister grin.

This was Sharon Gallagher.

"There is no escape from the pathway," Grace had admonished me. *"Yours is not an ephemeral ability, Eleanora. Once you're hooked, you can't discard it. You cannot walk away."*

All of Grace's examples that I'd emulated—all my lessons, careful imitations, and rehearsals—dissolved into a damp fog.

Instead, the familiar cold sweat, the racing heartbeat, the trembling, and the nausea of a panic attack emerged. I clenched my fists so my fingernails dug into my palms. I struggled to breathe.

Blindly, I reached backward, afraid I would stumble and accidentally fall over the limestone cliff.

Or be shoved by a watery hand.

For a long moment I clutched the nearby pine tree, hoping my vision would clear. I removed my sunglasses. Blinked hard. Rubbed my eyes.

Then I bowed to Grace with a quick apology, excused myself, and exited unsteadily down the path between the crowded benches into the solace of the shadowy woods.

Whispers followed. Whispers from those who turned to watch. Whispers that echoed eerily through the years. Whispers that rose like reprimands through the sheltering forest to haunt me even now.

4

*S*till having panic attacks, are we?"

Polly deftly maneuvered the car down the hill while I slumped in the passenger seat. My head was between my knees. She had assumed, correctly, that I wanted her to drive.

"You'll never guess who I saw."

My voice was muffled by my denim skirt. I was using it to swab the clammy perspiration from my face. And if I threw up, I didn't want vomit on the floor of my car.

Who *had* I seen, besides Bittner? I wasn't sure about Sharon; that may have been a hallucination. I might have imagined it.

Hallucination, my ass. It was Sharon Gallagher, all right; I had *not* invented her ghost! But I couldn't confess that to Polly; she'd race straight to the closest emergency room and claim I'd gone over the edge. Maybe I had.

"Who?"

"Huh?"

"I said *who* did you see?" Polly asked. "Who was it? Nellie, are you okay?"

"Bittner." I raised my head too quickly and felt dizzy all over again.

"*Our* Bittner?" Polly replied. "Mr. Bittner? Karl Bittner?"

"He was at the meeting. I saw him sitting there."

"Our eighth grade teacher?" Polly laughed. "That's freaking crazy! No wonder you panicked; I'd have zoned out, too! How'd he look?"

"Older, still handsome. It was really weird to see him, though."

"Weird to see him *there*," Polly added. "You suppose he's into Spiritualism now?"

"He was wearing a crystal around his neck. That's about all I noticed before . . ."

"Before you lost it?"

"Right. Before I lost it. Careful on these curves; I might lose more!"

We were silent for a long time as Polly retraced our route back to Madison. By the time we crossed Lake Wisconsin on the Merrimac Ferry, the sun was setting over the water and we got out of the car to stand by the rail and revel in the dazzling twilight.

"So, okay. What the fuck was that all about?" Polly asked, finally. "When were you going to tell me that you decided to become a *medium*?"

I shrugged, "I was feeling restless."

"Restless or reckless?"

"Try feckless," I suggested.

"Okay, sounds good. *Feckless*. What does it mean?"

"Irresponsible, I think. Maybe hopeless. Here's an example: One day at the market I found a grocery list in the bottom of the shopping cart I took. I bought everything that was on that list. Threw my own away. I still have groats in my pantry. What do you do with groats? I had to toss the kale."

"You're avoiding my question, Nell."

I had no clear answer.

"I just wanted to do something different with my life. When I was married to Michael I was locked into all these committee meetings—the country club, the library, the art museum, the YMCA, a bunch of charitable causes." I shrugged, took a deep breath. "I'm not saying they weren't worthwhile, but I couldn't do anything for *me*. I had to be so careful not to be seen doing something that reflected badly on Michael that I had to assume obligations I didn't want because I was a lawyer's wife. He could uphold his stern professional reputation as long as I was there to soften the edges. I hated it. Michael even got mad if I left the house wearing Birkenstocks, for God's sake!"

"You knew what you were getting into when you married him!"

Polly wasn't buying the poor-abused-lawyer's-wife story, so I tried another slant.

"Well, then there was the divorce. We both wanted it so that was okay, but Odessa left for New Zealand with her new baby girl and her boyfriend around that time, which broke my heart, and my son is never any help—Sky lives in Winnipeg and he never comes home. See, I was glad to be on my own at last but I was drifting without any sense of direction. Shopping for groats! Because I was desperate for someone to tell me what to do! I still had friends, like my book club and the women I golfed with, but when you get divorced, even if you and your ex-spouse are still speaking civilly to each other, your friends feel they have to take sides. As it turned out, most of our crowd chose Michael. And then there was the move. I hate moving! I hate messing up my nest and feeling lost. It all added up. Stress levels. You know, like that graph? I was flying off the chart."

Blah blah blah. I was pouring it out for Polly like water rushing over Niagara Falls. She probably knew much of this already. All my life I've acted straight from my heart, not from my head.

"Okay, so you were doing a story on this old-fashioned psychic and the next thing, geez, you're one of 'em. Did she hypnotize you?"

I couldn't tell her about Sharon's materialization; that would definitely have her thinking I'd *really* gone around the bend or off the deep end or whatever she wanted to call *crazy*. Instead, I explained how I'd thought it might be fun to get a feel for what being a medium was like. It was the truth.

59

"But Grace thinks I'm her protégé. I've been meeting privately with her and sitting in on some of her classes for the summer. I'm only pretending . . ."

"She must not be very psychic if she can't see through that facade," Polly cracked.

I ignored her and continued. "I took my grandmothers' names, Merrill and Chase, so I could do this medium thing 'undercover.' If I get enough background stuff, I'm going to write a book and call it *Medium Grace.* She has some mind-boggling stories and no one's really looked into the actual remnants of nineteenth-century Spiritualism that still exist. Like the Wocanaga Camp. I love the innocence of the place. I think it's really sweet."

"Nellie, do you think that's fair?" Polly shot me a critical glance. "You told me this afternoon that people revere Wocanaga. Isn't it disrespectful to denigrate their beliefs? Spiritualism is their religion, right?"

"I'm not *dissing* them!" I was becoming annoyed. "I'm just trying to *understand.* You know how I've always wanted to know why people believe the things they do and the unusual ways they express it. Their motivation for it. *That whole mystery of faith.* It's always interested me."

"Like your curiosity about Catholics when we were kids."

"Well, there's that, I suppose . . ."

"I guess you haven't changed," Polly decided, shaking her head.

"Neither have you," I said. "You still insist on being my moral guide."

"But you were right about one thing." Polly ignored my peevish outburst with a grin.

"What's that?"

"You said it would be fun."

"Fun?"

"It was funny as hell." She put her arm around my shoulders and gave me a hug. I began laughing, too. "Imagine Ada standing at an ironing board. My mother never ironed a day in her life! And you, the *inscrutable Merrill Chase,* standing up there telling some guy that *Paul* was happy now. I almost cracked up."

60

"I guess I got lucky," I confessed.

"Maybe it was this Saint Christopher medal on your keychain," she said, dangling it over the water. "Who gave it to you, anyway?"

"I bought it at Holy Hill. At the gift shop."

"I bet it's *blessed*."

"Well . . ."

"Who blessed it?"

"I don't know, a priest. Or a monk. He sprinkled holy water on the medal. And on me, too."

"He blessed *you*?" Polly whooped.

"Okay, so what's with this Tibetan rosary you have on your wrist, huh? Do you really believe in that?"

"Nellie!"

"Or that tattoo on your back, above your thong. In the first place, I can't believe you're wearing a thong at your age, and in the second place, what's Our Lady of Guadalupe doing there? She winked at me when you grabbed your luggage from the baggage carousel at the airport."

I could feel my mood brighten. This was definitely like old times, one of our lighthearted wars.

"And what's so bad about being blessed by a priest?" I added. "You make it sound ridiculous."

I grabbed my keys from her hand, intending to drive.

"I'll tell you what's ridiculous," she said, taking her place in the passenger seat as the ferry bumped the opposite shore. "*You're* ridiculous, Nell. Adopting other people's beliefs, 'just for fun,' and 'borrowing' their symbols and practicing their rituals without any consideration for their sincerity. I'm surprised you're not wearing a yarmulke. You haven't changed a bit. I don't think you're ever going to grow up."

But she didn't say it in an angry way. She was still teasing me. Polly usually tolerates my idiosyncrasies. Maybe, this time, she was scolding herself, too. I mean, the Tibetan rosary? And Our Lady of Guadalupe?

The real reason for Polly's visit was our high school reunion at Little Wolf the following day. I had managed to avoid all the past gatherings of our Class of '69 but by the time our thirtieth rolled around I called Polly and begged her to make an appearance with me. I even offered to shell out her airfare from LAX to Madison, but she didn't insist that I go that far. Still, it was a hard sell. She claimed she'd never wanted to return to Bear Lake again. I wasn't crazy about the location either, thanks to Sharon's final escapade.

"I'll make it up to you," I promised.

"I have at least a hundred of your worthless IOUs," she replied with a slight edge on her voice.

But she relented at last when I said, "We can't let ourselves still be haunted by something that happened so long ago!"

Of course that was before I encountered Bittner and Sharon at Inspiration Point. One more (important!) reason I couldn't tell Polly that I thought I'd seen Sharon's manifestation there.

Actually, the town where we grew up is about 150 miles north of Madison. Not really "up north," but far enough that people from Milwaukee have cottages on Bear Lake and think they're in the sticks. Anyone from Little Wolf who wants to go "up north" knows that means Minocqua or Star Lake, or even Lac Vieux Desert.

We left Madison early the next morning and took our time getting there. The appeal of the Wisconsin countryside in mid-August lends itself to a leisurely trip. If you take Highway 22 you go through lots of idyllic small towns with Victorian houses and tall church steeples. Blue asters and Queen Anne's Lace danced with black-eyed Susans. Sumac along the roads was beginning to turn scarlet and occasionally a wagon in a farmyard offered a surfeit of someone's garden harvest: fat red tomatoes, cucumbers, cantaloupe, sweet corn, bushel baskets of zucchini, and acorn squash.

Holsteins camped in the shade, placid old ladies, unperturbed, chewing their cud.

"Mooooo," Polly called to them, rolling down the window. "Moooooo!"

"I can never figure out why people do that," I told her. "Don't you have cows in California?"

"They're not like Wisconsin cows," Polly replied. "California cows have *attitude.*"

We made a brief detour to a cheese factory where we picked up a bag of warm cheese curds. Polly bought a green cap with gold lettering that said "Grateful Curd-Head" and put it on right away.

"I've been dreaming about eating these again," she said, offering me a handful of salty curds that were only minutes out of the vat. "Ummmm! Now *this* is Wisconsin!"

The curds were rubbery, warm, and squeaky. Munching on them, we sounded like a pair of gluttonous mice.

"Perfect," I admitted. "The absolutely perfect lunch."

Our reunion was at Bear Lake, only three miles out of Little Wolf. We checked into the local motel, then toured our hometown to see how it had changed. Of course the sentimental picture I carried in my heart no longer existed; that wasn't a surprise. Sheltering elms had disappeared; the sturdy oaks I'd strung my tent between each summer were long gone. Could this be the same sidewalk where I'd outlined my hopscotch grid? Where I knew every crack and frost heave by heart beneath my roller skates' scroll?

I parked in front of the bungalow where I'd turned my face to Teddy Carter's for lingering good-night kisses on Friday nights after he walked me home from the movie, both of us sweaty and breathless after an hour of making out behind the bandstand. We were almost the same height if I stood on the first step.

I'd been thinking of Teddy Carter a lot, lately. He was one former classmate I was curious about and definitely hoped to see that night. Hoped to see? Hell, he was the sole reason I wanted to come but I didn't want to show up by myself. Of course I'd never have confessed that to Polly.

I didn't share this with her either, but during sleepless vigils back in Madison waiting for Michael to come home from working late (his lame excuse), I'd lie in bed and manufacture outrageous fantasies in which I roamed the country to seek old boyfriends I'd dated in high school and college, guys I'd wanted to sleep with then but hadn't because only "easy" girls went all the way. I still fantasized about a secret F*** Quest to collect what was "overdue." Forget the fact that I was almost fifty! I tried to imagine Teddy Carter still boyish but with a mop of steel-gray hair, succumbing to my raptures. In each "Quest" I was slim and stunning. I had no idea what Teddy looked like now or even what he did. But in every dream I invented, he was easily seduced.

"Did I ever tell you about the time my mother asked me what *fuck* meant?" I asked Polly. "It's so casually thrown around now, but back when we were kids that word still raised eyebrows. So one day my mother, in her sublime but daffy ignorance, asked me what it meant, spelling it out. 'Don't laugh, Eleanora, but I'm not sure I know the meaning of F-U-C-K,' she said. She probably thought she'd go to hell for saying it out loud, so I replied, *'Fuck?'*"

"You always walked on the edge," Polly joked.

"I remember she was working in the garden over there, near those daylilies. She cringed when I said it, so of course I said 'It's like giving somebody the finger. Flipping the bird.' Mom was still mystified. So I told her, 'Why don't you ask Daddy?' because I thought it might be a test to see how much I knew, but she wasn't that savvy. 'I don't want to bother him, Honey,' she said."

"Your mother was really that clueless?" Polly asked, laughing. "I suppose Ada was, too."

"I explained it the best that I could, in seventh grade terms. I told her, 'It means to *do it!*' Remember that little booklet she gave me, *The Stork Didn't Bring You?*"

"Hey, I remember that book! We were traumatized by the entire prospect of even *seeing* a penis."

"It's all my mother's fault," I agreed, pulling the bill of Polly's curd-head cap down to her nose.

We were silent then for a while.

"Just think; the strangers who live here don't have the slightest idea of the little dramas captured by those walls. The Christmas mornings, the loose baby teeth, the spankings. I got more spankings with that damn ping-pong paddle than Buddy did!

"I learned to ride my bike and jump rope on this driveway. You and I built snow forts and jumped in leaf piles on this lawn, and we played Monopoly for hours on that porch."

"It was Sharon's Monopoly game," Polly reminded me. "She always had to be the banker. Her aunt's place next door doesn't look so hot."

Gloria Piekarski's property seemed cruelly diminished by the ruthlessness of time.

"Didn't she and Cookie move away to Florida? Neither of them wanted to stick around after what happened to Sharon."

"The whole town was traumatized," I said.

"Remember the way Sharon used to make us play church with her? *Just pretend!* she'd say. *Pretend the NECCO wafers are Communion wafers.* Remember? *Pretend that oak tree is Saint Francis, and that one's Saint Anthony . . .*"

Then Polly insisted on looking for the famous Our Lady's Garden Rosary. Sharon, Polly, and I had helped Cookie and Gloria assemble it in Gloria's backyard. My dad even lent a hand. "It was such an unexpected blessing, Mr. Grendon," Gloria told him, flushed with enthusiasm. "You wouldn't believe the folks we had to outsmart to get this! Fifty bucks! My husband, God have mercy, would kill me if he was still around." She crossed herself on the bib of her apron. *"Fifty bucks,"* he'd say, *"for a bunch of old bowling balls."*

But it was more than a bunch of bowling balls—it was *sixty* very heavy bowling balls, some all black, some black marbled with red or green, each cemented on top of a pipe that served as its pedestal. The bowling balls were placed in a circle, connected to one another by a big iron chain. The entire rosary, finally installed in Gloria Pickarski's garden, was 345 feet long with a 10-foot crucifix on the end that carried a realistic, aluminum Jesus. The pièce de résistance was the life-size plaster statue of the Blessed Virgin Mary that weighed 800 pounds and had to be set in place beneath the kitchen window with an end-loader. Mary came with the rosary for an extra $200 because Gloria couldn't bear to see them separated. The entire spectacle had been part of a convent in Canada that had gone belly-up.

Apparently the rosary was now defunct, too, but that didn't stop us from reminiscing about its installation. For two weeks, Sharon, Polly, and I had brushed the whole thing with several coats of white paint. Painting the chain was especially hard. Father O'Neil came down from Sacred Heart to bless the rosary with holy water. The display became a "roadside attraction" for Catholics and Protestants alike. On Sunday afternoons, strange cars clogged the driveway that we shared with Gloria, and I overheard heated arguments between my parents about the steady trickle of visitors who sauntered between our yard and hers to recite the rosary along the chain of bowling balls.

Mother's generosity of spirit became strained. "I understand these people are devout, but I cannot stand that eyesore," she'd complained. "Our privacy's being invaded. I can't even go outdoors! Only a couple of you-know-whats would fall for something as tacky as those darned bowling balls."

"To each his own, Margery," Dad told her.

She meant "Polacks."

*P*olly and I wrapped up our melancholy tour with a leisurely stroll down Main Street. These days she may call herself Polly Blue, but Cornbloom's had been her family's store. It seemed like every small town in Wisconsin had a dry goods store run by a Jewish family who comfortably assimilated into the community. Polly's dad belonged to the Masons just like my dad, and Ada was in my mother's Bridge Club. The Cornblooms went to Temple in Appleton on holidays. I knew they weren't Orthodox because Polly ate bacon and loved pork chops.

The Cornblooms lived in an apartment on the second floor of their store. The building was torn down after a fire in the 1980s. A tanning spa now shared the space along with an abandoned video rental shop. My father's insurance office had been across the street, next to Seger's Funeral Home. Which reminded me of Leonard Twyn and Sharon, so I changed the subject.

"What about those matching pajamas we had in eighth grade?" I asked. "All three of us had the same ones."

"With poofy bloomers," Polly said. "And polka dots."

"They came from Cornbloom's Dry Goods," I reminded her.

"That's probably why I hated them," Polly replied. "We had them in three colors: pink, blue, and green."

"Sharon wore hers with underpants instead of bloomers."

"I'm surprised she wore anything on her bottom at all. One time Sharon came into my dad's store to buy a bra," Polly continued. "I showed her where the dressing room was, then I watched while she tried it on."

"She let you?"

"Sharon? You know she loved to show off her tits."

Polly was right; Sharon did. And Polly Cornbloom adored Sharon Gallagher; she never made the slightest effort to hide it.

Business at Cornbloom's Dry Goods dwindled as shoppers were drawn to department stores in nearby cities or maybe the Sears catalog for their underwear, overshoes, tennis shoes, and housedresses. Nothing at Cornbloom's was stylish. Mother wouldn't shop there unless she was desperate.

Polly was often asked to help her parents at the store. If this happened to interfere with plans we'd made, I'd pin price tags on men's heavy work socks, long underwear, or overalls or straighten up the storeroom so she could get away.

One early summer afternoon I stopped by the store to pick up Polly for our Red Cross swimming lessons, as usual. We always rode our bikes together to Bear Lake. But before Polly could go, she had to unpack a new shipment of brassieres from a cardboard box and attach price tags, then sort them out according to cup size and arrange them on the counter.

"Hey, look at me," Polly said. She had looped one of the biggest bras over her shoulders and fastened it at the back. It must have been a size "F" at least because she started stuffing it with cotton work socks from the men's counter and, laughing, I helped her. When we were done she looked ridiculous and paraded around the counter like a movie star, the enormous brassiere ramming out in front like a pair of rocket ships strapped to her chest.

"Polly," I tried to warn her, but at the sound of her father's footsteps she turned around and right into him, poking Mr. Corn-bloom in the belly with her bazooms.

Polly did not go to swimming lessons that day.

❧

The population of our hometown had been around one thousand when Polly and I were kids. There were seventy graduates in our Class of 1969. For our reunion, maybe half of them arrived with their spouses or "significant others" and we shared a cafeteria-style banquet of the usual chicken and ham. I felt ill at ease with the forced gaiety that seeped through the noisy crowd; I'd been away from these unfamiliar people far too long. It was like a masquerade—inside every other middle-aged person (Time-worn? Ripened? Seasoned? Mature?) there must be someone I once knew, someone whose algebra I'd copied or who sat near me in history or whose naked body I showered with after gym. Someone who'd *mattered* to me then.

During the awarding of prizes ("most grandchildren," "married the longest," "lost the most hair") I excused myself to use the ladies' room. Then, instead of returning to my table I wandered outside to sit on the edge of the wide veranda of the Bear Lake Pavilion with my sandals off and idly traced designs in the damp sand as the sun was setting.

It was almost eerie, the way everyone had aged. Scrap Rollins combed a varnished rake of hair over from a part that cut a neat swath from his earlobe to his crown. Carolina Sawyer had gained at least forty pounds and had a triple chin. Hannah Larkin still looked pretty good but someone said she was having an affair with a married man, a professor at UW–Madison.

And there was Teddy. My *Teddy Bear.*

After catching my first glimpse of him I saw how rewarding my imaginary F*** Quest might have been. He looked terrific. As handsome as ever with a bright smile of recognition that triggered a hot flash from the top of my head to my toes. He still resembled the All-American Boy. You just knew by looking at him that even though his sandy buzz cut was a little thin on top, he was still athletic, fond of faded jeans and old baseball caps. In fact, I realized now, Teddy looked a lot like Brett Favre, quarterback for the Green Bay Packers. He was sweet, too, a little mischievous but not mean. I'd been crazy about Teddy since I kissed him in the cloakroom in kindergarten.

"I didn't think I'd ever see you again," I admitted, falling into his welcoming embrace.

"Your luck must've run out," he joked and held me tight. "You look fantastic," he whispered in my ear. My heart sang.

His wife was younger: tall, blonde, and stunning. One of those women with great bones who doesn't know the meaning of *concealer* and who can pull her hair back in a simple twist and look like a million bucks. So much for my fantasies.

He introduced her to me. I immediately forgot her name.

Later, seated on the veranda, drawing pictures in the cool sand with my toes, I was lonesome. Not for any one person—rather, for the way things used to be. The simplicity of childhood. I was choking with melancholy and ready to go home.

"Are you about ready to leave?" Polly joined me.

"Almost. Are you?"

"Anytime," Polly answered. "This place still has unpleasant vibes."

"I know what you mean," I responded. "Want to go back indoors? It's almost time for the big raffle drawing!"

"Whoopee," Polly said with fake enthusiasm. "That's almost as exciting as a spirit lightbulb that never goes out." She sat down next to me and shucked her shoes. "Do you remember 'No-Toe-Joe'?"

"No-Toe-Joe, the Old Crow . . . I wonder if Miss Khrol still has her little cottage across the lake."

"She probably died a long time ago," Polly said. "Everything's changed. Even No-Toe-Joe, if he's out here lurking in the shadows. That guy gave us the creeps. He must've been in his twenties when we were kids. He'd be old now, and toothless."

"No-Toe gave *everybody* the creeps, Polly. And the Old Crow may have been in a wheelchair but she wasn't really old back then, we just wanted her to be."

"So she was a *young* crow, not an old crow. If she's alive, she's probably watching us right now from the other side of the lake with her father's telescope."

"What made you think of No-Toe-Joe?"

"The smell of the water, maybe. This heavy fragrance, kind of fishy but fresh, mixed with the pines, the—"

"Beer," I interrupted.

"This place has always smelled like beer, even in winter when we came out here to ice skate."

"No-Toe always had a beer in his hand."

"Except at the movies. Then it was a bag of old maids from the bottom of the popcorn machine," Polly recalled. "Every Sunday matinee you'd hear him in the back of the theater, crunching old maids. He must've had awfully strong teeth."

"The guys all liked him because he let them look at his collection of dirty magazines."

"What?"

"Teddy told me that once. Maybe they weren't girlie mags; they could have just been calendars with pictures of nude women. That's why the boys never made fun of him; they didn't want to lose access to his pornography."

"Well, they *did* say he was made up of spare parts."

"Because his dad was the undertaker. Thanks for reminding me, Polly."

"If we went for a walk right now, I'll bet we'd run into No-Toe."

"He was right here that night we went swimming, remember?"

"Sharon's 'Chocolate Dip,'" Polly said softly. "He was chewing ice. Sitting on this porch."

"With a beer in his hand."

"Of course, with a beer . . ."

And then we were both thinking about Sharon again. Her presence, insistent, mingled with the musty warmth of the summer evening and merged into the sunset's pale afterglow of regret.

*W*hat're you two up to out here, anyways?"

Buck Springer and Duane Morris were leaning on each other.

"You gals still party poopers after all these years?" Duane asked. "Aw, geez, it figures."

Buck Springer had been Teddy's best friend. "We brought you a coupla Miller Lites," he said, hoping to join our conversation. We took the beers but, bored with our despondent mood, the guys soon went back inside.

"I Can't Stop Lovin' You," Ray Charles mourned in the background. *"I've made up my mind . . ."*

Polly and I sang along, unable to help ourselves.

"Oh, Polly . . . ," I breathed deeply and sighed, reaching for her hand.

"Oh, Nellie . . . ," she laughed, returning our secret handshake, something I'd forgotten in the thick gauze of intervening years.

Squeeze, squeeze, squeeze. One, two, three. That meant "I Love You." Polly's idea. It meant we would always be best friends.

The diet I'd been on to lose ten pounds, the ridiculous price I'd paid for my black linen sheath, the expensive cut of my salt and pepper hair, the crinkles hinting of deeper crow's feet soon to set in—none of that meant a thing to Polly. She saw through it all. On the other hand, this woman sitting next to me in a white tank top and long chambray skirt always had to hold my hand when she squatted to pee outside so she wouldn't lose her balance. One time she got bit by a yellowjacket on her bare butt. I could tell you when Polly began her period, smoked her first joint, shaved her legs, stopped shaving her legs. She, of course, knew exactly the same secret, personal things about me. Except I still shave my legs.

I couldn't possibly divulge what I had seen at Wocanaga, but I confessed, "I'm still thinking about Sharon."

Polly nodded. There was something in the summer night air that made Sharon's memory almost tangible, as if she were sitting right there on the edge of the veranda beside us. If she *were* here, though, she would be the life of this party.

"The Chocolate Dip was more than thirty years ago," I said, clearing my throat, feeling definitely weepy again.

"Thirty-four, thirty-five, something like that?"

Sharon had insisted on going for a swim after midnight. It still

71

didn't make any sense to me. The three of us were not bad swimmers, but Sharon was the strongest and made the deepest dives from the raft. I couldn't tell in the dark, but I didn't think the raft was still there now. It had been a jerry-rigged outfit, anyway—made of empty oil barrels lashed together. The barrels were topped with boards that were covered with canvas tarp. It was tippy, and causing it to rock back and forth was a favorite taunt older kids used to make little kids lose their balance and fall in the lake. On one side, the high dive projected from a tall wooden tower. I suppose now it wouldn't seem high at all, but then it seemed like every step up the ladder was an intimidating test. You could always cannonball from the high dive but you couldn't back down the steps.

One time Sharon dove from the raft and resurfaced holding a clamshell she'd found at the bottom of the lake. None of us had ever gone so far down into the chilling deep that we could bring back a prize like that. I had a fleeting suspicion that she had found the clamshell along the shore and secreted it inside her swimsuit. Still, I attempted, over and over, to get down to the mucky bottom of the lake, that frigid place where the sun never filtered and the water had an icy chill. But I could not get that far, even when I tore off my swimming cap and blew out most of my breath.

"I can still see Sharon on the raft with that damned clam shell," I said to Polly. "No one even noticed me, not even you. Each time I came back up, gasping for air and practically dying, everybody was still crowded around her, admiring the one she was showing off."

"You're still sore about that?" Polly said, mystified.

I guess I was.

The sky slowly turned from peach to amethyst and reflected in water ringed with silhouettes of cedar and pine.

Inside the familiar Bear Lake Pavilion, red and black balloons and crepe paper streamers (our school colors) were sagging in the humidity where the raffle for Green Bay Packer tickets was proceeding, the highlight of the evening.

"I think we should go back."

"What?"

"We should go back inside," Polly said. "I didn't fly all the way out here to avoid everybody else and sit in the dark with you."

Duane Morris won the Packer tickets. Eventually I bribed him—with the promise of another beer and a dance with me later—to keep Teddy's wife out of the way for a while. I didn't feel guilty about that at all.

Teddy and I danced to Elvis Presley's "Can't Help Falling in Love." That wasn't a coincidence; I asked the DJ to play it. It was our song all the years we dated and my only regret was that the song was so short. Teddy murmured the lyrics in my ear and I recalled how deeply I'd believed *some things are meant to be*. I overheard someone say, "Now it finally seems like old times, doesn't it? Nellie and Teddy, dancing together." Everybody was watching us except Teddy's wife. I had no idea where Duane had taken her. And I didn't care. We danced the next dance, too.

"Having a good time?" he asked.

"Now I am," I said, not at all embarrassed by my candor.

"So am I," he whispered in my ear as we deftly dipped and paused, then resumed the dance steps again.

I shouldn't have been surprised, the way I moved so naturally with Teddy. We had learned to kiss together and we had learned to dance together. There used to be a jukebox in the corner of the back room of Lulu's Dairy Bar where, sustained by Cokes and french fries, we danced to slow, romantic tunes and left with the smell of stale grease and cigarette smoke embedded in our clothes and our hair. It felt completely natural to be held in his arms.

I was tempted to tell him about my F*** Quest, but something held me back. Surely it wasn't my better judgment; I had abandoned that when I'd bribed Duane to entertain Teddy's wife, what's-her-name.

"You were the first girl I ever loved," Teddy confessed.

For a moment, I was absurdly alarmed that he might have a "Quest" of his own.

"I wonder what it might have been like, what our lives—"

73

"That was a long time ago, Teddy," I said, cutting him off, uneasy all of a sudden.

"I still remember the first time we kissed."

"You mean kindergarten?"

"No. At Buck Springer's. Our first *serious* kiss."

"Sharon dared us to do it," I recalled. "We were in sixth grade. One Saturday afternoon in fall. Afterward I rode my bike down the hill really fast. I have this very visual memory of dry leaves scattering like crazy in the wind behind my wheels."

"Sharon Gallagher," Teddy said her name wistfully. "I wonder what she would look like now."

"Like her mom. Plump and dumpy," I replied with confidence.

"You still have a problem with her?"

"Only because she flirted with you. Mercilessly."

"Well, I liked her; all the guys did."

"She would never have made it to graduation . . ."

"I told you once I thought she got it on with Bittner." The song had ended but Teddy was still holding me in his arms. "I've always been sorry I told you that."

"Mr. Bittner." I tensed in reaction to his name, nearly tripping over Teddy's feet. "Why?"

"Because you told me then you thought that maybe Mr. Bittner got her pregnant and caused her to drown. *You* were the one who told me that, Nell. You told me you thought that was what happened, but I never repeated it to anyone else."

"So . . . ?"

"So how come everybody else started thinking that, too?"

"We had our own 'code of silence,'" I said. "Like when we played Horses. Everyone kept quiet about it."

He seemed so remorseful that I realized Sharon was attending our reunion after all.

"Okay, I got the idea from a library book," I admitted. "I think it was *An American Tragedy.* By Theodore Dreiser. The guy drowns his pregnant girlfriend. It seemed logical at the time."

Teddy's wife was heading our way. He dropped his arm from my shoulder, and I continued, "This guy takes his girlfriend out in a

74

rowboat and he pushes her over the side. It was a movie, too, with Montgomery Clift and Elizabeth Taylor. One night when I was babysitting I saw the movie on TV and then I read the book. The bad guy gets the electric chair in the end. But I never said Sharon was pregnant . . ."

*W*hat's the difference?" Hannah Larkin said later that night.

We'd all had quite a bit more beer by then.

"I remember when you told me that all the guys on the basketball team went all the way with Sharon."

"I said that?"

"It didn't take much imagination, did it, Nell?" Carolina added. "The way they acted so stupid around her."

"Bittner, too," Hannah said.

"Oh, hell, the whole damn basketball team, *and* Bittner!" Lucy Bolton interrupted. "They were all completely disgusting. Sharon was disgusting, too. I never could stand that fucking little bitch."

"No one ever reached a conclusion for the definite cause of her death," Polly said.

"I thought the coroner said she drowned."

"Yes, but why? That never made sense. Sharon was the strongest swimmer of all of us."

"Well, we *all* thought that Bittner drowned her the night of my party," Carolina said. "Wasn't that your idea, too, Nellie?"

"How come we never told our parents that?"

"Somebody must've said something because Bittner quit teaching in the middle of the next school year and disappeared."

"Nellie saw him yesterday," Polly offered.

There was total silence.

"I thought I did," I said, grimacing at Polly. "I might have been mistaken. You know, thinking about the reunion and everything. He was probably on my mind . . ."

*E*ventually the party wound down. People began to say good-bye: "See you soon," "Take care," "See you in five years," all the typical farewells.

"Thanks a lot, Polly. You might as well have said I've become a spirit-medium and I'm haunted by my past."

"You and Sharon picked me up with your bikes and we went to Carolina's party together that night. The night she drowned," Polly argued as we walked a little unsteadily across the gravel parking lot toward the car.

"I don't want to think about Sharon anymore, ever! Give it a rest, Polly! Jesus! You think I'm still obsessed with Sharon; what about *you*, after all these years!"

"I remember lots of stuff, Nell." Polly wasn't smiling. "You and Sharon picked me up, and the three of us rode our bikes to Carolina's and we were together almost all that night. Like we usually were. Even for the Chocolate Dip. We saw No-Toe-Joe but we *never actually saw Mr. Bittner . . .*"

It occurred to me later that Polly may have wanted to say more about him, but I'd impatiently interrupted her.

"Look. Carolina told me she asked all our old teachers to our reunion this year, including from grade school, and Mr. Bittner's the only one she heard from. He sent his regrets because he had another commitment."

"Oh yeah?" Polly bent down to shake a pebble from one of her huaraches.

When I saw him at Wocanaga yesterday, I could have added, *he was there with Sharon's ghost.*

Instead, I said, "Apparently he teaches at the Wisconsin School for the Visually Handicapped, in Janesville."

She reached for my arm to steady herself. "The school for the blind?"

"I know what you're thinking," I replied. "We always used to say Mr. Bittner had Roman hands."

5

Okay, Frydeswyde Quimby. And Angella Wing.

I love old houses. I love the normal wear and tear, the scuffed woodwork, webbed cracks in the plastered walls, penciled marks on doorways that record someone's inch-by-inch progress from toddler to adult.

I also enjoy researching the stories of houses and imagining the secrets sealed in the creaking floors. I like to sense the conversations they've absorbed, envision the dreams they've assimilated and the hopes and even the despair submerged behind the decayed facades.

As I said earlier, I preferred not to leave our comfortable neighborhood when Michael and I split, so part of our divorce settlement included a long-vacant colonial revival of faded pea-green shingle and stone that his law firm had accepted as payment from a client years ago. It had a hip roof and an unkempt yard overrun with indeterminate shrubbery. Previous owners had altered the interior to create student housing. Cheap paneling was nailed over plastered walls and clumsy partitions divided spacious rooms that had coffered ceilings. Woodwork stripped bare had never been restored.

Beer cans, used condoms, litter from overnight parties and other dubious activities cluttered every room.

Any exterior modifications had to be approved by the National Register of Historic Places. When University Heights had been developed in the 1890s as one of Madison's first suburbs, an architectural challenge quickly ensued: who would build the most remarkable residence? Louis Sullivan was retained. So was Frank Lloyd Wright. Frideswyde Quimby did not develop into a significant architect but Frideswyde *was a woman,* which was most unusual in her day. My quirky pea green house was her one and only legacy. In 1894 she fled Madison with a tenor during a touring performance of *Rigoletto* and was never heard from again.

Of course, Frideswyde's story lent the house a sensational appeal for me. I loved that a woman had conceived such a wonderfully eccentric dwelling. The many nooks and crannies gave the house a fanciful character that I adored. Only a stone's throw from the Frank Lloyd Wright house, my pea-green goddess stood at the highest point where it was now hemmed in by many square miles of city and suburban development. I prized the unusual windows—some were oval stained-glass jewels, some clear and semi-circular with beveled rays that suggested a setting (or rising) sun. In many places, windows were clustered together like tall, narrow neighbors. I was convinced the two-story polygonal porch had originally been topped with a pointed roof but I needed documentation to persuade the National Register and could not proceed with my summit until I had their okay.

No permission was required to have the inside repaired, just a robust checkbook. The wide foyer offered access to the first floor sunporch on the left and the parlor on the right. A gracious, open flight of steps led to the hall on the second floor. Beyond the stairway there was a dining room on the right, and then the butler's pantry and the kitchen. Outward bays of three windows graced each of the largest first floor rooms.

Off the broad second floor hall were doors leading to the upper sunporch, a study or nursery attached to a large bedroom with

78

another bay, and an enormous bathroom. Toward the rear of the second floor were three bedrooms and another, smaller bath.

The third floor no doubt provided rooms for the servants. There was attic space there, too, and a narrow back stairway led down to an outside door on the first level, near my kitchen.

Contractors were able to bring back much of Frideswyde's original intention, but as I said earlier, I moved in before their work was complete. My budget was strained by that time and I figured I could handle the rest of the painting and a few other details myself. I didn't anticipate a lot of interruptions. That's when I took my first trip to Wocanaga, to research my short piece for *Meanderings*.

Soon after that initial visit (with Grace's chilling identification of the Lord's Prayer ring) I set aside the rolls of wallpaper, hung my paintbrushes out to dry, and enrolled in Grace Waverly's introductory class, Personal Development of Mediumship. I began collecting questions to ask her so when I finished my article I could embark on yet another project that I was tentatively going to call *Medium Grace*.

I drove up to Wocanaga every week, encouraging Grace to talk about her career in mediumship, where she grew up (Rochester, New York), her family (widowed with two daughters), and how she became interested in mediumship (her mother was involved with Spiritualism, too). She stressed that everything comes with a price. When she became a medium, Grace claimed, her life became more challenging. As her abilities increased, she began to suffer from unpleasant things because she could pick them up more easily, psychically. But she said she also increased her capacity for enjoyment at the same time because she was more attuned, more sensitive, more alive.

Grace remained patient and gracious throughout. She obviously enjoyed tutoring me as her protégé but she was careful to insist that my unfoldment must proceed slowly and with dignity.

"When you connect with Spirit, your lives are bound in an inextricable way."

My preliminary sessions with Grace were followed in late summer by the fiasco of my ill-fated visit to Wocanaga with Polly, and then Sharon's apparition or whatever the hell it was that scared the shit out of me—so any motivation I'd previously felt for writing *Medium Grace* flew away like thistledown.

All of this clarification is, I suppose, to justify the fact that after Polly returned to California following our class reunion I lacked incentive to do much at all. With the air out of my book project, I had no excuse, no worthwhile source of procrastination, to keep me from working on the house. There was no getting around the fact that the living room needed wallpapering and I had to do something about my bedroom and the rest of the second floor (the third floor could wait forever), but when I'm working on a menial task, even when I'm exercising, I find too many opportunities to think.

One day during my morning walk I began wondering if Michael and I had done the right thing by agreeing to divorce. He seemed happy to maintain homes in both Arizona and Wisconsin. Right now I knew he was currently on the *Queen Mary 2* for a month-long cruise with yet another female companion. Screw him! I would have enjoyed that trip.

Then I thought of Lee, my first husband, who was now teaching at Stanford. We'd kept in touch through the years because of the kids, but the children had gone their own way early. Odessa, in New Zealand, ran a vegetarian restaurant with her boyfriend. I can't find words for how much I yearned to hug Cassia, my new baby granddaughter! Sky did animation for websites in Winnipeg. I would see one or the other when they returned to Madison, which was rare. I couldn't recall the last time I'd been together with both of my children at the same time.

When I got home from my walk I tore through unpacked boxes in search of a collection of 8mm films that Lee took of our children with his old movie camera. They were only toddlers when he photographed them crawling, waddling their first steps, playing with a puppy, opening Christmas gifts. I prized those films more than any of my material possessions.

I set up the projector in one of the back bedrooms upstairs and dumped the carton of unmarked reels on the floor. I had to thread about a dozen films onto the projector before I found the ones I wanted. Then I pulled down the torn shades and had a good cry while images of Odessa and Sky flickered on the blank wall I used as an impromptu screen. I was looking for reassurance that I'd been a good mom. Here I was in my bikini, running through the sprinkler with my beautiful, naked children. I could almost hear our shrieks of laughter as the sprockets clicked and spun. Here was a family picnic. I held squirming baby Odessa in my arms while Sky pulled himself up on my skirt. Sky learning to ride his bike with training wheels. Odessa riding a tricycle, tipping over, screaming. Me, running to her aid and kissing her owies until Odessa was able to smile at the camera again and bravely climb back on her trike.

I *had* been a good mother. I had raised normal, healthy children who grew up knowing they were loved. It was inevitable that they'd leave home; I was aware of that always and dreaded the day when I would no longer be needed by them. In my dreams, Sky and Odessa were still toddlers that I clutched with a feverish hunger, wanting to hold them forever in my arms.

After an hour of screening such melancholy footage I felt a little rocky (all those fast zooms and pans) and whacked with an emotional thump. I turned off the projector and sat, still weeping, in the dark.

When I felt better, I went downstairs, drank some ginger ale, and sent each child a rambling e-mail telling them how much I loved them and missed them and profusely apologized for not visiting (a) Winnipeg or (b) New Zealand's north island. Maybe I would soon, I said. Then I ate half a bag of Cheetos and had five or six of those little dark chocolate candy bars with almonds for dessert.

I played a Janis Joplin CD for inspiration ("Try Just a Little Bit Harder") and dipped my roller into the paint tray again.

I could justify my tears over missing my kids or even the folly of my own blunders, but if I wasn't really careful, the memory of my encounter with Sharon Gallagher that afternoon at the Wocanaga Camp rose to the surface of my consciousness like a bloated corpse and that image could not be diminished with chocolate or rock 'n' roll. I had not returned to Wocanaga since that afternoon with Polly and I really had to apologize to Grace Waverly for my emotional display at Inspiration Point. After all the time and special effort she had invested in me, only a personal request for Grace's forgiveness would be appropriate. I kept putting it off.

My pea-green house lacked air-conditioning, of course. I solved that during hot weather by sleeping on the second floor sunporch where a small, upholstered loveseat folded out into a single bed. With the windows open to create a breeze, my increasing insomnia (just another fun aspect of menopause) granted me a special acquaintance with everything that happened in our neighborhood.

Normally a light and restless sleeper, I now awoke near dawn—often soaked to the skin with sweat—listening as soft footsteps approached, then paused, as if perusing my front door, before moving on around the corner. One morning I sat up in bed to peel off my wet T-shirt and crept over to look out the window. A man hesitated beneath the streetlight. Then I saw him gesture, heard him softly say "Heel," and I went back to sleep.

From then on, the once-menacing footsteps and "heel" became a reassuring aspect in the pattern of my day.

If I woke especially early I would anticipate their arrival, man and dog. I'm embarrassed to admit that once or twice I knelt naked with my chin on the windowsill, watching them come up the hill. Such pathetic behavior was excusable for someone who lived alone, I reasoned. If the man and his dog did not appear at all, I took that as a sign that I would have a difficult day.

The dog was of medium size with a rumpled black coat, legs spotted black on white, not a familiar breed. He lifted his leg to pee on the lamppost, always in the same place. I was more interested in the dog than in the man, but without my glasses I was fortunate to identify them at all. In my sleepy edge-of-dream fusion I privately referred to them as "The Man and His Spotted Dick" because the dog was male, had spots like raisins in pudding, and it was beneficial, just then, to begin my day with a smile.

You can imagine how astonished I was to run into them face-to-face at our neighborhood market. Actually, the dog was outside, tied to the awning, but the man—I now know his name is George—was selecting apples in the produce bin while I was reaching for a pear and our hands accidentally touched.

I overreacted.

Afterward, I wondered why I had not recognized the dog. Of course I had never seen Henry at ground level, only from above and in very dim light with my myopic gaze. As for George, well, I try never to look anyone in the eye at our little market because however far away you might be it always seems uncomfortably close due to the intimacy of the store. I usually assume a kind of trancelike appearance when I shop there for groceries—the look people get when plugged into their iPods. That way, if I accidentally fail to greet someone or have forgotten their name I can pretend I am merely absorbed in something else. Or if I look like crap (like I did that hot morning after my walk, sweaty in my oversized shirt and shorts with a bedhead badly in need of a shampoo) I can disappear behind my sunglasses and pretend, what the hell, I'm invisible.

So when our hands accidentally tangled I pulled mine back as if I had been burned.

"*Oh!* I'm so *sorry,*" I said, with too much emphasis on *sorry,* surely prompting him to wonder what I had done that was so bad.

"What?" he said, puzzled by my abrupt response.

Maybe it's because I hadn't touched anyone in weeks! Or maybe I was aware of who he was at the last minute. I don't think it was the long scar on the back of his hand because I barely noticed that—but whatever the reason, the magnitude of my startled backlash was way off. So I began to apologize. I even explained about the store being tiny and the dazed look I purposely assume in case I can't recall someone's name. All this while other customers were trying to maneuver their way around us with their loaded shopping carts. The aisles are very narrow.

"Have we met?" he finally interrupted. My monologue was into its third or fourth round. I believe I was recycling the part where I was explaining that I'd been holed up for a very long time restoring my house, the pea-green one on the hill designed by Frideswyde

Quimby, a not-quite famous female architect, and I had run out of snacks. As if that would clarify the bounty of potato chips, Cheetos, and ice-cream bars I was attempting to hide from view.

Although I had only seen him from above, and without my glasses, I sort of recognized his cap. It was dark blue, with an image on the front that I'd assumed was a "C" for Chicago Cubs. Now that I was *right there* I could see it wasn't a "C" but a toothy thing with fins and curved tail and lightning that zigzagged out of its rear end.

And this man wasn't a student, as I'd assumed—he was at least my age, or maybe even older. He was tall and weathered. His hair was gray and curled at his neck.

"George Stafford," he said, extending his hand.

"Nell Grendon," I replied, wiping my sweaty palm on my shorts and touching him intentionally this time. His hands were soft. "What's that on your cap?"

"This?" He removed his cap and pointed to the logo. "A killer whale. An orca. Vancouver Canucks."

"Oh, sure," I replied, as if I knew what he was talking about. A *Canuck*. Wasn't that a derogatory term? Well, at least I didn't say "Eh?" I'm surprised I didn't, because I was still babbling like mad. Amazingly, I didn't blurt out everything I was rapidly thinking— with no particular logic—or I would have exclaimed that I usually saw him without any clothes on. That's the state I was in at the time. Then I'd have had to explain about the Spotted Dick passing beneath my bedroom window each morning. Well, not really my bedroom, the porch attached to my bedroom. I waited for them every day. I watched his dog pee. And I was the one without anything on.

I was a mess.

"Allow me," George said, reaching for a pear and placing it in my shopping cart. "That should help round out your nutritional needs."

I began to rearrange the items in my cart, strategically placing the granola on top of the onion dip, and busily gathered tomatoes and lettuce and cucumbers, enough salad ingredients to feed a crowd, all the while mumbling some kind of nonsense about preparing for a picnic I was going to give.

I was so engrossed in this lie that when I looked for him again, George and his dog had moved on. Meanwhile, I had a whole lot of groceries to lug home and I lived on salads for the next few days. It was probably a good thing.

*A*t that point, I would have been content to avoid Wocanaga altogether. But I still owed Grace an explanation, and in my prior zeal I had registered for her *advanced* mediumship workshop. It was scheduled for Labor Day weekend; the Wocanaga Camp would close for the season after that.

I packed my laptop, closed up the house, and drove north. Before I left, however, I placed a blind ad in *Delve,* Madison's alternative weekly:

> Rooms for rent to serious graduate students.
> No smoking. No pets. No loud parties.
> Some skill with yard work and carpentry preferred.

*T*his time at Wocanaga I felt like an impostor. I was posing as someone who was still seriously interested in mediumship, which I wasn't (seriously) anymore. Everyone else possessed a surfeit of peace and serenity. They weren't zombie-happy, with the blank, mesmerized faces you see in a freaky cult, but they seemed truly blissful. It might be the bad drinking water. Or the fact that Spiritualists don't believe in death.

I didn't have a chance to speak with Grace before the beginning of our first class—which had a dozen students, including Spence, who had so graciously welcomed me there last spring. Even if I had been able to talk to Grace, I probably wouldn't have had the courage to back out.

Class was in Assembly Hall, a tilting two-story clapboard building. There were two rooms on the ground floor. The smaller one on the left was fairly empty; the other, much larger room was furnished with straight chairs and a long oak table, and the walls were heavily laden with frowning photographs of mediums past (passed!). That's where we met.

The morning session was pretty much a review of what I already knew. Leaning on her cane, Grace sketched a stick figure with a felt-tip pen on a tablet placed on an easel in front of the room. She drew a crude circle around the figure with rippled lines above its head that represented energy. "*Feel* the power. *Blend* with the power. *Trust* the power," she said. "Our mediumship is always developing, but Spirit won't give you any more than you've earned."

Then Grace repeated the Great Natural Law of Mediumship, or what I like to think of as the vibration explication: "All things in the universe are constantly vibrating and well-developed mediums are supposed to be able to intercept those vibrations." Here in the material world, vibrations are fairly slow, but Spirit vibrations are higher and more rapid, so one has to relax and go into a "trance" to intercept them, and then only for very short periods of time because, according to Grace, "you are apt to shatter the delicate mechanism of the brain and cause damage to the physical body."

When it was time for questions, I asked if there were such things as "evil spirits" who might want to communicate with mediums. (Of course I was thinking of Sharon.) Grace said there was a lot of misunderstanding about evil spirits, but they could sometimes cause serious problems. "One thing to watch for is this: when we go into a passive state and allow ourselves to become receptive to Spirit entities, the law of attraction sometimes governs such things," she said. "Good attracts good, and evil attracts evil. This is a Natural Law, and we cannot get away from it. So if an evil spirit is able to lead you to do wrong, it may be the evil in yourself that makes that possible."

That seemed reasonable enough, but I didn't like the implication. What evil in me could have made Sharon's apparition appear at Inspiration Point? *Pretending to be a medium?* That wasn't evil, it was just an experiment.

Spence asked, "How do you know if the spirit you're communicating with is an evil spirit or a good one? And then, what if an evil spirit attempts to possess you?"

"Ah," Grace replied with a wry smile, "you have asked questions that will take some time to explain." She reached for a chair and propped her cane against the wall as she gratefully sat down.

"There have always been spirits that were thought of as being evil," she said. "In the early writings of the Chinese, Hebrews, Egyptians, and Greeks we find all kinds of mental disorders attributed to demons that were believed to have taken possession. Even in the New Testament Jesus casts out unclean spirits, and exorcisms are still practiced in the Catholic Church."

"So it's possible one of us might be possessed by an evil spirit?" Irene asked.

"Well, it's unlikely," Grace replied. "We don't usually refer to it as such, but mediumship itself is a situation that requires a kind of possession. When nonphysical intelligence, what we call a 'spirit,' assumes some degree of temporary control of our physical body in order to communicate, it *is* a form of possession. But this usually occurs with our permission and cooperation. When it does *not,* when we allow ourselves to be dominated by a spirit that has unresolved earthbound intentions and does not disengage when we ask it to, then, Irene, we have a horse of a different color."

Grace stood again and drew more diagrams on the tablet.

"Sometimes there are spirits who don't actually know that they're dead. I didn't intend to talk about this today, but since it came up I might as well touch on the subject. All sorts of names have been given to such disoriented, earthbound spirits: soul wanderers, ghosts, poltergeists. They are not spiritually evolved enough to reach the Summerland—what we Spiritualists call the middle and upper planes of the spiritual afterlife. These kinds of spirits can cause all sorts of trouble."

It was time for lunch and the class was gathering its things to leave. Before Grace could get away I asked her privately, "How can we tell a good entity from a bad one?"

87

"If you're channeling—and we'll get to channeling toward the end of this workshop—you become very observant of what's going on," Grace said. "A lot of it has to do with empowerment. If you find the entity is trying to get you to follow it or is attempting to get you to give up your own power, then you really need to watch out. *It wants to take over.* One clue might be the temptation to do or say something that's contrary to your basic personality, out of character for you. This may be due to the influence of the so-called evil entity. So it's important to remember, a spirit cannot make you do anything against your determined will!"

Thoughts are things. If you project vibrations of doubt, you set up a shield that's difficult for Spirit to puncture. Doubt, Grace said that afternoon, is a negative force that tears down, rather than building up. One person can throw out doubt vibrations strong enough to spoil an entire charmed circle. Apparently my "doubt vibrations" were not as strong as I'd thought, or they were becoming weaker. At any rate, I was not yet "outed" as a fraud to Grace or to the group.

On Saturday we had a mildly interesting class on "psychometry." Psychometry is the practice of soul measuring, so we tried reading vibrations emanating from everyday objects that had absorbed vibrations from the person who had worn or handled them. Grace held out a tray and without anyone else watching, we were each asked to place an item upon it that held our own personal vibes. I'd brought the Lord's Prayer ring with me in the pocket of my jeans. The tray was later passed around the circle so we could choose an item to psychometrize. By the time it was my turn there wasn't much left—a pen, a few pebbles, an earring. I took the pen. Spence chose the Lord's Prayer ring.

I held the ballpoint pen and closed my eyes, actually attempting to feel something meaningful. In the end I faked it, as usual. I said the pen belonged to somebody who wanted to write but they felt the pen held the words; the owner of the pen didn't trust his or her own intuitive creativity and wanted the pen to do the work. It turned out the pen belonged to a shy little man, bald and wrinkled and dressed entirely in black, who flushed bright red when I said that and admitted it was true. Ha!

The funniest part was when the same shy little man opened his palm to reveal a shiny pink pebble. It was a polished piece of rose quartz that gleamed in the weak light through the windows (Grace wouldn't let us turn on the lights). "I don't know what this is," the little man said. "I seem to feel a heartbeat, but that's about it. It's warm. That's all."

"Whose item is this?" Grace asked, and Irene, sitting next to me, admitted it was her bra stone. We all said "What?" and she said it again, "It's my bra stone. I have a bunch of them. Every day I place a different one in my bra for luck."

Hearty laughter passed all around our circle, and the little man blushed even more this time. Even Grace thought it was peculiar. "I thought I'd heard everything," she said, "but a 'bra stone' is a new one even to me!"

When it was his turn, Spence said, "This is a ring with the Lord's Prayer inscribed upon it." He had his eyes closed. "It feels very cold. Almost as if it belongs to someone who has passed on." That gave me chills. In fact, I shivered so violently that everyone looked over at me and I did not have to admit that I'd been the one to place the ring on the tray.

I'd noticed that my hands were always hot after we'd been meditating. Irene told me that meant I had healing powers, but I took that and everything else with a grain of salt from a woman who carried stones around in her bra.

After class I waited for Grace and arranged to talk with her the next afternoon at three. Other students were standing around, waiting for a word with her and scheduling appointments for personal readings at Shadowlawn.

After I'd initially stumbled upon Wocanaga, I did a little research on fraudulent schemes used by nineteenth-century mediums—production of spirit pictures, slate writing, and how mediums read billet messages. Some mediums used artificial hands during séances so they could wander off and ring chimes and play the violin while the unsuspecting circle clutched the hands believing they belonged to the medium. Others employed trap doors, magnets, luminous paint. I even found some info on subterfuge with levitating trumpets!

Grace was so earnest that I was reluctant to bring up the subject of deceptive mediums at our appointment the next day. But I was still really curious, and as long as I was there I might as well get what I could.

Sunday was warm and humid but Rosebud, my little rustic cottage, was quiet and cool with a nice breeze from the pines. A full moon that evening was obscured by a welcome thunderstorm that promised to dissipate the heat we'd suffered all weekend.

We talked about auras in class on Sunday. Auras, and how to read them. I was a failure at that (and did anyone else really see something or were they all pretending, like me?). We were watching for teensy sparkling particles that were supposed to shimmer around each other's body like the movement of hot air from a stove, or the wavy mirage you see on pavement on a hot summer day but in various layers of colors. Clairvoyants are supposed to see auras more easily than most. Healers have auras that are violet or purple. Red denotes passion. Well, duh! How intuitive is *that*?

Here was Grace's official definition of an aura: a psychic soul atmosphere or magnetic body surrounding and holding the physical body intact. She said one's soul must have an aura at birth, or else it could not enter into the earth condition. I won't go into my notes about the various layers of the aura or what the different colors mean (for instance, yellow indicates intellect and is usually seen around the head), but the lines radiating out from the physical aura are supposed to depict that person's physical and mental health. And those colors are not always the same because our energy is never static.

To demonstrate what she meant by auric vibrations, Grace used a couple of copper dousing rods and showed how they moved apart when she approached a person and moved back together when she stepped away. Then she showed that this could be done with metal coat hangers, too. I was amazingly successful with the coat hangers.

I didn't know what was springing them apart, but I couldn't make it *not* happen, even though I tried.

I went to see Grace after our class and I explained the humiliation of my panic attack at Inspiration Point. She said that wasn't so unusual with beginners and not to worry about it. I didn't mention Sharon. I did say I'd been too busy to work on my book idea very much.

Tentatively, I mentioned the fraudulent practices I'd researched because I knew skeptics had their own ways of explaining the "levitating trumpet," for example. Grace readily agreed that there had been trickery in the past. She said there were probably unscrupulous mediums today, too. But "official" mediums had to pass strict tests before they were allowed to be admitted to the revered fold. Just this summer, she said, six candidates had applied to be certified to do readings at Wocanaga, but only one qualified. Each one had to do three private readings for people chosen by the Wocanaga Board, and then they had to go before the board itself to deliver messages to members. "We want hard evidence of spiritual contact," Grace said. "We have very high standards here."

The thunderstorms that raged all Sunday night continued into Monday morning. In honor of the full moon, we meditated in silence for an hour in class. Then Grace discussed channeling, which I knew very little about. Some channeling sounds like bad fortune cookies, she said. Fundamentalist Christians apparently consider channeling the work of the Devil. Others blame channeling on UFOs and extraterrestrial contacts. There were more weird descriptions that Grace offered (like saying Edgar Bergen channeled through Charlie McCarthy!), but because of what happened later, I was most intrigued when she admitted, "There is still no way to ascertain whether or not someone is genuinely channeling."

We went into another trance-meditation hoping Grace would channel a spirit for us and we were not disappointed. In the middle of the silence, with thunder echoing far away, Grace began to channel the spirit of "Enos." At first I thought she said "he knows," but later she said that after she first channeled him she looked it up in *Names For Your Baby* and Enos meant "man is mortal," which didn't seem appropriate, but Grace had no qualms and Enos spoke in a deep, rich, commanding voice that caused all of us to sit up straight and tall. I couldn't resist peeking through nearly closed eyelids when Grace began to speak in that strange masculine voice, mostly because it frightened me and I wondered if anyone else felt the same way. I saw Irene peeking, too.

Enos (Grace) explained that he was an elderly man, very ancient, and said this was a powerful time to be on this planet and we in this room had been chosen to carry the light, to be responsible. "There are no pockets in shrouds," he warned ominously. So we should not be concerned with trying to amass material goods because our soul would be the only thing we could carry with us when we left this plane and the only thing by which *we* would judge our progress; keep that in mind.

Then, when Enos left, almost immediately Grace began to channel a sweet, shy Asian woman named Blossom, who apologized for Enos's brusqueness. And after Blossom was done, there was silence, welcome silence, in which to digest all this strange stuff. The thunder in the distance was growing and suddenly Spence grunted, "HO!" really loud. I jumped about a foot off my chair and opened my eyes without intending to, but so did Irene and a couple others who were obviously as shocked as I. Spence kept going. He said his name (the spirit he was channeling) was White Horse, and he went on and on about stuff that sounded like gobbledygook, mind-speak, vague thoughts, and strung-together words that didn't make a whole lot of sense, but they were loud, sort of speaking in Indian-tongues.

To my immense impatience, Irene started to speak after Spence was done. Rain was dripping from the eaves and it resembled the tick of a clock, so she said she was the spirit of Seth Thomas and spoke in a bunch of clock metaphors, time ticking away, blah blah blah. I think she was trying too hard, maybe felt she was expected to participate. In fact, she wouldn't shut up. I wanted to consult my watch.

As for channeling, I was certainly not going to say a thing. In fact, I was hungry and eager to get out of there and use the restroom but we could not leave until Grace gave us permission to break our charmed circle and there was this air of expectancy after Irene finished with poor Seth Thomas. I knew Grace was waiting for me, but I tried to maintain my self-control.

"On the wings of a snow-white dove," I began singing. Singing! Later, much later, I remembered this was a song Ferlin Husky made famous in the 1950s. Who names their kid "Ferlin," anyway? And when I sang it in front of Grace and all the rest in my workshop I changed the words around. It's supposed to be "He sends His pure sweet love," but I sang, "She sends her pure sweet love," and then started speaking in a voice that didn't sound like my own. I didn't realize that either until later, when I played back the cassette I'd secretly hidden in my backpack to tape Grace's classes since she wouldn't let us take notes.

"On the wings of a snow-white dove, she sends her pure, sweet love . . ."

I am Angella Wing, and I am here to bring my love and gratitude to you, my chosen one, Merrill Chase. During my celebrity, audiences would have known me as one who portrayed a variety of personalities in radio drama, Broadway plays, early television, films, and such. When I passed I was known as the Woman of a Thousand Voices. Now my words will be delivered by you, Merrill, my child of the spirit. When we speak, the world will listen.

As I rewound and listened to the tape that night I barely recognized my voice. Surely it was the voice of another woman and I spoke with a confidence I know I could not have possessed at the time.

Grace, mightily impressed, encouraged me further after our class. She said my throat chakra was well developed and I should take advantage of it; this was my role. I had been chosen. My classmates were really wowed. But I still didn't know what had happened. I couldn't remember saying a thing.

I'd intended to drive back to Madison after our final class, but Grace invited me to a special "Home Circle" gathering at Shadowlawn that night with six elderly mediums. They gathered twice a week to communicate with their spirit guides and ask for guidance and instruction. Because of my previous faux pas at Inspiration Point and since it was a special invitation to an outsider like me, I didn't want to seem ungrateful. I never expected a séance, just another kind of "charmed circle." Now I know they're the same thing.

Grace had a gentle soul and was so trusting. If her psychic powers initially told her I had come there planning to do a number on Wocanaga, all of that was forgotten as she presented me to her friends as a promising medium named Merrill Chase whom she was very proud to have taken under her wing.

And while we were sitting around in this circle, another very odd occurrence took place: I began to channel again! It seemed as if Angella Wing had more to add to her afternoon message, but this time (thank goodness) she did not make me sing.

> *There is an old Chinese saying: "Only the Caucasian lives and dies alone." That was not true in my case. I lived many lives and passed over as I lived, in the company of my many selves. Now our world will be inspired by the messages that I deliver, through Merrill. I shall become her voice, her vision, her influence. Believe.*

Part 2

6

*O*kay, at first I thought it was very funny. Here I was *pretending* to be a medium when I accidentally, *spontaneously,* channeled the "Woman of a Thousand Voices." Terrific. She seemed to have really glommed on to me, too. Did that mean I'd eventually channel in a thousand different voices? One voice like Donald Duck and another like Stevie Wonder? Or maybe *Daisy* Duck and Wonder *Woman?*

Grace had briefly mentioned channeling in her workshop, but as soon as I got home I raced to the bookstore and loaded up with everything I could find, including books in which a friendly spirit named Seth spoke about individual self-development and expansion of consciousness. He was channeled by a woman named Jane Roberts who said she held "Seth sessions" twice a week but felt exhilarated by the experience, never possessed or invaded. A more analytical book about channeling told of a class that Jane and Seth taught together. Jane may not have felt "possessed," but one time when she and Seth were discussing sex in front of their class, Jane calmly unzipped her dress to reveal that she was not wearing any underclothes and then she challenged her students to do the same.

A text relating historical channeling repeated the advice Abraham Lincoln was given in December 1862. Medium Nettie Colburn Maynard channeled a spirit that advised the president to go ahead with the Emancipation Proclamation and "fearlessly perform the work and fulfill the mission for which he had been raised up by an overruling Providence."

There were books with channeled dialogues of spirits with names like Emmanuel and Michael and Lazaris, and the "Starseed Transmissions," channeled by a Missouri farmer, in which "Raphael" said, "Do you want a definition of angels? We are you, yourself, in the distant past and distant future."

Hmmm. Fascinating stuff. Too much, in fact. And some of it pretty weird. I should have taken a moment to sort out the books before I paid for them.

All I really wanted to know was, *What is channeling?* Responses to that question were all pretty much the same. In the most comprehensive and authoritative book on the subject, *Channeling: Investigations on Receiving Information from Paranormal Sources,* author Jon Klimo defined it as "the communication of information to or through a physically embodied human being from a source that is said to exist on some other level or dimension of reality than the physical as we know it, and that is not from the normal mind (or self) of the channel."

Inevitably I would find this contradicted by another book on channeling, in which a psychiatrist claimed that automatic writing, bizarre as much of it is, comes from the subject's own unconscious. Another psychiatrist spoke of cryptomnesia—hidden memory—in which automatic writing taps material to which the person has been exposed, or knowledge that has been subconsciously learned.

But I'm getting ahead of myself. We're not discussing automatic writing yet, just plain channeling.

When Angella first made her appearance, I was excited. And I was scared. Not as scared as when I saw what I thought was the apparition of Sharon Gallagher at Inspiration Point. (That was a 9 out of 10. Angella scored more like an 8. Give or take.) What if I wasn't actually channeling?

What if there was a more logical explanation, like I had a tumor ripening in my brain? Or I was suffering from "multiple personality disorder." Google told me that's now known as "dissociative identify disorder," five times as many women suffer from it than men, and (oh, God) "each personality has its own personal history and identity and takes on a totally separate name."

I tried Googling "Angella Wing" and came up with "Are you sure you don't mean *Angel* Wing?" Apparently the "celebrity" she spoke of had not left much of a trace.

What about the possibility that I was suffering from a nervous breakdown due to too much stress? In my youth, women didn't suffer from bipolar symptoms or clinical depression, they had "nervous breakdowns" that sent them to a spa or a sanitarium, where they were waited upon hand and foot and afterward everyone treated them with deference just in case they'd crack.

Pondering that, I actually *wanted* to be having a nervous breakdown. A month of pampering in a spa sounded exceptionally good.

I checked the Internet again and wondered if Dr. Burns would laugh if I told him I thought I had dissociative identity disorder. More than once, he had warned me against diagnosing my symptoms on the Web. But Wikipedia said "multiplicity is not always a disorder," and it could be normal for some people. Carl Jung thought it could be characterized as "hyper-awareness of one's personas." Could "hyper-awareness" be related to clairsentience?

After a cup of calming tea, deep breathing, and further, more rational deliberation, I realized it would have to be too coincidental if Irene and Spence and Grace Waverly—all of us—suffered from dissociative identity disorder. It had to be *channeling*. It was direct voice mediumship, a form of extra-dimensional communication. Like the Oracle at Delphi who wore a wreath of laurel and chewed bay leaves and sat on a seat with three legs when she prophesied.

Since channeling was a frightening concept to anticipate (having now had an opportunity to comprehend and reconsider), I decided I might be freed from doing it again if I chose never again to participate in a séance. My overactive imagination was probably stimulated by too much Wocanaga hullabaloo—a reasonable and logical diagnosis considering the amount of propaganda and indoctrination I'd hungrily absorbed during my fantasy mediumship. Since that's the only place Angella had "appeared," I would stay clear of the Wocanaga Camp and its afflictions, along with the panic attacks the place seemed to inspire in me. I had no desire to become one of those wacko channelers! My interest in Wocanaga had simply been for the purpose of writing an article. And maybe a book. Which wasn't getting anywhere.

And . . . yes, also to see what it was like to manipulate the beliefs of susceptible subjects. That's what got me in trouble.

I could tell that I had already changed from the person I had been. For one thing, I felt anxious all the time. In the past I'd used meditation to relax, but now it was impossible to let down my guard for fear this Angella spirit would make an unbidden appearance, so to speak (and so *to speak*!). Good grief!

I packed the unfinished manuscript of *Medium Grace* and all my notes from Grace's workshops and interviews in a plastic storage box, snapped the lid, and carried it up to one of the spare bedrooms where I buried it under more boxes of old children's books and toys.

Later that afternoon I tied the Lord's Prayer ring in the red bandana again.

Because I needed groceries, I drove to a big supermarket and loaded up so I wouldn't have to risk running into the guy with his spotted dog at the neighborhood store where I'd made a fool of myself.

I was aware that by doing just that I was *still* making a fool of myself. This was not the woman I had been, nor the woman I wanted to become! When Michael and I split I thought I'd travel and enjoy my singular freedom. That was before I'd sunk most of my savings into Frideswyde's relic.

I knew a shrink would advocate spending more time with normal people (i.e., not mediums). I would call a reliable friend, get a manicure, meet for lunch downtown. Would my old book club let me back in? I hadn't attended a meeting in over a year; I hadn't kept up with the list.

I gave that a try.

It might have worked out just fine if only I hadn't been so candid when one of the women asked, "Writing anything interesting these days, Nell?"

To be hospitable, the hostess, Nancy Anderson, mentioned my piece about the Wocanaga Spiritualist Camp that she'd seen in *Meanderings*. That prompted others to comment on it, too, and someone asked me to describe what really went on up at Spook Hill. Powerless in the midst of their praise, I asked Nancy for two metal coat hangers.

Even that might not have been so problematic if I hadn't chosen to demonstrate the existence of an aura around sweet little Doris Hackenberry with her cauliflower mop of white curls. Doris was a strict Episcopalian and a professor emerita of home economics, and she appeared not at all pleased to have her personal electromagnetic field described and her auric emanation revealed in living color before our book club. Doris sat frozen in place, eyes behind her bifocals staring back like those of a frightened fish, while the coat hangers approaching her opened up to resemble an enormous jaw.

"As you can see, the aura extends outward from the body in an egglike shape for about two or three feet," I explained to the others. "Your spiritual and physical conditions can be determined by the colors vibrating in your aura. It's widest and brightest around the head and shoulders, where the emanating color is the most dense."

There were ooohs and aaaahs and a bit of snickering at my back. I heard someone blow her nose, perhaps a misguided attempt to smother another giggle.

"Do it, Nellie," someone urged. "Read her aura!"

"The yellow in Doris's aura is an inspirational color," I offered, "and denotes mental activity. Then I see blue—this means high spiritual aspirations and thoughts. And red . . ."

I could feel a hot flash beginning to seep up from my chest and wash over my neck, my cheeks. My entire face was aglow.

"Red is a physical color," I continued, hastily wiping my forehead with my palm. "It represents . . . *passion*. Anger. Whatever."

I had to sit down. Nancy's living room had become so quiet I felt I *had* to say something, even if it was only a guess. Doris, passionate? Too late, I realized everyone must be astonished at my audacity in using poor Doris Hackenberry as my guinea pig and dumbfounded by the alien subject matter about which I'd hoped to enlighten them. In addition to those blunders, I should have asked permission!

Whatever happened to *"May I come to you?"*

"Would you like a drink of water, Doris?" Nancy inquired of her paralyzed guest.

"Could I have one, too?" I asked.

"Why don't we have our dessert now," another suggested.

≈

After our class reunion in Little Wolf, I'd queried my *Meanderings* editor about an Oktoberfest celebration at a local farmstead that had been converted from a hog farm into a replica of a Bavarian village. My editor loved the idea, so I found myself in Little Wolf for the second time in two months, this time smothered with featherbeds as soft and welcoming as any spa and enough German beer, gemütlichkeit, and oompah bands to wipe out any thoughts of Doris Hackenberry's aura, Wocanaga, or Angella Wing.

Fortunately, no one from Little Wolf remembered that I once played the accordion. I seldom revealed that to anyone. Buddy called it a "squeeze box." I only stuck with it for a couple unpromising years. When I was in fifth grade a shy man from a nearby town came to our house every Tuesday night at 6:30, took his big white-pearl accordion out of its case, and sat with me in front of my folding music stand in the dining room while I pumped out polkas on my junior-size red accordion that had "Nell" written in rhinestones on the front. Polly had wanted to know what would happen when I started getting breasts—wouldn't they get pinched in the bellows? I hadn't considered that, and Mom didn't know either but she told me not to worry about it yet. Actually, I gave up playing the accordion before breasts became a problem.

I was refreshed enough by my Oktoberfest weekend that before I returned to Madison I stopped at the local cemetery to visit my mother's grave. Since my dad moved to Arizona to live near Buddy, no one paid their respects to her anymore. I have a fondness for graveyards, especially those with ancient tombstones and pithy epitaphs. Mom's granite memorial was simple: her name, date of birth, date of death. I didn't have to concentrate very hard to connect with her enduring admonitions ("Take your calcium! Go to church! Write your thank-you cards right *now* before you forget!").

If spirits passed on to another level and could be contacted in a séance or message service, did Spiritualists go to the trouble of putting flowers on a loved one's grave?

As long as I was there, I stopped at the graves of my grandparents. If I walked around and looked for it, I could have found the spot where Leonard Twyn had been buried, too.

Sharon, however, was buried on the other side of the road. The Catholic Cemetery was separate, in their parish cemetery. I wouldn't have to look for Sharon's grave; I knew exactly where it was. But I didn't stop to pay my respects, as if that would pay her back for showing up at Wocanaga.

∎

When I was in Grace Waverly's workshop on psychometry and Spence had taken the Lord's Prayer ring from the tray and said its vibrations felt cold, for a quick moment I thought he had said "gold," and I could have sworn Leonard Twyn was present. Or the mean little spirit of Leonard Twyn.

Polly had been visiting her cousins for Passover when Leonard Twyn died. She would probably remember all the words to that spooky warning, "Don't laugh next time the hearse goes by." I'd have to ask her.

On Friday nights Mother and Buddy and I usually went to the library. The Friday night before Leonard Twyn's funeral, Mother had to help Dad at the insurance office because they filled out income tax forms for my father's clients. Gloria Piekarski came over from next door to stay with Buddy and me. My parents thought we weren't old enough to stay alone at night but I think they mostly worried that we'd fight.

"I've heard you practicing that polka, Eleanora," she said when she arrived. "You're getting a lot better."

"I have to take some books to the library but when I get back I'll play for you," I promised.

"I want to go, too," Buddy whined.

"Your mother didn't say anything about the library," Gloria said.

I did have books to return; that was not a lie. Since winning the Lord's Prayer ring I had become ultra-sensitive to lying and cheating. Possession of the ring, I hoped, would convert me into an even more honest and conscientious person in reparation for any liberties I may have taken in order to win the Bible Bee.

"Buddy, you play Yahtzee with Gloria. I'll walk fast and be home by eight o'clock."

The stores were open on Friday nights so farmers could do their shopping. All the taverns were open, too. When I passed their doors I could smell stale beer and cigarette smoke and hear people laughing and whooping it up inside. Sometimes they were singing along to polka music from a jukebox. I had never been in a tavern, so I was a little scared by the noise. Through the windows of the IGA and the Red Owl I could see people filling shopping carts with groceries for the coming week. Cornbloom's was open, even though Polly's family was out of town.

The library was in Village Hall but instead of actually entering, I quickly shoved my books into a slot in the front door where it said *Return Books Here*. Then I went next door to Seger's Funeral Home, which was really close to my dad's insurance office. If my father ever found out what I was doing, I'd get the ping-pong paddle for sure. All I wanted was a peek. I pulled the door toward me and inched my way through. It shut quietly. I was inside.

Silence. Quiet as a stone. The silence of the dead—a phrase my father sometimes used. Not a sound. Dead quiet.

A feeble glow from the streetlight shone through a window nearby and when my eyes adjusted to the darkness I could tell I was in the lobby. Another door stood ajar to reveal a large room where a pale shimmer of light at the far end spilled over Leonard Twyn's head, his shoulders raised slightly above the edge of a white coffin on a velvet draped catafalque. Surrounding him was a whole garden of flowers. Baskets of daisies and carnations, wreaths of roses, and vases of lilies and chrysanthemums—pink, yellow, red, purple, every color of the rainbow; I had never seen anything like it. One wreath of roses had a wide satin ribbon stretched across and the words *Beloved Grandson* in gold paper letters.

The entire scene was glazed by the glow of a lamp placed next to the spinet piano in a front corner. Leonard Twyn's face shimmered as if coated with moon-colored wax. He was dressed like a little man in a gray suit, white shirt, black bowtie. A sprig of pink rosebuds was pinned to his lapel.

Without realizing it, I slowly advanced on the thick blue carpeting that swallowed every sound, fascinated by the arrangement of Leonard Twyn/flowers/shadows. Now I was at the front of the room a long way from the door, and the silence, the heavy fragrance of the floral displays, and the sight of Leonard Twyn, absolutely dead, had me trembling.

I am seeing a dead person for the first time in my life, I thought, but he does not look much different than he did when he was alive. Maybe not even as pale.

I made mental notes of everything so I could tell Polly exactly what it was like. His head rested on a white satin pillow and a blanket of yellow and white blossoms was pulled up to his waist as if to keep him warm. I had expected this to be gross, but now, face to face with a Leonard Twyn who did not tease, did not smirk, did not whisper "gold" anymore, I was ready to go home.

I just had to check on Leonard Twyn's ring before I left. Both hands lay on his chest over a miniature Bible from which a red ribbon emerged like a thin spurt of blood. But it was his right hand that he always hid in the pocket of his sweater, his right hand where Leonard Twyn had worn the Lord's Prayer ring, his right hand now lying beneath his left. I had no choice but to reach in and move his left hand to find the ring. The very thought made me quake with revulsion.

At first timid touch, Leonard Twyn was so icy cold that I pulled away and waited another moment, breathing fast. For one frightening second I imagined that Leonard Twyn was breathing, too.

Again, I gently touched his skin. Then I forced myself to reach under the fingers of his left hand, searching blindly, anxiously, for the ring on his right. It was there. *Our Father, Which Art in Heaven,* the raised lettering identical to my own ring on one chilled finger and the lines where it said *forgive us our debts* instead of *trespasses* because debts took up less room. Was his ring gold instead of silver?

His left hand slid off the Bible and his right hand was visible. It looked gold, the ring looked gold! It did! The ring also looked too big for his bony finger.

Slowly, smoothly, in one quiet motion, I tugged at Leonard Twyn's ring and it was off, there, in my palm. With a similar motion, quietly, smoothly, I slid my own ring off my own finger and onto Leonard Twyn's. If his was gold, then he could have the silver one to be buried with.

A noise!

A triangle of light appeared outside the door that led from the entrance hall to this room. The wake! It was tonight! Voices!

My heart rocked so loudly in my chest that I was sure Leonard Twyn would sit up and ask, "What's all the fuss about?"

I dove behind the spinet piano where a bouquet of pink carnations sprayed out in a fan from a white wicker basket on the top. Crouched in the shadows, I listened.

"His hands slipped off the Bible," a man whispered, very close to the piano.

"Put 'em back, quick. Christ Almighty," another voice said with some urgency.

I prayed that no one would notice that Leonard Twyn's ring was now silver, that it fit him better than his gold ring had. Of course I also prayed that no one would notice *me*!

Then someone sobbed nearby, and a man said soothing things. As their voices moved further away I carefully parted the flowers on top of the piano to catch a fleeting glimpse of people shuffling past Leonard Twyn's coffin to murmur "Poor dear" and "Beautiful child" and "Looks so peaceful, like he's asleep." Someone said, "You have our sympathy, Mr. and Mrs. Twyn." It was my father's voice!

I leaned against the back of the piano, sweating hard. My vision broke up into tiny dancing molecules as my breath came faster and faster and my heart threatened to burst from my chest. *Head between your knees! Put your head between your knees!* Mother's instructions on such occasions came to me as I slid to the floor and bent over. At least I didn't throw up.

When the first sad notes of "Abide with Me" rang out from the piano, I jumped about a mile off the carpet; I wasn't expecting that! Everybody sang softly, as if they weren't sure of the words.

After the last note of the "Amen" died away, Reverend Bennett began to speak with the solemn, nasal voice I heard only in church. He bragged about Leonard's Sunday school attendance, signified by the pin with four perfect attendance bars; his diligent memorization of Bible verses; and the Lord's Prayer ring he had won only last fall in the Bible Bee, the ring he wore, even now, on his lifeless hand.

My upper lip tasted like tears. I wanted to go home. Reverend Bennett began to lead the gathering in the Lord's Prayer.

By habit, I touched his ring as I was accustomed to touching my own. The ring was too large and spun around my finger.

No, it didn't look like my ring. I couldn't really tell if it was gold or silver but it was not my own, it did not fit like mine had, and I wanted *my* ring back. I had trespassed and cheated to win that ring, and it was mine! I had paid a tremendous price!

Then, miraculously, the last voices threaded out beyond the door, the overhead lights were switched off, and the room was quiet again, lit softly by the yellowed lamp shade.

I crawled cautiously out from behind the piano and pulled myself up, holding onto the coffin, determined to switch rings again as fast as I could and get out of there.

But the coffin was closed. I tried to push the top open, even pounded on it with my fist to pry the heavy lid from the base. The coffin was sealed. Leonard Twyn and my Lord's Prayer ring were together and gone forever.

Outside, under the streetlight, I took a better look at Leonard Twyn's ring. It was silver, exactly like mine. That was for sure. The fact that it was not gold after all did not give me the pleasure I had thought it might. Besides, the ring was so loose; it did not fit, anyone could tell, especially Sharon—she would notice right away that it didn't fit. Polly would, too.

As if to emphasize my despair, Leonard Twyn's ring slid from my finger and clattered onto the sidewalk. But it didn't roll very far so I was able to find it before it got lost.

No-Toe-Joe was leaning against one of the gas pumps over at the filling station across the street. He was called No-Toe because his big toe had been bitten off by a muskie when he was a little boy, fishing up north with his father. I didn't think anything about No-Toe being there; his dad was the undertaker and I was sitting on the curb in front of the funeral home. If he had seen me switch rings with Leonard Twyn, No-Toe gave no sign. But, then, he never gave a sign of any emotion at all. That was the spookiest part about No-Toe-Joe. Polly always said No-Toe was like a walking corpse. And, yes, the guys whispered that he was made of spare body parts.

I tied Leonard Twyn's ring in the bandana and I never wore it again. Once when I was babysitting for Reverend Bennett's new baby he asked why I wasn't wearing my Lord's Prayer ring and I had to tell him I was keeping it in a safe place because I was afraid of losing it.

My parents seemed oblivious to the ring's absence, and only Buddy wanted to know where it was. Finally I told him I'd buried it out in the backyard so nobody would be able to steal it. Buddy wandered around the backyard with a shovel for several days, trying to figure out where to dig for buried treasure.

The whole point of winning the Lord's Prayer ring had been to impress Sharon Gallagher. Now I had nothing to show for my transgression. In fact, I carried the burden of that guilt with me for the rest of the school year, right into the following summer. Mother took me to a specialist in Marshfield. I was ready for him to diagnose leukemia, but he decided I was anemic and prescribed large, evil-tasting iron pills that upset my stomach even more than it already was. Every time I ran into No-Toe-Joe I got the creeps because I didn't know for sure what he had seen.

❧

Back in Madison in my pea-green mansion, my Oktoberfest article easily took shape. I was pleased with the results, until about an hour into my work.

Initially I thought it was because I was tired and typed a pair of keys at the same time by mistake; that wouldn't be unusual because I normally type very fast. But what happened definitely *was* unexpected and *very* unusual: Angella Wing made another uninvited appearance. I don't mean that I saw her face or spoke her voice; instead, her words were captured on my computer screen.

My darling Merrill, I have been waiting most impatiently. One might even infer that you were not impressed with my manifestation of Spirit at Wocanaga! You do realize our lives are now bound in an inextricable way.

All right, this time I really *was* troubled. This was my home, my computer, my territory, *my private space* that was being invaded. I had not *written* those words—they arrived, unbidden and unwelcome. Of course my fingers helped create the message, but my brain was disconnected from the process. It was either dissociative identity disorder . . . or automatic writing, a skill I had no wish to perfect.

Recklessly I asked, "Where are you?" and Angella replied:

I am here and I am everywhere. My existence is not an exact science but it may not be up to you to determine the time and place

109

for our exchange. This may not have been of your own volition, darling Merrill, but you have tapped into a realm unknown to most and now you are privileged to be a part of the chosen. There is no escape from the pathway, as you have been informed. This is not an ephemeral ability. You cannot turn your back and simply walk away. I have to speak. Your role is to listen and respond.

What an overbearing bitch, I thought, and immediately asked, "Why the hell should I?"

She said she refused to respond to such an idiotic question. So I turned off my laptop and left Angella hanging there. This was too much for one day; I needed to find out what was happening to me.

I poured a glass of wine and reviewed my newly acquired library of channeling books. The most familiar theme, "We Create Our Own Realities," seemed to me to have a solipsistic New Age attitude. I didn't know what Angella's intentions were but I was sure she wouldn't concern herself with ephemeral sermons or New Age philosophy. And I was not about to allow myself to become unzipped in front of an audience to reveal an absence of underwear before a crowd.

Was she the spirit of an actual deceased human being, as she claimed? Or an alien disembodied intelligence?

According to my own desperate logic, I hoped Angella was merely a person from my past whom I was regurgitating from my subliminal mind or unearthing from my own unconscious. Perhaps she was a potpourri of many people I once knew, like a dream. *Creating one's own reality?* Hey, it worked for me.

The only way I knew to contend with Angella Wing, outside of committing myself to psychiatric care, was to keep my computers turned off for now and let her twist in the wind.

I may be painting an extraordinarily pessimistic picture of what transpired that autumn. True, I was unnerved to the point of being unhinged by the presence of an intransigent spirit. But, on the other hand, my old buddy Polly Cornbloom returned to Wisconsin in

October! In fact, she moved back to Madison and set up a studio to develop her art.

Then Teddy Carter called with a startling invitation to spend some time with him.

Other odd incidents occurred—and I was reminded of Grace Waverly's comment that her life became more challenging after she became a medium. But I hid that thought in the random debris of my frazzled mind.

Polly would stay with me until the truck arrived with her belongings; then she'd move into the east-side building that would be her studio and her home. I felt I had to offer to rent her the rooms I'd advertised in *Delve* (to which I'd as yet had no response), but she said she preferred to live alone and needed an unusually specific kind of space for her work in holography. She attempted to explain but I tuned out when she started talking about lenses and mirrors and percentages of angled refractions.

October in Madison. The lakes reflect blue autumn skies and golden-hued maples mingle with Wisconsin's cardinal red as every Saturday assumes Big Ten fervor. Camp Randall stadium, only a few blocks from my home, echoes with cheers of the crowds and the enthusiasm of the band whenever the Badgers play football there.

On the Saturday after her arrival, Polly and I went downtown and joined the throng moving counterclockwise around the Capitol Square at the weekly farmers' market. This was one of the events I especially loved about living in Madison, and that day it was fun to just review the booths that displayed artisanal cheeses, crusty breads, abundant vegetables, and fruits that appealed to my need for physical *and* spiritual nourishment. I planned to get some apples, but we spent a long time just sitting lazily on a sunny park bench with morning buns and café au lait, enjoying the moment, watching the crowd.

But that October was a busy and unusual month and what happened next added to the peculiar tendency for synchronicity I seemed to be attracting (due to an increased sensitivity, I wondered? Clairsentience? Like exerting a pull on Angella Wing and her attendant irritations?).

I was digging around in my purse to pay for a bag of Honeycrisp apples when I distinctly felt something nosing into my crotch from behind. Now that's not a sensation I experience every day, nor was it particularly enjoyable. So I whirled around and discovered the Spotted Dick and his owner, whose name had never really registered with me. George Something. The dog's wet nose was the brutal culprit but, to be fair, there *was* a pressing crowd.

He (George) reined his dog in and said, "I'm sorry!"

I was curt, hurt, but Polly—who never misses an opportunity to gush over someone's pet—was nearly down on all fours, inspecting the breed.

"We've met," George said with an apologetic smile that, I decided, was supposed to make up for his dog's rude goose.

"In the market," I replied.

"George Stafford," he reminded me. "An apple a day?" he asked. "Have you run out?"

I mumbled an insipid response but it didn't matter; he didn't notice because Polly was practically enjoying coitus with his mutt.

George Stafford (*now* I remembered) again wore his blue Canucks cap with the killer whale.

"Nice dog," Polly said, finally, full of dog-slobber. "What kind *is* he?

"A Llewellyn Setter. A hunting dog. Not a very good one, either; that's why he ended up with me."

"What's his name?"

The two of them became deeply absorbed in canine conversation so I paid for my apples, tapped Polly's shoulder, said "I'll see you later," and continued around the Square. Sometimes Polly is exasperating. She insisted on embarrassing me; that was the only reason she made such a fuss. There's no way she could have such an overwhelming interest in that man or his dog. I glanced back once and they were still chatting, still in the same spot. Well, fine. I'd just go home. My stride increased. By the time I reached the parking ramp I was out of breath, still enraged.

He *was* from Canada, Polly said later. He was also a musician. He was a pianist, a visiting professor at the university's School of Music, and he also played gigs with a jazz band on weekends.

"Did he actually say *'gigs'*?" I asked, "or is that your own *cool* expression?"

"Musicians always say 'gigs.' It's what they do. Play 'gigs.'"

"*Gig* makes me want to gag," I offered. It's too cute.

"Well, he's playing a *gig* at the Bosky Lodge tonight and he invited us to come."

"No thanks," I said. I had to take my computers in to be fixed before the repair place closed that afternoon. I wasn't sure how I could explain to Polly or the computer geeks that I needed to have Angella Wing exorcised from my hard drives, but defragging, checks with my spyware, anti-virus tests—nothing had budged the spirit from either my desktop or my notebook and I felt prohibited from doing any writing at all. Thanks to Angella's intrusions, my Oktoberfest article was lodged in limbo.

On Monday the moving truck arrived with Polly's belongings. While she directed the placement of her equipment in her downstairs studio, I helped settle her apartment on the second floor. Afterward, I was relieved to have my pea-green place to myself again. I loved Polly like a sister. Maybe that's why I couldn't live with her.

Tuesday afternoon the doorbell rang and George Stafford stood there with his dog.

"I understand you have some rooms for rent," he said. "Do you allow pets?"

Of course I knew. He hadn't come because of the blind ad in *Delve;* Polly had directed him.

I looked into his dog's liquid brown eyes, recalled those lonely early mornings when their walks past my house brought me such a sense of wellbeing, and confessed, "The rooms need a lot of work. I'd hoped whoever rented them would be skilled at carpentry."

"No problem," George replied. "I'm okay with that. This is Henry, by the way."

"Do you have a piano?"

"Yes, I do. It's a small one, though. Will that be a problem? I occasionally have a student stop in to play for me."

I reluctantly offered to show him the rooms on the second floor and the rear entrance that led to them. While we toured the house, I told George about Frideswyde Quimby. George agreed that the varied assortment of windows and the polygonal porches were curiously unique.

When I opened the door to one of the vacant bedrooms my precious 8mm films were still scattered all over the floor. I lifted the shades and began tossing the films back into the box with the projector.

"Want to see some footage of my daughter learning to walk?" My voice cracked.

George ignored my comment, walked over to the window, admired the view (you can see Lake Mendota from there), and inquired if I'd given any thought to making that part of the house into an apartment. It seemed so obvious when he explained it, I was convinced that he'd been pondering the scheme for some time (Polly, again?). "If you'd decide to go ahead, I'd be happy to do most of the work myself, in exchange for rent. Then after I'd leave, you'd have a nice little flat."

What could I say to that? I believe I sighed.

I told George I'd have to see some references and check with the city zoning about renting the rooms (a major detail I'd overlooked) and that I'd be in touch. George went down the front steps but Henry remained by my side as though we were already the best of friends and looked up at me.

"You're a good boy, Henry," I said, giving his head an affable scratch.

Honestly, Henry had the most amazing eyes. His spotted coat was exceptionally soft and he seemed very well behaved. It might be good to have a dog around, I thought. And, okay, a man.

But we'd have to have a pact, George and I, not to get personally involved with one another or to interfere with one another's lives.

How could I approach that subject without admitting I'd imagined the possibility of involvement? Sometimes I made my life more complicated just by visualizing supposings and what-ifs.

7

 My computers came home stripped of every unnecessary cookie and jpeg file, but Angella Wing still fluttered around like a bothersome moth. The first time I turned on my laptop, she already had a message waiting:

Oh, my dear, you cannot rid your aura of me so readily! Your life is shifting in a very real and very dramatic way. Prepare for change.

I knew all about change. I was struggling with a lonely bed and night sweats and irregular periods; I felt irritable and bloated most of the time. *Change,* my ass. I didn't want to talk about changes of any kind.

I was so annoyed with Angella's imposition that I went back out that same day and purchased a new expensive laptop with all the bells and whistles, one that was not "cleansed" of Angella, because she had never inhabited it. Then I set the old one aside hoping it would gather dust instead of "mystical" messages from the ether.

I deliberately did not open the box with the fancy new laptop for several weeks; I didn't even check my e-mail, which was an excruciating temptation. Instead, I sorted through boxes and called Goodwill to pick up items that I had collected through the years and would never use again. All those elaborate dresses I'd worn to social gatherings with Michael! If I never wore another sparkly sequin, I figured I'd survive. In fact, getting rid of all that excess debris was refreshing.

When I'd finished cleaning and unpacking, I went out for a new haircut and a pedicure to celebrate. It was a mere coincidence, of course, that spiffing up my image coincided with the arrival of a new man on the scene.

Each autumn I found myself immersed in a melancholy ennui, but this fall my blue mood diminished with the prospect of having George Stafford in the house, even though initially he'd be ripping out walls and creating a dusty mess. George taught only on Tuesdays and Thursdays, so the rest of the week he arrived early in the morning, entered by the back door near my kitchen (I'd given him a key), and went up the rear stairway to work on his apartment. Henry usually trotted along, but once in a while he chose to linger with me.

There wouldn't be much of a problem making the second floor into two separate residences as the central hall would conveniently divide them. George was making one of the back bedrooms into a kitchen and removing traces of kids who'd trashed the place plus tearing up wall-to-wall shag carpeting, the revolting remnants of a previous landlord.

George's half would be entered by the rear stairs but the door to my upstairs hall would provide emergency access or egress.

Restoration work on my side of the upstairs had been pretty well completed. My large bedroom occupied a front corner of the second floor and featured a fireplace and lovely bay. A bath carved out of an adjoining room opened off the master. Also connected was the smaller room that I used as a study. Then there was the second floor sunporch, where I'd been sleeping when I first spotted the Spotted Dick.

After a couple of weeks of heavy traffic—his students coming and going, pounding noises, shouts, stomping, loud music—the house grew quiet. One morning I took an early shower, fixed my hair, put on some mascara and blush, and took George a mug of fresh coffee and a loaf of banana bread. I wanted to appear neighborly without being pushy. I also thought I might ask if he could recommend some books on modern jazz. If he seemed especially friendly, I'd hint that I wouldn't mind a short lesson in jazz appreciation.

I climbed up the back stairs because that route was closest to my kitchen. Henry greeted me with enthusiasm but George had his back turned. I noticed, then, that he had his own coffeemaker that held coffee, freshly brewed. I cleared my throat.

"I brought you some coffee," I said, wondering why my voice wobbled. "But I see you already have some."

At that moment his cell phone rang.

"Thanks," he said. "Leave it on the counter, will you?"

I did, and I felt stupid. I dropped the banana bread there, too.

"Just my landlady," he said into the phone.

My landlady! I motioned awkwardly that I wanted to take Henry for a walk, a quick escape. George nodded and indicated the leash hanging near the door. I hooked it to Henry's collar, took him over to my side of the second floor, and led him down the wide front stairs so I could grab my jacket and get out of the house. My face was burning hot.

After Michael, I had determined that I was never going to get involved with a man again in my life. Polly had heard me say the same thing, many times. I had refused invitations for dinner with divorced colleagues from Michael's firm, and had turned down dates to movies from well-meaning widowers. I thought it was prudent, considering my bad track record, and except for my fantasy of making love with Teddy Carter (which I still allowed myself to indulge in), I was confident I'd never find anyone interested in a gray-haired woman approaching middle age; a grandmother, for God's sake, whose breasts were succumbing to gravity and whose hormone level fluctuated between steaming hot and lukewarm.

So, walking Henry, I analyzed the maddening adolescent fascination I was developing toward George. Maybe it was his husky voice, the way his face crinkled when he smiled, and the warmth of his eyes. Hazel eyes. And the recordings I heard playing when he was home. Soft jazz. Very sexy. Duke Ellington. Thelonius Monk. Bill Evans. I wasn't completely ignorant about jazz.

George had revamped the servants' quarters on the third floor as a music studio. I'm not ashamed to admit I checked his place out every day, after he'd left. The kitchen carved from the back bedroom had a little dining area and living space. It was sunny and inviting. Of course I looked his bedroom over, too. And I tried the mattress on his king-sized bed, which he had already brought over.

I was his *landlady*, after all! I brought him coffee. I walked his dog. I would gladly be his doormat. My grip on reality was not all that firm.

*P*olly informed me that George's trio played at the Bosky Lodge on Friday and Saturday nights. I figured that's why on Sundays he didn't arrive at the house until mid-afternoon. One lazy October Sunday I watched him unload boxes of books from his car.

"I'll do the Big Move the middle of next week," he said when I held the back door open. "I still need to pick up a few things for the kitchen."

The day George's piano was moved was the day he stayed overnight. It was a Friday. He planned on having dinner out with friends before his *gig*, he said. Henry would have to stay behind, alone. George warned me that I shouldn't be surprised to hear the dog whimpering while he was gone. "In a day or two he'll be content."

Poor Henry. When I went to bed I could hear him crying from the other side of the hallway door that separated George's apartment from mine. His forlorn whimpers nearly reduced *me* to tears, so I unlocked the door and Henry ran around in circles of joy. I left a sticky note on George's side inviting him to leave the door ajar, if he was comfortable with that, so Henry could return when he wanted to. The dog looked like a speckled ragdoll with his floppy black ears and he was really very sweet. After several failures, he learned to scamper quickly from the hall so he could accomplish the leap up onto my bed, where he curled at my side while I read. He was still there in the morning, but when I stirred he jumped off and went in search of his master and his dish of kibbles.

That was a Saturday. There was a Badger home football game, so my neighborhood was transformed. Residents park cars in their yards and stuff in as many as they can, bumper to bumper, while their kids beg "Park Here" in an attempt to rein in visiting fans and their willingness to shell out a few dollars for convenient parking. If you're a UW alumnus, the roar from the nearby stadium warms your heart and makes you more than a little nostalgic. On football Saturdays I'll wear a red sweatshirt that says "Go Badgers," even if I'm not going to the game.

Michael and I had season tickets, but now I'm content to watch on TV or listen to the radio play-by-play. I can hear the band even without opening the windows during halftime or the Fifth Quarter.

Teddy Carter called that morning. He was in Madison for the game and asked if I was free to join him for dinner. I warned him that bars and restaurants would be crowded but agreed to meet him at the Bosky Lodge. I figured, being located on the outskirts of the city, it wouldn't draw a lot of football fans. I'd never been there before. Maybe we could hear George's trio.

The Bosky Lodge, situated on the edge of Lake Waubesa, is built of logs and surrounded by a thick stand of fragrant pines. It's an intimate place, with a bar and a dining room, neither of them very spacious. The décor is faux Northwoods—birchwood picture frames, mounted antlers, a bearskin stretched along one of the knotty-pine walls. Teddy had already secured a booth and he waved to me when I came in.

My first clue should have been the huge black motorcycle parked in the lot. It was a honkin' big machine, heavy with chrome, studded mud flaps, and lots of dials on the dash. But I had no reason to connect the cycle with Teddy. Back when we dated, he had never shown any attraction to them.

Then I saw the black leather pants and the black leather jacket he was wearing. Thick buckled boots with tall heels made him even taller than he already was, so when he hugged me my face was buried somewhere beneath his massive leather chest.

"Teddy," my greeting was muffled.

"Nell, great to see you! Did you go to the game?"

He said he'd ridden his bike down to Madison with a bunch of friends. They were all spending the night at someone's home and everyone else had gone out drinking, but he wanted to see me.

We ordered steak sandwiches and covered all the requisite small talk. His wife was fine, the marriage was great, they had three grand-children, and he was eager to retire from his position as district at-torney of Northland County.

"Teddy," I said, choking back laughter, "you don't look like a DA with that thing wrapped around your head. What's that called?"

"It's a skull cap. Or a do-rag," he said. "We don't wear helmets. Maybe you didn't notice at the reunion," a pink blush broke out be-neath the freckles that still dusted his boyish face, "but I'm getting a little thin on top. The do-rag keeps my head warm."

He adjusted the cap a little bit and grinned.

"But it has little flaming devils all over it! And it says 'Bad Boy!' under each one!"

"So maybe I'm just freeing up my inner child," he shrugged. "What're *you* doing for fun, Nellie?" When he smiled that disarming smile I was fifteen all over again. He was still my *Teddy Bear.*

"Writing. Articles for a magazine. I've been working on a book but sort of lost interest in it. Nothing very exciting, I'm afraid . . ."

"And what's Polly up to? I heard Wolly Doodle moved back."

I told him about Polly's warehouse and studio and the exhibition she was preparing, as much as I could relate.

"I was listening to an oldies station on the radio the other day and remembered the quartette you girls had. Couldn't remember what it was called."

"The Starlettes."

"*The Starlettes,*" he mused, drawing the name out slowly as if he was savoring it. "You tried out for Ted Mack's Amateur Hour."

"I've tried to forget that," I laughed. "Let's talk about something else."

"How can I forget Sharon Gallagher in that sparkly miniskirt and her go-go boots!" Teddy teased. "Her bad leg came back pretty well!"

I kicked him under the table for that jibe. "Have you forgotten I wore a sparkly miniskirt and go-go boots, too!"

Then I *had* to laugh. The unfortunate night we sang at the county fair didn't seem so horrible anymore.

The lighthearted mood continued after we left the Bosky Lodge. I noticed a poster advertising the George Stafford Trio: they began playing each weekend at 9 p.m. It was almost nine but I didn't see George. Just as well.

Teddy followed me home and parked his enormous bike in my driveway. I felt I should comment on the shiny vehicle, so I said that it looked new and not only did Teddy say it was brand new, but he also told me the model and how great it was and would have gone on for hours about all the trimmings had I not encouraged him to come inside.

I built a fire in the living room and put on some soft music. Henry heard my voice and ran downstairs to jump around and bark at Teddy, but soon the pup curled up on a chair and went to sleep. Teddy and I snuggled on the sofa. It was like old times. Not exactly as I'd pictured it in my Quest, but this was my Bear and I was in his arms again.

So why wasn't I thrilled?

I dozed. I know Teddy slept because he snored. Kind of embarrassing. Maybe we were too old to be lovers! I woke him, joking about that, and Teddy gave me a kiss. The kiss was pretty nice. After that it didn't take very long before we knew where we were going.

"Are you sure?" I asked. "I mean, you *are* married . . ."

"And how many years did we make out hot and heavy before we even got *this* far?" Teddy wanted to know.

He was trying to pry off his heavy boots.

"We never got this far," I admitted, fumbling with the zipper of my jeans.

In my fantasy we'd undressed each other slowly, murmuring charming little endearments all along the way, head to toe.

I pulled my sweater off and had just tossed my bra over a lampshade when I noticed his shirt on the floor. I held it up.

"Okay, I get the do-rag and the leather, but what does this mean, on your shirt: *Mark 5: 11–13*?"

"The Gadarene Swine," he said. He was sitting on my Persian carpet and tugging at his tight black leather pants with considerable effort. "You know what they say about leather pants. If you can get 'em on and off too easily, they're not tight enough."

"Gadarene *what*?" I asked.

"Swine," he grunted, and I had to subdue another laugh. "In the Bible. Mark 5, verses 11 to 13. Jesus casts a bunch of devils into a herd of pigs and they run over a cliff and they're killed. Those pigs are martyrs. It's our club's citation. HOGs for Christ."

"Jesus."

"No, Christ. HOGs for *Christ*. A HOG is a member of the Harley Owner's Group. HOG. I'm a HOG."

"I know what a HOG is."

"For Christ."

"For Christ," I replied. "So, what does one *do* as a *HOG for Christ*?"

"We provide Christian witnessing to all motorcyclists, for one thing."

"And . . ."

"And we do evangelistic outreach. It's a motorcycle ministry. Bound by brotherhood and bikes. We go *Full throttle for Jesus*. That last part is mine; I thought it up," he said with a grin of pride.

"Teddy, you're Catholic . . ."

"I thought I told you, Nellie—I'm born again!"

Teddy stood in front of the fire, completely naked, wearing only

123

his devilish do-rag and a broad smile. The earnest removal of my clothes had decelerated. HOGs for Christ had taken me by surprise. It wasn't exactly a turn-on.

"Are you really 'born again'?" I asked, astonished. "My parents didn't want me to date you because you were Catholic!"

"Nell, have you seen Henry?" George came through the door to the living room.

"Hello," Teddy said to George, making no effort to cover himself.

The dog scampered over to George.

"Good evening," George greeted Teddy congenially and reached out his hand. "George Stafford. I live upstairs."

"Do you?" Teddy said, returning the handshake. "Ted Carter." He turned to me with raised eyebrows and I saw something else was raised, too. Oh, shit.

"Nellie and I were sweethearts, back in school," he said, as if that explained . . . everything.

"I'll see you George," I said, slipping my sweater back over my head.

"This isn't going to work, Teddy," I told him moments after George was gone.

"I gathered that."

He squeezed back into his leather garb and, with a swift kiss good-bye and a "See you later," hit the road. I could hear Teddy's Harley roaring into the distance with its distinctive reverberation fading away: Potato Potato Potato Potato, which has something to do with pistons and cylinders and the crankshaft. I wasn't paying much attention when Teddy explained how it worked.

So. That. Was. A. Huge. Blunder.

How stupid of me.

The truth was, the fantasy of seducing Teddy had been more exciting than the real thing. Now I could abandon the dream.

$\mathcal{I}$ needed a few days to recover from that encounter and did my best to avoid running into George. Eventually, I decided that since I survived the incident with Teddy and had gone a few weeks without

Angella I was less troubled by the consequences of her presence. It was not as if I'd regret never hearing from her again, but the prospect of waiting to see what transpired in her next message wasn't all that alarming anymore. As long as I could keep her on my screen and out of my mouth I could always pull her plug. It was like getting e-mail from outer space. Or "communicating with another plane of existence," as Grace Waverly would insist, "by means of automatic writing," another form of physical mediumship. If I got good at it, I should be able to read a book at the same time I was typing Angella's messages. How cool was that?

In my heart I knew wasn't suffering from multiple personalities or dissociative identity disorder. I wasn't (alas) threatened with a nervous breakdown, either. I was channeling Angella. That's all. I was a channeler just like Shirley MacLaine and that crazy California lady who claimed she channeled Barbie, "the archetypical feminine plastic essence," as she referred to it.

So, I rationalized (one of my champion skills coming into play), what's the worst that could happen? Sure, Angella could continue to interrupt my work, keep me from writing my little stories for *Meanderings*. But if I brought out the manuscript on old-fashioned mediumship to work on *Medium Grace,* perhaps Angella Wing could be of help.

Before I invited her back, however, I wanted to see what else I could find. Google still asked, "Are you sure you don't mean *Angel Wing?*" but there was another source I had to access. The location was too convenient to pass up.

The Wisconsin Center for Film and Theater Research, located within the Wisconsin Historical Society building, has an international reputation as one of the world's major archives of materials from the entertainment industry. Its vaults hold 15,000 motion pictures, TV shows, and videotapes, two million still photographs and graphics, and thousands of sound recordings. If there really had been an Angella Wing known as the "Woman of a Thousand Voices," perhaps I could discover more about her by digging there. A search on their website was futile, so I e-mailed a reference request. That turned up nothing. I accepted the archivist's suggestion to come down to campus on Monday to check out the files. I don't give up easily.

Granted, I had little to go on. If I could just hear her voice, on a radio recording! Or see her in a film! Well, that would be something. At least I'd know she'd survived somewhere besides the dusty crevices of my tortured brain.

I love burrowing around in historical artifacts and those items treasured by scholars in the past who valued old books for their wisdom. I even love the *smell* of old books. Pulling them from a myriad of floor after floor of dusty stacks to carry over and read at a table I've claimed near a window is one of the finest activities I can think of pursuing on a rainy day. It's not just that finding the book you're looking for is such a kick; you know that at least ten books on either side will contain interesting material, too.

The Wisconsin Historical Society is located on the campus of the University of Wisconsin, just across from the Memorial Union, which is on the shores of Lake Mendota. It's a practical place to visit because afterward you can have coffee at the Union or sit out on the terrace by the lake to review your notes or just pretend you're doing something constructive when you're really enjoying the sun or watching the sailboats or eating a bratwurst and killing time.

The historical society building itself has multiple floors of white marble and a vast atrium supporting a graceful stairway on either side. Lit by a ceiling of skylights in the center, the interior has an otherworldly glow that seems appropriate for this crypt of antiquities.

The Archives Research Room is on the fourth floor. I stuffed my handbag and jacket into a locker, then filled out a form for patrons at the desk inside the reference room with its ultra-high ceilings and individual tables where silent researchers wore the requisite white gloves and wrote with pencils; pens are not allowed.

The stacks in the archives can only be accessed by an archivist, so I discussed my search for "Angella Wing" and "Woman of a Thousand Voices" with a woman who worked on a computer where we tried all kinds of variations. The archivist even looked at files of unprocessed material that, she told me, they had tons of down in their vaults. But nothing seemed even remotely related to Angella or my search.

$\mathcal{D}$espite my failure, I felt buoyed by my modest attempt at exploration. I was not going to let some unknown spirit dictate my moves. If Angella "spoke" again, I would get her to reveal more personal data. Opening my brand new laptop might be like opening Pandora's box, but I still had not completed my Oktoberfest piece for *Meanderings* and I had a deadline ahead.

When studying old-fashioned mediumship, one source suggested creating an "Inner Sanctuary" to meet spirit guides and visualize a place in nature or a castle in the clouds. Take the phone off the hook. Fragrant candles could be used to alter the vibrational rate of the environment and to entice spirit guides.

I was then supposed to close my eyes, do some deep breathing, and imagine myself walking through a lush natural habitat.

Angella couldn't wait for the candles or deep breathing; she came rushing in as soon as I placed my fingers on the keys.

Whatever stardom she may have enjoyed, with whatever pseudonym, Angella Wing must have been a lonely woman. In a freaky, inexplicable way I warmed to her honesty. I had the impression that Angella still needed a *stage,* a place to expound and express herself. The Drama Queen was still itching to perform:

> *I'm laughing at you, Merrill! One thing you can't do is out-think me, dear girl. I feel the slightest nuance in your every thought.*

Was she referring to my visit to the film archives? That was eerie. I was trying to learn more about *her;* what did Angella know about *me?* It didn't seem to matter, because Angella was predictably self-centered about the stories she wished to convey.

> *I may be expecting too much of you because you are not an actor, and no one truly understands us but other actors. I, you will*

127

*soon find, am more complicated than most. The best of us journey
to the darker sides of their souls where we dig up bits and pieces to
illuminate the human spirit. I have to be honest, so you know what
you are getting into. Together we are bringing up the curtain on a
brand new show.*

I met Polly for coffee at the Terrace a few days after my encounter with Teddy, while walking Henry. I told her I'd seen Teddy, but I left out the colorful details. I didn't mention Angella, either.

During our conversation, she mentioned that she was writing a blog for the Museum of Holography in Chicago. The blog was mostly confined to the art of holography and challenges of that difficult form of artistic expression. I understood little about holography and even less about blogs, so I asked her to show me what hers was like.

"It's like a personal journal, but it's on the Internet," she said, bringing it up on her laptop.

"So you share it with the world," I said.

"Right. Anyone can access it and even add their own comments, if they want to. The kind of art I do is rather obscure, so it's a way for other holo-artists to keep in touch."

Eureka! On our walk back home I told Henry all about my inspiration for Angella. I told him if he stopped to pee more than fifteen times, that was a sign it would be a success. I lost count.

I had placed my computer on my lower sunporch, where I lit some candles. That evening when Angella began writing I replied that I had a very special idea: I would create a personal platform for her narrative expression and donate a few hours every week for her to "speak" through me, as her mediator. In return, she would promise to avoid interrupting me at will.

I explained that I would create a blog and a chat room for her. Of course Angella had no idea what a *blog* was; she had no idea what the *Internet* was. Personal computers were a mystery, too—even though she seemed quite content inhabiting mine!

A "blog," I explained, was a place to share her own private thoughts with whomever clicked onto her site. In other words, it was an exclusive place where she could write on an ongoing basis. Her newest entries would appear at the top. Visitors to her site could read them. In the chat room, readers could comment, and she could respond to whatever they said.

For me, it meant that rather than merely channeling her messages, I would *mediate* them. I would retain the ability to act consciously between Angella and those who wanted to hear her voice. I would know with whom I was in contact; there would always be an awareness of the nature of the message and how best to convey it. Perhaps most importantly, I would be able to turn my perceptiveness on and off at will.

If she was aware of "every nuance of my every thought," however, she must have been aware that I was operating on ignorance and bravado. I had no practice in being a "mediator," and even though Polly had told me of a free site that led me carefully through each step, it took me a long time to set up Angella's blog.

"Take Wing," I called it, after a line in a Byron poem. I felt it was the most appropriate title for her blog because I never knew what kind of mood she would convey. When I wrote her entries, I pulled a cap over my eyes so I couldn't see what she was saying, did some deep breathing exercises, and invited Angella to speak.

TAKE WING:

A CONVERSATION WITH

ANGELLA

O God! It is a fearful thing
To see the human soul take wing
In any shape, in any mood.

Byron

A spirit named Angella occupies this blog and wishes to share her thoughts. During her life on this plane, Miss Wing was an actress celebrated as the Woman of a Thousand Voices. Her words cannot be quelled; she has many marvelous things to say. I hope you will take her communications to heart and share your own concerns.

Peace and love,
Merrill Chase

Well, I can't say it was a resounding success at first. For once, Angella was at a loss for words and made a few erratic comments. She quoted Isadora Duncan, who said, "Before I go on stage, I have to put a motor in my soul," which made little sense. Then she offered this advice:

> *The changes that occur when you become attuned to the spirit world are major and irreversible. As a former radio actress, I might liken it to moving into a higher frequency. When this happens to you, it will be accompanied by adjustments in how you react to situations and how you respond to others.*

After I had completed my Oktoberfest article for *Meanderings*, Angella had no responses to the entry on her blog. Disappointed, she added the following:

> *I wish, if you are reading this, that you would reply to me. I need to hear your voice, as the mediums say; I need to know we are on the same frequency. As an actress I need to break through the "fourth wall" and receive a response from my audience. Believe me, I am desperate to know you are there.*

Within the next several days there were several exchanges between Angella and fascinated bloggers who had questions about energy vibrations and what happens if you can't accept losing friends and family once you become more spiritually attuned. Angella replied that the changes we make to our "vibrational" or frequency levels are irreversible and once our journey to enlightenment has begun there is no turning back. That gave me a chill.

But "Take Wing" was working. Angella had taken flight and I hoped I would soon be free of her.

❧

It was Polly's idea that we check out the George Stafford Trio at the Bosky Lodge. "You can tell a lot about a performer by their relationship with their audience," she said. If that was truly the case, one would deduce that my friend Polly Blue was incredibly idiosyncratic. Her area of artistic expression had progressed from portrait painting to performance art and now this weird interest in holography. I knew she went down to Chicago every week to teach workshops at the holography museum in addition to writing their blog. And she was currently working on a new show for a Chicago gallery that she'd tried to explain to George and me but it was a complicated affair that seemed to require smoke and mirrors and way too much elaborate math.

When Polly talked about her work, she became animated and beautiful.

Unlike Sharon, Polly had not been an attractive child. She'd pulled her straight dark hair back from her forehead with a plastic headband and besides being slightly overweight she was doomed in the fashion category. Of course the poor girl had to wear clothes from Cornbloom's Drygoods. I often wondered if that had an influence on Polly's rebellious behavior as an adult, because she enjoyed being unconventional, and when she bleached a stripe in her hair (her early California phase, after she'd abandoned "Cornbloom" in favor of "Blue"), she insisted on the blue wave seductively covering one eye. "It looks sort of Veronica Lake *punk*," I told her when I felt comfortable saying it. "Polly Blue isn't punk," she insisted. "It's my signature."

*I*t would be gauche to get there before the music begins," Polly assured me. "We don't want to seem too anxious." So the trio was well into the first set by the time we found a vacant table in the back of the darkened room of the Bosky Lodge, beneath a wall of taxidermied fish.

George had no advance notice that we were coming, and that made me a little uncomfortable, but, I decided, the man was going to be living with me, or (let me rephrase that) living in my house, so I had a right to hear what his original musical tastes were like. Before long I'd probably be hearing the blissful notes of his piano seeping through the walls and down the halls.

"He's not gay," Polly blurted out as if she'd only just been reminded.

"How the hell would you happen to know that?" I asked, as a waiter set a Dusky ale in front of each of us.

"I asked him," Polly replied. "One day when you were locked in your little porch I went up the back stairs and played with Henry. George asked me a lot of questions about you, so I felt it was only fair to inquire about his personal background, too."

"What did he want to know?" I asked, worried about Polly's fixation for details.

"How long had I known you, what happened in both your marriages, did you have kids, had you ever committed a felony, were you hot for him, the usual things."

Sometimes my old pal could still be exasperating!

"So, what'd you say?"

"All my life, your husbands were jerks, no jailbird, two kids, and probably."

"Probably?"

"You were hot for him."

I chose to ignore that.

"I got the idea he was checking you out. What's the difference? It looks like you passed," Polly grinned.

The trio played a combination of modern and traditional jazz. Besides enjoying the music, it was fun to see George perform before an audience. The bassist and drummer were both about George's age only not as tall and the bassist was bald. I recognized them as the guys who'd helped move George's piano up the back stairs.

Midway through the second set, a couple asked if they could join us at our table. They said they'd driven down from the Twin Cities and were big fans of George's music and thought George was "really cool." I think they would've said they went to all his "gigs" if I'd encouraged it. As it was, they seemed content to tap their feet and didn't say much, even when the trio took a break.

Polly and I stayed until after the final set, and then went up to say hi. George introduced us to his pals, calling me his "landlady," which didn't seem like a joke. Then he gave us each a copy of their latest CD before he had to chat with other fans who were waiting, and we said good night.

⟨✦⟩

Between sessions for Angella's blog I was again working on *Medium Grace*. I prowled eBay and found out-of-print copies of Spiritualism books from the 1800s that gave vivid examples of the use of ectoplasm, a word derived from the Greek words *ektos* and *plasma*. Emanuel Swedenborg referred to it as "a sort of stream which poured from [his] body and formed into rats or reptiles," a symbol of a poisonous condition of his constitution.

I found materialization to be the most fascinating aspect of old-fashioned mediumship, but sex in the séance room was not all that unusual, either. One famous Boston medium sometimes conducted spiritual séances in the nude, to rule out fraud. During these sessions, carried out in total darkness, she often threw her feet into the lap of one of the participants while her head lolled in the lap of another. Numerous accounts stated that her ectoplasm had a propensity for emanating from her vagina before its restoration to that orifice.

Other female mediums enjoyed orgasmic reactions during séances. And there were male mediums who took pleasure in debauchery with sitters, treating women of their choice (in the dark, of course) to especially passionate action. I didn't think Grace would have anything relevant to add to that.

*H*enry preferred to stay on my side of the house whenever George was gone. I had never had a dog, and neither had my children because their father was allergic to them. My brother, Buddy, had several dogs in succession, each one killed by a car. After we'd sobbed through three backyard funerals in one summer, Mother put her foot down and said that was enough. I'd never liked Buddy's dogs much anyway, they were little yippy rat terrier mutts that Mom had to nag Buddy to feed every day and they did not like to be petted or cuddled.

Henry was fluffy and sweet. Henry loved to be hugged.

As I mentioned earlier, George taught on Tuesdays and Thursdays and he held office hours and rehearsals during the week. I tried to keep track of his comings and goings, but his schedule was inconsistent. I knew he kept a calendar next to his telephone in his apartment, so if I had a question I could always clandestinely check a specific date.

I made another unproductive check up two weeks after my first visit to the film archives, this time asking the archivist to run a search on "radio actresses." There were hundreds, but none had names that remotely matched "Angella Wing." Afterward, I sat on the terrace with a cup of coffee and a slice of fudge-bottom pie (the Union's signature dessert) to scan another pile of musty old mediumship books from the historical society.

George unexpectedly sat down at my table with a cup of coffee of his own. Without speaking, he began paging through the book on top of the stack.

"I'm writing a book on old-fashioned Spiritualist mediumship," I explained, "and this is grist for the mill."

George put that book down and began to page through another.

Why had I never paid much attention to the scar on the back of his left hand until now? The raised line creased in an irregular pattern that must have made it difficult to reach an entire octave of keys. But I couldn't ask. I also couldn't take my eyes away.

"You know, the sociology department is sponsoring a seminar that you might be interested in," he offered, still flipping pages.

"What about," I mumbled, sipping coffee that was already cold. I was ready to get out of there.

"I saw a poster about it on the corner kiosk," he motioned toward Park Street. "The PseudoScience seminar is put on by the Committee for the Scientific Investigation of Claims of the Paranormal, or

CSICOP. They investigate extraterrestrials and aliens, that sort of thing."

"I'm not interested in UFOs," I said with my mouth full of the last bite of delicious chocolate fudge. I'd have to walk Henry an extra mile to make up for the pie, but it was worth it.

"One of the speakers is going to talk about psychic hotlines. Another's going to speak on channeling. The seminar could give you another perspective on this subject."

"Maybe it would," I agreed, albeit reluctantly. And maybe it would help me sort out my clandestine relationship with Angella Wing.

"I'll even go with you," he suggested.

"What?"

"I'll go, too. I'd like to hear what they have to say."

I must have looked bewildered because he added, "I have a friend who wants to attend, but she has to be out of town. I promised I'd take notes."

The PseudoScience seminar was provocative but raised more uncertainties for me than it resolved. While I appreciated the statement that 95 percent of channelers are not conscious frauds, I found many of the hypotheses put forward unsettling. Like the one that claimed some people who channel have split personalities, exactly what I'd worried about, dissociative identity disorder. "Everyone has the potential," the scientist claimed. "People have enough information to act out hundreds of personalities. Creative artists and writers can learn to tap this potential. It can also appear when one is hypnotized, sick, or deprived, or during a mystical ritual."

I was very much aware of the woodsy scent of George's cologne right next to me and had trouble focusing my concentration on anything but him.

My favorite diagnosis of the evening turned out to be "magical thinking," a theory proposed by a British professor of psychology who suggested that our minds easily make causal connections and patterns that may not actually exist. Perception is a creative act that involves not only the sensory apparatus of the brain but also memory, emotion, personal hopes, and fears. We fill in our observations of reality with the way we think things should be, based on our expectations. And when these misperceptions become part of our memory they can create new perceptions and interpretations, a suspicious "false memory" syndrome.

Or a channeled "entity," I thought.

After the seminar, George and I had coffee at Hava Java on State Street. I was pleased when one of his students, a young man who'd helped paint George's apartment, remembered my name.

Again, I found myself studying the scar on the back of his hand when he sipped his coffee and had to hold back from tracing the wound with my finger.

"What's that from?" I asked, lightly touching it.

"Something stupid I did when I was a kid. Believe me, you don't want to know."

But I did. I wanted to know everything about him. Especially now that I knew he had once acted in an irresponsible way. I could identify with that!

"So what do you think about the seminar?" George asked, changing the subject. "Are you in agreement with the skeptics or still enamored of your Spiritualist pals?"

"One has to have an open mind," I offered cautiously.

"Having an open mind isn't the same thing as having a hole in the head," George joked. "I think people are searching for transcendental meaning in their lives because they can't handle the simple fact that this is all there is. Right here."

"That's understandable, isn't it? No one wants to believe their life is just a meaningless accident. Some people want to be reassured that there's a grand plan involved, an explanation for what's happening."

"So they ask a psychic to tell them. Makes perfect sense," George said with a crooked smile.

"Hasn't that always been the case?" I challenged. "Aren't people always looking for meaning? Where would we be without all the philosophers who expounded on that need? And besides, I can't see where psychics—real ones, not the frauds—are doing any harm, after all."

At the risk of tarnishing his estimation of me, I took a nosedive and told him about the Wocanaga Camp, where mediums deliver messages that tell people to take care of their health, or live life to the fullest, or go ahead and take a trip they've planned.

"And none of those mediums at Wocanaga are frauds?"

"I can't guarantee that, but I don't think they're harmful or give dangerous messages. That's all."

"Look, any fool could come up with 'messages' like that, don't you see? It doesn't take psychic ability to realize how many insecurities someone has. If you look carefully at what they do, I'll bet those mediums just tell people what they want to hear."

I knew for a fact George was right about that. "So maybe some people just need a little prodding," I replied. "Permission. A little common sense. There's nothing wrong with that."

"But if they call themselves psychics or mediums, then they're deluding themselves or the public, or both. I say they're no more psychic than you or I."

"Suit yourself," I said. "I have a psychic vibration that says you're full of it."

"And I say you ought to join *my* church, the Church of Savior Fork."

"Savior *what*?"

George sat back, picked up a fork, and tried to stifle a grin. "What do they say when you're at someone's house for dinner and they clear the plates; what do they say? They say, 'Save your fork.' That means there's something really good ahead, like chocolate cake or lemon meringue pie. The best is yet to come. *Save your fork.* I want to be buried with a fork in my hand. *The best is yet to come!*"

"Fork yourself," I said, pushing my chair back and grabbing my jacket.

We established a routine together, George and I, that kept us out of each other's way and protected our privacy. I knew when he was

137

home because I could hear him playing the piano (which I loved) or he played CDs that became calming background music to the hassle of my days. Billie Holliday. Alberta Hunter. Ella Fitzgerald. Much of it, though, was jazz by musicians I did not recognize.

Part of our routine was to walk Henry through the neighborhood every morning. We'd take our time wandering the curvilinear streets that hugged the rolling landscape. We developed a comfortable, casual, neighborly relationship. I wanted to avoid, at all costs, any suspicion on his part that I "was hot for him," Polly's jocular remark. Although I sort of was.

When we walked in the morning he told me about his family, his former marriage, his music, and his students. I told him about growing up in Little Wolf, my marriage to Lee, and my life in Madison. I mentioned how much I missed Sky and Odessa. I explained my marriage to Michael. I even related my fondness for Teddy, evoking the embarrassing moment they met.

Often, we'd leave the door between his apartment and my second floor ajar so Henry could enter and exit without invitation. The rest of the time the door remained closed, and my key, one of those old-fashioned skeleton keys, was securely stationed in the keyhole.

$\mathcal{I}$ wasn't meant to see them, of course—George and his friend, Breeze Quinn—but I did, and that preoccupation soon became as enticing and as strong as my initial desire to learn more about Angella Wing.

It was one of those Saturday nights when Henry was already on my side of the house so I left the upstairs door ajar when I went to bed. I'd stayed up late, working with Angella's blog, and didn't shower until midnight. If I hadn't still been lying awake, reading, I wouldn't have heard the laughter: a woman's voice, muted, and then the subtle click of the interior door I'd left open.

As I said, I always left my key in the lock, and George did the same. This night, however, the woman who closed the door from the other side and turned the key must have removed it afterward.

I'm not proud of what I did. It was an unconscionable invasion of my neighbor's privacy. But I could not get to sleep while listening for George's voice and the woman's, in what was, practically, a room right next to mine.

At first I thought I'd just stand next to the door and see if I could make out their words. Then I removed my key to hear better, and I saw the beam of light that meant his key was not there.

From that small window of sly opportunity, I saw Breeze Quinn for the first time. If George could see me kneeling at the keyhole on the other side of his door at one o'clock in the morning wearing my ratty chenille bathrobe, hair still wet from the shower, muzzling Henry so he wouldn't whine—well, I knew how contemptible I really was.

I knew how miserable I really felt.

Breeze Quinn. Lithe, slender. Auburn hair that could be an illustration for a shampoo ad, glossy and rippling in a reddish-brown shimmer down over her shoulders. Green eyes, flawless pale skin.

I just took it for granted her eyes were green. All I could see of her during that primary keyhole preview was a quick glimpse as she traversed the space between George's bedroom and the bathroom across the hall. There was a flash of red hair and ivory flesh. The rest was left to my imagination.

But my imagination was so agitated, my jealousy so fierce, I lay awake the remainder of the night hearing the wind scream around the eaves while I envied Henry's contented snuffles.

No one stirred at sunrise except Henry, who was desperate to get outside. I pulled on jeans and a heavy sweatshirt and grabbed his leash from the back hall just as George stepped off the bottom of the stairs, wearing only a towel. He had been letting his hair grow long so it was a tangled mess and his unshaven beard made him look like a homeless wreck. His eyes were red-rimmed and bleary.

"Get a fucking haircut," I snapped. "And shave that stupid pussy-beard goatee. You look like a goddamned bum."

I followed the dog outside and let the storm door slam. Sure, I instantly regretted what I said but he had a sweet Breeze in bed to soothe his sore ego.

$\mathcal{P}$olly gathered details later that day. When we met for brunch I nonchalantly mentioned a red-haired woman with a British accent that I thought George might be seeing, and Polly called back that evening with information that Breeze Quinn managed the Bosky Lodge, the brewpub where we'd heard his trio. She, I decided, was most likely the stylist behind his new "look."

Monday morning, when George and I met out in front to walk with Henry, I avoided his eyes. Few words were spoken but when we got home I said, "I think we need to draw up a contract."

"Meaning rent?" George said.

"Meaning rent and personal responsibilities."

"If it's a privacy issue," he assured me, "I promise I won't ever set foot on your side again without invitation!"

"I mean," I said coolly, unclipping Henry from his leash so he could romp in the leaves, "I'm your landlady, and you're my tenant. So I have the right to disregard what's happening in your life, just as you do in mine. I appreciate the fact that you've managed to over-look what happened when Teddy was here. And I'm very sorry about what I said yesterday. That you looked like a bum. That was un-called for."

I just then noticed that he'd shaved off the beard. He pulled off his baseball cap and revealed he'd had a haircut, too.

"*Now* you tell me!" he grinned. "At least I wasn't wearing an earring!"

Of course, I thought he looked more handsome than ever.

I laughed so hard, Henry leaped up to lick me in case something was wrong. And then I couldn't help it; I had to give each of them a hug.

As a rule, I don't like secrets, but in addition to what had become my chronic keyhole surveillance of George and his wafty Breeze, I concealed my channeling of Angella for a fairly long time.

In Little Wolf I could go for days, sometimes an entire week, privately pretending that a camera crew was filming *A Day in the Life of Eleanora Grendon* for a very special movie. A pleasant narrative voice ran in the background of my mind: *As Eleanora Grendon enters the front door of her school, classmates greet her with joyous enthusiasm. She is the most popular girl in her home town.*

But sustaining a secret takes a lot of effort.

Eleanora enjoys an order of french fries and a Coke at Lulu's Dairy Bar while listening to Mama Cass singing "Dream a Little Dream of Me," her favorite record. She overhears malicious gossip about Sharon Gallagher and saves it to share with her best friend, Polly Cornbloom, who is inserting another quarter into the jukebox.

Keeping secrets can be tedious work. For example, there was Miss Khrol, otherwise known to us kids as the Old Crow. Polly and I liked to pretend she was a witch and we made up stories to scare Sharon when she was visiting her aunt.

"The Old Crow lives on a swamp near Bear Lake."

"She's over a hundred years old and dresses all in black and walks hunched over with a scarf tied over her head."

"It's like a babushka. And it's printed with mysterious symbols!"

"She gets more humpbacked and shrunken every year. Her nose has a wart on the end!"

"A *huge* wart!"

"Her nose is so big it's like a beak and from the side she looks like a crow."

"And she's a *crone,* too," I added; then I defined the term because Sharon looked momentarily puzzled. "That's a witchlike old woman. In the old days she was originally called the Old Crone, but it was shortened to Crow because her nose kept growing and besides, a lot of people were so stupid they didn't know what a *crone* was."

"Nellie and I sneaked up to her garden once," Polly lied, "and she said if she saw us there again she'd cast an evil spell over us!"

In truth, Polly and I had never seen the Old Crow, which only enhanced my yearning to learn more about her.

In the middle of sixth grade, Sharon and Cookie appeared at Gloria Piekarski's front door and asked if they could move in. Mother explained later that "Cookie flew the coop" when Mr. Gallagher beat her up one time too many.

Most of our sixth grade class already knew Sharon because of her summer vacations in Little Wolf. Polly made sure Sharon felt comfortable and filled her in on where we were with everything. Because of her leg, Sharon couldn't play on our girls' basketball team after school, so she watched from the bleachers. Sometimes I thought Polly showed off for her. In fact, I was more than a little jealous about the special attention Polly gave to Sharon. But the three of us were seldom apart for very long.

I can't explain exactly how it happened, but Sharon became our leader. She was taller, older, and very good at math, which became important as soon as we were introduced to long division. If we asked her, she didn't mind sharing the right answers with us. Her withered leg was getting stronger, too, and she was able to go without a brace for longer periods of time. The brown oxford she wore on that leg had a built-up sole so her limp was not as pronounced.

Mr. Gallagher was allowed to see his daughter once a month. He adapted a girl's bike so Sharon could strengthen her deteriorated muscles. During the summer between sixth and seventh grade we rode our bikes in the country a lot, purposely avoiding hilly roads.

In late June, Sharon said she wanted to ride bikes out to Bear Lake and see the Old Crow's cottage.

"It's too hot," I said, feigning weariness.

Sharon was persistent. "Oh, c'mon, Nell. I'll get Cookie to fix us some sandwiches with bologna and cheese."

"I'll bring some potato chips," Polly added, urging me to agree with Sharon, who seemed more loyal to her than to me at times like that.

"I don't know," I said, stretching like a lazy cat with a desire to be cajoled. "My dad says the Old Crow is just a little Bohemian."

"Is that a big deal?" Sharon wanted to know.

"It's like being a hippie," Polly offered.

"She's no hippie," Sharon insisted. "She's a witch. You told me so! If you're too scared to come along, Nell, then Polly and me will go by ourselves."

Sharon knew I would respond to that threat.

The June day was almost as perfect as June days can be and wild blossoms and birdsongs embellished the countryside. Pedaling became harder on the gravel that led to the Old Crow's, but Sharon did not complain.

When we reached a grassy space overlooking the swampy area where her home was hidden in the trees, we lay our bikes down and ate our lunch on a log. Cookie had mixed a thermos of cherry Kool-Aid, which we shared in paper cups.

"If I tell you guys a secret, promise not to tell?" Sharon said. "Cross your hearts and hope to die?"

Polly and I solemnly crossed our hearts.

"I started menstruating."

"No kidding," Polly said, glancing over at me. This was a subject we had never discussed.

"Cookie got me one of those elastic belts at Crandall's Drug Store that you hook your Kotex onto and boy is that ever uncomfortable. I had bad cramps, too. Cookie says she calls it 'getting the curse,' because it's so awful. And she says now I can have babies," Sharon added. She pulled her hair back into an impromptu ponytail and wound it with one of the rubber bands that had secured waxed paper around the sandwiches.

The ponytail move struck me as such an unconsciously grown-up gesture, as if Sharon were moving on ahead of the rest of us and Polly and I would never catch up.

Sharon as a mother: it was a perplexing thought.

"Cookie says down in Tennessee girls can get married when they're eleven, and I'm already twelve," Sharon added.

"They're hillbillies," I said. "You're not a hillbilly, you're . . ."

The minute I said it, I knew she'd be angry at me. It didn't take much to get Sharon mad; all you had to do was make a casual allusion to "Polacks," even just teasing, and she'd lose her temper.

"That was a stupid thing to say, Nell Grendon," she spat back. "It's almost as stupid as thinking Teddy Carter is your boyfriend. He told Buck who told Merry and she told Carolina that he wants me to sit next to him at the show next Friday night."

It would be an ultimate humiliation for Teddy to publicly choose Sharon over me. We always met *inside* the Lenore; that way my parents didn't know I sat with Teddy when I went to the double feature on Fridays. Almost all of us were paired up now—Carolina and Duane, Buck and Merry, Hannah and Robert. Teddy always held my hand.

"I don't believe it," I said. "He wouldn't do that."

I could envision Sharon in high school, tall and beautiful, with no acne on her forehead and a plaid miniskirt and matching tight pink sweater with a scoop neckline that the boys couldn't turn their eyes from because her breasts were really big. Even Teddy could probably be seduced.

"For Pete's sake, Nellie," Polly said. "Don't get mad at Sharon. Teddy's the one who said it, not her."

"Teddy did *not* say it! Neither of you know *anything*," I shouted at both of them.

"I see him at Mass every morning. He's Father O'Neil's altar boy," Sharon bragged. "He looks really cute in his cassock and surplice, too. I think Teddy would make a cute priest."

"Teddy does not want to be a priest," I said. "I know for sure he doesn't want to."

"I know for sure that you're too chicken to sneak up on the Old Crow," Sharon suggested slyly.

"You really want her to?" Polly eyed Sharon suspiciously. "She might cast a spell on us!"

If we stood up on the log, we could see the sagging fence surrounding the Old Crow's garden and the patchwork of shingles on her cottage roof.

"I don't mean *all* of us," Sharon answered. "I just mean Nell. I want to know if she's got the guts to do it. I think she's a chicken. Cluck, cluck, cluck!" She pranced around, wiggling her elbows like chicken wings. "Cock-a-doodle-dooooo. Cluck, cluck, cluck! Nellie's yellow! She's a *yellow* chicken!"

If only I could tell her I touched Leonard Twyn's dead body, she'd change her mind about that!

"I'm not a chicken," I said. "I'll show you I'm not afraid of the Old Crow or anybody, not even you, Sharon Gallagher, not even you and your stupid lies."

I tramped through the cowslips in the marsh so carelessly that my tennis shoes became soggy right away. I hated the squish that came with each wet step. Mosquitoes and gnats swarmed around my face and some got between my glasses and my eyes. It was awful. I paused to look back and saw Polly and Sharon standing on the log, watching me.

When I reached the fence around it, I found the Old Crow's

garden tangled with ferns and vines and musky herbal scents. Her house was worse than it looked from a distance—held together with tar paper and shingles and rusty chicken wire. No one was in the garden.

I couldn't see Polly and Sharon anymore, so they would never know how brave I'd been unless I presented them with proof. I pried the boards of the fence apart, sucked in my stomach, and slithered through.

Scattered here and there, little plaster and plywood figures popped up like surprise greetings—a large frog, a sundial, a bird-bath, a fake deer, two gigantic plaster toadstools, a mirrored ball on a pedestal, and beneath it a little garden gnome about six inches high that leaned next to a bunch of nodding yellow pansies. Red paint flaked from the pointed cap on his head.

Quick as a flash, I slipped the garden gnome under my arm and crept back across the swamp. When I reached Sharon and Polly, I held him out to show them where I'd been and what I'd found.

"Ta-Da!"

Sharon was impressed, but I didn't like Polly's scowl. "You better put it back," she said.

"There's so much junk over there the Old Crow will never miss it," Sharon boasted. "Did you see her?"

"Just her shadow," I fibbed. "I waited until she slinked around a corner then I grabbed this and ran."

"We better get out of here." Polly was already screwing the cap back on the thermos.

"She doesn't scare me," Sharon boasted, but I noticed she was packing up her picnic stuff, too.

I took the gnome home in the basket of my bike. I didn't really want him, but that wasn't the point.

Mother was in the yard when I rode up the driveway and she spotted the gnome right away. I tried to make it sound like I hadn't stolen him when she asked me whose it was.

"Eleanora Grendon, you're going to ride right back out there and take this up to Miss Khrol's door and apologize," she declared.

146

So that was her name: *Khrol.* It even sounded like *Crow.*

It would be bad enough coming face-to-face with the Old Crow at any time, but to confess that I'd invaded her garden and stolen something . . .

"She might cast a spell on me," I muttered.

"You should have thought about that before you took something belonging to a shut-in, of all people," Mother said bitterly. "Stealing is wrong, it's against the law, and I won't have any child of mine trespassing like that. How could you, Eleanora! Trespassing on someone else's property! Wait until your father finds out! You have never done anything like this before; what's gotten into you? I might expect this kind of behavior from Buddy, but *you* know what *trespass* means!"

"Does Daddy have to find out?" I asked.

He and Buddy were up north on a fishing trip with the Cub Scouts.

"We'll see about that," she said, which meant there might be some leeway to make a deal.

"I'll wash dishes every day for a month," I suggested. "Then could we not tell him? Please? I'm really sorry."

"Return this ornament to Miss Khrol. Tell *her* how sorry you are. Then we'll talk."

I wasn't feeling well by then—too many potato chips or my jumpy stomach. I felt so sick that I couldn't eat any supper. Mother relented a bit and said she'd take me to Miss Khrol's in the car. "Let's get it over with and stop at the A&W on the way home. C'mon."

But she refused to walk up to the door of the Old Crow's cottage with me.

"This is your doing, Eleanora. It's your responsibility. I'll wait right here."

Mother stayed in the car.

I wished I could just set the gnome down by the Crow's front door and run.

Miss Khrol opened the door only a crack and stuck her head out before I had a chance to knock. I couldn't see inside because it was so dark in there. I did notice, however, that she had enormous hair—black hair, frizzy, that sprayed out all over her head like a gigantic Afro but her skin was unusually pale. And there was no wart on her nose but thick glasses balanced there made her eyes loom huge and owly.

An even bigger surprise: she wore a pink shawl and was seated in a wheelchair.

"I have something," I began softly. "My friends and I had a picnic over there today . . ."

"I saw you in my garden," Miss Khrol said in a whispery voice that sounded sinister but it could have been my imagination. Maybe she had a cold. "I saw you break through our fence and take the little gnome."

"I'm sorry," I said, handing it over. "It wasn't stealing, really. I just borrowed him. He's all right. I hope that's okay? That I borrowed him?"

I gently stroked the tip of the gnome's red cap. He was sort of cute.

"Please don't cast a spell on me," I wanted to add just in case, but I thought that might be asking too much of her.

"You might have asked," she said. "I would have let you show him to your friends."

So all along she knew why I'd "borrowed" him.

"He doesn't seem the worse for wear," she said as she inspected the statue. "Can you step inside?"

"My mother's waiting." I indicated her, sitting in the car.

"Oh, that's Mrs. Grendon. She buys strawberries from us."

"She does?"

Miss Khrol waved to my mother, then whispered, "Come back one day, by yourself. When we can talk."

By the time Mother and I arrived at the root beer stand I was ready for a hamburger and a black cow, a mug of root beer with a big scoop of vanilla ice cream.

The actual face-to-face meeting with the Old Crow wasn't the worst outcome of that experience. The next morning I had to contend with Sharon's scorn.

"Of course your mother made you take it back," she said. "Stealing is a sin. 'Thou Shalt Not Steal,' it's one of the Ten Commandments."

"I know it is," I said, thinking of the Lord's Prayer ring hidden in the knot of my cowboy bandana.

"I never asked you to *steal*," Sharon continued sourly. "Stealing's a *venial* sin. You can spend about ten years in purgatory for stealing, I'll bet!"

"But I wasn't stealing," I could hear myself whining. "I just wanted to prove to you that I was in her garden. I always planned to put it back."

"I think she's telling the truth," Polly said, supporting me.

"If you commit a venial sin, you need to go to confession to obtain absolution," Sharon replied. "Want to play Confession?"

It was a cloudy day with drizzle and there wasn't much else to do. Cookie and Gloria had gone to Waupaca to buy some support hosiery they couldn't get at Cornbloom's, and my mother was at Priscilla's Circle. I thought about the confessional at the Catholic Church in Waupaca—the little wooden house that looked like a dollhouse with two rooms and a woven metal window in between. Did one feel an enormous relief after confession? Could you actually start out fresh again, with everything bad erased?

I had already thought of going up to Sacred Heart and confessing to Father O'Neil because Sharon said priests kept your secrets no matter how bad they were. I imagined myself entering the confessional and falling to my knees. I knew the words to say: "Bless me Father, for I have sinned," and he would say, oh, so kindly, "What have you done, my daughter?" and my guilt would dissolve when my secrets were revealed. I would confess that I took something that didn't belong to me. And I knew it was wrong, so I returned it. Well, actually there were two things, really, two things that I stole and one of them I couldn't put back because the coffin was locked—which would, in retrospect, have the potential to bring up even more uncomfortable issues.

"Might as well," I shrugged in response to Sharon's question.

"How do we play Confession?" Polly wanted to know.

149

Sharon led us to an upstairs closet in the spare bedroom where her belongings had been moved, although she was still sleeping in the same bed as Cookie in another room. The closet smelled of mothballs and held Gloria's winter coats squeezed next to some scratchy suits on hangers—maybe Mr. Piekarski's old clothes that Gloria hadn't had the heart to give away after he died.

"You get inside," Sharon said to me, "and Polly and me will hear your confession. I'll be the priest."

"What's Polly going to be?"

"She's my altar boy."

I didn't think altar boys had anything to do with confession. Teddy never told me about hearing anybody's confessions, but I didn't want to bug Sharon because then she might get mad and the whole game would disappear. I went inside the closet and kneeled, as she ordered, on the floor, facing the door. There wasn't much space: a sewing machine and a vacuum cleaner were in the way.

The closet door clicked shut. I could see only a dusty crack of light near my knees.

"What should I say?" I asked.

There was giggling in the bedroom and I didn't like that.

"You say, 'Bless me Father, for I have sinned,'" Sharon ordered, muffling laughter.

I repeated the words.

"Louder, Nell. We can't hear you out here."

"Bless me Father, for I have sinned!" I shouted, feeling silly and deciding this game was really stupid. I reached for the knob and tried to push the door open.

"We're not letting you out until you confess," Sharon said.

"C'mon, Nellie," Polly encouraged me, "tell the priest what you did and she'll let you out."

"What are your sins, my child," Sharon sputtered in a fake-deep voice.

"I don't know how to say it," I pleaded. "Tell me what to say."

"You disobeyed your parents, didn't you?"

"I guess so . . ."

"And you fought with your brother."

"Well, sure, I did that."

"Okay, start with those. And then you also had impure thoughts."

Impure thoughts? What were they?

"Nellie . . . ," Polly pleaded, as if to say, don't make this go on any longer than necessary.

The closet was stuffy and sweat was running down my forehead, stinging my eyes.

"I disobeyed my parents," I said.

"How many times?"

"Four," I said. Who knew how many times I disobeyed them? Who really cared?

"And I fought with my little brother, two times."

"Are you sure it was only two?"

Sharon could really be mean.

"Okay, three times. Sharon, I want to get out of here!"

I was beginning to feel as if I couldn't breathe enough air.

"And you had impure thoughts?"

"Yes, I had *impure thoughts.*"

"About Teddy Carter?"

"I don't know what they are . . ." My voice was trembling; I was ready to cry but I would not let her make me cry, I would not cry!

"Nellie, play the game!" Polly hinted. I could tell she was tired of it, too.

"Say you had impure thoughts about Teddy Carter, Nell. Say you want him to kiss you a thousand times!"

"Then will you let me out?" My heart was thumping loudly and quickly and I couldn't get enough oxygen into my lungs. A deep hum pressing on my eardrums made everything echo. I was going to suffocate in this closet and it would all be Sharon's fault when I died.

"Say you want Teddy Carter to do it," Sharon urged. "Say it!"

Her voice sounded as if it came from miles away.

"I had impure thoughts about Teddy Carter," I said weakly. "I want Teddy Carter to kiss me a thousand times."

Was wanting him to kiss me "impure," I wondered? Then I *did* have impure thoughts. My head swirled with fizzy little dots. I fell against the door.

"And you want him to touch your private parts."

I wouldn't say that. Never!

"You want him to diddle your titties."

"SHAAARON!" I screamed.

"Sharon," Polly warned. "That's not fair."

"Let me out of here!" I sobbed.

"There's something you forgot," Sharon cautioned, imperiously.

"I took something that didn't belong to me," I admitted softly.

"Stealing is a very serious sin," Sharon's fake-deep voice intoned. "You will have to be punished to earn some indulgences and your penance will be to say an Our Father at each bowling ball in the Our Lady of the Garden Rosary immediately, even if it's raining. This will be a good act of contrition, my child."

"Let her out," Polly ordered.

The door opened a crack and cooler air rushed in. I was faint from the fumes of mothballs. My bangs were glued to my forehead.

"You're all white," Polly said as she helped me to my feet.

"You must make your revolutions of the Our Lady of the Garden Rosary right this very minute," Sharon demanded. She was wearing a man's white shirt put on backwards so the collar was like a priest's. Over that she had buttoned one of Gloria's black sweaters. Polly rolled her eyes and mouthed "sorry" behind Sharon's back.

Rain was falling hard by now, but Sharon would not give up the game. I made my way around the Our Lady of the Garden Rosary, reciting the Lord's Prayer and kneeling in the wet grass at every bowling ball. It took me over an hour, at least. Sharon assured me if I were Catholic this would take a year off my stay in purgatory. But I didn't feel any better afterward. In fact, I was certain that I was going to get pneumonia.

Trespass. It was becoming a regular part of my life, crossing the line into places where I wasn't wanted and did not belong.

Eventually I took my bike out to see the Old Crow again. I had to build up my courage but she had asked me to come and she was crippled, so how dangerous could she be?

She was alone, sitting in her garden. And she wasn't as old as I'd thought, maybe around my mother's age, so that would make her about forty, but it was hard to tell for sure because of her Coke-bottle glasses and owl eyes.

"Sit down and enjoy the sun with me. Isn't it sybaritic this afternoon?"

She spoke slowly, her whispery voice so musical and so expressive that it was almost like singing. Again, she was seated in an old-fashioned wicker wheelchair. I had no idea what sybaritic meant, but I plopped down on a bench in the sun and agreed, "It sure is."

Violets were scattered everywhere. They danced around the weathered wooden fence and along the crooked path through the swamp. I picked one from the grass near my feet and inspected the purple five-petaled blossom and the heart-shaped leaf.

Miss Khrol wore a shawl this time, too, a pretty paisley print that concealed much of her long, soft gray dress. She also wore a fraying straw hat. It had a large and crooked brim and was tied beneath her chin with a red scarf so her wild hair wouldn't throw it off.

The only scary thing about Miss Khrol *was* her hair—black and blustery, it spun out around her head in a halo like cotton candy. In a weird and wonderful way, I decided, she was beautiful.

"Do you know why they're called violets?" she asked after a while. I admitted that I didn't. "The plant has many names in many cultures," Miss Khrol said. "Apothecaries call it *Herba Violaria,* from the Latin, *Viola.* V-I-O-L-A," she spelled. "If you eat them, the flowers will act as a laxative. And, for the ladies, a concoction of violet flowers in olive oil produces a lovely *huile de violette* for the hair." She blinked her eyes fast and made a funny dancing gesture with her bird-thin hands. "Hair oil, in French," she explained. "Now you've learned something, haven't you?"

"Yes, I have," I said, staring at the delicate purple bloom I had clutched in my fist.

"Are you familiar with mythology?" Before I could admit I wasn't, she continued, "The Roman god Jupiter turned his love, Iö, into a cow."

"A cow!" I said. "If he loved her, why would he turn her into a cow?"

"*Because* he loved her," she answered, smiling. "Cows were precious possessions and dearly loved. Then the earth brought forth this special flower for Iö, and because of that act, the flower was given her name. I-O in *violet* is the part named for her."

"Neat," I said. And then I asked, boldly, "Do you need these violets for casting spells?"

Miss Khrol actually laughed. "Is that what you children think I do?" She laughed again, a dry laugh that caused her to cough.

I was searching for a way to respond when she cleared her throat and continued.

"Violets are not only one of the most modest and beautiful flowers, but also one of the most useful herbs. 'Root, stock, and branch,' as they say. But enough of violets! Come inside and we'll have a cool drink of lemonade. Can you help with my chair?"

I was wary about entering the ramshackle cottage with its shabby exterior and windows cocked at odd angles, but there was something almost magical about Miss Khrol that was irresistible to me. She possessed a wisdom of things unknown that I alone was being invited to share. Not Polly and Sharon and me, *just* me. I liked feeling special, even if I was still a little bit scared.

Her cottage was damp with a sour odor and there was no electricity so it was lit by oil lamps and lanterns. Her father cooked meals on a huge black cast-iron cookstove that lurked in one corner, she said. A deck of cards lay on a worn wooden table.

"I sell magazine subscriptions," she said. "I try to do my part but I'm limited." She pulled back her shawl to reveal her useless legs. "Polio. I was stricken as a child."

Before I could comment, she added, "And I play a lot of Solitaire. Do you ever play?"

"Yes," I said. I didn't add that I sometimes cheated so I could win.

154

She demonstrated several different layouts that were unfamiliar to me: the Carpet, the Travellers, the Clock, the Star, Rosamond's Bower. I played a much simpler kind.

"Napoleon was reputedly fond of Solitaire. And Queen Victoria's husband, Prince Albert, played frequently. It was originally called Patience," she explained. "The origin of the name is French. I don't know how that name came to be, except that one must exercise a great deal of patience when playing! But in modern French, Solitaire is more often referred to as *réussite,* meaning "success," or "favorable outcome," to distinguish it from *patience,* which now means "jigsaw puzzle.""

The layout she was now undertaking had four aces in the center.

"Playing cards have been around for centuries, you know. The ancient term applied to cards was from a Hebrew and Arabic word that meant "to foretell." So it may be that cards originated for the specific purpose of fortune-telling, not Gin Rummy or Poker. In fact, the French word *réussite* is explained as a combination of cards by which one may try to divine one's fortune. You ask a question while dealing, and if the game succeeds, *réussite,* the answer is favorable. Otherwise not."

"I've tried doing that," I admitted, "but sometimes I deal so I can win.

Miss Khrol smiled. "Don't fret about it. I sometimes finagle, too. Now here's a little fortune-telling game that's over a hundred years old. You can try this with your friends, because you need three or more players. The four aces are laid on top, like this, and hearts represent *loved;* diamonds, *courted;* clubs, *married;* and spades—well, they represent *single blessedness,* a state with which I am all too familiar," she said as she gave a shrug of mock-regret and smiled ruefully.

"The idea is this: After you set out the aces, you deal the rest of the cards to your friends and yourself, and the players place them, face down, in front of them. One by one, the players turn their cards up."

She dealt four imaginary hands and went through a sample game.

"If you finish off all your cards on one of the ace packets, it shows what your fate will be; but if your cards work off on your neighbors' packets, the oracle is veiled, and your fortune remains untold. It's a very old-fashioned game. I can imagine elegant young ladies seated around a card table in beautiful long satin dresses with glittering jewels draped from their necks . . ."

She was quiet for several moments and seemed off in another world, so I said, "My friend Sharon had polio."

This broke her reverie.

"Tell me about your friend Sharon," she said, gathering up the cards that she had set aside.

While we sipped our lemonade, I told Miss Khrol about Sharon being so smug about being Catholic and even about the Bible Bee at our Methodist church and Leonard Twyn and the Lord's Prayer ring I had stolen from his dead body. It was as if she had turned on a faucet and out spilled all the secrets I'd been holding inside. After that I felt hollow. There was nothing left to say.

"Without pain there is no growth," Miss Khrol told me, taking both of my hands in hers. "Remember that all your life. You will have to change, in some ways, as you mature, but you will not have an easy time. I can see this in your soul. You are an inquisitive child and I hope you will be allowed to keep your sense of childlike wonder. Once lost it can never be recaptured. But this is not a world for gentle people, Eleanora. You must be prepared for that."

I was so stunned that I didn't question how she knew my name.

After that day I frequently visited Miss Khrol. She showed me more old-fashioned card games and sometimes she asked me to return library books for her.

I told Mother where I was going, and she approved. She even said she was proud of me. Every time I visited Miss Khrol, Mother sent along a fresh batch of brownies or a plate of cookies or a loaf of banana bread.

Let Sharon have her pagan babies and rosaries and saints and medals.

I had my own honest-to-goodness missionary work with a shut-in.

*T*oo quickly, it seemed, the end of my summer was in sight.

"Come back and visit me again, Eleanora," Miss Khrol said from her front door as I hopped on my bike. "Don't forget me."

"I'll be back," I promised as I pedaled down the gravel road toward town.

But I saw Miss Khrol only once more that summer, and then not again for thirty-five years.

9

I was in kindergarten when I begged my mother to tell me I was adopted. "Are you sure?" I'd ask, knowing in my heart I must truly belong to a family that was more exotic, a family that loved passion and adventure like the traveling gypsies that came through town each summer in dusty black Cadillacs and camped out at Bear Lake under the pines.

"I'm sure," Mother would say again wearily. "Five o'clock in the morning. Waupaca hospital. The birds were singing. I remember as if it were yesterday. Don't ask me again."

"Are you sure?" I'd ask, because I really felt that I was so different from everyone else. Buddy fit fine—he was just a regular kid.

"Are you really *sure* I'm not adopted?"

❧

After we went to the PseudoScience seminar together I told George about my adoption request because the seminar had also discussed the consequences of being "fantasy-prone." Apparently fantasy-prone people scored high in tests that measured daydreaming, creativity, and hypnotizability, and they often experienced vivid hallucinations.

What I didn't share with George was my identification with the statement that, while fantasizing, fantasy-prone personalities (FPPs) are prominent among mystics, sensitives, . . . and channelers.

It was even suggested that voices heard by mediums or channelers were actually spawned by their own imagination or internal thoughts, gleaned, albeit innocently, by familiar means. That "sounded" familiar. Maybe I was assimilating part of myself with Angella Wing because I was an FPP.

For days after the seminar I watched for clues that might indicate that I was an FPP. One reassuring sign that I was not: without any physical stimulation, fantasy-prone personalities are supposed to be able to reach orgasm merely by imagining a sexual encounter. I tried that (visualizing George of course) several times and failed. It was one of those win/lose situations.

❧

"Take Wing" still flourished, and Angella's audience had multiplied. "Lark," who almost never missed an opportunity for comment, recently inquired about the adaptation of one's inner life to the challenges of developing mediumship. Angella's response to this reminded me of what Miss Khrol had said to me. I'd never forgotten that woman's quiet admonition that this was not a world for gentle people and that I must be prepared to change in order to survive.

Of course, Angella added her own dramatic embellishments when she delivered her reply to Lark:

Many years ago Laurette Taylor, the great theatrical legend who played Amanda Wingfield in "The Glass Menagerie," said to me, "How can you give it if it hasn't grown inside?" I had to learn to use my anguish to hone my talent. Keep that in mind.

At first, while I was "working" with Angella (I don't know what else to call it), there was a sense of being absolutely okay with the

159

world. Then gradually she demanded increased attention. If I dared to ignore her I received a reprimand.

It was not merely by chance, Eleanora, that our lives became intertwined. You cannot untie a knot by pulling on it!

After each of her "Take Wing" entries, Angella's chat room buzzed with activity. No matter how late it was or how dumb the questions seemed, it was up to me to make sure Angella remained responsive. She relished the attention.

So how could this possibly be my *hyperactive magical-thinking-fantasy-prone imagination* speaking? How could I have regurgitated this character from my unconscious and re-created her with subliminal glue?

As long as Angella hadn't forced me to walk in front of a speeding train or make a *complete* fool of myself, what harm was there in letting her speak? All it cost me was my time.

Take this response, for example, that she offered to the unrelenting Lark. I could never have thought *this* up:

In the mid-1950s I had one of the greatest comedy roles ever written for a character actress, in "Anniversary Waltz," which played for three years in San Francisco. It's a beautiful city but has a cold, windy, rainy, foggy climate and what with being cooped up in a hotel room and a dressing room at the old Alcazar Theater (now torn down), I lost thirty pounds in those three years and was a skeleton when it finally closed.

༄

The hostess for our November book club meeting was Doris Hackenberry. Again, I hadn't read the assigned book, but because of my impulsive gaffe with the coat hangers when we met at Nancy Anderson's I felt an obligation to make an appearance as my old "normal" self.

My book club has been in existence for about thirty years, but

Doris is the only member who goes way back to the very beginning so she is treated with deference. Her home was warm with firelight and a Thanksgiving cornucopia spilled a bounty of well-loved paraffin fruits and vegetables onto a linen tablecloth embroidered with little turkeys. Doris always hosted the November meeting and had prepared her pumpkin cheesecake bars, the recipe for which she never conceded to share though we asked every year, as a matter of course.

I'd feared I might be shunned following my abominable aura demo, but there seemed to be more esteem extended in my direction than usual. It was due to the holiday warmth, I figured, and I smiled a great deal.

When she brought my coat as I was leaving, Doris handed me an envelope. "Don't open this until you get home," she whispered.

I lived only a few blocks away, but the certainty that I had been secretly blackballed by my book club troubled me with every step and I paused beneath a streetlight to rip open the envelope:

Dear Nell, I hope I am not being presumptuous, but are you able to—or would you consent to—do a Spirit reading for me? I have, in the past, driven to Milwaukee for such readings, not wishing to divulge my esoteric proclivity to my Madison friends in academe. I feel I can trust you. Please give me a call when convenient.

Warmly,
Doris

I'd grabbed a bunch of free books and pamphlets after the PseudoScience seminar and among them was one that discussed how to give "cold readings." When Miss Khrol gave me examples of many more ways to tell fortunes with cards, she had advised, "When someone comes to you to have their fortune told, you'll be wise to tell them what they want to hear."

Even Sharon had been impressed with my newly acquired "knowledge" of fortune-telling. In fact, the *golden rule* for telling fortunes is just this: *tell people what they want to hear.* It turns out that giving a fake reading is much the same, and I wondered if that was what most mediums flew with, too.

To give a "cold reading," you have to buy into the assumption that people are more alike than they are different. Except for those who want to cause trouble (like scientists or well-meaning friends who enjoy debunking psychics), people who come for a Spirit reading or tarot reading or palm reading mostly want answers to questions about money, love, and health.

In the old days of Spiritualism (could I ask Grace Waverly about this or would she be insulted?) there might be a wily assistant on hand to go through a client's purse left in an outer room and sift through papers to obtain hints. By examining the label on the coat, for example, he could gauge how much it cost or where it was purchased.

Today, most bogus readers have to be more cunning. The reader will casually study the client's clothing and her physical features. Hands can be very revealing so the medium will explore the hands for jewelry, calluses, scars, a recent manicure. Manner of speech, gestures, and eye-contact—all are meticulously scrutinized.

When you give a reading, you begin by professing modesty about your talents. This will catch your subject, usually a female, off guard. Emphasize that her cooperation is absolutely necessary, and if you don't happen to convey the exact meaning of the cards or the message you're passing along due to difficulties of translation or the vagaries of verbal communication, the subject should interpret the message in terms of her own vocabulary and her situation in life.

This is a crucial move—because the subject will strive to fit your generalities to her particulars, and thus let you off the hook. She needs to believe. In fact, her *need to believe* is stronger than her need *not* to believe. This need to believe sometimes exceeds not only logic but also sanity.

And if you're a good listener, your client will divulge lots of clues.

I gathered a bunch of stock spiels that would apply to anyone. For example: "At times you are extroverted, affable, sociable, while at other times you may feel more introverted, wary, and reserved. You pride yourself on being an independent thinker . . ."

Doesn't everyone fit this mold? As a reader, all you have to do is personalize it for the client and she will be convinced. Above all, appear absolutely confident in what you are saying. Give the impression that you know a lot more than you're offering. Once your client is convinced that you are in possession of information about her that you could not have obtained through normal channels, she will assume you know *all*. She will then let go and confide in you.

Tell the client what he or she wants to hear. Even Sigmund Freud observed that the adroit fortune-teller predicts what the client secretly wishes to happen. When I gave bogus fortunes as a child, that's what I usually did. Unless I had a reason not to.

I faced a quandary. I wanted to keep Angella and my ongoing interest in mediumship a secret from Polly and George. Each of them knew of my interest in Spiritualism, but both agreed that mediumship was a foolish endeavor to explore and even worse, it was terribly dishonest to fake.

If I began doing readings, it would take a great deal of deception on my part to keep Polly and George unaware. With the added stress of Angella's demands, I'd have very little time to spend with them anyhow.

I already had a room set up, the downstairs sunporch that I now called Angella's Lair. A little incense, some crystals, a tinkling fountain, a New Age CD with flutes and crickets, and the Medium could be IN. Naturally, Angella was all for it.

I will be greatly pleased to observe you offering private messages. Remember, I am always nearby and ready to be your guide. Spirit entities can often see ahead through time and convey visions, ideas, and teachings that are immensely prophetic.

I dug out the worn deck of cards given to me by Miss Khrol and reviewed the method of divination that had become my favorite. As I shuffled and practiced a few layouts, I thought about Grace Waverly and how long it had been since I had seen her. Angella may have given her permission, but Grace was someone I could ask for advice.

Ever since Angella took over my life, I had been ignoring dear Grace. When I took her class, there *had* been something there—and consider the oddity of Sharon's apparition! Grace said I was clair-sentient; would that help me give honest readings? It sounded a lot simpler than platform work with its corresponding audience on tenterhooks and my penchant for panic attacks!

I immediately called Grace and arranged to visit her the next day.

*T*he Wocanaga Camp season ended on Labor Day and the camp closed down after that. Abandoned beneath November's gray skies, the place looked even more run-down.

A bronchial infection had weakened Grace, whom I found slouched in a rocking chair, wrapped in a wool blanket. I was alarmed at the transparency of her skin and her weak grasp when I took her hand.

"Is there a chance you could spend the winter with one of your children?" I asked her.

I was worried about the isolation she might experience if the roads became icy or Wocanaga received a lot of snow.

"They have their own lives," Grace replied, "and they're busy with their families. I don't wish to be a burden to my children. Besides, my friends look after me here. I'm feeling a great deal stronger now than I did just a month ago, but thank you for asking."

Over tea, I confessed I was still hearing from Angella Wing.

"Oh, I knew you would be," Grace said, reminding me in famil-iar terms, "Have I not told you that you cannot walk away from your talents?"

I explained how Angella manifested herself on my notebook computer in automatic writing and gave Grace printed copies of Angella's messages from the blog. "It's a kind of ongoing diary but for the public. She often writes about her life as an actress. I should have brought my laptop so you'd get a better example of what it's like. You could have asked her a question."

164

I thought of Angella and her tendency to ramble on and on.

"Grace, in your workshop you mentioned spirits who were 'deceivers.' Can you tell me more about that?"

She seemed at a loss. "I'm not exactly certain what I said," she apologized, "but I do know that it's important to keep your psychic energies strong because if your protection weakens, a malicious spirit can move in and interfere with your work. Such a deceiver can be harmful, especially if you are now engaged in automatic writing. I cannot emphasize this strongly enough."

"Why is writing so dangerous?"

"When you're writing, energy is transmitted through your aura by the communicating spirit. This energy spreads through the nervous system, too, causing movement in your arm and your hand. It can create havoc with the delicate balance of energies between your aura and your physical body.

"I've known cases where a deceiving spirit has taken possession of a medium's hand and made her write *whenever* and *wherever* the spirit wished. When it went on for a lengthy period this became quite exhausting for her. Sometimes the writing consisted of nothing but nonsense, but if an effort was made to quit, the spirit became troublesome in other ways."

"Like . . . ?"

Grace waved her hand in the air, as if to brush them away.

"Oh, just trivial things. Little accidents. One medium fell down her basement stairs and broke her arm so she had to give up her writing. Another suffered a dog bite to her hand. That sort of thing.

"So," she continued, wiggling a finger at the teapot to indicate she would like me to pour more tea, "if you're becoming more closely involved with this 'Angella,' I would caution you to guard against deception. It must not be taken for granted that Angella is everything she claims to be. There are spirits who 'play up' to our weaknesses and wheedle the vanity of those to whom they communicate, you know."

She gave me a curious look, as if she were convinced that I might be susceptible to flattery.

"How can I tell if I've contacted one of those?" I asked.

"Wait and see. If you feel Angella is causing you to do ridiculous or foolish things, you can gently but firmly *refuse* to submit. But you will have to be very strong. Not a few mediums have had their vanity tickled or their ambitions aroused by crafty and domineering spirits."

"The blog was my idea," I offered. "So far, Angella's been agreeable. Verbose, but cooperative. And she is willing to respond to readers of her blog who have questions about . . . well, a lot of things. In fact, I asked her once about 'negative energy.'"

I read Angella's answer, which I'd brought along with me:

In my acting career I knew liars and thieves, drunkards, perverts, gangsters, and whores. There was no depravity that I didn't come across. I went without meals, I dressed in stinking basement dressing rooms in cheap vaudeville theaters, I lived in filthy boarding houses or cheap hotels on the road sometimes playing four shows a day. But none of this negative energy rubbed off on me. I was in it, not of it. Keep your own vibrations strong.

"Isn't this the same thing you're saying?" I asked.

Grace was silent. She busied herself with adjusting the blanket on her lap. Finally, she told me, "Eleanora, I do hope this 'Angella' is not a disturbing influence for you. Mediumship of this sort needs the help of other people, you know. It's a fundamental fact. I wonder if I emphasized that in my workshop?"

"I'm not sure you did."

"Sitting alone as you must to develop Angella's writing may fascinate you, especially when you're feeling lonely. But I would be more comfortable with the situation if I knew you had a friend, or a group of friends, present. A friend can help guard you from any psychic shock that might occur if the telephone rings or if someone unexpectedly opens the door. And you should be allowed to sleep for a

166

short time afterward. Friends should look after you and see that you get enough rest."

Impossible. I had to do Angella's blog alone. There was no way to explain this conviction to Grace, so I changed the subject, mentioning the request I'd received from Doris for a private reading. "Would it be all right, do you think?"

"Do you feel ready to do readings?"

"How would I begin?"

"How do you channel your Angella Wing?"

"I sit quietly and meditate, and wait for her to *speak*. Or to write."

"It's much the same," Grace said. "These sessions are sacred, like our message services. You can trust a loving message. But also remember your personal responsibility."

"Should I sit at a table, or . . ."

"Each medium works in a different way. I usually sit at my dining room table, as I did with you the first time you came. Whatever is most comfortable for you and for your client. If your message is accurate, ask your client to acknowledge it because that enhances the flow of energy. Trust your initial instincts," Grace advised, "and do not apologize."

$\mathcal{I}$ called Doris the next day and said I'd be glad to read for her. I had installed blinds that could be adjusted to darken the porch, and a little fountain rippled soothing sounds over smooth black stones.

Doris arrived on Thursday afternoon at one o'clock. I'd chosen that time because I knew George would be teaching his class. Not that he'd necessarily know what I was doing on my sunporch, but I just felt better with his skeptical vibes out of the house.

Before we began, Doris asked how much I charged.

"I insist on paying you," she said, "and we might as well get that out of the way. In Milwaukee, the fee is understood in the beginning and then I leave an envelope on the table."

"I can't charge you anything," I said. "This is my gift for embarrassing you at our book club. When I tried to read your aura."

"Well, all right," Doris replied. She set her purse on the floor and placed her hands primly in her lap.

A gift? More like a pretense. But Doris was so solemn. I did not want to disappoint her.

"You understand that your cooperation is necessary. If I don't convey the *exact* meaning of the message I'm passing along—you know, due to difficulties of translation between this world and that . . . that one—you should interpret the message in terms of your own vocabulary and your own life."

"I understand," she said meekly.

Her husband's name. What *had* his name been? He'd gone only by his initials, Professor O. D. Hackenberry. Oscar? Oswald? Oglethorpe? Not many men's names began with O. I should have looked it up. Damn.

I closed my eyes, relaxed my breathing, and said what I thought Doris needed to hear.

"As I come into your spirit vibration, I sense a deep heaviness in my lungs."

This was true; I was not making it up. Suddenly I could barely inhale, and I hoped I was not precipitating another panic attack. I forced myself to breathe more slowly. Deep breath. Release. Focus.

"Did someone close to you pass on due to problems with his lungs?"

Doris said, "My husband had lung cancer."

Score one for me, I told myself. Now if only I could come up with a name beginning with "O."

"I feel the influence of a man. O . . . Oil . . . Oliver . . ." I was fishing. Could she tell? "Orville . . ."

"Orville was my husband's name."

"Orville is concerned about your welfare," I reasoned. "You must make an effort to see that the accounts are in order. Do you understand that?" I asked.

"Yes," Doris replied, nodding, even more solemn than before. "Ask him if I should consult our son about the investments."

I waited, musing, then replied, "Orville wants you to consult your accountant. He seems quite stubborn about that."

Doris seemed relieved. The furrows on her brow smoothed.

I continued, reciting whatever came into my head, to her apparent pleasure. As I wound down, she asked if I would consult the cards.

I confessed, honestly, "I'm not very experienced at reading cards."

"I don't mind," she offered. "Let's see what comes up."

I asked her to shuffle the deck, which she did. Then she cut them, at my request, and handed them back to me. I spread the deck face down on the table and had her choose thirteen at random. These I arranged in a row, face upward, in the order in which they were chosen.

My memory of *which* cards meant *what* was never very good. With a fortune-telling deck you usually removed all the twos, threes, fours, fives, and sixes, leaving only thirty-two cards. But there was still too much to keep track of, all those symbols; each one indicated something unique and then something different depending on where it ended up in the layout and whether the questioner was male or female. For example, if the consultant is a woman (like Doris) the King of Hearts may be interpreted as her lover or the object of her affections. If Doris were a man, the King of Hearts would be a rival in love. I could remember that much, at least.

In this case, the card representing the questioner, the Queen of Hearts, was surrounded by cards that fit nicely with her spirit-message.

"I can see that your question is about material success or well-being." Well, duh! What else would frighten an elderly widow?

"From this card," I said as I pointed to the ten of spades, "I can tell you that the opposing force to your well-being seems to be a fear of destitution. Loneliness.

"In your past there seems to have been some loss of property. Or loss of status. There is a possibility of further reverses. But these cards—clubs—seem to counteract the influence of some of the preceding ones and direct you toward the path of success."

I could hear Doris sigh.

"Most likely you have been worried about what you see as your impracticality. Those around you fear you should exercise more care. You agree, and you do not want to repeat the same mistakes you once made."

"What can I do?" Doris asked.

"Here," I pointed to the final card, a King of Clubs. "A man is going to be helpful to you in the fulfillment of your hopes. This man may be a councilor, advisor, a good friend. He will offer sound advice and you should listen to what he says."

After a moment of silence, I gathered the cards and gave Doris a smile of encouragement.

"I am so grateful, Nell," she said, nearly in tears. "Thank you. That was exactly what I wanted to hear."

𝒯he next day I had a call from Nancy Anderson, asking if I would do a spirit reading for her, too. I wondered if my entire book group would line up at my door, and, one by one, they did. Their friends began calling for appointments! I quickly printed some business cards. And I got a cell phone just for Merrill Chase. The medium was IN!

Merrill Chase
Medium

By Appointment:
(608) 555-0155

10

*C*ash in the sealed envelopes surreptitiously handed over to me began to add up. Between Angella's blog and chat room and my readings on Tuesdays and Thursdays, I had very little time to devote to *Medium Grace.* Actually, I had very little time to do anything for myself. Angella was piqued to receive less of my attention but Grace's concern over Angella's potential "disturbing influence" caused me to be less generous in my response to her dictates. Nevertheless, my friends were ignored, phone calls went unanswered, I hadn't replied to my kids' e-mails in weeks, and one of these days I had to do some serious grocery shopping because I was down to mostly yogurt and eggs plus some unidentifiable moldy stuff in my refrigerator.

I wasn't walking Henry with George in the morning, either—I claimed I was way too busy with my book. When I caught a glimpse of myself in the mirror there was a ghostly pallor around my eyes that was scary. I really needed a haircut but I couldn't get away.

Every spare moment was taken, almost. My life was not my own anymore.

From the calendar in his apartment next to the phone, I observed George's agenda while he walked the dog and arranged even more appointments for readings when I was certain he'd be out. That gave me more hours during the week besides Tuesday and Thursday to receive clients, and late on weekend evenings when he was playing at the Bosky Lodge I squeezed in a few extras.

To allow the next client to enter while I was finishing with another, I hung a laminated card from a nail on the front door that said, simply, "Come In."

I slipped up one evening when Polly came over for a dinner I'd planned for her and George. The dinner was an effort to pay more attention to my own needs for a change. Carelessly, I'd forgotten to remove the note. Who would have thought such a simple little misstep would cause a momentous change in my life?

⚬⚬⚬

Grace had called to see how my readings were going. I came across her message on my answering machine a couple weeks after our visit at Wocanaga, and when I called her back she asked if I was getting enough rest.

"Oh, probably not," I joked. "Things have been kind of crazy around here. I never dreamed this would take off like it has."

"Please do me a favor, Eleanora," Grace pleaded, "and give yourself some time to build up your strength. I can clearly sense the tiredness in your voice. You must remain strong to avert any mishaps and to contend with Angella."

"Don't worry, really, I'm fine."

I was curt with Grace, brusquely shrugged off her questions, and after I hung up the phone I realized I hadn't even inquired how she was.

⚬⚬⚬

A winter storm warning had been issued by the weather bureau. It would be our first big snow of the season and for Wisconsinites that means a trip to the market to stock up as if you were hoarding for a

172

blizzard or might not be able to get out of the house for a month or more. It's silly, I know, but it happens every year. The aisles are filled with excited shoppers, everyone wound up because a Big Snow is on the way. We feel tough; we'll ride it out. And our appetites change, too. Even if we've been dieting, eating veggie salads, and nibbling on fruit, a winter storm warning makes you think of hot chili or a savory beef stew. With a loaf of homemade rustic bread, red wine, and a plate of warm apple pie!

I checked with Polly and George on Wednesday. I hadn't seen nor heard from either of them in a very long time, so they were both pleased to accept my invitation to dinner on Friday night. I anticipated a blinding snowstorm, comfort food, and a cozy, crackling fire. George said if the threatening forecast came true, he wouldn't be going out to the Bosky Lodge so we could enjoy a leisurely meal.

Thursday, of course, I was busy all day with clients. Friday morning I fought the crowds and bought groceries. I was home by noon.

The gray sky was heavy with clouds. I checked the weather station on TV and hoped the storm wouldn't fizzle with only a couple of inches. That was always a disappointment, like foreplay without a climax.

Schools were closing early—a good sign. Blizzard warnings predicted up to a foot of snow with winds of 35 miles per hour by Saturday morning. I heard a city truck pass the house, already spreading sand.

According to his calendar, George had a faculty meeting that day and I had a backlog of urgent requests so I crammed in two appointments for readings early that afternoon. Light snow was in the air when the first woman arrived at one o'clock. When she left, at two, the second woman was waiting in the living room. She turned out to be a lingerer and insisted on a second card reading and then a third. I had placed a small clock on the wall behind my clients so only I could see it. Usually gathering the cards and telling them thank you was signal enough, but I had to physically escort this woman to the door. The high heels of her stylish boots clicked on the polished hardwood.

"I have to laugh at myself," she said from the front steps, which were now snow covered. "When I was sixteen I thought I had everything figured out. Now that I'm seventy, I'm still amazed at how little I know! Thank you again."

"Don't slip," I warned her, but it was too late. She had already crumpled down to the sidewalk and I hurried to help her get up.

"Nothing hurt, just my pride," she laughed. "I'm fine."

We brushed the snow from her coat. I handed her the purse she'd dropped and opened the door of her car.

"Miss Chase, I'm so embarrassed . . ."

"Don't be," I assured her, "I have to put some salt on those steps!"

I searched for the chemical crumbles to put on the steps, convinced that my client would get home and find out she had a broken hip. I brought a snow shovel up from the basement. It was almost four o'clock and I hadn't even begun the stew. Or the bread. Or, of course, the apple pie. All of which I'd boldly promised with my guarantee of a splendid comfort food feast.

Before reporting to the kitchen I had to check in with Angella's blog. Her arrogance was escalating and she was turning out to be a bit of a snob. She refused to answer mundane queries, so I was obliged to make up replies to some of the more minor chat questions without her "inspiration."

Lark appeared every time Angella was online. Lately someone called RillCashmere was being a *rill* pest.

I opened the chat room and allowed Angella to announce her presence.

Today I want to talk about creativity and how it affects one's personal vibrations. There is no question in my mind but that the nearer a creative person is to genius, the nearer he is to madness . . .

And on and on. Then Lark came online to ask how it was possible to be certain it was someone from the other side who was communicating and not one's own imagination. Angella said it didn't really matter and summarily brushed him off. After Lark was answered, RillCashmere entered the chat room.

> Hi. I've been trying to get this guy to like me and envisioning that he will, but it's not working, not even with spirit help. Do I need to focus harder because he's Canadian and into jazz?

And so it went. I paid scant attention to Angella's conversations while I ran between the porch and the kitchen until I said to hell with it and set the laptop on the kitchen table. In between sautéing the beef and peeling apples, I wiped my hands on a dishtowel and responded to someone named SuZ-Q with Ouija board questions and Lark, who needed more assurance. Angella deigned to add her two cents' worth every once in a while as I concentrated on my recipes.

> *Believe me, Cashmere, if you are a healthy, ardent woman, it's damned important to have a man who's good in bed. Keep trying. I don't know about jazz musicians; I've never had one. I could never even imagine loving any All-American Boy, and a Canadian, it seems to me, would be as boring as a loaf of bread. Give me a Jew or an Italian any night. I've had some truly marvelous lovers, and you can't take that away from me, tra la. One word of warning: don't mistake the way a musician plays for the way he is in bed. I once fell madly in love with a great tenor's voice—but, oh, brother, the voice was not the man!*

I was kneading sticky bread dough when I heard Polly shout, "Helloooooooo! Anybody home?"

"I thought you might be in the shower," she said, showing me the laminated "Come In" note that I'd forgotten to remove.

"Nope, just up to my ears in ciabatta," I said, "and didn't want to take time to run to the front door."

"Smells great!"

"The beef. It's simmering with onions. Here, peel these red potatoes and slice the carrots."

"Nellie, you're ordering me around and I haven't even had a welcome hug!"

"Oh . . ." I went to her with floury hands held high and hugged my dear friend.

"Polly Wolly, I haven't seen you for such a long time!"

"I know. Where have you been? It's been weeks."

"The last time I saw you we had lunch, after we went to the Bosky Lodge to hear George's trio. When you told me about Breeze Quinn."

"Right," she said, grinning as she unwound her scarf and unbuttoned her jacket. "Is the Beautiful Breeze still blowing?"

"I guess so," I shrugged. "Haven't seen her around in a while."

"Snow's really piling up out there," Polly said, hugging herself. "I'd forgotten how thrilling the first snowstorm can be!"

"California girl," I teased, then went back to shaping my loaves, urgently aware of my laptop open on the table and Angella's message flashing like a warning beacon.

"I'll build a fire in a minute," I said. "Why don't you bring in some wood from the backyard?"

It didn't take Polly long to notice the screen.

"What's this? Your latest work of genius?" Polly sat down at the table and read the message.

"This is a chat room, Nellie! You asked me how to configure a blog. What's going on?"

She was quiet for a minute, reading. "Hey, are you still messing around with Spiritualism?"

She scrolled up the screen and came across the heading, Take Wing, and my pseudonym, Merrill Chase. Then she read some of Angella's entries, including the final one, which she read, dramatically, aloud.

"Believe me, Cashmere, if you are a healthy, ardent woman, it's damned important to have a man who's good in bed. Keep trying. I don't know about jazz musicians; I've never had one . . ."

176

Where the hell did *that* come from? I didn't even remember typing that response!

I banged around the kitchen and set my ciabatta loaves aside for their final rise, trying to ignore her. I started rolling out my pie dough. Through the kitchen window I could see the snow falling heavily now, illuminated by the streetlight. Henry sauntered in—he'd been sleeping under my desk on my sunporch (to which the door was still open!)—but Polly was too enamored of Angella's erotic communiqué to even welcome the dog.

"Would you mind walking Henry? He's been sleeping and he needs to pee."

If she'd only leave the house for a minute I could stow the laptop and close the porch door.

"Are you kidding? I have to read more of this. Who's Cashmere?"

"Polly . . ."

"Nellie . . . ," Polly imitated my pleading tone. She did that when we were kids and I hated it then, too.

I heard George coming downstairs. Henry ran to the back door so I hollered, "The dog needs to go out."

"Polly, please," I pleaded desperately, turning to her and keeping my voice to a whisper. "I'll explain everything after dinner. Don't mention this to George, okay?"

"Why not?" she asked. That was my Polly, all right. Full of questions.

"Because. Because he thinks psychics and Spiritualism, stuff like that . . . well, he's a skeptic. Nothing wrong with that, but he is. So I don't want him to know. About me. What I'm doing. Polly, c'mon! Please!"

"Is this connected to that day you took me up to Wocanaga and had that seizure?"

"I did not have a seizure!"

"Okay, a panic attack, then. You said you were 'Merrill Chase,' a name I see right here. 'Take Wing, a Conversation with Angella.' And Merrill Chase is Angella's mediator. You're channeling her!" Polly shouted.

"Quiet," I said, in a loud whisper.

"Nellie! What is going on? What *are* you doing?"

She would not lower her voice.

"What's going on?" George wanted to know, brushing snow from the shoulders of his dark red sweater.

"Nell is channeling," Polly said.

"Right this minute?" George teased.

"Look at this . . ." Polly showed him my computer screen and read out loud:

> "*If you are a healthy, ardent woman, it's damned important to have a man who's good in bed. Keep trying. I don't know about jazz musicians; I've never had one. I could never even imagine loving any All-American Boy, and a Canadian, it seems to me, would be as boring as a loaf of bread.*"

"Wooo, woooo," Polly sang. "Who is saying all this stuff?"

"A Canadian jazz musician?" George read. "Hmm, wonder who that could be."

I wanted to die, of course. I wanted to disappear. I took advantage of their preoccupation with Angella and slipped away to close the door to my sunporch. That's when my cell phone rang. My cell phone that I'd left in the kitchen.

"I'll get it," Polly called.

"No . . . ," I yelled, but it was too late.

"Merrill Chase?" I heard Polly saying. "This is Merrill Chase; may I help you?"

"Give me the phone," I whispered, trying to wrest it from her.

"An appointment? For a reading? Can I get back to you?" she purred.

George was reading even more of Angella's blog and frowning.

Polly snapped the phone shut and glared at me.

"Nellie Grendon, *what are you doing*?"

My hands were shaking as I poured the sliced apples into my pie shell. "The bread is still rising, but everything will be ready in about an hour," I said, my voice failing me. "Maybe two hours. I'm going to start a fire. You two can join me in the living room and drink this bottle of pinot noir or you can stay here and read that fiction."

Of course I was frantic, and in my anxiety I knocked the bottle onto the floor, the clay tile floor, where it broke, splashing red wine and shards of glass everywhere. Henry yelped and ran upstairs. At that moment I would have given anything to run upstairs after him and hide in my bed with a pillow over my head.

George turned off the computer. He snapped the cover shut.

"I'll start a fire," he said. "Polly, you can clean up the mess in here."

I found another bottle of wine, but George insisted on opening it and pouring a glass for me. I took it into the living room and watched him build the fire. Polly joined us with a glass. George had coffee. We sat in silence, listening to the snap and pop of the logs and the snow sifting against the windows, until I began to talk.

I finally admitted with a wobbly voice, "I wanted this to be a nice evening. I wanted the three of us to have a comfortable time on a snowy night."

"Not good enough," Polly said stiffly. "Don't give me that 'poor little Nell' shit. It's time for *confession*, babe. What have you been up to?"

George sat next to Polly and shot me a very dark look.

I shuddered, sighed, wiped my nose on my sleeve, and checked my watch.

"The bread can go in the oven now."

"No," Polly declared. "Tell George about Merrill Chase."

"Who's Merrill Chase?" he asked.

"Me," I said.

"Her," Polly added. "It's a name she invented out of both of her grandmothers' last names. It's the name she uses to channel that 'Angella Wing' character."

"I believe Merrill Chase also does readings," George added, holding up one of my business cards. "Is that right?"

"Only on days when you're gone," I said.

179

"I hope she's better at telling fortunes now than she was when we were kids," Polly mentioned. "She told me I was going to marry a farmer and have at least eleven kids."

"I never said *eleven,*" I argued.

"And Sharon was going to be a movie star."

"I was just pretending. I was making everything up."

"Are we to presume that you're still pretending?" George inquired.

"Sometimes. Most of the time. I think. There's a term in Spiritualism, or in some aspects of it anyway, that refer to this, what I'm doing, as being 'open to myself.' That means—I know, okay, some mediums have been and are frauds. But if it's just magnets or sleight-of-hand, or whatever, it's for a good purpose and doesn't do any real harm.

"And I also believe some mediums, like Grace Waverly, really do get genuine vibrations. From Spirit. And that's what really counts. I *meant* to . . . I don't know. Be somewhere in between. I can't always control what happens. It's very confusing to explain. I thought I could carry it off—the charade—at Wocanaga. But then Sharon . . ."

"We had this friend, Sharon Gallagher," Polly explained to George.

"I saw her at Wocanaga," I told Polly in a rushing tumult. "The day you went up there with me. I saw her. Or I thought I did. Her apparition. She was standing right behind Mr. Bittner. That's why I ran off. It wasn't because I had a panic attack. Well, I sort of did feel like I was going to have one, but *I saw her ghost.* She was wet and tattered like she'd risen from the lake in a torn white dress and she stared at me with hollow eyes."

Now Polly was quiet. Despite the warmth of the wine I was overwhelmed by violent chills and began to shudder.

George led me to a chair by the fire and took a blanket from the back of the sofa to wrap over my shoulders.

"Nellie," Polly said, obviously shaken by my news about Sharon, "how could you keep that a secret from me? If I'm your best friend; I had a right to be told! Besides, I was right there with you that night, when she drowned . . ."

Polly was hurt. She wouldn't trust me with anything now, and I deserved her misgivings.

It was up to George to lighten the mood.

"We haven't even addressed the fact that your spirit thinks I'd be as boring as a loaf of bread in bed! Was that *you* speaking . . . *pretending* . . . or is this Angella spirit for real?"

"I'm really sorry about that," I said. "Angella's pretty unpredictable. And lately she's been annoyed with me. I don't know where she comes from. I honestly don't."

George stood there for a moment, looking at his hand, holding his empty coffee cup, and then he smiled. "I think I'd like to tell you how I got this scar," he said.

He went into the kitchen and came back with his cup refilled. Polly poured herself another glass of wine and one for me.

"I don't drink alcohol much," he said, settling into the chair opposite mine by the fireplace. "You may have noticed. There's a reason. Loaf of bread, my ass.

"All through my childhood and teenage years I had this friend named John," he continued. "He was one of those bookish guys who was always trying to figure out how things worked. You know the kind. Well, when we were eighteen, John figured out how to make a batch of sloe gin."

"What's that?" I asked. Then I explained, "I was raised a Methodist. My parents didn't drink much. Isn't gin just *gin?* What makes it slow?"

"S-l-o-e," George spelled. "It's made from blackthorn berries and it was pretty gross stuff with a horrible sweet taste. The overtone was kind of like creosote, as I recall."

"Wait a minute, I'd better check the bread," Polly said. "This sounds like it might take a while."

"We were already out of high school," George continued after Polly had returned, "and John had moved into a tiny house by himself in Vancouver. It was in an odd little backwater neighborhood that still had a couple pockets of woods but was closed in all around by the city.

"Well, one night I was over at his house with a few other people. We started listening to records and we all got pretty tanked on John's sloe gin. Me especially. A very manic but physically uncomfortable high. At some point a storm came up and there was a tremendous crash of lightning and thunder and the electricity went out. It later turned out that the lightning had fried the record player—which was mine, by the way; John was only borrowing it."

"Were your records okay?" Polly wanted to know.

"I guess so. I don't even recall," George confessed. "Probably Jefferson Airplane. Anyway, the others started looking around for candles to light, but I jumped up off the couch and yelled, 'That really pisses me off!' and headed for the back door. Actually, I think the lightning strike had come close to scaring the shit out of me. I wasn't sorting through things very well just at that moment. Apparently someone asked me where I was going and before I went out the back door into the wind and the rain, I screamed, 'I'm going to piss at the storm gods!' Pissing in the wind was more like it really.

"In any case, when I got outside in the storm, I stripped off my clothes and took off running through the woods like a berserker. I was having some kind of 'Ride of the Valkyries' moment."

"George, you?" I asked, incredulous.

"Yes, me," he continued. "But there's more. I ran through the woods and got to the neighbor's fence and climbed over, then headed for the barn. The neighbors boarded a couple of horses there and kept a couple of their own. For some damned reason I went in the barn and got on one of the horses, an old sway-backed mare who was probably just peacefully living out her days. Well, I gave that old mare a wild whoop and we took off. Even with the noise of the storm the neighbors heard me and woke up and saw me leave. The mare was scared to death and she took off across the field at a good clip. I was bareback, of course, naked as a baby, hanging on to her mane and feeling no pain."

I suspected the scar on his hand would involve the horse. I didn't really want to hear the rest, but he went on.

"The neighbor pursued us on foot across the field, in the rain. He found me on the ground naked, dazed-drunk, with a big gash on my

182

left hand. The mare was on the ground, too. She'd stepped in a hole in the dark and had broken her leg. The neighbor's wife called the cops. The Royal Canadian Mounted Police, to be exact. They got there in a few minutes and one of them put the mare out her misery with his pistol. She hadn't been ridden in quite a while, and, anyway, that was probably the most excitement she'd ever seen.

"They took me to the station where I was dressed in a jumpsuit, and my hand was sewn up and bandaged. In court, I made a big demonstration of remorse. And the judge was lenient. It turned out that the cops had been extremely ticked off at me for putting the horse through that—they were Mounties, after all, and really felt for their own horses—but by the time the trial came around, one of them had noticed that this was the first case of horse stealing in Clark County for almost eighty years. I told you this all took place inside the city limits. They were all part of a city police force. And then, there I was in court, such a complete idiot. It turned out that the judge and the prosecutor had come to see a certain amount of humor in the whole thing."

The oven timer went off.

"Wait a minute," Polly said. "That's the bread."

I wanted to laugh at the irony. I mean, God, it was embarrassing. Here the guy was spilling his guts to prove he wasn't bland and the bread was done baking.

"So, was that the last time you drank alcohol?" I asked.

"Pretty much," he said.

Polly was back. "Did I miss anything? What happened to your friend, the one who concocted the sloe gin?"

"John? I'm not sure where he is. I haven't seen him in a while. Last time I heard anything about him was some years ago. One of our friends told me that John had found his way down to Oaxaca. He'd set up a big greenhouse to hybridize marijuana but was spending most of his time trying to communicate with some extraterrestrial arachnids who lived in some other dimension."

With that, George smiled at me, in a pointed sort of way, I thought.

"Okay, I don't mean to be rude," I told him, "but why are you

183

telling us this right now? I mean, I did want to know about the scar on your hand, but . . ."

"Because we all do stupid things, that's why. Things that we're embarrassed about, or painful things that betray someone's trust," he nodded at Polly, "or just dumb things we can't explain. It's not the end of the world. We might end up with some scars, but that's life, isn't it?"

"Angella says, 'The best of us journey to the darker sides of our souls where we dig up bits and pieces to illuminate the human spirit.'"

I thought that might be comforting for George.

"What else does she tell you, Nellie?" Polly asked, gently.

The bread was okay, the stew was simmering. Dinner would have to wait.

I took a deep breath and told them everything.

11

As usual with the earliest snow of the season, drivers had to get accustomed to slippery roads and there were dozens of fender benders. I suffered worse than that: a motorist skidded through a red light at the intersection of Regent and Allen and hit me sideways, smashing my car and sending me careening into a telephone pole. Luckily my airbags inflated and I only suffered a sprained wrist and a mild concussion. My first thought was that Angella had caused the accident. The car was totaled. With my sprained wrist I wasn't very adept at test-driving so George and Polly were happy to help me select a new car.

I couldn't do much with my laptop, either. That meant Angella, if she'd encouraged the accident, had momentarily lost her "voice." It served her right. I used my freedom to sit by a comforting fire and read. Henry slept next to my feet.

Angella Wing. No more blog, no more chat room, no more channeling—it was a welcome reprieve. I made an announcement for my answering machine: Merrill Chase was no longer giving personal readings. I thought of calling Grace to tell her what happened but decided I'd rather make a visit to Wocanaga and see her in person. Eventually.

Polly and George stopped in every day to make certain I was okay. George brought in fresh loads of firewood and Polly fixed tea. I thought maybe they weren't exactly certain Angella *hadn't* been involved in my accident, and one night I confessed: "I've been reading about disembodied spirits in this book and I'm convinced that's what Angella is."

"So, what's a 'disembodied spirit'?" Polly asked. "It sounds like one of my holograms."

"They're the spirits who don't go on to the upper planes of the astral domain but instead they hang around here. Earthbound. They're attracted to our physical realm and believe they still exist on our level. And they really enjoy being channeled. Especially channeled by someone who isn't all that sure of what she's doing."

"Like you," George added.

"Like me," I agreed, chagrined. "When they try to possess a channeler—and that's what they want to do, to *possess* someone, mind, body, and soul—they take over somebody's entire nervous system! And they do it spontaneously. That's how it was with me. I had no intentions of channeling when Angella began speaking through me at Wocanaga. I didn't want to channel at all! And spirits like Angella are more concerned with controlling than communicating. That's why she gets so mad when I refuse to carry out her wishes. I wouldn't even be surprised if Angella was responsible for having Sharon appear when she did, when I had my panic attack at Wocanaga. She knew that would weaken my disbelief."

Polly rolled her eyes. "You said you hadn't channeled Angella yet when Sharon's ghost appeared. Can't you get your story straight?"

"Oh, whatever," I threw the book angrily on the carpet, where it landed among several others. "Fuck you, Polly. I'm serious about this; I'm really getting scared. If I start doing weird stuff . . . *weirder* stuff, then maybe you'll believe me."

"I believe you," George said softly. "I believe you're afraid."

"You guys can go to hell," I sobbed. Then I limped up the stairs and went to bed with Henry.

186

$\mathcal{F}$or the first time in many years, Madison enjoyed a white Thanksgiving.

I had a late dinner that day at Polly's apartment. Before I went over there each of my kids called with holiday greetings and I got all teary. Odessa's baby, my granddaughter, Cassia, burbled, "I wov Nana Nell," and I was ready to buy an airline ticket to New Zealand right away.

"You're welcome any time, Mom," Odessa said. "I don't know when we'll be back in the States."

Then Sky called from Winnipeg and said he'd be back in Madison for the summer. I was cheered somewhat to hear that but still felt so far removed from my family. Being independent had advantages, but pretty soon I might have to think about moving closer to my children.

Polly did her best with the turkey. It was only one of those molded turkey breasts with a plastic packet of gravy. But she was never much of a chef. While it was roasting, she tried valiantly to explain the exhibition she was preparing for her gallery opening in Chicago. The holography setup involved a lot of glass and numbers and I was lost from the very beginning.

"I liked your paintings," I said.

"I liked painting, too, but it got boring after a while," Polly replied. "The flat dimensions didn't offer much of a challenge for me. When I did installation art, that was just being goofy. Now, I absolutely love experimenting with light and mirrors. It's so neat to be able to create an illusionary aspect that doesn't demand a subjective response."

"Huh?"

She said the viewers' response to holograms depends on the way the holograms are presented and the intention behind their presentation, not the esoteric criteria one takes for granted as a painter. That part made sense for me, at last.

But then she said, "Think of light as a form of wave motion."

I tried. Light is wave motion. Everyone has a vibrating aura. Mediums throb to the frequency of spirits. Thoughts are things; things are not always what they seem.

"A hologram is a kind of frozen photograph, but it has three dimensions and the light source is a laser," Polly patiently explained. "Oh, never mind, Nellie; I can tell you're zoning out. You might as well wait 'til you see my show," she promised. "I guarantee my new images are really wild!"

We were enjoying the pumpkin cheesecake I'd brought over when the lilting tone of my cell phone jingled.

Polly advised, "That's your Merrill Chase phone, right? Who'd call her on Thanksgiving? Let it go."

Karl Bittner would call on Thanksgiving. Grace Waverly gave him my number (or Merrill Chase's number) because he'd learned that I was now doing private readings and claimed that Merrill Chase "owed" him a reading since last summer when she "gave him the brush-off at Wocanaga."

He sounded grumpy. Maybe he'd had a few too many hot toddies.

"I'm so sorry," I told him sweetly, "but Merrill Chase no longer does personal readings. I appreciate your recognition of her work."

"And I have a great appreciation for Angella Wing's presence on the Internet," he interrupted. "I think it would be in your best interest, Miss Chase, if we could schedule a meeting, reading or not."

I took his number and said I'd have to call him back.

I hated that Bittner's stern voice could still make me shake in my shoes.

Polly advised me to meet with him out of curiosity, to see what he had in mind. I refused. But then we shared a bottle of Riesling and plotted a scheme that seemed hilarious. Later, I blamed it on the wine.

◈

My mother used to refer to the "pope's nose" as the tail of the turkey, or the part of the bird that goes over the fence last. When I fix a turkey I always cut off the tail and throw it away. It's greasy and disgusting, like an extremely large nose with great big pores. Since Polly had only roasted a faux turkey for Thanksgiving, she did not have to contend with the tail.

Protestants began calling the turkey's tail the pope's nose in the late seventeenth century. It's also known as the parson's nose. In the Middle East it's called the sultan's nose. The actual name is "pygostyle," which has nothing to do with *anyone's* nose and can be found in more than 18,000 references on Google, where I learned the tail's swollen appearance is due to the oil glands that turkeys use when preening. One more reason I'll definitely continue to cut it off. A person can do too much research, it seems.

I mention all this because the Pope's Nose was the Chicago restaurant that Polly and I chose for my reading with Karl Bittner. It's a fun and irreverent Italian restaurant on Taylor Street where their signature dish is a white bean turkey soup featuring, of course, the fatty pygostyle. Dessert offerings include Nun's Farts, little cinnamon rolls.

We chose it not for its *zuppa di tacchino* but for the décor. The restaurant consists of semi-enclosed booths; three sides of each booth are ceiling-high and painted with murals that depict Italian village scenes. The fourth—through which the waiter peers to take your order and serve your food—is curtained off with thick drapery, thus providing a sense of privacy for your dining pleasure.

I did not want to meet with Karl Bittner in my home or God forbid a hotel room, so steering him toward the Pope's Nose was Polly's inspired solution. It worked, too, because we were able to arrange for my meeting with Bittner to occur on the same day as Polly's gallery opening in the city so I'd naturally be in Chicago. Polly wanted to hear what Bittner had to say and I felt more comfortable having her there.

I'd told Bittner that "Merrill Chase" would be available at one o'clock. Polly and I reserved adjacent booths at the Pope's Nose and we both arrived at noon. I carried a baby monitor turned to "transmit" and set it just inside my purse, which I carefully placed at my side; Polly had her module set to "receive," so she could hear every word that transpired. We practiced sending and receiving silly messages to each other for about twenty minutes. I was glad I'd inserted fresh batteries in each.

Polly reminded me of the times we rode to basketball games in eighth grade with Mr. Bittner. We were cheerleaders and Sharon was the only one who'd sit next to him in the front seat of his car because he loved to take what he called "opportunity corners" that would throw her against him.

I asked Polly if she recalled how he taught us about "perdiddles." When you met a car with only one headlight, Bittner said, you were supposed to shout "perdiddle!" For every perdiddle you got, you could demand a kiss from the other person. Bittner always told Sharon he was saving his perdiddles up for her. He said that right in front us! (Well, Polly was alone in the back seat; I had to sit in the front seat, of course, squeezed between Sharon and the door so I wouldn't throw up.)

I asked for a glass of wine to steady my nerves and Polly reminded me that she had to return to the gallery by two thirty, so she went ahead and ordered lunch. My waiter understood that I would not be ordering until my companion arrived.

Bittner was early. He was ushered into the booth with a flourish of sweeping curtains and a gust of his trademark Old Spice fragrance. A menu was handed to him before he sat down. Apparently our waiter felt we were already usurping more than our allotted dining time.

"Wine?" the waiter inquired.

Bittner deferred to me. I declined another glass, but he ordered the house Chianti. It seemed we were going to eat before the reading. I was too nervous to dine but picked at some strozzaprete with shrimp and sun-dried tomato. Strozzaprete, a long curved pasta, means "priest strangler." Bittner went for the turkey soup with pope's nose and beans.

I was agitated for all sorts of reasons. Across from me sat the man who had casually fondled the majority of my female classmates, including me. Today he'd easily be charged as a sex offender! There was also a very good chance he had assaulted and murdered one of my childhood friends. I would *love* to be able to prove that!

Prior to my Wocanaga panic attack (which I hoped to hell I wouldn't have today, thus Polly's reassuring presence nearby), I had not had an opportunity to scrutinize Karl Bittner very closely. Now I thought I detected that he'd had a little work done on his face. Eyelids, maybe? Jowls? A tweak here and there? If you weren't aware of his seamy past you might even find him handsome: a charming, tanned, well-toned, and very fit gentleman wearing corduroys and an argyle sweater over a blue button-down Brooks Brothers shirt. Mr. Suave. *Mr. Debonair,* flashing a diamond pinkie ring. He must have been in his early seventies by now but easily appeared ten years younger.

Did I mention that I wore sunglasses? I told Bittner I'd recently had cataract surgery and my eyes were super-sensitive. I watched carefully but saw no sign that he recognized Eleanora Grendon.

Bittner sipped his *zuppa* and I rearranged my pasta. Small talk. The weather. Approach of the holidays. Chicago. Nothing personal.

"Merrill Chase," he said finally, after our plates were cleared and coffee mugs were filled. He pronounced my name slowly, as if he were declaring my sentence of death. "I haven't forgiven you for doing one helluva number on me at Wocanaga last summer."

"Running off, you mean?"

"Setting me up, giving me that look. Your rudeness was devastating for me. I need to know—did you see dire indications in my aura? Can you at least tell me that? I've held back for six months, but now I have to know the message you had for me."

Unfinished business. I should have known he'd ask.

"Um . . . honestly, all I remember is that I wasn't feeling well. If I gave you a funny look it was because I was going to throw up. That's why I rushed off, why I left as quickly as I did. Some kind of virus. Maybe something I ate. Diarrhea, vomiting, really disgusting stuff. I had to find a bathroom right away. I was sick for about a week."

A flurry of coughing erupted from the neighboring booth, as Polly could not resist commenting on my lie. So I gleefully plunged right into another.

"As for the message, I don't recall. It must not have been important." I took a deep breath and gave him a fresh smile. "Whatever it

191

was, our lives are always in flux so the messages Spirit gives us are always altering, too. A reading you might have been given last summer would not be appropriate for today, anyway. Shall we try again?"

I was radiant. I was sweetness. I was Merrill Chase, a most compassionate medium, who had just agreed to give him another reading despite her earlier refusal on the phone.

But beneath that saccharine facade I was still Nellie Grendon, battling memories of sitting at my desk in his eighth grade classroom with Polly and Sharon and Teddy and all the rest, watching this same man pace in front of us with a stick of chalk in his hand, this man but much younger, his hair not yet silvery gray, his handsome face not yet lifted, waiting for him to wander down my row followed by a strong waft of Old Spice and lay his hot palm on my shoulder, run it slowly down my back, and casually snap the elastic of my bra. I shivered with the memory and reached for the deck of cards in my handbag. As I did so, the baby monitor clattered to the floor.

"My phone," I explained, ducking beneath the table. "Clumsy idiot," I told myself under my breath as I retrieved it.

More consumptive coughs from Polly.

"Would you like me to read your cards first, or are you more concerned with a spirit-message?"

"The cards," Bittner said. "Unless you sense someone trying to get through."

"Well, let's see."

I still had a bandage on my wrist from the sprain, but I was able to shuffle the cards, set them aside, then place my hands with palms down on the table in front of me. I closed my eyes (he couldn't see me do that but he must have known that I would) and hoped to hell the bedraggled image of Sharon Gallagher wouldn't pop into the booth.

Thirty seconds passed, and then an entire minute. I *had* to mention Sharon.

"As I'm coming into your vibration from the spirit side of life I am getting a name. I think it begins with S."

I could feel Bittner squirm on the Naugahyde seat across from me.

"I'm hearing . . . Sheila? Sandra? Shirley, maybe Sherrie? . . . Do any of those names resonate with you? What about *Sharon*?"

"I knew someone named Sharon. She passed on. A long time ago."

"Sharon," I repeated. "Sharon . . ." Then I crossed my hands over my chest and coughed, as if I couldn't breathe. It was grossly over-dramatized but Bittner caught the symbolism. I grabbed my neck.

"She drowned," he said as I noisily gasped for air.

"Sharon says . . ." I slowed my inhalation and turned my head just slightly as if I were listening.

"Yes?"

"She tells me that she has not forgotten you. She wants you to know that."

"Thank you."

"She says she learned more from you than from lessons in any book. Does that make sense?"

I opened my eyes in time to see Bittner nod, then closed them again.

"I see words, all these words are bombarding me, paragraphs. Pages of words, turning, turning. Sharon says there's a 'story.' A 'problem.' Maybe a 'story problem.' Do you know what I mean by 'story problem'?"

"Hmmm," he said, nodding again.

"Story. I am definitely getting that word. Maybe there's a problem attached to it. I don't know if it's your story or Sharon's or someone else's. Could it be a story you're supposed to tell? A problem you're supposed to solve? Are you a writer?"

"No, not a writer," he said. "But I do have a connection with books."

I paused. That part I hadn't faked. I decided the inspiration came from seeing Mr. Bittner in my classroom, holding a book. So it was a reasonable guess.

I paused, as if musing. "There is a *story*, a story that must be told . . . to resolve this . . . this problem."

There, I'd said what I needed to say. No response from Bittner, except, "Let's see what the cards reveal."

Thus far he was giving me nothing I didn't already know. I'd hoped for more of a reaction to my declaration of Sharon's name.

I could always draw on what I knew of his past. Or at least a portion of his past. I could work with that, if I had to. But I hoped I could come up with something else.

Books. He said he had a "connection" with books. Was he a collector? Should I press the "story" idea?

"I'm not always terribly accurate with cards," I apologized. "So please take what I give you with a grain of salt. Okay? Everyone reads them differently."

He issued a deep sigh, sat back, and ran both hands through his perfectly coiffed hair. Bittner was nervous!

"Have you had your cards read before?"

"Tarot cards. Not regular playing cards, like these."

"It's much the same. You should have a question in mind. Concentrate on the question. It should be something you want the cards to reveal. Don't tell me what it is. Put all other thoughts from your mind while you shuffle the deck."

He took the cards with trembling hands. Interesting. Did he have a drinking problem or was he merely scared? He shuffled the deck several times and cut it before giving it back.

His cards were unremarkable, but I took the "story" clue and concocted what I could.

"Here, the Jack of Hearts is the augur of success in an enterprise you are about to undertake. This spade warns against a most unfavorable change and as this is the ace it intensifies the danger. But this ten of clubs is the bringer of extreme good luck and will probably offset the spade."

He probably wanted me to say that he'd be successful at some written endeavor, so that's exactly what I told him.

"The heart in this position foretells happiness and possibly fame . . ."

A quick glance at Bittner's face indicated that reference was correct. I decided to quit guessing while I was ahead.

"I used to be in education," he admitted, "but some years ago I started a little publishing house. We don't do a lot of books, only three or four a year, mostly on contemporary religious or New Age subjects. You didn't happen to read *What Would Judas Do?* did you?"

"No," I admitted honestly with the slightest feigned note of regret.

"I'll be candid with you," Bittner said, swallowing the dregs of his coffee and setting the mug aside. "When I spoke with Grace Waverly a while back, she alerted me to Angella Wing's weblog, Take Wing. I'm a regular reader. I occasionally add a comment or two under the name of Lark."

"Lark," I said. "I remember seeing comments from 'Lark.'"

So I wasn't the only one masquerading as someone else!

"I insisted on meeting you," he flashed a grin that revealed new too-white teeth, "because I am very interested in publishing Angella Wing's memoirs. Her *channeled* memoirs. Channeled by Merrill Chase!"

"Oh, no!" I gasped. He must have thought that was an expression of surprise, instead of absolute denial.

"As you're obviously aware, Miss Wing is a tremendously fascinating woman. I think this kind of book would sell very well for us. It fits our niche of readers and it's your chance to be an author!"

I am an author, you dunderhead, I wanted to scream, but of course I did not. There was another bout of coughing in the next booth and a flurry that seemed to indicate the neighboring customer was about to leave. I checked my watch; it was quarter to three.

"I . . . I guess we'd have to leave that up to Angella, wouldn't we?" I tried to sound as pleasant as I could manage. "I'm obviously flattered, Mr. Bittner, but I'll have to see what *she* says about it and let you know."

I knew in my heart she'd be thrilled.

I was appalled.

$\mathcal{D}$ecember is a beautiful time to walk around downtown Chicago. The shimmering lights and festive displays create a jovial mood on Michigan Avenue. Even the most entrenched Scrooge would surrender to such vibrant joy. But my relief at having finished with Bittner's reading was tempered by the further complications of his ridiculous plea. *A biography of Angella Wing.* Channeled by *me*? Not in *this* life, you moron!

I did not doubt such a book would be a success, of course, and then I would be encouraged to admit my identity to the world. I didn't mind having the local women who'd been given readings on my porch think of me as "Merrill Chase, Medium," but book reviewers and interviewers? Critics who'd titter behind my back? I definitely did not want back-titterers. And to write the book, I'd have to deal with Angella 24/7. Whoo-ha! No matter what Angella said, I knew my final answer was *absolutely not.*

The little gallery celebrating Polly's art was located on a side street not far from Neiman Marcus. The opening reception wasn't until six o'clock so I had time to kill and did a little shopping that, blessedly, took my mind off everything bugging me. I should go shopping more often; it's so therapeutic.

"Friendly Phantoms" was the name of Polly's show.

When I saw her work in a gallery setting, I *was* tremendously impressed. Polly was depicting photographic images of body parts in three dimensions. The large white room had a variety of tables and wall hangings that resonated with three-dimensional images of legs, arms and hands, legs and feet, torsos tangled together. There are a lot of odd aspects about holographs, like when you view the object from different angles, the object is also *seen* from different angles. I could see why the process fascinated Polly. Subjectivity was not an issue, here.

I was in awe of the way she mixed artistic and technical skills to achieve these bizarre images. It was magic. Seeing was *not* believing. You look through what seems to be an almost clear piece of glass as if you're looking through a window, and on the other side is a three-dimensional image that looks like *something* but it only exists in the form of light. People wandering around the room reacted with astonishment and disbelief. I saw one woman reach around the glass and try to grab a foot but her hand went right through the foot and she squealed.

On one wall, this quote from science fiction writer Ray Bradbury was inscribed:

Not so far off across the sill of tomorrow,
three-dimensional holograms will "visit" your house.
These friendly phantoms ... will delight, edify, and educate ...
Built upon the very fabric of light and air in any room.
View them from North-South-East-West.
Walk round them.
They'll have as many sides as you have angles.
Watch for these friendly spirits.

I wanted to talk with Polly about her amazing art and report on the rest of my lunch with Karl Bittner. I wanted to tell her about his interest in Angella's life story. I knew this wasn't the time, but just the same, I couldn't wait. She was still wearing the same raggedy jeans she'd had on at lunch and was surrounded by fawning admirers who were gesturing and shouting about her "incredible personal style." I was enormously proud of my old friend.

"How do you like the music?" a familiar voice spoke in my ear as his arm fell over my shoulder in a casual hug. I'm embarrassed to admit that my knees really *did* get weak! What a schmuck I am.

"George!" I could not conceal my delight. "Isn't this an outrageous show?"

"I hope you'll notice the music isn't that bad, either . . . ," he continued, teasing. "Polly wanted jazz flute, so I scored this for one of my students."

The music, ethereal but with a raw edge, threaded through the bodily images and could have been emitted by their otherworldly glow.

"It's perfect," I told the girl, obviously the flutist, who proudly stood next to George with a couple other kids. We all chatted for a while about the exhibit before they took off to help themselves to refreshments and George was left to congratulate Polly with me. She seemed almost embarrassed—very unlike the Polly Cornbloom I had known almost all my life. Then again, *this* was the newly discovered holo-artist, *Polly Blue!* A reporter was waiting for a few words, so she had to go.

"By the way, great performance, Nellie," Polly mumbled quickly, turning. "Breakfast tomorrow, okay? See you then."

Before he could ask, I said to George, "You want to have dinner?"

He agreed, then helped me gather my shopping bags from the back room.

George's trio was playing that weekend at a small jazz club in the city. He insisted on getting a cab so I could drop what he called my "plunder" back at my hotel. "They're Christmas gifts," I argued. "I have a granddaughter to spoil!"

"A black cashmere sweater from Neiman Marcus?" he teased. "That's one sophisticated toddler!"

Over dinner, I confessed that I had done a reading that afternoon. He'd heard all about Sharon and Karl Bittner during that fateful November night I thought of as My Snowy Night of Shame, but I hadn't filled him in on Bittner's Thanksgiving phone call and our meeting at the Pope's Nose. When I told him Bittner logged on to Angella's blog as "Lark," George immediately replied, "Of course. That's an anagram for 'Karl.'"

He wanted to know who else logged in. I gave him a few names, and it didn't take him long to figure out that "RillCashmere," the one who'd asked about making love with a Canadian jazz musician, was an anagram for "Merrill Chase."

"No!" I reached across and slapped his hand for emphasis.

He wrote it on a paper napkin and turned it around so I could see. Oh, my God. He was right. I wanted to die.

Angella was playing a dangerous game with me; the evil bitch.

At least George was laughing. I was mortification made flesh.

"I really need to figure out how to cut off my contact with her," I confessed. "When I started channeling Angella I was pretty much consumed with wondering if she was a real spirit or a product of my fantasy-prone imagination. Now all I can think about is getting her out of my life."

"Ah . . . before you take any extreme measures," George hesitated, "I need to ask a personal favor of you."

"What? Something that involves Angella? I thought my being a medium was anathema to you!"

"It may be a bit strong to put it that way," he said simply, reaching across the table to take my hand in his. This was extremely unusual behavior from him.

"Breeze Quinn, you've met her? The woman who runs the Bosky Lodge? Well, she's a believer in the kinds of things you do. Or that you've been doing. And she asked me if I could arrange for her to have a spirit reading. I told her that was unwise and besides, you were not doing readings anymore. But she insisted that I ask you anyway. Breeze can be very needy. Frankly, sometimes I feel like her gigolo. If we didn't need the bookings . . ."

"George, it's okay."

"No, I want to explain. You and I have already been free with each other in sharing some embarrassing behavior. Please allow me another turn. But it isn't easy . . ."

I looked down at my hand. His fingers were entwined with mine. I clasped them as tightly as I could.

"At first Breeze was an interesting diversion, and I can't say there weren't pleasant compensations. She manages the Bosky Lodge where we play, and she came on strong. I didn't need a whole lot of encouragement, I'll admit."

"She's very beautiful," I added. "What I've seen of her . . ."

I didn't mention that most of what I'd seen of her was through a keyhole.

"But she insists on my being with her *all the time*!" George continued. "I take more hours than I really need to meet with my students, just to steal some solitude for my creative work. But that's in my office; I want creative time at home. Alone! I built a great studio on the third floor where I've seldom even been. She has fallen into this habit of dropping by whenever she thinks I'll be around. I stupidly gave her a key early on so sometimes I'll get home from school to find her waiting for me! I even think of telling her I'm going on a trip and then hiding in my apartment without turning on the lights."

"George . . . ," I interrupted, not wanting to hear this but really *wanting to,* if you know what I mean.

"I don't know if you noticed, but last week I changed the lock on my apartment door, at the top of the stairs. She's been begging me for a copy but I keep *forgetting* to have one made."

I lifted my hand and brought George's fingers to my lips.

"It's okay. I'll do the reading."

George took my face in his hands and kissed my forehead.

"One more time won't make any difference," I told him. "And, if you want, I could skew her reading. Fake it. Tell her what she wants to hear. Or . . . what she doesn't."

"You'd do that? Bend the rules?"

"Hmm. *Rules.* There aren't so much rules as *standards.* The usual operating procedure. But of course I would bend them. Matter of fact, I usually do. I don't seem to be much of a medium when it comes to intercepting spirits—except for my nemesis, Miss Wing."

"You'd even tell Breeze to stop stalking me?"

"That depends," I teased, wanting to add "What's in it for me?" but I didn't say those words because I already knew what I wanted from George.

"You stop Breeze from suffocating me, and I'll help you get rid of Angella."

"That's a deal," I said, and we sealed it with a kiss.

My luck was turning. He must have read my mind.

*M*other had always spoken of the Palmer House as if it were Windsor Castle, so that's where I always stayed when I went to Chicago. Polly was there, too, and at a champagne brunch the next morning we read reviews of Polly's exhibit and she shared her congratulatory cards. Finally, over coffee, Polly asked me what had happened with Bittner after she left.

"I need to tell you something, Nell, that I've never told you before," she said.

The stars seemed aligned for me to receive confessions from my friends. What now?

"When we were in eighth grade, I had to stay after school one day. I hadn't finished my math assignment or something idiotic like that. I can still remember how weird it seemed with the whole school empty and so quiet. Mr. Maxwell came in to sweep with his big broom. He scattered that red sweeping compound and he swept around all the desks and along the edge of the room while I finished my homework. I was glad he was there. After he left and we were alone, Mr. Bittner called me up to his desk."

I cringed, already confident I knew what would come next.

"He made me come around to the side, and then he caught me between his thighs. He wouldn't let me go. He put his hand up under my sweater to fondle my breasts and said he wouldn't stop until I kissed him. He said Jewish girls were supposed to have remarkable boobs."

Polly wasn't crying, but I had enough tears for both of us. Bittner never went that far with me but now I felt a fresh desire for revenge. I would wreak real havoc with that sleazy degenerate.

"He did that more than once. I don't even know how many times."

"How come you never told me?" I demanded, borrowing her napkin to wipe my nose because my own napkin was already wet.

Polly's eyes were welling with tears. "He made me touch him, too."

"How could you let the bastard get away with that?"

Polly just shook her head and shrugged. "I don't know. I was scared. He convinced me it was my fault. And I couldn't tell my parents! Hell, I couldn't even tell you. We thought Sharon was so depraved for flirting with him. I worried you might think I was immoral."

"Oh, Polly. I never would have thought that you were like Sharon. You were *never* like Sharon! She was . . . she was . . ."

"She was Sharon," Polly said. "And I'm so glad you told Bittner that she hadn't forgotten him. If he drowned her, that might give him at least a few sleepless nights."

I finally remembered to tell her that Bittner wanted me to channel Angella's autobiography.

"Are you going to do it?" Polly asked.

"Are you kidding? I'd rather destroy him," I replied. "Wouldn't it be ideal if I could figure out a way to use Angella to punish that son of a bitch? Let me give it some thought so I can come up with a plan."

12

Teddy Carter called when I got back from Chicago. We'd said good-bye so awkwardly when we were together in the fall that I agreed to meet him again. Part of me wanted to tell him about my lunch with Bittner, but then I'd want to tell Teddy about Polly's recent admission and my vision of Sharon and Spiritualism and my readings and Angella—it was all just too much. I wasn't sure he'd understand my mediumship and, if he did, I felt certain that a born-again Christian would not approve.

I purposely did not turn on my computer so I could avoid contact with Angella Wing, who would beyond a shadow of a doubt be wildly enthusiastic about having her channeled autobiography in print. I could not bear to think of sitting through more of her melodramatic musings, much less writing them down. Much *less* signing my name (even my pseudonym!) to them.

I had wondered what it would be like to be a medium; that's what brought me to this. Now I knew. Like anything else, mediumship could get boring and tedious. But I hadn't figured on the hazards that might be involved.

To free myself from Angella, and from Karl Bittner, too, I would have to free myself from Merrill Chase.

❧

It was not Hogs-for-Christ Teddy who called for me; instead it was Ted Carter, Lakeland County District Attorney, in a conservative dark suit with a modest paisley tie. He could have passed as a partner in one of Madison's law firms on the Square. I felt much more comfortable with this Teddy instead of the one with the demon do-rag and black leather.

Because we had reservations at an upscale restaurant downtown, I'd gone shopping, a Madison spree I hadn't engaged in for a very long time. As in Chicago, the stores were pushing holiday spangles but I chose a dark purple silk skirt with matching cashmere sweater. You can't go wrong with cashmere unless it becomes part of an anagram for Merrill Chase. I even bought new leather boots and a new winter coat.

Dinner was leisurely and enjoyable. I wondered if anyone who saw us thought we were just another married couple, maybe celebrating our wedding anniversary. We reminisced about high school (Teddy had been a high school football star and went on to play at the University of Illinois) and our fellow classmates at Little Wolf. I asked a lot of questions about his work in the Northwoods, quite a drive from Madison, an area of lakes and pines where my family had a summer cabin that we didn't often visit because Mother had to clean up so much mouse residue whenever we arrived. Eventually she refused to go and, against my objections, Daddy sold the place. I still felt bad about that.

Teddy and his wife had six kids and ten grandchildren. *Catholic,* Mother would've nudged me with a sharp elbow to the ribs. But Teddy spoke of his family with such affection that I became choked up and when he asked me about my own grandchildren I was barely able to respond.

"One granddaughter," I said, clearing my throat. "She lives in New Zealand."

"That's too bad," he commented, and then I could see he was sorry he had.

"I really *do* need to get down there one of these days," I replied. "I miss my daughter and I had only a few days with Cassia after she was born."

"You look like you could use a vacation," Teddy agreed.

"Do I really look that bad?" I teased.

He studied me for a long moment before he spoke, and then I could tell his words were carefully chosen.

"Nellie," he said leaning forward, "you have always looked beautiful to me."

Teddy seemed about sixteen when he said that and he reached across the table to clasp my wrist.

"I've only loved two women in my life," he continued. "Nellie Grendon and the woman I married."

Old *what's-her-name*, I said to myself, awkwardly digging a Kleenex out of my purse with my free hand.

"Teddy, that's very sweet . . ."

"So if I think you look tired, it's because I still care about you."

I blew my nose.

"It's okay," I said. "I still care about you, too, Teddy."

"C'mon up and visit us next summer," Teddy urged, loosening his tight grasp on my arm. "Bring Polly along! We'll show you a good time and you can fish and swim or golf, or just rest if you want to. We built a big log house right on the water with five bedrooms. I'll have my wife give you a call so you two can decide on a date."

I was dying to ask if his wife—whose name I still did not recall and wasn't sure if I ever did know it—was also "born again." Maybe she was even a *Hoggette* for Christ.

"Personally, Nellie, I think you could use a rest *right now*," Teddy said. "You really are looking pretty rough. Is anything wrong?"

I told him I'd just returned from Chicago, where I saw Polly's show and did my best to explain what holo-art was. Then I mentioned—I couldn't help it—that I'd run into Mr. Bittner down there. I offered no details on how that happened, just said it did.

"No kidding," he said, truly impressed with that. "How'd he look? What'd he have to say? Did he remember you from Little Wolf? What's he been doing? Retired, I suppose."

I asked if he'd read *What Would Judas Do?* but Teddy said he'd never heard of it. "Bittner has a publishing company," I said. "That's one of his books."

"Judas, huh? Figures. Son of a bitch. I still don't think he drowned Sharon, though."

"Do you recall a coroner's report ever being released after her death?"

"Nope. But if there was one, it'll still be on record."

"Would it be a whole lot of trouble for you to look it up?"

"Ah," he said. "That's what assistant DAs are for."

Lying awake the next morning in the pale light of December, I fantasized that George was sharing my pillow and it was his breath falling softly on my cheek instead of Teddy's.

But it was Henry, sweet, docile, furry Henry, who was snoring next to me. The warmth of his shaggy body snuggled so close to mine was reassuring. I loved his unconditional loyalty. And I was grateful to be in my own bed!

Floating in and out of sleep, I fondled Henry's feathery ears and the dog sighed, stretched his long legs, then burrowed closer to my face to bury his moist nose beneath my neck.

"Oh, you're my sweet Henry," I whispered.

My murmured affections were rewarded by generous ear licking, which tickled and caused me to move away slightly—encouraging Henry to bound off the bed and announce with a woof that it was time for our morning walk.

I attempted to push aside my regret about the night before.

After dinner we had gone back to Teddy's hotel, as anticipated. Apparently adultery was not forbidden in Teddy's born-again handbook.

"Wait a minute," I said, placing my arm on his when he turned off the motor of his car in the parking lot. "Let's make out right here, like we did in high school. Then, instead of taking me home, we can go up to your room."

I was not about to totally give up my fantasy.

Teddy sighed and took my face in his hands.

"Nell, you're still a dreamer, aren't you? Why waste our time here in the car? It's freezing outside! Pretty soon it'll be freezing in here. In two minutes we can be in my room, in a comfortable king-size bed. I don't want to make love in the back seat with a seventeen-year-old Nellie Grendon! We can't relive the way things were any more than we can recapture our youth. Why would we want to? I still find you a fascinating woman."

"You could put your hand up under my skirt," I said, "the way you used to, and I could . . ."

"Sure, and some Madison cop could pull up and shine a light in the window and find out I'm the Lakeland County DA. That'd be cute, too."

He backed away from me. A chime sounded as he opened, then slammed, his door.

Silently, I followed Teddy to his room. We made out on his bed with our clothes on, a concession to my request that we engage in some serious foreplay for old times' sake. My silk skirt got pretty wrinkled and my cashmere sweater was stretched. I untied Teddy's necktie and slowly unbuttoned his shirt. I'd already taken off my boots and had worn a garter belt and stockings, looking forward to this moment. Okay, so I had shopped at Victoria's Secret, too. It felt very sexy to wear black lace underwear beneath cashmere and silk.

Heavy breathing. Fumbling. It was not as graceful as I'd hoped, but we finally slid beneath the sheets.

"Well, this is a first," Teddy mumbled, stretching out.

"Took us long enough to get here," I replied, working my way down his chest with nibbly kisses. His navel. The line of pubic hair that led to his groin.

"Nell . . . ," he warned, but not soon enough.

"Dammit!" Teddy groaned as he came all over my breasts, my neck, my face. He even hit my right eye, which began to sting like crazy.

"Jesus, I'm sorry. You made me wait so long, I couldn't help it!"

I hoisted myself back to the pillows, still wiping my eye.

"It's okay, Teddy. Really. It's no big deal."

Later he recovered enough so we could try again. I knew before the earth moved (and after so much foreplay it was only a minor tremor) this would be the first and last time I slept with him. It wasn't worth the risk and certainly wasn't even close to my imagined passion.

While George and I plodded through snow flurries with Henry the next morning, my mind was still in the hotel room with Teddy.

Fantasy-prone, indeed; the ruin of my illusions served me right. The most excitement occurred when the heavy silver cross Teddy wore on a chain around his neck whacked my face with his every thrust. I ran my fingers over my jaw. I suspected it was bruised.

When we said good night, Teddy had again invited me up north, then added, "God will forgive your sinful ways if you take Jesus Christ as your Lord and Savior." He must have seen my frown as the light came on when I opened the car door because he said he was only joking. That may have been true; I conceded that I didn't know him very well anymore. My Teddy Bear had become a prose-lytizing fundamentalist but wasn't saintly enough to avoid a casual fuck.

I laughed aloud so abruptly that Henry stopped in his tracks and I stumbled over the dog.

"What was that about?" George wanted to know as he helped me up. He already knew the worst of my secrets and I knew some of his; how could telling him about last night with Teddy change anything between us?

"Well, if his wife has any suspicions, he can cross himself and claim he didn't have sex because there wasn't any 'penetration,'" George joked after I'd finished my story of woe.

"You guys are all alike," I said, trying to shove him into a snowdrift. "And he wouldn't cross himself, because he's been Born Again. Jesus."

"Praise the Lord!" George sang, waving his hands above his head.

"I remember when I was grounded for stealing a few of my mother's cigarettes for Sharon. And then I heard that Teddy went out with her. I was *so* mad! I wanted to kill them both."

"One out of two," George remarked dryly.

"C'mon, that isn't funny," I told him. "Last night Teddy told me about the time he siphoned gas from Father O'Neil's Chevrolet so he and Buck and Duane could take Sharon for a ride. Teddy didn't even have a driver's license and he used his father's station wagon. They gave her a Coke with an aspirin in it; that was supposed to make her drunk. Teddy said Sharon let them each kiss her and feel her up. The next day he had to serve as altar boy and his breath still smelled like gasoline. He was afraid to blow out the candles in case a stream of fire appeared and he'd explode!"

"Okay, now *that's* funny," George said. "Flames of Hell were already reaching out to get him. I hope Sharon was worth it."

Everything began to escalate the summer after eighth grade. Crazy things happened, and if I had truly been "clairsentient," I would have realized how volatile our lives would be as we grappled our way through adolescence.

Polly decided she was going to become a stuntwoman. She filled a couple of pipes with sand and began lifting weights. Then she practiced doing somersaults on the grass at the end of a lengthy run. She said she got her ideas from movie stuntwomen and tried to copy the stunts she'd seen them do.

One night Sharon got the idiotic idea that we should throw rotten eggs at the Old Crow's house. I don't know where Polly was that night; maybe she was with her family in Appleton at their synagogue. She would celebrate her bat mitzvah soon, and when she wasn't lifting weights she was studying Hebrew. Sometimes, she told me, she did both at the same time.

No one knew where to find "rotten" eggs, so Sharon decided regular eggs would have to suffice. I tried hard to dissuade everyone, but I couldn't say a whole lot or they'd suspect I had some kind of personal relationship with Miss Khrol, which I surely had.

The eggs made a horrible mess. Even if the eggs weren't rotten, the boys had great aim. Even Teddy. One egg cracked a window. Sharon called me a chicken for not joining in and did her stupid chicken dance sticking her elbows out like wings and cackling in a squawky way. It didn't take long for the others to start cackling and mocking me. I rode my bike home while they kept on throwing eggs. I probably cried.

The day after the egg throw I rode back out to the Khrol's and began picking up eggshells. I took a pail from behind the cottage and tried to wash down the splashes of yolks on the side of their house with water from the lake. Mr. Khrol came outside and used a broom to scrub the weathered boards and tarpaper while I threw water on them. He was old and weak so it was a hard thing for him to do.

I didn't want to be a tattler and a goodie-goodie, but I did mention to Miss Khrol that the eggs had been Sharon Gallagher's idea.

"Is that girl always so insensitive?"

I related the story of Sharon locking me in the closet for my "confession," when I had to make the rounds of the bowling ball rosary in the rain.

"Damn shame," Mr. Khrol mumbled. He took out his handkerchief and made a honking sound as he blew.

Miss Khrol again repeated her warning that this was not a world for gentle people. "You are right to learn to look out for yourself at an early age," she said, "because there will be times in your life when no one else will be looking out for you. I am fortunate to have my father. I can't imagine what I'd do without him even though I try to be as independent as I can."

"Jesus Christ on a cream-colored cross . . ." Mr. Khrol was still thinking about my "confession."

"Pa," Miss Khrol warned, "watch your language when we have guests."

"This one's a thoughtful young woman if you ask me," Mr. Khrol said as he stuffed his handkerchief back in the hip pocket of his overalls. "You want to go fishing?"

Miss Khrol said, smiling, "I want Eleanora to do a few things for me. Maybe another day."

I thought it was a nice gesture and said, "Thanks anyway," to Mr. Khrol as he went out the back door. I could not imagine going fishing with the old man, but his invitation was very kind.

"Now," Miss Khrol said with a sly smile, "I'm going to teach you how to change your friend's aspect."

She reached for her deck of cards.

I laughed. "You mean I can change the way Sharon is?"

"Girls like Sharon can be easily manipulated. Remember, we are all more alike in this world than we are different."

With Sharon, she said, I could influence her "fortune" through my own imagination and resourcefulness. It was an ingenious suggestion. I couldn't wait for an opportunity to carry out the plans we made.

Polly had her bat mitzvah at the synagogue they belonged to in Appleton. It was with a couple other Jewish girls and my family wasn't invited.

I took confirmation classes and was confirmed in our Methodist church.

When their bishop came to Sacred Heart, Sharon had her confirmation that summer, too.

I didn't see much of Polly until July, except when she tried to give me Hebrew lessons. My own confirmation involved going to classes with Reverend Bennett and memorizing the Apostles' Creed and the Beatitudes, plus learning more details about the Methodist Church. It was monotonous, but I hadn't expected much. The Sunday of my confirmation I was allowed to wear earrings and high heels for the first time. I had this neat dress that was like a Mary Quant design. I showed my mom what I wanted and she had a local seamstress sew it for me, but it still wasn't as short as I'd hoped. I had my hair cut in a new geometric cut, too. My parents gave a party and my aunts and uncles came. We'd already had grade school graduation and this felt almost the same (except for the memorization part and going up to the communion rail to drink Welch's grape juice from tiny glasses and chewing little cubes of Wonder Bread). I got presents both times.

Sharon's confirmation was, as usual, colorful and exotic. She said she was blessed by the bishop with chrism oil that smelled like Christmas and became a "Soldier of Christ." That meant she had been enlisted to fight the war between good and evil. Polly and I couldn't help giggling when we heard that because we suspected she was on the "evil" side more than "good."

Sharon even got to choose another name. A saint's name. There was much discussion about this when the three of us were together, and we weighed the qualities and qualifications of a variety of saints.

Sharon suggested "Agatha," a saint who was a martyr and had her breasts cut off. Polly chose "Catherine," for Saint Catherine of Siena, because Sharon's book of saints said, "If you want a hard-charging saint to go to bat for you, Saint Catherine of Siena doesn't take no for an answer."

I liked Grace, but it turned out there was no Saint Grace.

"Grace is a gift, not a name," Sharon told me after I told her to ask Father O'Neil why there wasn't a Saint Grace. "You're in a state of grace after you go to confession and do penance and are cleansed of your mortal sins."

I still loved the name Grace, and since Sharon wasn't taking it, I took it myself.

Sharon finally chose Maria, for Saint Maria Goretti. I loved all the dramatic saint stories. When she was twelve, Maria was raped by a farmhand who tried to choke her and stabbed her fourteen times after she yelled that it was a sin and he'd go to hell. Before she died, she forgave her attacker. Then, after she was dead, she appeared to him (in jail) and handed him an armful of lilies that turned into flames.

For my own "Saint Grace," my inspiration was much less gripping. My mother had a small plaster frieze on the bedroom wall that was a miniature of the Three Graces. I loved the smooth whiteness of their naked, angelic bodies. Mother told me they weren't angels, they were Greek goddesses named Aglaia, Euphrosyne, and Thalia. That was good enough for me.

Eleanora Merrill Grace Grendon. It thought it had a nice ring. "Merrill" was for my Grandma Merrill, my mother's mother. She was a really sweet old lady, the epitome of what a perfect grandma should be. Her cookie jar was always filled, her hugs were warm and soft, and she smelled like lily of the valley toilet water.

Years later, when I assumed the pseudonym "Merrill Chase," I realized it sounded a great deal like "Merrill Grace," and I didn't mind that at all. Of course I also caught the resemblance to Grace Waverly.

Sharon's Catholicism was exasperating—not because of what Catholics were all about, but because she made her personal beliefs seem like such a major issue. Polly and I had plenty of other Catholic friends but it was just part of their life—it wasn't something they held over our heads and bragged about.

On Ash Wednesday, for example, Sharon refused to wash her face so you could still see the smudge on her forehead on Thursday and sometimes on Friday, too. I think she wore a Band-Aid over it when she slept so it wouldn't rub off.

Polly and I were affected by Sharon's inability to eat meat on Fridays. That meant we had to order a cheese pizza instead of pepperoni shared between the three of us. Or we'd have toasted cheese sandwiches instead of cheeseburgers.

Near the time she was confirmed, Sharon was given a scapular. You would have thought she was an incredible martyr for wearing it. "It itches," she complained. "It itches so horribly bad."

"If it itches so much, why don't you take it off?" Polly suggested.

"Because it's an outward sign of protection."

213

"Can we see it?" I asked. "What does it look like?"

Sharon claimed, "That's for me to know and you to find out."

Eventually, of course, she relented and showed us the scapular made of two small rectangles of brown wool taken from the robes of Carmelite monks. There were pictures sewn to the wool, one of Our Lady of Mount Carmel holding a scapular. That side said "Pray for Us" beneath the picture, and the other side had a picture of Saint Simon Stock kneeling before the Blessed Virgin Mary, who was giving him a scapular. That side said "Pray for Us," too. The pieces were joined by two strips of brown ribbon so you wore one square on your back and the other on your "scapula," the bone that joins your arm bone with your clavicle. Teddy told me what his own scapular looked like and showed it to me before Sharon showed us hers. They were the same.

"We can't be friends after we die, you know," she'd remind Polly and me after we'd pledged our friendship to the death.

That was just another way for Sharon to elevate herself to angelic status, a way to look down on everybody else.

Naturally, I'd expected my friends to be my friends forever. But our loyalties to Sharon began to falter late that summer as we were about to enter high school.

By then, Sharon and Polly and I and Carolina Sawyer belonged to a girl's quartette, "The Starlettes." We had matching costumes with tiaras made of tinfoil stars and star-spangled red shorts that we wore with white go-go boots. We sang at Lion's Club meetings and Women's Club teas, and we were featured at Friday night summer band concerts in the park. It was fun. Gloria Piekarski was our accompanist. We practiced after school and at night during the summer. In the beginning, our repertoire consisted of sappy "star" songs like "Would You Like to Sing on a Star and "When You Wish upon a Star," but we had been working on a couple pop tunes that we hoped would make us famous.

Ted Mack's *Original Amateur Hour* had been on television for a long time by then. The television audience voted for the winner by mailing a postcard for their favorite. The show always opened with a wheel that was spun to decide the order of appearance of the talented guests. While the wheel spun, Mr. Mack always said, "Round and round she goes, and where she stops nobody knows." Tryouts were held in little towns across the United States.

The Starlettes auditioned for *The Original Amateur Hour* in the basement of a hotel in Waupaca with about fifty other contestants. We sang "My Boyfriend's Back" and "If I Had a Hammer," and we were really excited when we were chosen as one of a dozen acts who would perform in August at the county fair where a winner would be selected to appear on the TV show. Wow! Our mothers sewed new costumes, although they balked a little when we explained we wanted mini-skirts. Sharon belittled our competition, which included a chubby baton twirler, a juggler who looked just like Janis Joplin, and a trumpet player who wore a leather cowboy vest and chaps. While our mothers labored over the pleated white mini-skirts with gold sequins attached painstakingly by hand, we found white tank tops at Cornbloom's in sizes that would fit each of us.

I can still feel the sense of anticipation we suffered as we waited to go on stage in front of the county fair grandstand that night. There was a big crowd on the bleachers. Spotlights shone brilliantly toward the stage.

We wore rouge and false eyelashes. Our go-go boots had spindly heels. We'd tanned our legs and our arms to a perfect bronze. I had a pouf of fake curls pinned to my scalp for additional height. Polly's hair was cut like a boy's but she wore a tinfoil star tiara like the rest of us. Sharon was going to wear a blonde pageboy wig.

But Sharon was late. Carolina was about to go crazy with fear that she wouldn't show up, and Carolina's mother, who was acting as our "chaperone," kept tapping her watch to make sure it was still working. Gloria bit her nails.

We didn't know where she'd been, but when she arrived, Sharon's lipstick was smeared and her wig was a snarled mess. Her tiara was gone. She smelled like marijuana and there was beer on her breath, too. One of her false eyelashes was flopping; the glue had come loose.

We had no time to waste—we were being called out onto the stage.

I could feel the start of a panic attack, although I didn't know then what it was. I was sweating and dizzy. My heartbeat was erratic and I thought it was going to rock right out of my chest.

Gloria Piekarski began the introduction to "Blowin' in the Wind," and Sharon started to giggle. Carolina, who never could hold a straight face if someone else was laughing, began to giggle, too. Polly and I started singing, but it was no use. Sharon forgot the words and Carolina was way out of tune. Then Sharon put her hand over her mouth and burped. Next, she vomited all over my go-go boots. The smell made me feel sick, so I ran off the stage. The winner was an obnoxious little girl who lip-synched the words to "Alley-Oop."

I was really pissed off with Sharon for screwing up our chances for stardom. I could have played my accordion and won that contest by myself!

It seemed only right for Sharon to be embarrassed and apologetic after that. She wasn't. Not at all. So I decided to make my move.

A bunch of us girls were lying on the sand at Bear Lake one afternoon in late August, resting on beach towels in the sun. I casually pulled my deck of cards out of my beach bag.

"Anybody want their fortune told?"

I knew Polly didn't approve, but I went ahead with it anyway. Sharon, of course, insisted that she be first in line.

I told her to ask a silent question. Then I had her shuffle the cards and cut them with her left hand before she gave them back to me. I spread the deck face down on the towel and asked Sharon to choose seven cards at random. Those I arranged in a row, face up, in the order in which they were chosen. I intended to read out the meanings of the first, fourth, and seventh card as I saw them (or, in this case, as I wanted them to be). These would represent her past, present, and future. No matter what the cards were, they would have *nothing* to do with what she wanted to hear.

In the past, I said, I saw that she had undergone great pain. This was represented by the nine of spades. For the present, the Queen of Hearts, I divined that she had great hopes to attain her heart's desire (which was, I knew, romance, Hollywood stardom, and success). Then I pretended to be shocked by the ace of spades, her third card, which had been revealed upside down. I covered my mouth and shook my head, insinuating that the ace represented something sinister. I told Sharon, as I swallowed hard, that her future . . . was too devastating for me to divulge.

We had to stop, I alleged, because it was too risky. I gathered the cards and put them back inside my bag.

"C'mon, Nellie," Sharon begged. "That's not fair!"

"Go ahead, Nell," Polly suggested. "Tell her what it says!"

A chorus of girls protested, so I finally said, with apology, "I saw sorrow and death come to your family, in that card."

That part of her fortune was close to true: I knew an ace of spades could mean something similar, if it were reversed. It might have to be in combination with another card, though. I could never keep it all straight.

The girls stared in awe at Sharon. She told me with a huff that my magic tricks didn't mean anything and she didn't care, anyway, even if they did.

Miss Khrol had told me this was a way to "alter Sharon's aspect." She had *not* advised me to threaten Sharon with images of anguish and death.

But I was still mad about the county fair and our loss to the "Alley-Oop" kid. I wanted Sharon to worry. I wanted to pay her back. I wanted her to have to beg her guardian angel to protect her. I wanted her to make circles around the bowling ball rosary on her knees and wear an even deeper groove in Gloria's lawn than was already there.

⁓⁓

Henry was with me for Christmas. Breeze had insisted on joining George in Chicago, where his trio was playing again. Polly had flown to California for a couple weeks.

217

On Christmas Eve, Henry and I went for a walk after dark to peer in the windows of houses in University Heights. I missed my kids terribly; or, I missed the children they used to be. The dog and I paused to watch Christmas lights framing happy gatherings, gifts being opened, and homes that were dark because their inhabitants were probably in church. Or out of town, staying with their families. Chimes from a neighborhood steeple rang out Christmas carols.

When Henry and I got back to the house I fixed a mug of hot chocolate and got out Lee's old 8mm films again. I set up the projector in the living room and with only the sputter of fading firelight I reveled in melancholy, watching the happiness of Christmases long ago—Sky in a playpen filled with leftover Christmas ribbons, looking like a chubby gift himself when I pressed a sticky bow to his nose. Odessa and her first cowboy boots; Sky with a ventriloquist's dummy. Then Odessa got skis; Sky, a red bicycle. Every year, it seemed, Lee had recorded each Christmas morning's surprise with his old movie camera. There I was, with my beautiful children beside me. I was always in my bathrobe and nightgown and they were still in pajamas, a mountain of gift wrap nearly enveloping us. We were laughing and making funny faces. Sky made rabbit ears behind my bad hair.

Near the end of the reel we were outdoors, with snowmen. There was Rudolph, with a lightbulb for a nose (probably red), and a snowman who resembled Burl Ives with his goatee made of broom bristles. I never liked his character in that holiday cartoon because of the song he sang:

> *Silver and gold, silver and gold*
> *Ev'ryone wishes for silver and gold . . .*

It was Leonard Twyn, and his "yours is silver, mine is gold," all over again, unpleasant memories. *Everyone wishes for silver and gold.*

*I*n flickering black and white I use the broom to whack the snowman's head off. Sky and Odessa, shocked at first, attack me with mittened hands. Then we all join in ruining Frosty or whoever he is, push him over, tumble in the snow, collapse in hugs, and throw snowballs at the camera, which dips and dives and finally goes dark.

Did I watch these movies because it hurt so much? I wondered if I craved the anguish they brought because it was deeply familiar to me, or if I simply missed those precious years with all my heart.

13

The way I remembered it, early in September between eighth grade and high school, Polly and Sharon and I were invited to a slumber party at Carolina Sawyer's to celebrate her fourteenth birthday. It was a Saturday night, and we all rode our bikes there.

School would be starting next week, after Labor Day, and all we could talk about was going into high school. Mom had taken me to Appleton to get new school clothes. Polly came along and spent ten dollars on a light blue knit top to wear with jeans. I thought it was nice of her Grandma Cornbloom to give her the money because most of Polly's clothes had to come from her family's store, where the stock was tough and durable but hardly stylish. I bought underwear at Cornbloom's, but that was about all.

Polly adored Julie Andrews. Cookie and Gloria took us to see *The Sound of Music* at the Moonlite Drive-In and we sang the songs everywhere we went—especially "Edelweiss." That was my favorite because it had such nice harmony. Polly had hair cut short like Julie Andrews', kind of boyish. I was still trying for more of an angular Mary Quant look but it never stayed in place even with barrettes and a lot of hair spray and I usually ended up with a very stiff and sticky style. Marilyn Monroe had been dead for a couple of years and I was waiting for Sharon to peroxide her hair so she could achieve her goal of looking more like Marilyn but it bleached a lot lighter in the summer sun, anyway. We'd spend hours lying out on the roof over Gloria Piekarski's back porch, rubbing lemon juice in our hair to bleach it and Man Tan on our skin to hurry the bronze shade that was so desirable. When the Man Tan ran out, we mixed baby oil and iodine. We had orange palms all summer.

To show off my tan legs, I wore white shorts to Carolina's birthday party. Polly had on cut-off jeans, and Sharon wore a flowered mini-skirt, which was the latest rage. She loved really short skirts, but we told her she'd be in trouble wearing them in high school because the principal made you kneel down and if the hem of your skirt didn't touch the floor, you were sent home to put on something more appropriate.

At first, Carolina's party was pretty unremarkable. She and her mother had attempted to embellish the knotty pine rumpus room in their basement with blue and yellow crepe paper streamers that swooped languidly in the humidity and ultimately draped over and around us as we did the twist and danced to the newest Beatles album. It smelled like a mildewed basement down there, because it was. Everyone brought their latest albums and we blared the volume as loud as Carolina's record player would go.

No boys were allowed since it was a slumber party, but we knew they might show up anyway in case we'd sneak out in our pajamas. Carolina's mother was notorious for guarding the back door during sleepovers so Teddy had said they might not waste their time.

Around nine o'clock we had snacks, popcorn and cheese puffs, and Carolina's mom brought down some frozen pizzas she'd baked plus some cold Tab. We stopped dancing to sit on the damp tile floor and eat. I hated Tab, but they didn't have Coke or Pepsi, just Tab or orange Kool-Aid.

Music was playing while we were eating, I remember that. It's so strange how some things pair up in your memory as if they belong there, even though if you looked at them separately they'd be totally unrelated. "Do You Wanna Dance," from the new Beach Boys album was on the record player when Carolina asked if we wanted to see her make-out doll. She ran up to her bedroom to get it and made it dance to the song. It wasn't even clothed.

The ratty old thing flopped around and stuffing hung out of its lumpy fabric body. I thought it was sad, really, but everybody laughed. Even the doll's poor hairless head tossed from side to side as if it were enfeebled. I thought Carolina could at least have found some old doll clothes to give it a little dignity.

"This is what I practice kissing on!" Carolina laughed so hard she tumbled over backward, clutching the doll to her chest. Sometimes Carolina laughed so hard she peed her pants. Or she liked to claim she did.

"You mean, you practice kissing *Herbie* on," Merry Hudson teased.

"Show us how you do it!" Dottie Ogden begged.

"Yeah, show us, Carolina," I urged sarcastically, and she obliged by passionately planting her pursed lips wetly onto the tiny pout posed by the baby doll. It was disgusting.

"Let me try it," Dottie cried, caught up in the game.

Dottie wiped the doll's mouth with a napkin dipped in Tab, then kissed it like Carolina had.

"Mmmmmm," she moaned. "Oh, Herbie, you're so groovy!"

"Let's see that," Sharon said, taking the doll away from Dottie. "Here, Polly," she offered. "You kiss it now."

The rumpus room grew quiet.

Polly took the doll from Sharon and held it, but then she shook her head.

"This is stupid," she said. "I'm not going to kiss a doll."

"Then kiss Nell," Sharon ordered. The other girls whooped in delight. "See what it feels like," Sharon snickered, "and Nell, you have to kiss Polly back!"

It was like I was back in sixth grade when Sharon demanded that Teddy kiss me in front of her and Buck. I refused this time, too.

But the group of giggling girls would have it happen. Sharon stood behind me and held my arms in a tight grip while Carolina pressed Polly forward.

"Nellie?" Polly asked plaintively, as if we had a choice.

"Oh, go ahead," I said. "It won't kill us."

In fact, I kind of wondered what it would feel like to kiss a girl.

So we kissed. A quick kiss. Polly's lips were firm, like a boy's. Everybody shrieked and applauded.

Sharon let go of my arms so I grabbed Polly's head and pulled her toward me to kiss her again, to demonstrate that I wasn't a bit scared. This time it was Polly who pulled away and I noticed her eyes were wet.

More screams, and Carolina's mother opened the door at the top of the stairs.

"Would you girls please settle down? We have to get up in the morning and go to church. Now I'm *not* going to tell you again!"

But she did.

Around eleven we gorged on potato chips, which I was certain would cause my acne to erupt with obscene pustules on my forehead. I had little enthusiasm for dancing or entertainment of any kind. In fact, I felt a little sick. I noticed Polly was curled up in a corner, pretending to sleep.

But Sharon wasn't pooped. She announced that she wanted to go for a "Chocolate Dip."

"Is that an ice-cream cone?" Dottie asked. "Because if it is, I don't think there's any place open where you could buy one; it's too late."

"Oh, my God, Dottie," Sharon squealed, "I can't believe you guys are so dense! It's like a skinny dip, except you do it in the dark. I'm going to ride my bike out to Bear Lake. Anybody else want to come along?"

"My mother won't let you out of the house," Carolina warned, but Sharon said she'd wait until Carolina's parents were in bed.

I tried to imagine what it would feel like, swimming naked at night. Pretty good, I guess, but I was getting tired.

Polly stupidly said she'd go along with Sharon but then added, "I don't have my swimsuit," and everybody laughed. Polly blushed. A couple other girls said they'd go along just to *watch,* but Sharon said, "If you're coming along you have to take off your clothes and go into the water. Those are the Chocolate Dip rules."

"*Your* rules . . . ," Polly mumbled.

"Sharon, I don't think it's very nice of you to come to my slumber party and then leave before we even have the birthday cake and sing 'Happy Birthday' and not let any of the rest of us come along," Carolina pouted.

"She's right," I told Sharon. "It *is* Carolina's birthday party . . ."

"And I'm going to open my presents pretty soon, too, so I think you'd better stick around."

Sharon was quiet for a while, but she warmed up again when Carolina opened her gifts that included a new Beatles album and the game Operation, which consumed our interest for maybe another hour.

"Okay, girls! Now that's *really* enough. I'm through warning you," Carolina's mother shouted through the din. "Lights out! And I'm *not kidding! Go to sleep!*"

She flicked the switch at the top of the stairs and the lights went out.

We spread our sleeping bags out on the vinyl tile floor and copies of *Modern Romance* were passed around the room. The more lurid parts were read aloud by flashlight and there was much muted shrieking at stories like "My Dentist Made Me His Love Slave" and "100 Ways to Discover If He's Cheating on You."

Mrs. Sawyer lost it. "If you girls don't quiet down, I'm taking every one of you home! Shut the hell up and *go to sleep, goddammit!*"

She didn't seem to notice that Dottie and Merry were sharing a cigarette.

*L*ater, after we could hear a few snores of contentment, Sharon whispered across my sleeping bag to Polly, "Let's go."

I was on the verge of sleep but I didn't want Polly to go swimming with Sharon because Polly wasn't a very good swimmer and Sharon was.

So, as it ended up, Sharon's "Chocolate Dip" was endured by the three of us. We crept up the basement stairs and out of the now unguarded back door of Carolina's house as if we were burglars.

"I wish we could wait a while," I told Polly when we got on our bikes. "It probably hasn't been an hour since we ate birthday cake and I don't feel so hot."

"You can stall so you don't get cramps," Polly replied. "Besides, it'll take us half an hour to bike to Bear Lake."

Sharon was pedaling way ahead of us already and couldn't hear the two of us agree that we wouldn't have to go in very deep, just far enough to cover our shoulders. We could squat down in shallow water so Sharon wouldn't know.

The village was silent and there was very little traffic, which was a good thing because we didn't have lights on our bikes. The moon was bright, though, and it helped to illuminate our way.

On Saturday nights, wedding dances were frequently held at the Bear Lake Pavilion. That night's dance was winding down because it was close to bar time. Couples were wobbling out to their cars. No-Toe-Joe sat on the veranda, looking vacantly out at the lake as if there was something out there to see.

A middle-aged man in short sleeves leaned near the door where rice granules littered the floor like sleet. He didn't seem to notice we were wearing our pajamas. "Can I offer to buy youse nice girls a drink?"

"Why are we stopping here?" I asked Sharon while straddling my bike, crossing my arms over my chest in modesty. "I thought we were going to the beach . . ."

"I'll take a beer," Polly said, showing off for Sharon, who already had a dripping cold bottle of Schlitz in her fist and was chugging it down like a pro.

"I don't drink," I offered primly. At Methodist church camp earlier that summer I'd signed a pledge to treat my body like a temple. That meant no drinking, no smoking, and probably (although it was unspoken) no going all the way until I was married.

The drunk pulled more chilled beer and bottles of soda from the washtub of melting ice, then tipped it off the edge of the porch and onto our feet, causing us to jump and stumble over our bikes. He thought it was hilarious, before he slipped and fell.

The ice bath was so freezing cold in the still-warm summer night that it felt as though my legs were seared with fire instead of cooled.

"Here," Sharon teased, sticking a slab of smooth ice inside the elastic waistband of my pajama pants.

"Stop it, Sharon!"

"Let's go," Polly said.

No-Toe-Joe must have witnessed all of this.

I was afraid Polly would get sick from drinking beer. After all, Sharon was older. And Polish. They drank beer over at her Aunt Gloria's all the time. "Those Polacks are guzzling again," Mother would say, tsk-tsking, while Dad looked out the dining room window with a kind of wistful glance.

Tall pines grew in a dense grove not far beyond the pavilion. Their aromatic scent blended with the humid summer night and the sour tang of beer. We propped our bikes against rough trunks sticky with pitch and stood in the shadows, waiting.

Pretty soon the drunk was gone and No-Toe was, too. The band had finished playing. Cars were leaving the parking lot.

We stood apart to take off our clothes. Polly and I were shy about our nudity. "You go first," I whispered from behind a tree.

"No, you!"

The lake was stirred with quiet magic in the breeze and the moon's muted glow.

From where we stood, we could see Sharon clearly enough. She was ripping her pajamas off right out in the open, on the grassy shelf that bordered the sandy decline to the water's edge. The whiteness of her skin was soft with the creamy wash of moonlight.

Polly hit the water first, but I think that was so Sharon and I wouldn't have time to notice her. All of a sudden, there she was on the sandy beach, dashing in. She flopped under the surface; then her head emerged and she was laughing.

"Come in, you guys! This is really fun!"

I followed, in a swift and shrieking race to the shore where I kicked up camouflaging sheets of water until I was far enough in the lake to bend my knees and cover my chest.

"Last one in is a rotten egg," Polly shouted at Sharon.

I turned, having reached Polly's side, and we watched Sharon, standing alone.

"She looks like a goddess," I said. "Like Diana the Huntress." It was my favorite sculpture.

"I know," Polly added, gasping. "She really does. Maybe it's the moon."

Sharon was standing, ivory white and innocent in front of the pines, when a gauzy layer of clouds caught the moonlight like a shawl of sheer chiffon. She didn't seem real. I don't know how much time passed but I heard Polly suck in her breath and I did, too. Then I dunked my head underwater, so Polly would think that was why.

Sharon looked like a movie star, I thought when I came back up and wiped the water from my glasses.

Still pausing, as if listening to far-off music or frozen by moon-light, Sharon struck a dramatic pose and I was certain that she smiled.

"She's smiling," I whispered to Polly.

"I know," Polly said. She hadn't taken her eyes off her.

Sharon walked out to the end of the pier with a Miss America walk, like she was balancing books on her head—something Polly and I tried when we read that's what models did. There was a neat shadow of pubic hair visible low on Sharon's belly when she moved. When Sharon reached the end of the pier she paused, opened her arms wide, drew them above her head, and dove off, barely breaking the water and leaving only the slightest ripple as proof.

You could only see her limp when she was barefoot, I realized, and only barely then. Maybe she walked on tiptoe with one foot to make up for it. I didn't know. But I was certain that I had never seen Sharon look more beautiful than she did that night.

Polly and I watched her swim out to the raft, where she pulled her-self up to the tarpaulin surface. Drops of water glistened and spilled from her gleaming body. Then, calmly, gracefully, with deliberate

227

poise, Sharon climbed up each step of the ladder to reach the high dive. Again, Sharon paused, posed, then swept her arms and completed a perfect swan dive into the pond. Another sleek entry. Sharon swam like a seal.

As soon as she slid into the water we heard the whistles.

"Yeah, Sharon!" A boy's voice shouted.

There was applause. Boys hooted and yelled, "Do it again" and "Let's have another look!"

"How 'bout them jugs!" another guy rudely snorted.

I worried that it might be Teddy and Buck. I didn't want them to see me without any clothes on! Then I worried they'd steal our pajamas as a joke and we might be stuck in the water all night.

Instead, it was worse. My glasses were drizzled but I could see who they really were: high school boys, five tough boys I didn't know who were from another town. I'd seen them hanging around. Sharon had stopped to flirt with them once when we were walking home from school and I had left her there with them because they scared me.

Now the boys raced out to the end of the pier, one after another, beer bottles in their hands, dropping their pants as they ran, laughing and tripping in their eagerness to dive in and surround Sharon.

"Should we rescue her?" Polly asked, worried.

"She isn't calling for help," I said, "or trying to get away!"

Actually, it seemed that Sharon was enjoying herself. A fast and efficient swimmer, she swam ahead of the cluster of boys, who had trouble keeping up. When she had a good lead, she flipped over on her back and leisurely did the backstroke for a while, lifting her head to check their pathetic process. One by one they dropped behind, exhausted in their effort to capture the elusive mermaid.

"Little prick tease!" one of them shouted.

"Stupid fuck!"

"Goddamn cunt!"

Sharon laughed and slipped away with an easy sidestroke. Polly and I could see her watch them as they turned back.

Luckily, we must have been practically invisible to everyone else.

"I don't think those guys even noticed us."

"If they did, they didn't care," I said.

We were both shivering, hugging our shoulders. I was covered with goose bumps. I knew my lips must be turning blue.

"Let's go," I whispered, after we heard the squealing tires of a departing car.

"What about Sharon?" Polly asked.

Sharon was almost over on the other side of the lake, floating on her back in undulations of moonlight, taking her time. If she kept going, she'd soon end up in front of the Old Crow's.

"I'm going, Polly. You can stay here and wait for her if you want to."

Lights in the pavilion were being turned off, one by one.

There was a long pause before Polly said, "I'm coming, too."

"We're leaving, Sharon," I cupped my hands to my mouth and called to her.

Polly called, too, "We're going . . ."

"Okay," she answered.

I think she answered. I really thought I heard her voice.

I asked Polly over and over if Sharon answered, and every time Polly said yes. *Yes,* Sharon knew we were leaving and that we were going back to Carolina's before we got caught.

I felt really cold, riding my bike in damp pajamas. I felt guilty leaving Sharon behind, but Polly must have felt even guiltier because we hadn't gone half a mile before Polly insisted, "I'm going back. Wait for me at the bandstand."

She turned her bike around and headed for the lake. "Make it quick," I called. "If Carolina's mother calls my parents . . ."

I didn't have to finish the sentence.

"Be careful," I whispered after her but Polly was already enveloped by the night.

$\mathcal{I}$ don't know how long I waited. I was shivering cold but I might have dozed off in the grass. This was where Teddy and I made out after Friday night movies, right beside the slanted metal door that led underneath the bandstand where the music stands and the folding chairs were stored. The grass there was deep and soft.

"Let's go." Polly was standing above me. She seemed in a hurry.

"Where's Sharon?" I asked, noting with dismay that the eastern sky was already pale with approaching dawn.

"I don't know where she went. Maybe those guys came back again."

Poor Polly. I knew she wanted to help Sharon if she needed to be rescued. She would like to be a hero and impress her. It always seemed so important to Polly to win Sharon's respect.

"I found this." She held out her hand and in her palm lay some brown ribbons with small cloth rectangles attached.

"Her scapular," I whispered with astonishment. "Where'd you find it?"

"On the shore. In the sand. Maybe she took it off before she went in the water."

"And then, afterward, she couldn't find it in the dark," I suggested. "Maybe she's already at Carolina's. She could've beat us back there; you were gone for so long!"

"Maybe . . . ," Polly said, hopefully. But I knew she doubted the odds of that happening, just as I did.

We stole back down to the rumpus room and slid into our sleeping bags as the sun was coming up. Sharon's sleeping bag was still empty. Those boys had probably come back and she had gone with them. That was so like her. I was angry because she caused us to worry. Of course she would turn up later.

I went to sleep.

On our way back to Carolina's, Polly and I had made a pact. In case, just *in case* Sharon wasn't waiting back at Carolina's, just *in case* Sharon had gone off somewhere to drink beer with those boys, we *would not tell anyone* about going for the Chocolate Dip with her. Never. And Polly promised she would hide the scapular.

"She's so boy crazy," Dottie and the other girls agreed the next morning when Sharon still had not returned.

"She's probably with Teddy Carter," Carolina said, grinning wickedly at me.

"I saw her touch herself once," Merry offered, "in the shower room after the rest of us played basketball. She wasn't even sweaty, but she took a shower with us anyway."

"I heard she let Mr. Bittner kiss her," Hannah said, her voice scornful and sour-edged.

Polly and I exchanged wary glances, making a big production out of rubbing our eyes and yawning and saying how well we slept and how hungry we were for breakfast, how we had not heard a thing when Sharon had gotten up out of her sleeping bag at night. We certainly were not aware that she had left! Were the pancakes ready? Polly even ate some bacon.

In the back of my mind was the toxic fortune I'd told for Sharon weeks ago. But that had absolutely nothing to do with Sharon's swim. The Chocolate Dip had been Sharon's idea, not mine.

You can believe anything if you tell yourself over and over that it's true. You can be pretty convincing.

They found her body the next afternoon, washed up on the shore of the lake. At first, reports claimed Sharon probably suffered a cramp. She had eaten a lot at the party, Carolina's mother explained (as if she knew). What about beer, I wondered, but Polly and I kept silent. We both knew Sharon was an excellent swimmer.

Everyone at Carolina's party had heard her say she wanted to go for a Chocolate Dip, but the others said nothing when we were each questioned by the county sheriff. I can't say for sure, but Carolina's mother may have had a few words with Carolina. Polly and I were questioned first and the most because we were Sharon's best friends.

Polly and I kept our pact about not admitting we had gone with Sharon for the Chocolate Dip. We didn't want our parents to know that we'd taken our bikes on the highway in the dark, and we sure didn't want them to know that we'd gone swimming in the nude!

There was water in her lungs, the county coroner said. Sharon Gallagher was a victim of accidental drowning. Sad but true. Little

Wolf mourned the loss of a beautiful young girl who had overcome the terrible afflictions of polio and a broken home and was loved by everyone. That's what newspaper articles said all over the entire state of Wisconsin.

The case was closed.

14

*H*enry rode along as Polly and I drove to Little Wolf. Curled up on the back seat, Henry was content. Polly, seated next to me, was not.

"Why did you insist on coming along if all you're going to do is bitch?" I complained.

Polly and I had been quarreling ever since I picked her up at her place around ten o'clock. "You're acting as if it was my fault that my car had a flat tire. I wanted to get an early start, too, if you'll recall. George wasn't home so I had to call a garage and with that little temporary tire you're not supposed to go more than fifty miles. So I had to get a new one. Stuff it, okay?"

There had been no flat tire; it had been Angella who'd kept me from leaving, who had been inspired that morning to write another chapter for her autobiography. This installment was about her mother, *the ogress who had to be propitiated at any cost*. According to Angella, she had been beaten by her heartless mother every day.

I had very delicate skin and I was always a mass of black and blue welts and cuts that bled.

Angella said she was pulled down the front stairs by her long hair and her head banged against the wall. When she screamed, her mother said she'd give her something to scream about (which made *me* want to scream because it sounded so trite but I had to keep writing!). Once her mother hit her with a heavy tortoiseshell comb that broke in two. Despite the pain suffered from being struck, Angella was happy because the comb had been her mother's favorite. So she dared to laugh in her face. And on and on and on.

I suspected, but could not prove, that Angella was embellishing her stories to enhance the manuscript that Bittner was hot to publish, so she scooped up hours of my time to reminisce about all her lovers and exhaustive aspects of her attention-grabbing past. I worried that she watched my every move so she could capture me when she wanted. This morning, for example, I explicitly said I had no time for her.

Oh, but my dear Merrill, we are connected by an invisible bond. If you don't follow my wishes, I warn you—I am capable of causing great discomfort!

The "invisible bond" crap was trying my patience. And I already suffered discomfort: Angella and her harassment were affecting my life in ways that proved disagreeable for me and for my friends.

"You didn't have to come along with me, Polly. You *wanted* to."

"Oh, shut the fuck up," she said. "I'm tired of hearing you whine."

How I would love to be able to spit that at Angella!

The March countryside would have looked pretty dismal even without the rain. It was too early for green sprouts to relieve a landscape worked over by the hostile scour of winter. Holstein cows were dredged with mud, leftover snow on the edge of the road looked like something from the Pleistocene Age, and farmers with manure spreaders had bestowed an undercurrent of nose-pinching fertilizer on their fields.

"After you left Little Wolf, how much did you think about Sharon?" Polly asked.

234

"Not much at all," I admitted.

"We didn't talk about her in high school."

"We were busy with other stuff."

"You didn't think about her when you were in college?"

"Nope. Did you?"

"I don't think so. But what about when you were married to Lee, or when you had kids, or when you were married to Michael . . ."

"Thanks for reviewing the dregs, Polly."

"Your kids aren't dregs."

"I didn't mean my kids."

"You're saying you didn't think about Sharon until you saw her at Wocanaga?"

"Her apparition, you mean."

"Okay, her *apparition,* her ghost, whatever. Didn't you ever wonder why she chose that time and place to start haunting you?"

"She's not *haunting* me, Polly!"

"Well she's been annoying you like crazy, that's for sure. Every goddamn thing reminds you of Sharon. You went on and on about her at our class reunion last summer 'til I wanted to gag. You want me to remember every little thing I can about the night she drowned. You get all worked up quizzing Teddy about her and how she was in love with him and now you want to talk to No-Toe-Joe who for all we know might even be dead! No-Toe never uttered a word thirty years ago; what makes you think he'll talk to you now? Or that he can even remember who Sharon Gallagher was?"

"He'll remember Sharon," I said confidently. "He was there that night at Bear Lake."

"And since when have you turned into Nancy Drew? You connected with Sharon's spirit up at Wocanaga, too, just like you connected with Angella's. Nancy Drew, woo, woo wooo. . . ."

"You know, you didn't have to come along today—you could've stayed in Madison and played peek-a-boo with Henry."

I didn't mean to sound quite so huffy, but Polly still got on my nerves.

As it happened, finding No-Toe-Joe turned out to be much simpler than I'd thought. I stopped at the post office and they said

235

he was living with Miss Khrol. He had moved in to help care for her after her father died.

"Pretty bizarre, huh?" I asked Polly.

"Opposites attract?"

The decrepit little cottage had been replaced with a well-worn mobile home in roughly the same area. Somewhat more substantial than the Khrol's tar-paper shack, the trailer had a big rusted dent in the front and sat on a definite slant.

I'd been pondering how to explain my surprise visit, if either of them were still alive. Bursting in from the past and asking someone to recall everything they could about a tragic event that occurred thirty-five years ago was a bit of a stretch, but I was determined to try. I'd carefully pinpoint the date and time for them (which was clearly in *my* mind) and recapture the feeling of that evening—the full moon, the humid night, the stillness of the water. I knew Miss Khrol's father had bad eyesight and never went out at night so he wouldn't have had anything to add, even if he were living. Which I now knew he wasn't.

The former site of Miss Khrol's home was only a mound of weeds. There was a ramp to the front door of the trailer. No-Toe-Joe (wordlessly) invited us inside where the living room was neat and clean, albeit skewed toward the lake.

No-Toe had not grown any more talkative through the years. His hair was gray but nicely trimmed. He carried himself straight and tall, as always. I would say he walked like a stiff, but that would be more cruel than humorous.

Miss Khrol, however, was crumpled in her wheelchair and looked like a discarded doll. She seemed to have shrunk. The tiny little woman was bent over and supported by pillows, her hair as wild as ever springing around her head in a feathery white cumulus.

"Who is it?" she asked. Her voice rose barely above a murmur. "You have to tell me. I'm blind."

No-Toe offered us coffee from a sooty pot on the stove. Black syrup in chipped cups, the same delicate teacups Miss Khrol had always used. I wanted to weep.

"It's Eleanora Grendon, Miss Khrol. I visited you when I was a little girl. We played cards," I said very loudly.

"You're the girl who stole my garden gnome."

"Well, yes, that too . . ."

"Naughty. Naughty girl. Bad girl. You should have been spanked!"

"Nell," Polly intervened softly, "Henry probably needs a walk."

"Who's Henry?" Miss Khrol demanded. "Is that another naughty girl?"

"It's my friend Polly," I told her. "She's going to walk the dog."

"Dog? I don't have a dog. Joe doesn't have a dog, either. What dog are you talking about?"

"Miss Khrol," I tried to gain some control of the visit, "I wondered if you might remember the night Sharon Gallagher drowned."

"Good luck," Polly mumbled as she went out the door.

"Never heard of her."

"The girl who drowned. In the lake. Right out there," I pointed, forgetting for a moment she was blind.

"Nice," No-Toe sputtered. "N . . . ice."

Wow. He said something. I was stunned. *Nice*. Of course he thought Sharon was nice. All the guys did.

"Do *you* remember that night?" I spun around, asking him. "You were at the pavilion when we rode out there on our bikes. It was after midnight. Do you remember?"

"N . . . ice," he said again, his face so red it looked as if he'd been boiled.

"Ready to go?"

Polly was sticking her head back in the door.

"N . . . ice," No-Toe said to Polly.

"Nell," she said quickly, "I think this is a lost cause."

I said good-bye to Miss Khrol and shook No-Toe's hand and thanked him for the coffee. Truthfully, I could not escape from there fast enough.

"Satisfied?" Polly asked. "A crazy old blind woman and a crazy old man who can't say a word. You hit the jackpot."

"Oh, shut up," I replied. "I'm going to drive around the lake to the beach."

"Let's not," Polly said. "I'd rather go home."

"I want you to show me where you found Sharon's scapular."

"What for?"

"Just because. Because you never mentioned it again after you showed it to me that night. And because I didn't tell the sheriff. You didn't, either. I suppose you still treasure it . . ."

"I don't know," she said vaguely. But when I looked over at Polly her face held a telltale blush. "I might be able to find it. What do you want it for?"

I knew she would laugh if I told her I wanted to try to psychometrize it, like I'd been taught in Grace Waverly's workshop. Maybe the scapular held a secret that now, after all these years, I'd finally be able to discern.

Of course I told her. And of course, as predicted, she laughed.

We shared a pizza at Bear Lake and afterward walked down to the sandy beach where the frozen lake was beginning to melt. Henry, freed from the car, was eager to romp and frolic. Polly threw a tennis ball into the grove of pines for him to fetch while we stood by the shore. I told her I'd had an e-mail from Teddy.

"So?"

"So, he found some old newspaper clippings that mentioned Sharon's death. The coroner's report said she died from drowning."

"So? We've known that all along."

"Yes, but did you know who the wedding dance was for that night? Teddy discovered it was for Karl Bittner's sister."

"I knew he was here."

"Of course," I replied, then I paused. "Polly . . . how did you know he was here?"

Polly took the ball from Henry's mouth and threw it into the pines again.

"I haven't told you everything," she said, finally.

"What do you mean?"

"About that night. The Chocolate Dip. Sharon . . ."

"I'll bet it's about the scapular," I said, certain that she'd kept the artifact for more than simply a souvenir of our old friend.

"In a way, I suppose it is," she admitted. "I *did* find it on the beach, in the sand. Isn't that what I told you?"

"Yes," I agreed. "So what's the rest of the story?"

I knew I sounded flippant, but she had just accused me of obsessing over Sharon so I was weirdly satisfied to hear there was something *she* had obsessed about for almost forty years, too.

Polly stared at the damp yellow ball that Henry had brought back to her. Her expression had changed. I thought she was going to cry.

"I came back here on my bike, and Sharon had come out of the water."

"You told me you couldn't find her!"

"Sharon was out of the water and still wet but when she saw me she covered herself up with a man's shirt."

I leaned over to pick a little white snail shell out of the sand. I didn't want Polly to know I could see how upset she was. I also didn't want to say anything to interrupt Polly's impromptu confession. The snail shells were tiny calcium spirals, wound tightly, empty now. I used to like to break them apart in my palm and trace the whorl inside, a minuscule world.

"She was surprised to see me. I thought the shirt belonged to one of those boys and she was going to go with them. I guess she really wanted us out of the way all along. Then she said . . . some stuff."

"Like what?" I asked.

"Just a minute. I've got to blow my nose."

I dug a tissue out of my purse and handed it to her.

"Sharon said some hurtful things. It was probably my fault. I told her she'd better get back to Carolina's or she'd get in trouble. But she said she didn't want to go back; she had other plans. And we were the ones who were in trouble. You and I. And would I please get the hell out of there."

"I don't get it," I said.

"She said I was queer and you were a fairy because we liked kissing

239

each other at Carolina's house that night. And everybody knew we did that all the time. And we were perverts."

"Oh, Polly . . ." That sounded like something Sharon would say, all right. But Polly had never revealed these callous words. Not in high school. Not in college. I loved my dear friend Polly, but there was nothing sexual about our relationship. Polly was simply . . . she was my Polly. I loved her for who she was.

"I got mad," Polly continued, "so I took her pajamas and I threw them in the lake."

"Did she get upset?"

"She was like a rabid dog! She whirled on me and tried to knock me over. We fought for a while. Remember, that was the summer I wanted to be a stuntwoman? She was bigger, but I could take her down."

"So . . . what happened?"

Polly blew her nose again. I handed her another tissue.

"Oh, shit," Polly said, her voice filled with remorse. "Her weak leg," Polly sighed. "I'm not proud of this, Nell."

I took the tennis ball from her and threw it for Henry, to quiet his whimpering. This time he dropped it in the frigid water, splashed in himself, and lapped a long drink.

"While Sharon was sitting here on the beach rubbing her bad leg, I ran and got some of that ice they dumped out of the beer tub. I came back and she was trying to get up so I tackled her again and sat on her and stuffed it down her throat."

"Polly! The ice? What the hell?"

"I wanted to punish her for saying what she said, Nellie! I wanted to wash out her mouth with ice. But the more ice I stuffed in her mouth, the more I wanted her to choke. I even thought if it melted she'd breathe it down into her lungs and everybody would think she drowned."

"You were that angry? *Polly!*"

"I wanted to hurt her, that's all I wanted to do."

"I don't get it . . ." I was silent, envisioning the scene clearly in my mind, and the burden Polly had carried all these years.

"There's something else. The man's shirt. The one she put on to cover up with. When I tackled her with the ice I smelled Old Spice."

"Jesus. Bittner was here, on the beach?"

"He was *somewhere*," Polly said. "He wasn't far away because Sharon was wearing his shirt. I was mad at Sharon and when I smelled Old Spice I was mad at Bittner, too."

"Wow," I shuddered. "All these years, you've wondered if you drowned her?"

"I didn't really want to know," Polly admitted. She was hugging Henry tightly to her side, unaware of how wet he was getting her with his whapping tail.

"Sharon was still okay when I dragged her onto the pier and pushed her in the lake. I heard her gag. Then I got on my bike and rode into town where I found you. I never turned around to look. But just now, over at the Old Crow's . . ."

"I wish you wouldn't call her that."

Polly released the dog and threw the ball.

"Okay, over at Miss Khrol's, I heard No-Toe-Joe say 'n . . . ice.' *Ice!* I think he might have watched me try to choke her. I think he knows. I'll bet Bittner does, too."

"If either of them thought you were responsible for her death, why didn't they come forward at the time?"

Polly shrugged. "I don't know."

Henry came when I called, then shook himself right next to me.

"Let's go," I said and reached out to hold Polly in my arms. "I'll love you forever, you know that; we've been best friends almost all of our lives. I'd have been angry with Sharon, too. And you know how much I detest Bittner! But there's no way you caused Sharon to die. I know you didn't. I'll bet there's a way we can prove it."

I wasn't sure about that last part, but I'd give it my best try.

"Don't you think it's weird that you didn't think about Sharon until you saw her at Wocanaga," Polly asked, getting in the car. "After you took your mediumship lessons? Don't you think that's strange?"

"What? That I saw her apparition or that I didn't think of her until then?"

"Both. It's like what you were doing at Wocanaga brought Sharon back to you. And maybe that day when she showed up it was because I came along."

I turned the heater on high to dry Henry's wet fur. I was shivering, too, not only because Henry got my jeans wet.

Although she knew nothing about Spiritualism, this time Polly might have been right. I was well aware that beginning mediums were susceptible to the intrusion of malicious spirits, but I'd only been thinking about Angella in that light.

"That's when Bittner came back into your life, too," Polly continued. "It's like you caught a spook virus up there or something."

"C'mon . . ."

"I mean," Polly continued as I steered the car back out to the highway, "if you hadn't gotten involved with spirits up at Wocanaga and being a medium and everything, you might never have been bothered by Sharon again. You didn't think about her when you had children of your own, or when you were married to Michael—it's only been the last year or so, right?"

I had been so busy with Angella that I had not taken the time to examine the capacity in which my recent concerns about Sharon had originated. But Polly (much as I hated to admit it) had made a valid point. Sharon may have been another "deceiver," just like Angella Wing.

Part 3

15

If you shape a bolus out of coconut-oil butter and herbs and stuff three of them into your vagina at the same time, every night except Sunday (a day of rest), the evil entity that's possessing you is supposed to be cast from your body. Roll each bolus into the size of a finger and include squaw wine, yellow dock root, comfrey root, marshmallow root, chickweed, goldenseal root, and mullein leaves.

Sure, I was desperate, but what would I tell my gynecologist if I developed a vaginal inflammation and he discovered all that garbage in there?

Another source advocated exchanging entities during sexual intercourse. Fine and dandy, but wouldn't that mean having sex with someone you hate?

It was a limp substitute, but I looked all over town and found a small topaz to wear in my bra. Irene, the bra-stone woman from my Wocanaga workshop, claimed topaz has powerful protective characteristics and is helpful in dispelling negative energies and negative magic. The lump was slightly uncomfortable and I worried the pebble might fall out and get lost, but Irene had said it was important to wear the stone next to one's skin so every day after my shower I taped the topaz between my breasts with fresh surgical tape.

What a paradox. Just as I'd spent an inordinate amount of time trying to comprehend what it meant to be channeling Angella, I was now devoting way too much of my life to get rid of her.

With a guaranteed publisher for her memoirs, Angella would not shut up. She woke me from sleep to note her latest inspiration. If I lay awake, resolute in my refusal to go to my computer, I became so thirsty I could barely swallow. Or hungry! One night I devoured an entire carton of Ben and Jerry's New York Super Fudge Chunk.

Or Henry needed to pee. Or *I* did, too.

When it came to recording her life story, Angella had no shame.

For at least a week she went on about her lovers. How she taught them, how grateful they were, how she tired of them after a while and treated them as shabbily as some of them had treated her. Educating the lovers in her life to be better in bed was her way of feeling superior to them, she said. Afterward she received letters (all of which she kept) thanking her for "improving them." I wondered how many women were the unknowing recipients of Angella's seductive skills.

She seemed captivated by whatever random "gem" of memory inspired her at that moment. Such as:

> *Montgomery Clift was the only authentic genius we had in the acting department, and I worshipped him.*

Almost every thing else was abandoned in the dust of her personal reflection. Her blog no longer contained anything about Spiritualism, but she still had readers.

> *Actresses are a breed apart. We're easily upset, easily hurt, and ravenous for love and acceptance. Sir John Gielgud said the only way to deal with us is by using "ruthlessness combined with politeness," because an actor's perceptions are so delicate and complex. We are more than mere intermediaries for the writers' words.*

Damn you, Angella—was that supposed to be a joke? That's exactly what I was for Angella: a mere intermediary for her words.

I sought chapters in mediumship manuals that warned against allowing one's self to be under the influence of a spirit who either cannot or will not withdraw. One book advised invoking the assistance of a powerful medium who possessed the strength to deal with it. Another book counseled the opposite: "You should not go to this, that, and the other person for advice and 'cure'—the power to overcome is within!"

If I discussed Angella's domination with Grace Waverly, for example, such an admission would only strengthen Angella's certainty that I was her plaything and powerless to resist.

❧

Spring Break. Polly was teaching at the Museum of Holography in Chicago again. George and Breeze flew to Paris, where George's trio was playing at an international jazz festival. I wondered, but did not ask, if George had invited Breeze or if she had insisted on going along.

At least I had Henry as my companion. His bladder and other bodily needs took me outdoors several times a day where I breathed fresh spring air that cleansed my brain of numbness and fatigue. Like a perennial whose dormant root beneath the surface begins to stir in the spring warmth, something shifted inside me. Henry and I raked dead leaves from the flowerbeds. We cleaned out the garage. We sat in the sun and debated how to ruthlessly (but politely) get rid of a chronic pain in the ass.

I decided to take a chance and talk with Grace. I had been rude the last time we spoke—hard to believe that was last Thanksgiving!

Wisconsin was enjoying an unusually early, warm, and sunny spring. I set my jacket aside and wore a hand-knit cardigan with my jeans.

Henry and I arrived at Grace's cottage in Wocanaga just in time for the picnic I had brought along to share. She was now very weak and frail, and without too much trouble I was able to help her into my car by myself. I drove off the path and close to Inspiration Point, where I unfolded a couple of plastic lawn chairs under the dancing new leaves of an oak.

"This is such a treat, Eleanora," Grace said, patting Henry's furry head. "I haven't been down here in such a long time. And how glorious to sit in the sun! What a lovely gift you've given me!"

She ate only a small portion of the cheese and tomato sandwich I had prepared, and if I say her "spirits were good" that could sound like a really bad pun but the truth is, Grace was in good spirits. I don't know how else to express her upbeat attitude.

That all changed after I packed our picnic things away.

I had never before had the courage to make my way down to the broken rim of the point. Chunks of limestone steps led there, and the flat limestone plate slanted unevenly. The slightest lapse in judgment—stumbling on a stone or a patch of slippery lichens— could send one skidding over the brink.

The question spilled out before I had an opportunity to swallow.

"Would you like to go down to the edge?" I asked Grace. "I'll take your arm and we'll see what things look like from there."

She resisted, her arthritic knuckles white from clutching the plastic chair.

"You may never have this opportunity again," I cajoled, taking her arm. "I'll bet this isn't called 'Inspiration Point' for nothing! You can trust me—I won't let go of you, I promise."

"I don't know . . ." Grace's voice was weak with uncertainty. "The steps . . ."

We were seated near the tall pine where mediums, their backs to the abyss, performed their readings at message services. This was the spot where I, as "Merrill Chase," had looked out over my audience to see Sharon's apparition behind Mr. Bittner. This was where I clung to the tree when I felt I would certainly faint.

Mediums, as far as I knew, never ventured down the rocky incline with its protruding roots. I did not know anyone who'd attempted those treacherous steps out to the point.

"I want to go back, now," Grace said, her eyes pleading with mine. "Please don't make me go down there with you!"

"Grace," I said sternly, "this is very important to me."

Roughly, I pried her hands from the arms of the chair and pulled Grace to a standing position. She shuffled, unsteadily, as I guided her down through the snarled roots and crumbling limestone. I supported her with one arm around her waist, practically carrying her slight body. With my other hand I clung to random branches, fighting the impulse of gravity.

"Please, Eleanora," Grace begged, "don't make me do this . . . I'm afraid . . ."

She wrested herself from my grasp and collapsed to her knees. I lost my balance and fell, too, slipping away from her on damp moss, pine needles, and gravel.

The sound of my sunglasses sliding off the edge seemed so strange. What was I doing there? What had I done?

Any further movement would send me over the precipice, too. When I finally stopped skidding, my head hung in space; my fingers frantically tried to find purchase in fragmenting stone.

All I could see was the tops of trees above me. I could hear pinecones and bits of gravel slip and fall onto the trees below. In my peripheral vision I could barely see Grace beside me in a broken heap.

"Grace," I called, uncertainly, "are you okay?"

I tested my balance and reached around to find something to grab. With every movement I could hear more limestone cascading. My heart was barely beating. I don't think I breathed. Desperately, I continued searching for a branch or root. I found a root and pulled, but it broke under my grasp. I found another, smaller one. I pulled. It held.

Amazingly, I was able to find a way to wedge the toe of my shoe in a crack of the limestone and that gave me enough stability to use the stable root to pull myself up over the edge with one leg, one arm, and another rush of stones.

Safe now from plummeting, I paused a moment to rest.

Grace lay still next to me, her body limp. But she was calling my name.

"Grace?" I called again. "Grace, can you hear me?"

She blinked, unseeing, but cried out, "Eleanora?"

"Don't move," I pleaded. "Don't move! Stay very still!"

Carefully, I slipped my cardigan from my body. I wrapped it around Grace, tied the arms, and inched my way back up the incline on my knees, pulling her.

Jesus Christ, what an insane thing I'd asked her to do! Angella! Damn you, evil bitch! You tried to kill us both!

It was a huge struggle, but I gradually got both of us back up the rocky slope. Grace's face was bruised, her arms were bleeding, her dress was torn, and I hurt inside and out My palms were painfully raw.

Henry was napping by the car. He had ignored all the excitement.

Back at her cottage at last, I insisted on calling a doctor but Grace just wanted to lie down. First I cut off my broken and bloody fingernails. Then I bathed her bruises and put salve on her cuts. It did not appear that she had broken any bones, but her knees and ankles were swollen.

"Oh, Grace, I am really, *really* sorry."

I told her it was Angella. She had been responsible for my urging Grace to walk down to the point. I was certain she had tried to push us off the cliff. "Or pull us," I added, remembering Angella's words about her mother pulling her down the stairs.

"I've heard enough of this, Eleanora," she stated flatly. "When you told me of your automatic writing, I warned you of the dangers," she said crossly. "It looks like your Angella has succeeded in possessing you."

She pounded on my arm with her bony fist, emphasizing every word. "You must not wait one single moment longer to get rid of her!"

"But I don't know what to do," I confessed tearfully. "That's why I'm here! Grace, I need your help!"

Grace fell back on her pillow. "Having once had a physical body of their own, undeveloped spirits want to use the body of another because it is familiar to them. Angella may have examined several hundred people before she found someone, like you, who fit her needs."

The dear woman was exhausted. I was still trembling, too.

"I feel responsible," Grace admitted, before fading into sleep again. "I brought you along in your unfoldment. I encouraged you to channel. I am troubled by your anguish. But I have so little strength of my own these days, I don't know how I can be of any aid!"

I hung around for an hour while Grace napped intermittently. On her refrigerator I noticed a note with a telephone number for Spence. He and his wife were now living in the village of Wocanaga and he arrived at her door within a few minutes. I was humiliated and embarrassed to explain the situation. Spence was consoling. He called Grace's doctor and while we waited for him to arrive he gave me an exercise to practice that he called the "Auric Egg."

*M*aybe hope is like helium. I felt lighter when I drove back to Madison. Grace's injuries were superficial, her doctor said. Spence promised he and his wife would watch her closely for several days.

Then I was reminded of Sharon's scapular, which I'd intended to bring along for Grace to psychometrize. Damn.

I called Polly on my cell phone and asked if she'd located Sharon's scapular. She admitted that she'd forgotten to look for it.

"Well, find it, will you?" I asked, with more impatience than I'd intended. "You'll be glad to know I'm finally giving up all this "medium*shit*," as you call it, but before I do, I want to see if I can get any vibes from Sharon's scapular."

"I'll look for it, I promise," Polly said. "It's just . . . the memories, you know?"

As soon as I got home, I announced to Angella's readers that Merrill Chase was closing down "Take Wing." I gave no excuses, only stating that her blog and her chat room would no longer exist.

Angella slipped in a small personal note:

When I was acting, I would ask myself, What secrets do I know? How much of what I say is actually meant or truthful? What is left unsaid? What needs to be done to obtain your objective, for instance? What must remain private? Get the picture?

The day after George returned from Paris, we walked Henry in the morning. I told him I'd give Breeze a reading but it had better be soon because I was giving up my mediumship.

"You've seen the light!" he said, with a smile.

"Or the dark side of the moon," I replied, and told him about my visit to Grace and our tumble down the hill.

"I'm going to need your help really soon," I said. "Don't forget, when you asked me to give Breeze a reading, you said you'd help me get rid of Angella. Does that mean you *believe* in her?"

"It means I believe in *you*," he replied, ruffling my hair.

16

*N*ow I second guessed everything. Depression overwhelmed me without notice. I was anxious all the time. When I couldn't sleep, I would find contentment in the piano jazz so beautifully cascading from George's studio on the third floor. The music brought pleasure in a couple of ways. First, it meant Breeze was not staying with him; and second, it was intimate to listen while he composed new work. It soothed me in a visceral way, too. Excuse the pun, but it gave me strength to ignore Angella's overtures. Sometimes I sat out in the hall in my pajamas with Henry's head in my lap. Sometimes I spread a blanket on the floor and lay down with a pillow. I envisioned the expert touch of George's fingers on the keys, imagined the touch of his fingers on my skin.

*B*reeze was aware that I was doing her reading as a favor for George. He brought her to my front door, introduced us, then left us alone. She was much nicer in person than I wanted her to be and much more beautiful, too. I worried about what I might say (with Angella's help) but my promise to George was vital.

In the bright afternoon sunlight my sunporch now seemed tawdry with a definite tendency toward carnival. I pulled the shades.

Because of my growing feelings for George, I had been balancing the risk of revealing a fortune that would encourage Breeze to fall in love with someone else (certainly easier said than done), make her move *far* away, or do *something* to get her out of his life.

She received my stock pre-reading spiel and her green eyes (I knew they'd be green!) looked frightened.

I told her to relax, recommended some breathing exercises, asked her to meditate, explained I wasn't always accurate and she should interpret whatever I said through the lens of her own experience, blah blah blah. The shtick was getting old. I was getting stale. I didn't give a damn anymore.

Her incredible green eyes were artless and innocent. I was touched by her lack of guile. She had a habit of tossing her silky auburn hair back from her face with a graceful sweep of her head like an impatient mare or brushing it from her eyes with long fingers and impeccably manicured nails (pale orange polish). She crossed her legs—long, flawless, slender. Color rose in her cheeks when I told her to place her feet squarely on the floor, close her eyes, and concentrate on a question that she would like to have answered.

Asking her to close her eyes was not essential but it helped me concentrate because I found her credulous glance difficult to avoid. I sensed a strong appeal for wish fulfillment. I didn't know if I could grant it. Or if I wanted to.

"As I come to you from the spirit side I can feel someone reaching out in a motherly way. I don't know if this is your actual mother or a stepmother or godmother, but it's someone who has had a motherly influence over you. And she is saying, I hear her tell me to let you know . . ."

Then suddenly I was blank. Silent. I began again.

"I'm sorry, I was interrupted by another spirit whose name begins with an L."

No reaction from Breeze.

"Lance? Leo? Lawrence?"

She still sat across from me, motionless, eyes closed.

Then I blurted out, "Leonard? I think . . . it sounds like Leonard. A young man named Leonard. He wants you to know your ring is silver, not gold . . ."

Geez, get a grip! She deserved more than that, I told myself. And how the hell did *he* get in there, anyway? Angella, no doubt.

"Leonard," I continued, fumbling. "Well, I do think it's something about a ring. Maybe not a gold or silver ring; it could be platinum."

Yeah, right, a ring. Ringing in my ears. That's what I was hearing! I was fashioning a sinister fortune for her on the spot.

"You're going to get a ring," Breeze smiled at that. "Or maybe it's more like ringing you up." She frowned. "You'll receive a special call, something meaningful."

"Let's see what the cards have to tell us," I offered.

I let her shuffle, then cut, then hand the deck back to me.

I told her the Queen of Diamonds represented a wealthy but malicious widow or divorcée who would be personally involved with her future affairs. There was mutual love between her and a young man but the Jack of Spades was reversed so some kind of deceit would attempt to separate them. In fact, Breeze would reject this man's offer of marriage (!) because of treachery. She must be cautious; there was danger lurking everywhere, mischief that could be very damaging.

I felt a little bit sorry about her fortune but, hey, this involved George and if I didn't look out for my *own* interests, who else was going to? Some of this I invented out of thin air, some seemed to come from the cards, and I knew Angella had her hand in it, too.

*T*hat evening I was quickly checking my e-mail when Angella slipped in and left a message. I was puzzled by her tone.

I can be filled with hostility for everyone and anyone who has taken advantage of me or thinks me weak and/or stupid. Lately you have been showing signs of indifference. I have the pleasure of making you sweat, of you not knowing from day to day whether

255

or not I will pay you back. I want you to remember this. Get the picture?

Then she called me her "Darling Merrill" and said she was issuing me a challenge. Implicit was the promise that if I followed her directions, she would consider departing. Her words were brusque. I had no idea what kind of "challenge" Angella was referring to, but she had said "Get the picture" before, and that was unlike her usual message. What picture could she be talking about? Or did she mean it sarcastically, like "Understand?"

Hey, if it would get rid of Angella, I'd get her goddamn picture and shove it up you-know-where.

I closed off my bedroom so even Henry couldn't slip in through the door and dutifully practiced Spence's "Auric Egg" without interruption twice a day, morning and night, as he had advised. I tried not to laugh. Seated on my bed in the lotus position I imagined a string attached to the top of my head, pulling up my spine. Then I visualized myself inside a huge egg, three feet in each direction from my navel. Pure white light seeped down through the top of the egg into my head and into my body.

It might sound silly, but Spence was right: the Auric Egg exercise brought serenity. It also made me very sleepy. Often, I found myself taking an unintentional Egg nap.

*S*ome people claim to be possessed by animal souls. And a few patients who've had organ transplants say they've experienced strange dreams and developed bad habits and cravings that mirror those of the original owner of their new liver, kidney, or heart.

I had no idea where Angella came from, but she was a tough nut to shake. When I began to list some of the little triumphs she'd had (my car accident, the fall on the ledge at Inspiration Point, inserting Leonard Twyn's snarky gold and silver remarks into Breeze's reading), my hand—still sore—routinely touched the topaz taped between my breasts. Was there a stronger gem?

She'd claimed she was issuing me a challenge. Hell, she was already enough of a challenge, herself; what additional test could she possibly require of me? As much as I dreaded the discovery, I asked her outright the next time she made an appearance.

It is part of my great insecurity that I have to be in control of a situation. Here's a lesson for you: the most important elements in acting are the <u>objective</u> and the <u>obstacle</u>. The successful way for an actor to use an objective is to realize not only what your character wants but also why he or she wants it. Get the picture? The pursuit of an objective must be expressed in both physical actions and verbal actions (words). Characters <u>do</u> things to <u>get</u> things. Are you so obtuse that I need to spell this out for you again?

"Get the picture." No, I wasn't stupid; I was getting the message. This was a test of *my* control versus hers. It was war.

"Get the picture." I asked George what he thought it meant.

"She might mean an actual picture," he suggested, "like a photograph. What does Polly think?"

"Polly and I haven't been in touch for a while," I admitted. "We had a . . . well, a kind of emotional incident a few weeks ago when we drove up to Little Wolf. I'll fill you in later. Right now, let's just think about *Get the picture*. Does she mean *Understand? Figure it out? Comprehend? Recognize what I'm saying?*"

"Maybe it's simpler than that," George suggested. "What about a *moving picture*? Angella was an actress . . ."

A moving picture! How had I missed that? It was certainly worth a try.

There was a new sign on the front door of the historical society. All who entered were warned that video surveillance was now everywhere. My comfy mausoleum had developed sinister undertones. Materials stored there were practically sacred; I couldn't imagine anyone daring to steal them.

The film and theater archivist was a pleasantly disheveled woman named Linda, who wore jeans and a flannel shirt. She welcomed me back into her cluttered office, where metal shelves were crammed with boxes of old films in rusty canisters and several desks held tilting towers of papers and files. Posters of 1950s films like *Love Me Tender* were taped to the walls.

I liked the informality, but it was a claustrophobic room with no windows. Linda was the only one working there. I felt less anxious when she left the door ajar to the Archives Research Room instead of closing us tight inside her jumbled closet.

"Pardon the mess," Linda said. "Our intern is on vacation but that's not much of an excuse; it always looks like this."

If the building was a mausoleum, the film research area was a tomb in the middle of the catacombs.

"How can I help you?" She offered me a chair.

I told her I was doing a thesis on early actresses who'd made the jump from radio to film, and I had come up with several words or terms that might bring more of them to light. She whipped through an advanced computer search much faster than I could. Linda tried *Angella, Wing, Ring, Twyn,* and *Leonard.* I even suggested *Breeze,* on a whim. *Quinn, Twin, Leo, Sharon, Khrol, Joe, Jack, Spade, Queen, Heart.* Mix and match. Nothing seemed to correspond.

I was ready to leave when she pointed to the screen.

"Um, I don't know if *this* is of any interest, but here's an unprocessed box of miscellaneous films from something called Twiningham-Lennox. Apparently it was a small U.K. film company, active for only a short time in the 1930s. There are several 16mm reels and an 8mm home movie. That's kind of odd."

Twiningham-Lennox. It was like Twyn, Len. Leonard Twyn. Was this another of Angella's heartless jokes?

"I think I'd like to have a look at that box," I said. My heart was pounding so hard that my voice quivered.

"No problem. But you'll have to submit a reference request. I can pull it from the vault and have it ready for you to view tomorrow."

$\mathcal{T}$ime. This was taking so much time. But this *picture* might be a lead. The relief of booting Angella had me almost diabolical with glee.

It was a plain cardboard box with a number on it, nothing fancy. It didn't even have a lid. There were some rusty film canisters inside, a few with labels, most without. Linda gave me a pair of white cotton gloves, mandatory for handling photographs or film, and took me further back into her labyrinth to a viewing room that not only had no windows but was also mostly meant to be used without lights. She threaded the first 16mm on a Steenbeck—a flatbed film-editing table with a mysterious assortment of gates and rollers that scans the frames of the film that are then visible on a screen. You can make the film speed up or slow down to a stop by turning a dial.

I had no idea what I was looking for, though I kept up my pretense of my "thesis." Linda told me to let her know if I needed any help. Then she turned out the lights, left the room, and closed the door.

There was no air in that room. It smelled vaguely of chemicals, maybe some kind of volatile film cleaner. I had to do a few deep breathing exercises to calm down but rejected the Auric-Egg. Meanwhile, the first Twiningham-Lennox movie chattered through the gates: *The Respectable Pearsons.* In about ten minutes I called Linda to show me how to rewind it (I didn't need to see it all, just enough to have a feeling that Angella Wing was not one of the actresses in the film) and she lined up the next one, *Hangtown,* a gruesome sci-fi thriller. No interest there. Linda threaded the third.

Ultramarine was about life in a futuristic English fishing village. I sped through that one pretty fast, too. *The Blue Flame* followed a shy country girl to her new life in London where she fell prey to temptations of the flesh. I'd have spent more time with that because the costuming was interesting, but it was almost noon.

If Angella had a message for me in one of these films, I was totally unmoved. Not a clue. I didn't sense that any of the actresses was Angella (I had no reason to believe that she had been cast in a British

259

film). Nor could I draw any conclusions from the titles or plots or locations or credits. Absolutely nothing rang a bell.

At the bottom of the box was a small cardboard container that Linda and I decided must contain an 8mm home movie. She dug out an 8mm viewer and set it up on another table. The lightbulb was burned out, so she went in search of a replacement. I told her I'd be back to have a look at that last film after lunch.

I had a quick sandwich at the Union and was back in half an hour. Linda was gone, but she'd left a note telling me to go ahead on my own.

The 8mm film, simply strung from reel to reel and passing over a light, was revealed in a viewing box much as the Steenbeck but the setup was more primitive. Rather than speeding it up or slowing it down by turning a switch, I cranked this little film by hand. It *was* an early black-and-white home movie. Linda had told me 8mm cameras were not introduced until 1932, and this was obviously a pioneer film of its kind.

It looked like footage of a party in California, probably Los Angeles but that was just a guess. Glamorous women waved at the camera and toasted it with martini glasses while whoever was holding the camera walked through the crowd and around the swimming pool. Men in pin-striped suits nipped at the waist were smoking pipes and cigars. I found it hard to watch the film and not get seasick with all the movement, but I regulated the speed and stopped every once in a while.

I was sweating. The little room was warmer now that it had been this morning. My stomach felt rocky; the pastrami on rye with all that mustard—not a good idea.

In the film, the cameraman had the camera grabbed from his hands by one of the women who focused it back at him. He was tall and dashing, broad shouldered, an obvious matinee idol even by today's standards. Then the camera caught a woman who smiled through the lens of the camera, directly at me. It was a personal smile, one that jumped out from the black-and-white film so that I instantly put my hands up to shield my eyes. Was *this* Angella?

There was something about her that made me back up over and over and note every little detail of her appearance. Obviously, I didn't know this woman, yet I had a feeling that I did. She was gorgeous, glamorous, with an upswept hairdo that was probably deep red. Her lipstick was dark, her slim eyebrows were carefully penciled, and her skin was velvety clear. She wore a dusky satin gown that clung to her lissome body (seems like the right word for this period), and the gleam of the fabric revealed every curve.

Then the film went dark. When an image again appeared, it was as if a curtain was pulled open and morning revealed. This was indoors, certainly a bedroom. In the center of the frame was an enormous bed with numerous pillows, a plush headboard, and a nude woman, asleep. The camera moved forward and the figure on the bed stirred. She must have been startled (did someone tell her, "Look this way, Darling!"?), for she sat up clumsily and clearly said (although silently,) "Go away!" as she covered her breasts and shook back loose curls that fell over her face.

But the camera would not leave. It seemed merciless, capturing her like this, unprepared for such a rude intrusion. The woman (the same one who'd smiled at me!) gestured again for the cameraman to quit filming. He did not.

The film continued moving through the gate and onto the little screen. Now I was mesmerized as the woman swept aside the sheet she had covered herself with, revealed her nudity, and threw herself at the lens. There was a blurry closeup of her enraged face before the film went black.

Wow. I rewound it. The scene was fascinating and clandestine. This bed had the impressions of two bodies in its silky depths. I studied the woman's face more closely and decided her expression was *not* one of rage, as I'd initially thought. Instead, she appeared to be expressing mock anger. As the film ended, on the very last frame, I was certain I caught a grin.

"I'm back. Need any help?"

"No, thanks, I'm wrapping things up."

I swiftly rewound the film and placed it back inside the box.

261

"Find anything of interest?"

I was eager to leave and peeled off the white cotton gloves.

"Would it be possible for me to come back on Monday and view this again?"

Linda said that wouldn't be a problem. She placed the box on one of her shelves and told me I could come in and help myself.

Before I left the archives, I had to stop at the reference desk and present my notebook for inspection. The rules for using the archives were clearly stated in a handout available there: Penalties for archival theft included a $10,000 fine and a prison term up to ten years.

I'd found a film, but I was blindly grasping for clues and awaiting written hints from a disembodied spirit. I had no idea if the film was relevant to Angella or not. Her evasive comments didn't help.

> *Oh, you are clever, my dear girl! I'm laughing now, Merrill. Haven't I told you I feel every shift in your mind's eye, the slightest breeze (and I don't mean that as a joke)?*
>
> *Half my life I practiced the Christian ethic, but I think the laws of Judaism work better—an eye for an eye; a tooth for a tooth. I will give everyone a fair shake to begin with but if someone considers this a weakness in me, and tries to take advantage of me, I will fight him until I win or die.*

Angella's resistance was astonishing. Her comment on the laws of Judaism gave me the idea to propose a "tit for tat," this for that, or quid pro quo. A blow for a blow, an eye for an eye, a tooth for a tooth, just as Angella had vowed. I'd "get the picture" for her if, in turn, she'd do something equivalent for me.

But even when she realized my intention of obtaining the Twiningham-Lennox film, an illegal act that put me at great risk, Angella's rhetoric remained severe:

> *My greatest weakness, Merrill, is my sensitivity to rejection by anyone I love. I cannot tolerate rejection. Because of my love*

you could hate me and I'd still admire you for all that you are, but please don't dismiss me!

Oh, give me a fucking break! Where were the sniveling violins? Rejecting Angella and suffering the consequences was a gamble I didn't mind taking anymore.

Once I'd psyched myself up to do it, I had to move quickly before I backed out.

Lee's box of family films, still unsorted, was in my upstairs study where I'd stowed them after my tearful viewing on Christmas Eve. I knew a few had been duds—overexposed or underexposed or never exposed at all (he'd left the lens cap on). I found what I wanted: an unexposed 8mm reel. I tucked it inside the waistband of my jeans and put on a hooded sweatshirt that I could zip up to conceal my impending criminal behavior.

My unpredictable obsessive-compulsive gene kicked in at the top of the stairs and I suffered a momentary pause. But I firmly subdued the temptation to view the film and make certain it was actually blank so I could press onward with my burglary scheme. If I began viewing Lee's home movies I'd become immersed in melancholia and . . . well, there'd go the entire afternoon.

Linda was at the film archives. The Twiningham-Lennox box was on the shelf where I'd left it.

"You think that holds some treasures for you?" Linda asked.

"Could be," I said. "I want to look at one of the films again."

"Help yourself. I have someone scheduled to use one of the Steenbecks at three o'clock but until then the room is all yours."

"Those stairs," I said, to cover up my rapid breathing, "I waited for the elevator but it didn't show up."

The truth, of course, was that I was on the very brink of panic. I wiped sweat from my upper lip with the sleeve of my sweatshirt and went in the viewing room. Closed the door.

It was suffocating in there. I wanted to peel off my sweatshirt, but that wasn't possible. The silence was unnerving. I had to do what I'd come for, *tit for tat,* do or die, make or break, sink or swim.

263

Why did I think of that? *Sink or swim.* I felt like I did at Seger's Funeral Home, at Sharon's wake. Or at Leonard Twyn's, where I'd initiated the little incident with my Lord's Prayer ring.

Silver and gold, silver and gold . . .

I was humming that irritating tune from *Rudolph the Red-Nosed Reindeer,* for God's sake. Confinement in this airless room was like being buried alive. Wasn't that where these films were kept, in a vault?

> *Everyone wishes for silver and gold*
> *How do you measure its worth?*
> *Just by the pleasure it gives here on earth . . .*

I had to get out of there before I fainted. Because if I fainted, they'd find me on the floor with a film tucked into my jeans and then I'd have a fine of ten thousand dollars or ten years in prison to tuck under my belt, too.

I really ought to check out the film I brought along from home. What if it *wasn't* a blank one after all? It could be one of my cherished films of my babies. What were the chances of that? Why had I grabbed it without reviewing it to make sure?

But if I set it up on the 8mm viewer now and Linda came in, she'd find me looking at one of my own films and have questions about that and maybe become suspicious and my brilliant scheme would fall through.

Just then the door *did* open, and Linda handed me a pair of white cotton gloves.

"Forgot to give you these," she said. "I'll be right out here. Give a holler if you need any help."

I had to sit down and put my head between my knees to drain the blood back into my brain. God, I was a lousy burglar.

I'd hoped merely to substitute one film for the other. But the Twiningham-Lennox home movie had a different kind of metal reel that I hadn't noticed before. Now I felt I really should wind *my* film on *their* reel to make sure it would not arouse undue suspicion. That would be a great plan, Nellie, if your hands weren't shaking so much.

I placed the Twiningham-Lennox film on the left and wound it onto a blank reel on the right without slipping it into the gate so it could be viewed. Then I removed the Twiningham-Lennox film now wound on the right reel, exchanged it in my sweaty waistband for my worthless home movie, which I then placed on the right side of the viewer, and wound it backwards, onto the original quaint Twiningham-Lennox metal reel. If this doesn't make sense, take it for granted that I made the switch as quickly as I could. I was sitting down but my knees were doing the Saint Vitus dance. Sharon told us about Saint Vitus. Did you know he actually *was* the patron saint of dancers? And actors? He was also known for exorcising evil spirits, so maybe this was appropriate.

Why do the synapses of the brain collect bizarre information like that and then pass it on at the most incredible times! It's like you've got a filing system up there that zaps with extra electrodes and explodes with trivia or a vague buried memory that's ancient history, long gone.

Okay, I was done. But if I left abruptly, Linda might suspect something was up. I had to wait for a reasonable period of time. I sat there until three, sweating and needing to use a bathroom, when a man came in to use one of the Steenbeck tables. Linda came in with him, so I said good-bye, thanked her for her help, put the box of films on her metal shelf, and hoped that my guilt would not be evident when I stopped at the reference desk in the Archives Research Room to "prove" I had nothing to hide.

The stolen film glowed like a hot little wheel of fire under my shirt and against my skin, branding me as a thief.

"Minnie," the staff member commented when I boldly held out my hands at the desk and gave her my warm, ironic, "innocent" smile.

I was flustered by her comment and not certain I heard her right.

"Many . . . what?" I said, my blazing face surely giving me away.

"Minnie," she repeated. "You're going to look like Minnie Mouse if you don't take those white gloves off."

I laughed with relief and evidently too loudly; all the intrepid researchers in the research room looked up from their desks to glare.

When I returned home from the archives, another message was waiting on my laptop.

By your attempts to free yourself, Merrill, you risk meaning nothing to me. I may still love you, one of the few rare people I've known with a good, forward-looking mind, great sensitivity and beauty, and genuine talents, but if you cast me aside there is no way I'll ever have anything to do with you again. Is this your wish?

I was in the kitchen cleaning rhubarb from my backyard garden to bake a rhubarb pie when I cut myself. It was stupid, really, but it happened. Blood from my finger spurted everywhere and I hated to throw away the rhubarb so I washed it off and hoped no one would notice (and no one did).

But while I was slicing the rhubarb, and before I cut myself, a piece fell to the floor and Henry raced to pick it up. I bent down to get ahead of Henry and when I straightened up I cracked my skull on the corner of a cabinet door that I would swear had not been open.

The next afternoon, Henry slipped through the front door (who left it ajar was a mystery) to race after a squirrel. This was very unlike Henry, who sped across our street directly in front of a car. I heard the screech of brakes and someone shouting, so I ran down the front steps screaming for the dog and anticipating the worst. In my reckless haste, I missed the final step. Henry was fine. My ankle was sprained. The neighbor was upset.

I may have understood "get the picture," but Angella, hurt and angry, apparently remained reluctant to say good-bye. A threat loomed in her farewell message, but at this point I was ready to face whatever she threw at me.

I will prepare for my bravura curtain call, Merrill. We will finally be out of touch. The seed of crime bears bitter fruit.

17

I don't need to tell you that I grabbed the wrong film. Not the Twiningham-Lennox film, the home movie with the naked woman awakening at dawn—that one was safely stowed in the bottom drawer of my desk. But the 8mm home movie of Lee's, the one I thought was unexposed and switched for the other—that was my favorite film of my children at Christmas and I no longer had it. Angella was having the last laugh. One final taste of evil mischief.

I could blame Angella for taking up so much of my time that I hadn't yet had those films transferred to DVD. But that was really due to my own procrastination. Pure laziness, nothing more.

At least I knew the film of my children was safe and sound. How much safer could it be than in a vault in the film archives? I knew where to find it and that was the important thing. It wasn't sealed away like my Lord's Prayer ring, inside someone's buried coffin.

Anyway, I was really too elated with my freedom to be depressed. Angella Wing had been silenced. Her last message mentioned that she wanted to bow out with a "bravura curtain call," so I hoped the film switch was the one final trick up her ghastly sleeve.

For several days I expected her to contact me again. I wasn't convinced that she had completely closed the door. But sleeping through the night without being disturbed by a disembodied prima donna was glorious. During the day I accomplished things that had been pushed aside due to Angella's intrusions.

Then I conducted a test and found I could at long last use my computer *without* having her words appear! Right away, I queried *Meanderings* about some new story ideas I had.

My sprained ankle had kept me from walking the dog with George and Henry each morning, but I was nearly ready to toss my cane. There is nothing more discouraging to a (relatively) vigorous woman than forcing her to depend on a cane to get around. I had to avoid catching sight of myself in a mirror or the reflection of a store window to keep from sobbing.

It was with some disgrace—but not enough, obviously—that I found myself on my knees before George's keyhole again. Henry had spent so much time on my side by then that his little doggy brain was befuddled. At George's place he had food and water dishes, beds, toys, half-chewed bones, and the same at mine. When the door in the hallway was left open, Henry laid claim to the entire house. Lucky dog!

I had other words for Henry, however, when he decided he didn't want to miss Breeze's birthday party. I hadn't been invited either, but thanks to Henry, I made an accidental appearance.

The group gathered at George's after his "gig" (I still can't comfortably use that word) that Saturday night. I'd already showered and would have been asleep, but I'd begun a new mystery novel that I couldn't put down and was still awake, reading in bed, when I heard the commotion.

Henry raised his head to give me his very cute questioning look with his head cocked to one side before retreating back to his dream. I pressed ahead into the next chapter, but even the suspense of who-killed-whom-and-when was not enough to keep me from the temptation of poking my nose in.

Unfortunately, that's exactly what happened. I was kneeling at George's door, peeking through the keyhole at his party, when Henry, apparently deciding he was missing the excitement, raced from my bed and used my back and my head as a ramp to leap at the door, which then fell open. Shoved off balance by Henry, I fell inside the door, too. On my face. In my T-shirt and boxer shorts that I normally wore to bed. And now with a bloody nose, to boot.

"Henry, sweetheart!" Breeze crooned to the dog. "Everyone, this is Nell Grendon, George's landlady."

I tried to get up but my sprained ankle let me down. There was blood on George's floor and my T-shirt was drizzled with it.

So I backed up on my hands and knees, pulled the door shut, and stretched up to insert the key without saying a word. Maybe they'd forget all about my ungainly entry. I could only hope. A mere blip in their evening. But Henry would be in the doghouse for a few days, as far as I was concerned.

*T*he late April sun lured me into the midst of soft breezes, the fragrance of damp earth and the refreshing bloom of bright crocuses, tulips, and daffodils. I sat in the backyard, propped up my leg, and read more of my mystery. My black eye and bruised nose were barely noticeable with dark glasses on.

With my ankle wrapped in an elastic bandage, George and I were able to resume our early morning walks with Henry. I felt healthier in mind and body than I had in almost a year. George commented that I seemed like a different person.

"I am," I agreed, "but I still make dumb-ass mistakes."

"I'm still trying to get rid of one myself," he confessed. "Breeze."

"Her *bad fortune* didn't take?"

"Not yet," he replied. "But you warned me you weren't very successful at fortune-telling."

*L*ife was good but it could have been better if I had not encouraged Bittner to continue to correspond with Angella via her fake e-mail address, which I had not erased. Don't ask me why I felt compelled to answer him as "Angella" and keep it going. It was perverse, I know. But I still felt a strong compulsion to bug the hell out of him.

As Angella, I shamelessly flirted. I threw little darts at him as if he were a voodoo doll.

I remember meeting Maurice Chevalier in Paris when he sang "Thank Heaven for Little Girls" especially for me. What a delightful June evening that was.

Or another time:

While in Paris I recall thinking, "Lark's on the wing, / The year's at the spring," just as Robert Browning wrote. And here we are, "Lark" and "Angella Wing." Isn't that remarkable? And at the same time of year. All these similarities. How fortunate we are!

After a couple weeks of that masquerade, "Angella" told "Lark" it was time for her to withdraw from this plane and although she appreciated the interest in her autobiography, Merrill Chase was not currently able to fulfill Bittner's request in channeling it.

Bittner wrote back and *demanded* that Merrill Chase continue channeling Angella. Then he asked to see me (Merrill) in person and discuss it further. He even offered a nice advance; he was so certain Angella's book would be a best seller.

All he had was Angella's e-mail address; he didn't know where Merrill Chase lived.

At that point I met Polly for coffee. I told her what I was doing and that Bittner must really believe he was talking to two different people, Angella Wing and Merrill Chase, but he was actually talking to *three,* because of course Nell Grendon was there, too! So which of us was the craziest, Bittner or me?

"I feel such a deep need to destroy this man," I confessed.

"You need to get something on him," Polly suggested.

"Don't we already have something?"

"I mean, like blackmail. You could hint, just mildly insinuate, that you've heard *rumors* about Sharon."

I'd asked Teddy Carter months ago to dig up a copy of the coroner's report regarding Sharon Gallagher's death. Now I sent him a note and told him it was urgent that I see the report. He replied right away that he was bringing some papers down to Madison in a couple weeks.

Polly and I were invited to meet him and his wife (what's-her-name) at a "Hell-raiser Rally."

❧

Of course, after she drowned, I had been expected to go to Sharon Gallagher's wake. My parents didn't question it, as they had only a few years earlier with Leonard Twyn. In fact, I'd not been to Seger's Funeral Home since that awful time. My grandparents were still alive, and no one else had passed away, so I'd been freed from re-visiting the scene of my crime. Of theft. From a dead body. Leonard Twyn's dead body, which, on its rotting digit, wore my own Lord's Prayer ring. That still makes me cringe.

I'd hoped maybe Polly and I could go to Sharon's wake together. Or the group of girls that had been together at Carolina's slumber party. But it didn't work out that way. We were each doomed to accompany our parents.

Still, none of us had mentioned a word to anyone (or to each other) about Sharon's desire for a "Chocolate Dip."

Mother was apprehensive about Cookie's health. She hadn't seemed her old jolly self since her separation from her husband, and Gloria Piekarski had recently developed a very bad cough that Mother whispered might be *cancer*. That word was always spoken in a confidential tone with sinister undertones. "I don't know how they'll manage," Mother said. "That beautiful girl was their whole life!"

Dad handed me a little holy card from a stack near the sign-in register where Mother was signing our names. It had a picture of a guardian angel watching while a little girl walked across a decrepit bridge, maybe from this world and into the next. On the back it said,

> Angel of God, My Guardian Dear
> to whom God's love commits me here.
>
> Ever this day be at my side
> to light and guard and rule and guide.
> Amen,

So where was Sharon's guardian angel when she took her Chocolate Dip? Maybe it flew off when she so casually removed her scapular and dropped it in the sand so she could begin her parade.

And what happened to those wild high school boys who knew Sharon's name and chased after her? Would they come to her funeral? Did they even know she'd drowned? Were they with her when she did? Polly and I couldn't tell anyone about them being there because then we'd be admitting we were there, too!

Cookie's husband, Sharon's father, came down from Stevens Point to be at the wake. I saw him as soon as we walked away from the guest book. He was kneeling at the front of the room dressed in his best Sunday suit. When he stood to greet visitors, I noticed Mr. Gallagher had a piece of tissue stuck to a place on his chin where he must've cut himself shaving. Why didn't anyone say something to him? That didn't seem fair.

Gloria Piekarski still had her back to us. She was kneeling in front of the casket, too. I focused my eyes down toward the familiar blue carpeting I'd come to know so intimately when I'd visited Leonard Twyn in that same room.

Again, the fragrance of flowers suffocated me with the mixed perfumes of their overpowering scent. Adorning the warm room in heart-shaped wreaths, huge fans of gladiolas, baskets of carnations, and roses and lilies perched on high wooden stands. The arrangements draped with beribboned banners spelled out "Beloved

272

Daughter," "Niece," and "Friend" in shiny foil letters. What was with the labels, I wondered. Did they expect Sharon to know who sent them to her? Did they expect her to care?

The somber tones of the grim crowd, the slow shuffle up to the coffin and back. Despite my effort to not even listen (for once!), I could not help but hear the murmurs of mourners.

"Cannot imagine . . . what a tragedy . . . the shock . . ."

"Pray for her final salvation . . ."

"Just had the bad fortune to be at the wrong place at the wrong time . . ."

"Such a dear girl . . . she was an angel . . ."

The fortune part was kind of scary, but how could I say so? And Sharon was no angel.

Suddenly, before I was ready, I stood before an elevated bronze casket draped with a blanket of white roses. Resting inside was the incredibly beautiful body of my friend, Sharon. She wore earrings. And rouge, lots of rouge. Her hair framed her lifeless face in long, childlike ringlets again.

"Oh, Nellie, Sweetheart . . ."

It was Cookie and she was all over me, sobbing wetly into my neck.

"Sherrie was so crazy about you, Honey. I don't know what we'd have done without you to help her get acquainted. She had *so many* friends! But you were the best; you right away made my Sherrie feel welcome. From the very start."

"It's okay," I replied, gently pressing her back, wanting very much to escape Cookie's damp grasp.

"Oh, my Sherrie," she said, releasing me at last and caressing her daughter's motionless face. "Oh, what will we do without you, Nellie and me?"

I thought Sharon appeared waxy, as if her features had been molded in an unfamiliar way. Maybe after you got all shriveled up with raisin skin after being in the water so long, the undertaker had to plump you out again.

Cookie bent down to kiss Sharon's lips. I was totally grossed out.

"Go on, kiss her," Cookie suggested. "Kiss Sherrie. Tell her good-bye."

Cookie was erupting in tears once more. I felt my mother's hands on my shoulders, guiding me toward Sharon's body as she and my father offered their condolences over my bowed head to Cookie and Mr. Gallagher.

"Bye," I said, hovering my palm just above Sharon's hand but not actually touching her. She held a pink crystal rosary that was artfully arranged to cascade in a graceful arc. "I hope you don't have to spend too much time in purgatory with the other poor captive souls and the devouring flames while you're getting purified." I added softly, *"Even though you probably deserve it."*

I shook Mr. Gallagher's callused hand and gave Theresa Piekarski a quick hug. My parents mingled with the crowd, grieving over the loss of one of Little Wolf's most beloved young women.

We took a seat on folding chairs near the middle of the crowd. I didn't want to look around. I didn't want to know if Polly was there, or Teddy, or Mr. Bittner, or anyone else. I refused to raise my eyes. I wanted to leave.

Father O'Neil, wearing a black suit with his Roman collar, led the group in prayer and said a few things about faith and hope. I knew that pretty soon everybody who hadn't already done so would whip their rosaries out.

I wanted to throw up. Not only because I was reminded of my panic during the Leonard Twyn debacle but also because Sharon was not worthy of all this fuss. Of course she was dead, that was something, but she'd caused me a great deal of distress while she was alive and I wasn't as sorry as I could have been. Was that a sin?

Quietly, I got up and slipped out the door and walked home alone. When my parents came back I told them I'd had a "nervous tummy," their term for my panic attacks. The truth was I found the entire event repugnant. And, well, there was the matter of the fortune I'd told her, that her future "was too devastating for me to reveal."

"I don't think I can go to the funeral tomorrow," I told my parents later with as much sorrowfulness as I could rally. "Sharon would understand. I wouldn't want to faint or make a fuss when she should be getting all the attention . . ."

That was enough. I was excused from attending.

I played Crazy Eights with Buddy, something I usually avoided, but it was joyful penance for avoiding a horrible sequel to the wake.

Polly stopped in afterward to fill me in on the details.

"Did you cry?" I asked her.

"No," she said. But her eyes were red so I knew that she had.

⌘

I still don't know Teddy's wife's name, but in early May the two of them came down to Madison with a bunch of other Hogs for Christ for their Hellraiser rally just outside the city with other Evangelical cyclists. It was called "Born Again / Born to be Wild." Teddy invited Polly and me to meet the two of them out there for coffee because Teddy had brought along some papers that were related to Sharon.

I'd never before seen so many shiny motorcycles or so many scary-looking people with tattoos.

Teddy's wife wore black leather head to toe, like he did. No helmets, just colorful do-rags tied in back. It didn't seem very safe to me but, let's face it, I will never be a Biker Babe.

We sat beneath a big tent where a country and western band was tuning up for an afternoon event. Teddy spoke softly so the rest of us had to lean toward him to hear. Right away, Polly knew I'd told him about the ice she'd stuffed down Sharon's throat because he said he'd checked with a friend who was a doctor and he said it simply was not possible to choke someone with ice and expect it to look as if they'd drowned.

Polly got up to leave, but I caught her arm and pulled her back.

"Sit down and be quiet," I said. "I told you we'd try to figure this out."

Polly returned to her seat but I knew she felt betrayed.

"He said," Teddy continued, "if someone was unconscious you could stuff a fair amount of crushed ice down their throat but that

275

would probably initiate a gag reflex and they would puke it all back up. Probably aspirate what they vomited. And then they'd suffocate on that before the ice melted enough to be sucked into their lungs to imitate drowning. Plus, you'd have to plug their nose somehow or get the ice past their tongue to block their ability to breathe through their nose . . ."

"Okay, that's enough," I stopped him. "I'll take your friend's word for it."

"He said it's actually very difficult to drown unless someone doesn't know how to swim or float or they have poor reflexes due to intoxication or medications. And we all know Sharon was a good swimmer."

I heard Polly's deep sigh but I didn't know if it was caused by irritation or relief.

"So I told you the wedding dance that night was for Bittner's sister, right?" Teddy asked.

"Right," I replied.

"And I got a copy of the county coroner's report."

Teddy placed a photocopied document on the picnic table.

"And this here's something we never heard about, at the time. The next of kin ordered an autopsy."

"What?"

"It was at the Gallagher's request. Autopsies were more routine, back then. Sometimes it was done to help the family's grief process or to reassure them that nothing else could have been done to save her life. It wasn't that uncommon. But the results were not made public. Sharon wasn't a virgin, the autopsy found. And apparently she had had sex with somebody that night."

"Surprise," Polly said wryly.

"Polly, shut up," I said.

"Was she pregnant?"

"No, she wasn't."

I had to evade Teddy's eyes. He continued, "And . . . even though the coroner said Sharon almost certainly died from drowning, he didn't add that the autopsy showed she had suffered a significant blow to her temple."

"How come *that* wasn't made public?" Polly wanted to know

"Because it wasn't used as evidence. I mean, the autopsy was only requested by the family, for their knowledge, not because the sheriff suspected foul play."

We all looked at Polly.

"I didn't hit her on the head," she said, her voice cracking with emotion. "All I did was tackle her. And the ice . . ."

"The ice didn't kill her," Teddy added. "Somehow she got a bad bump on the head. Could've knocked her out."

"Bittner?" Polly said.

"Or those high school boys from out of town who you saw hanging around?" Teddy wondered.

"I'll put my money on Karl Bittner," I told them.

𝓜r. Bittner. Wow.

We are blessed with selective memories and, fortunately, the pleasant ones seem to have more staying power than the bad. That didn't mean that I'd ever forgive Mr. Bittner for his egregious behavior toward my female classmates and me in Little Wolf. And it didn't mean I wouldn't still pursue the possibility that he'd killed Sharon. But it *did* mean I wouldn't mind transferring Angella's malevolent attentions to him. The man definitely deserved the punishment of her possession.

◦×◦

What about a visit to a spa, I queried my *Meanderings* editor. There were several new spas in Wisconsin including one near Milwaukee that sounded especially interesting. She agreed.

The spa was called Chocolate Bliss. Everything they offered had chocolate involved. "Chocolate antioxidants paired with massage therapy detoxify your body," their promotions claimed. "Rich chocolate body butter soothes and hydrates your skin."

Following a Hot Chocolate Body Wash I experienced a Chocolate Mousse Body Wrap and then a Chocolate Gatteau Massage with warmed chocolate mousse massage oil. After I got home I told Polly *that* was the ultimate Chocolate Dip.

I also asked her, again, if she'd looked for the scapular. Polly sounded irritable. She said she was working on a new project and anyway, it was just a souvenir of Sharon that she saved so she'd have something of hers; was that such a crime?

The weekly farmers' market on the Square had begun again. The next Saturday morning George and Henry and I walked counterclockwise with the crowd and admired the tulip gardens around the Capitol and placed spears of asparagus, morels, and baby spinach in a fabric basket George carried for me.

We weren't far from Polly's loft, so we took her a bag of croissants.

First, of course, Polly made her usual fuss over Henry. He, of course, gobbled it up like fresh meat. Then she brewed some coffee.

Where was Breeze, she asked George. (I knew this was probably a slam at me for revealing her secret about the ice to Teddy.) Breeze was back at the apartment, still asleep, George admitted, "missing all the fun."

Polly disappeared for a moment, then she said, "I'm working on a new series of holographs that I haven't shown to anyone else. Want to have a look?"

Without my asking, Polly handed over an envelope with the scapular inside. I placed it in my pocket while George and I went down to her studio, where we were shown the holographic torsos Polly had created. They were stunning. Ghostlike. Surreal. The sort of images one imagines might appear during a séance. I told her she should call her exhibit "Ectoplasm Central."

In one hologram that possessed an eerie greenish hue, the smiling image of a woman seemed to look out of a veil, which could have been a shroud, through her own translucent fingers.

George was curious about the technical aspects. I tuned out, as usual, when she explained things like the parallax effect and pseudoscopy, spatial coherence and monochromaticity. I preferred to think of Polly's holograms as if they were magic. Like flying. If I truly understood why a plane could stay in the air I'd freak out and try to pry open the exit door. Some things, I figured, it was best not to know too much about. This particular image, for example, gave me chills. It was very freaky.

Then Polly made the entire ghoulish hologram move! As it revolved, so we could see all sides, the image raised her hands and placed them over her eyes, wiping them down over her cheeks as though wiping away a web of bad dreams. It was phenomenal.

"It looks like someone who's been raised from the dead," George said.

The figure, pale green but perfectly formed and lifelike, continued to rotate.

"Polly, I need to borrow this. Would that be possible?"

"Borrow it? Nellie, you've got to be kidding!"

It was complicated, both as a concept and as an actual procedure. But if it worked, I was sure Karl Bittner would be punished. He would flee from my life and Polly's and never ever return again.

It would also be a grand way for me to exit from Wocanaga and Grace Waverly and the astonishing lessons I had learned there.

After a lot of fast talking on my part, George and Polly agreed.

Neither George nor I were as cognizant of the technical aspects and difficulties of moving the hologram somewhere else. Polly was. I also thought she may have been more reluctant because she was still annoyed with me, but she eventually came around. Of course George owed me for doing the reading for Breeze. He was flying to Vancouver for a jazz festival but hoped to be back in time.

Here's the plan: We would conduct a séance. A spirit-circle. Or... we would pretend to do so. And the presumed intention would be to have Angella Wing speak through me there. With the hologram, we would all observe "Angella" making her final statement. Bittner wouldn't be prepared for Angella to say farewell, but when she did he'd finally have to let Merrill Chase off the hook.

Various locations and settings were discussed—Polly's studio, my living room—but I finally voted in favor of Assembly Hall at Wocanaga where I'd initially channeled Angella. I'd also see that former members of that workshop were invited, too. I wanted to stir up as much psychic energy as possible, to (a) help convince Grace Waverly that this would seemingly make up for the fact that neither Polly nor George were experienced "sitters" at séances, and (b) help Bittner believe that what he was being exposed to was absolutely real.

I could not bring myself to tell Grace the truth about the hologram.

I had no doubt that Bittner would attend.

Looking back, I guess I was indifferent to the possibility that Angella might actually return. She had been as silent as a stone for weeks, and she had seemed resolute when she assured me, "There is no way I'll ever have anything to do with you again."

And while I suggested the idea at Polly's, I didn't yet realize the séance would also be a way to dispose of Angella's film. It *was* a complicated project, but when it came together in reality like it came together in my mind, the end result would be worth our phenomenal effort.

If I set aside my indolence and blamed Angella for keeping me too wrapped up in her to have my personal 8mm films transferred to DVD, now that she was out of the way there was nothing to keep me from having that carried out. George said he wouldn't mind sitting through a few of my home movies, so we settled down one rainy evening with a bowl of popcorn to have a look. He was curious about my marriage to Lee and had never seen my kids. He'd never seen me as a young woman, either. About five minutes into the show I apologized for the bumpy ride—Lee wasn't the steadiest cameraman.

Of course the Christmas film was my favorite, and that wasn't there.

"Would you like to see something really bizarre?" I asked, after I put the last of Lee's films away. "I'd appreciate your assessment of this."

I reminded him of Angella's challenge to "get the picture." I also told him how the Christmas film ended up in the archives' vault.

"When I have my family's films copied onto DVD, I'll have this Twiningham-Lennox film copied, too. Then it's just a matter of sneaking the original back into the film archives and exchanging it for my own. It should be a lot easier getting this one in than it was taking it out."

"Will Angella be upset if you don't hold on to the original?"

Was he joking?

"I have no idea. I had no instructions to destroy it, just 'get the picture.' So, I did."

"'Tit for tat,' you said. 'Quid pro quo'?"

"Getting it was 'tit.' Getting her out of my life was 'tat.'"

"So selecting this one was just your own intuition, right?"

"She gave me a few clues. But, yes, I was only guessing."

I explained my suspicions about Twiningham-Lennox. George had heard about Leonard Twyn and the Lord's Prayer ring long ago. Breeze had already told George about her reading and the intrusion of "silver and gold."

"Well, let's see this 'tit,'" George said, settling back in his chair. "I'm ready."

"There's more than one," I said. "You'll definitely notice two."

At least he would in the bedroom scene.

Because I had only watched the Twiningham-Lennox film on the small screen of the viewer in the archives, seeing it on a large screen made it much more lifelike.

Here was the glitzy pool party with its martini toasts and glamour girls. The dashing matinee idol. The irresistible allure of the woman I thought might be Angella.

After the film went dark and the bedroom scene appeared, I slowed the film so we could view it frame by frame. Certainly, it was the same woman who had appeared in the previous scene.

"What the hell?" George said when that scene faded away. I flipped a switch and started rewinding it again.

"Wait a minute, there's more," he said. "The film hasn't run out."

"It's just black," I replied.

"Play the rest of it anyway. This doesn't make any sense. Why would she want you to steal something so benign? It's just early Hollywood footage, a private party. Somebody's boudoir."

"Well, she's naked," I announced, as if that fact were not blatantly apparent. "Maybe Angella doesn't want any nude footage of herself preserved for perpetuity. I sure wouldn't!"

Meanwhile, the film was moving ahead again. The screen was indeed dark but after a few seconds there was a picture again. It was grainy and brief and not quite in focus. Enough of the image could still be discerned.

We again saw the patio where two women lay together in a nude embrace upon an Art Deco lounge. Then these same women, now wearing bathing caps, frolicked in the kidney-shaped pool where a third woman, a blonde, sat on the edge and dangled her feet in the water. It was very jerky footage, and crooked on the screen, but suddenly the blonde was pulled into the pool, where her head was held beneath the surface for what seemed a long time. The other women laughed wildly. Then the camera was obviously thrown aside and the tail of the film made a flipping sound in the room.

"Holy shit," I said. "I wonder who that was."

"Doesn't matter, does it?" George replied. "Obviously it was someone Angella wanted whacked. I'm not so sure you should risk returning this to the archives. Not if you want her out of your life."

"Okay, I could sneak a truly blank film into the archives and rescue my Christmas one. But what about this? Should it be buried? Burned?"

"Why not see that Karl Bittner gets it. He's still fascinated with Angella, right?"

It took me only a moment before I knew what to do.

"With a little more planning, I think we can carry that out," I said. "When Bittner comes to our séance he'll be given more than one surprise."

Polly came along to Wocanaga when I visited Grace to consult with her about conducting the séance. I had to convince the elderly medium to participate so I explained why such a séance was necessary to rid me of Angella. Meanwhile, Polly looked around Assembly Hall to see how she could set up her equipment and carry out my scheme.

Grace was home alone. Her bruises and cuts had healed, but her white hair wasn't fixed in its usual neat braid; it was down around her shoulders. She was attempting to brush it but her gnarled hands had difficulty grasping the brush. So I brushed and braided her hair for her.

"The last few weeks have been difficult," she admitted, patting her chest with a fragile palm. "My doctor says it wasn't due to the fall, merely an 'affair of the heart.' Not all that unusual at my age, you know."

Grace readily agreed to participate in the séance so I might attempt to set Angella free.

"You may be taking advantage of my fondness for you," she said, fussing now with the fringe on a crocheted shawl. "I'm not certain this spirit-circle is truly a good idea. But since you have invited the students from my autumn workshop, I'm bound to go through with it, am I not?"

"Karl Bittner is a dangerous person," I explained. "The spirit-circle will help in diffusing his disturbing vibrations."

"If you'd like to use the trumpet, perhaps he can hear Angella's voice."

"We can have it available," I said, knowing the hologram would be enough to scare the wits out of everyone.

I couldn't confide this to Grace, but I had no intention of attracting actual spirits to this séance. It was going to be bogus all the way. It wouldn't matter if Polly and George had never been to one; it wouldn't matter that Angella was not actually speaking through me or that my attitude would not be one of devout belief. This would be acting. It would be absolutely fake. A mirage. A phony sham.

I did explain my wish to have the flame of a burning candle on the séance table. It would be encased in a large glass box.

"That's fine," Grace agreed. "It sometimes helps for participants to have a candle to focus on."

This flame, this candle, would also be a hologram. Compared to the torso hologram, Polly said the candle was a piece of cake.

$\mathcal{B}$ack home, I realized I'd once again neglected to take Sharon's scapular along to Wocanaga for Grace to psychometrize. Dammit! I found the envelope, opened it, and dropped the scapular on my desk: the rich brown ribbon connected two squares—remnants from the rough woolen robes of Carmelite monks. Just as I remembered, one square held a picture of the Our Lady of Carmel. The other was Saint Simon Stock, receiving his scapular.

I was a failure at psychometry, so I didn't even bother to give it a try. Just touching it made me shiver, though. I put the scapular back in the envelope and set it aside, vowing to show it to Grace when I went to Wocanaga for the séance.

That was all set for the following week.

18

*C*oming events cast their shadows before them.

The original poem by Thomas Campbell must have been wildly popular among nineteenth-century mediums; I saw it repeated many times in my books on old-fashioned Spiritualism. You know how a song gets so implanted in your head that a segment of the melody repeats itself with annoying regularity? Well, these lines—where a wizard is warned of impending doom—had firmly attached themselves to my neurons:

> 'Tis sunset of life gives me mystical lore,
> And coming events cast their shadows before.

Not that I'd admit to anyone that I was within light-years of the "sunset of life," but the past year had added a few wrinkles that couldn't be palmed off as laugh lines.

Obviously I was doing a lot of reflecting on my astonishing venture that began only last spring. Would returning to Wocanaga now help me rediscover the appeal of its "mystical lore"? Did coming events *really* cast their shadows before them?

285

On the day of our séance, I deliberately went right past Grace's cottage and drove through the welcome gate to the air-conditioned motel, where I parked my car. Since we'd have to dismantle our equipment after the séance and that might be well after midnight, I'd rented a couple of rooms. Besides, I wanted a place to meditate and change my clothes and freshen up before the Big Event.

Polly's bag was on one of the twin beds so I dropped my luggage on the other and began revisiting the grounds with a personal promise in mind.

It was evident that winter had been pretty brutal to the Spiritualist camp. Or maybe it was because I was making an attempt to rewind my memory tape and appreciate the setting all over again. For whatever reason, the worn and weary aspects were more apparent than ever.

Many features of Spiritualism were still unfathomable to me, but I sensed an aura of sorrow dogging my footsteps like a sad little phantom. My whirl in this extraordinary world had been unusual (to say the least) but it was time for Merrill Chase to bid her mediumship good-bye. That caused a little pang of heartbreak. She was fun, in her own preposterous way.

Buildings may have needed paint and roofs were missing shingles, but the vast grounds of Wocanaga wore the fresh green of spring and were carpeted here and there with purple violets. In the shadows, white trillium appeared spectral against a background of unfurling ferns. The tall pines, fragrant and still awe inspiring, moaned with deep sighs in the slightest spring breeze.

I'd never had the courage to spend more than a few nights in the dear little cottages—I regretted that now. Innocent and simple, they were tiny comfort zones of joy with their green shutters and joyful flowerboxes of plastic geraniums and trailing ivy.

Men were ripping off the remaining rafters of cabin 7. "Snow caused her to cave in," one of them explained to me. A stack of fresh lumber confirmed they were not ready to let it give up the ghost.

"Might get rain," I nodded at the cumulus clouds building in the west.

"Well, we need it," one of the men shrugged. "Gotta think of the corn."

I wished them well and continued along the path.

In fact, the weather forecast—while not unusual for Wisconsin in early summer—was the ominous kind that since childhood has caused me to wring my hands and obsess over being spun away in a tornado like the one that flung Dorothy and Toto into Oz:

> The Storm Prediction Center has issued
> a Strong Risk for severe weather today.
> Super cells capable of producing tornadoes could develop
> later this afternoon in western Wisconsin, evolving into a line
> of thunderstorms producing damaging winds and large hail.

The afternoon was already uncomfortably warm and muggy for May. I wore shorts but had brought a change of clothes—a beige linen skirt, violet T-shirt, and sandals—to wear for the séance. A skirt seemed more refined for Merrill Chase and her last hurrah. Besides, it was what I'd worn on my initial visit last spring.

To achieve *personal* closure on Merrill's "career," I thought it might help to replicate the first time I'd channeled Angella. That was in Assembly Hall during the final day of Grace's Labor Day workshop, where we'd hold our séance tonight. Polly and George had driven up from Madison together and were supposed to be in there now setting up Polly's holographic equipment. The complicated arrangement would take hours of preparation and testing. And it would be unbearable in this heat, too. After this production I was going to owe them both. Big time.

My path took me past the dining hall, where the opening ceremony for the summer season was scheduled for the first of June with a potluck luncheon after a morning prayer service. According to the newsletter I'd received, the schedule called for a flag raising and the Pledge of Allegiance, followed by a verse of "God Bless America."

One of the mediums would then recite the Declaration of Principles from the NSAC—the National Spiritualist Association of Churches:

We believe in Infinite Intelligence. We believe that the phenomena of Nature, both physical and spiritual, are the expression of Infinite Intelligence.

We affirm that the existence and personal identity of the individual continues after the change called death. We affirm that communication with the so-called dead is a fact, scientifically proven by the phenomena of Spiritualism. We affirm that the precepts of Prophecy and Healing contained in all sacred texts are Divine attributes proven through Mediumship.

And so on.

There would be casseroles of cheesy whipped eggs and sausage at the potluck. Maybe some fried chicken. Or ham. Jell-O salads. Sliced meatloaf and a four-bean hot dish with bacon. Fruit pies seeping with juice, their tan crusts flaky with lard. My clairsentience seemed to get really strong whenever I returned to Wocanaga. So did my appetite. I had an apple in my purse and a chocolate bar in my pocket. I chose the chocolate. It wasn't much of a contest.

I spotted members of my Labor Day workshop having an early picnic beneath the pines. The little man in black; Spence, and his wife, Barbara; and Irene of the bra-stone were there and would round out our séance table later that night. They returned my wave. I hoped Spence would reprise his "White Horse" and say "HO" loudly like he did before so Polly would be scared out of her sandals. And Irene . . . had she discarded her affair with Seth Thomas or was she still "ticking"? The anticipation caused my stomach to clench up a bit. I knew I should have had more than a candy bar but I hadn't eaten much for a couple of days. Anxiety does that to me. I still kept the topaz taped to my chest, too. Why take a chance?

Grace had said there should be no fewer than four but no more than twelve around the séance table. And there should be an equal number of both sexes rather than a preponderance of women or men. Of course Karl Bittner was coming so there'd be eight of us altogether. Polly had to stay out of the séance room to tend to her equipment in the adjacent space, but the "official" word would be that she'd never attended a séance before and had merely come along with her "boyfriend" George (who had not attended a séance before, either, but received special dispensation for this one).

"Everyone in the séance room must take part," Grace advised. "We cannot allow anyone in the room who does not sit in the circle."

I knew that would not matter. Polly's hologram would appear whether we had more than a dozen, or fewer than four. First, the candle would burn with a dithering flame before going out. Then, "Angella's" torso would sprout up from the table and revolve no matter who was there and awe us all.

It had been only a few weeks ago that I'd come to Wocanaga and had driven to Inspiration Point with Grace. Naturally, I asked myself afterward, "What got into me?" And, naturally, the answer was always Angella.

My hands had not yet healed entirely but my tire tracks in the grass were overgrown.

You'd think I'd avoid this place with all its bad memories. I mean, it was bad enough seeing Mr. Bittner here and then Sharon's dripping apparition. And then of course there was the tumble toward oblivion that I'd irrationally goaded Grace to make. With me!

Coming here today was a test of my personal resolve: if I wasn't scared to death that Sharon would appear again, or Angella would tempt me over the edge, then I was okay after all. *All manner of things shall be well.*

I paused at the pine tree and turned around as if delivering a message from Spirit instead of facing rows of weather-bleached benches. With my eyes closed I tried to re-create the panic I experienced when seeing Bittner and a drenched specter of Sharon behind him. But I felt perfectly calm. I patted the pocket of my shorts where I carried Sharon's scapular. It was still in the envelope where Polly had kept it. This time I would *not* forget to give it to Grace to psychometrize.

Then I proceeded to cautiously climb down the crude steps to the precipice. Clinging to one small pine tree and then another, I gradually made my way to the edge of the limestone escarpment that leaned over the deep valley like a shelf. This was a challenge to Angella, a bold statement. Her power had waned as I had taken over. Stealing her film had vastly altered our relationship.

The way she'd encouraged me to entice Grace reminded me of Sharon's old "chicken!" taunts. As if I would be so brazen as to test Grace's resolve! The poor woman didn't have a chance to resist; I'd grabbed her poor frail body and might as well have thrown her over the edge. Or perhaps the weight of her body was intended to carry *me* over the edge. It was irrelevant, now. I put it out of my mind.

Solitude would be calming, and I still had plenty of time. This was a truly beautiful spot, moist with dapples of lichens and spangled sunlight through the leaves.

I would concentrate on achieving a tranquil state of mind.

But Sharon was near—I could sense her subtle presence and attributed it to her scapular in my pocket.

I pondered Polly's question about why I'd not thought of Sharon until I became associated with Wocanaga. Would all my thoughts—guilty thoughts—of Sharon be dismissed when I left?

When I first saw Sharon's apparition I was afraid *she* might push me over the edge and I had clung to that stout pine tree in fear. If she were actually here now she would egg me on with "I dare you to jump" or "See what falling feels like, Nellie!" How clearly I could imagine that little bitch taunting me. Trespass, intrude, infringe, encroach—whatever you wanted to call it, Sharon had always enjoyed coaxing me to go over the line.

"This time it's not going to work." I spoke those words firmly, addressing the memory of her wraithlike vision. I felt a bit silly doing so, but this was a day of transformation and there was no one nearby to hear.

After a few breathing exercises I decided to try "Blowing into the Sun." It was another aura exercise from Spence, who had told me you could blow a picture connected with your past into the sun to obliterate it. By "blowing it" you vaporized the effect of the experience. You could not erase its memory, but the emotional charge it carried would be dissolved and the energy would be recycled into your aura, golden and warm.

I shifted my position so the sun fell directly on my face and closed my eyes. The sun was already seeping into my bones.

I took a deep breath while bending my head backward and blew my resentment for Sharon into the sun. With another deep breath I blew my frustration with Sharon's haunting memory. Then I blew the hostility I'd developed toward Angella toward the sun. I blew my long-held hatred of Mr. Bittner. I blew and blew again my impatience with my own vulnerability, my impulsive actions, my failures, my naiveté.

With all that heavy breathing I hyperventilated, but there was a real awareness of peace when I put my head between my knees. No messages, no inspiration, no visions. This truly was good-bye. I would never visit this mysterious and wonderful place again. My inquisitive nature had questioned what it would be like to be a medium and now I had a pretty good idea.

Although Grace had warned, "Once you're hooked you cannot walk away," I was taking giant strides to remove myself from Sharon's ghost, from Angella and her provocations, from Wocanaga and Grace Waverly (dear creature though she may be), and I was ready to enter a fresh, new period of my life when I could focus on things that were more important to me *now,* like my children and grandchild and friends I'd grown to love.

I moved back into the shade and repeated a few mantras just in case.

All shall be well, and all shall be well, and all manner of things shall be well . . .

Then I stood and climbed clumsily back up to the tree. With every cautious step I repeated my mantra, just in case.

It wasn't all that easy to push those extraneous uncertainties from my head. Over and over again I told myself, *this will be fun.* Best of all, Angella would be untied. Like a helium balloon, she would lift up, up, and soar away. Bittner would disappear from my life along with Angella. And with any luck, Sharon would soon fly off with them, too.

I should have screamed with joy. Instead, I ended up crying. It was like when you find yourself shedding tears after having sex. It doesn't mean it wasn't good; it's merely a release of emotions. It's *good* crying. In all probability the sex was great. They're good tears. Everything is all right. All shall be well. *All manner of things shall be well.*

That's what I kept telling myself as I sat down on one of the squeaky benches for a long session of weeping.

Yet I was reminded, *Coming events cast their shadows before.*

Damn. What did that mean?

*P*olly and George were busy with technical stuff at Assembly Hall and I didn't want to interrupt. Any appearance of mine at that time would have resulted in apologies for their efforts in the suffocating heat and for requesting their help in the first place. *All shall be well,* I kept thinking, and *What a sucker I've been!*

So I killed more time by walking back to visit with Grace at her cottage. After saying farewell to Merrill Chase I wouldn't see Grace after tonight, either.

Grace sat in her rocking chair and fanned herself with a Wocanaga newsletter. She was more weak and listless than ever. Even with the windows open, her cottage was unbearably hot. As I'd requested, she was again wearing the pink organdy dress with violets embroidered on the bosom. It was sweet of her to comply, although the dress no longer fit her emaciated frame.

I asked if she had an electric fan. She said there should be one in an upstairs bedroom but she hadn't been up there in years so was not certain just where it might be.

Wow. I was glad she'd never invited me to spend the night. Everything up there had been chewed by mice and their excrement was all over the place.

I found the fan in a jam-packed closet among boxes of papers and gadgets, little hinged slates and pens for writing on them, and a cracked crystal ball wrapped in blue tissue paper. Another box held a massive length of black silk and a small can of luminous paint. The black silk made me smile; this was a staple of old-fashioned mediumship.

The room was oven-hot and the stench was too awful to linger. Besides, I wasn't interested in this stuff anymore, remember? But I was *so tempted!* What if there were more hidden historical gems? With a newspaper, I flicked away enough mouse feces to clear a big enough space on the bed to sit. A shoebox I selected at random held "spirit photos," most of them clumsy double-exposures. Several featured Grace as a young woman, with a man. There were pictures and postcards of Wocanaga as it must have appeared fifty or more years ago. Here was the chapel—now in ruins—with lines of people streaming in through the doors. I could almost hear them singing "Bringing in the Sheaves." At the very bottom of the shoebox I found a tiny dark green velvet bag tied with a ribbon that broke when I pulled on it and into my lap spilled a collection of charms, medals, amulets, all tarnished or rusty but fascinating to examine.

Grace called up the stairway with an urgent note in her voice.

"Eleanora, are you all right?"

"I'll be down in a minute," I assured her, reluctantly stowing everything back in the closet. The door would not shut again, so I left it ajar. Grace would never know.

"I hope this works," I said when I came downstairs, soaked with sweat. I brushed a couple mouse turds off my ankles, dusted the fan, and plugged it into a socket despite the frayed cord. It was one of those oscillating fans that rotates slowly, back and forth. Every few seconds each of us was the grateful recipient of a limp current of air.

Then I had to wash my hands!

I'd planned to use this time, as we waited together for the appointed hour, to convey my appreciation to Grace for her teaching and her compassion. She had already expressed her dismay that Merrill Chase was signing off and my mediumship was concluding.

"Eleanora . . ." Grace sent me a pained look as if she had been pierced straight through to the heart. "Come over here next to me; pull your chair closer to mine."

Dabbing at my face with a damp paper towel, I sat near her chair.

"Of course I understand that what you've gone through with this devious spirit has been extraordinary. But you exhibited more talent than any of my students since . . . well, perhaps *ever.*" Her voice grew softer, almost strained, as the effort to speak became arduous and she reached for my hand. "For the life of me, I cannot imagine why you would not want to cherish this. Many make attempts, but not everyone can achieve your prospects!"

Grace had opened her heart to me. I didn't want her to think I had been taking advantage of her.

I gripped her hand with mine and spoke as tenderly as possible.

"Grace, you have been so kind, and you were always available when I had questions or needed you. But you, of all people, must know that this unexpected 'talent' has complicated my life so much that it's impossible for me to have a life of my own. Besides," I smiled weakly, "I seem to have a strong attraction for mischievous spirits. Even if I got rid of Angella, how would I know it wouldn't happen again?"

"I know, I know . . ." Grace's breathing was quick and shallow.

"In the first place, I'd only hoped to familiarize myself with the belief of Spiritualism. Then I was drawn to it because it seemed like it offered an inexplicable inner light. Now, instead of illuminating, that inner light has blinded me to nearly everything else! I'm so sorry to be a disappointment to you, but I really do have to get out!"

Was that a hint of hysteria in my voice?

Grace appeared solemn. She slowly shook her head.

"It's true, you didn't have much talent for psychometry or for reading auras." She tried to return my smile. "But your channeling was exceptionally sharp. I'm going along with your 'farewell to Angella' tonight, Eleanora, but only out of the goodness of my heart. I needn't tell you again—I don't have an especially good feeling about this spirit-circle."

"It's her wish." I was trying to sound as if I had more control over my emotions. "Angella insists on a *bravura performance,* to say fare-well. She always insists on achieving acclaim of some kind."

"And you will deliver her message? It's not always possible to predict who will speak, you know. Spence will be there . . ."

"And Irene. And my friend George Stafford, who brought his . . . um, his girlfriend, Polly. They are also my personal friends."

"They're not Wocanaga mediums," Grace interrupted, "or even experienced sitters . . ."

"George and Polly have been really considerate," I told her. "When Angella consumed my life in a negative way, they took care of me. You said it was important to have friends nearby when channeling. Well, during my moments of extreme exhaustion, Polly and George were there."

"It's your séance, Eleanora," Grace said finally, releasing her grip on my hand. She patted my arm. "You can have your way, certainly. Obviously you have thought this through and know what you want. Why you even want me to be involved . . ."

"Grace, you're my mentor!"

I got up from my chair and began to walk around the room.

"I've always considered you the expert, the wise medium who guided me along the frenzied path I made for myself. You have to be there to make sure I do this séance right. To lend legitimacy to it, too. I've never led a spirit-circle on my own!"

"Patience," Grace replied, sounding very weary. "Patience is es-sential. You must maintain a cheerful attitude. An expectant atti-tude. Do not be demanding. Spirits do not like to be commanded to appear. My best advice, Eleanora, is to persist but go cautiously. And whatever happens, be sure you do not falter."

She said she would appreciate an hour or so to rest before the circle convened. She refused to eat supper. One should not eat heav-ily before a séance, she said, and fasting would be wise.

"I brought sandwiches," I offered.

"Thank you, but I prefer to fast. Rest and fasting helps produce stronger phenomena. I have an impression that you will be in need of all the influence I'm able to give you."

Grace looked as if any moment she would nod off.

I found Sharon's scapular in my pocket, placed it in her hands, and told her when she felt more refreshed I'd appreciate having her try some psychometry with it.

Then I went down to Assembly Hall to check on Polly and George.

19

*P*olly was really proud of her creation— I could tell by the way she stood back and squinted to take in the entire room. Her shirt was soaked with sweat. George's shirt was completely wet, too. He didn't say much. I figured they were both tired.

A tall, square glass box sat in the center of the long oak table. Eight wooden chairs, one at each end and three on each side, were carefully arranged. Darkness would enhance the visual image of the hologram, but even in the dusky room the revolving, pale-green, disembodied torso inside the glass box could be seen as a ghostly, phosphorescent glow.

"Oh, my God, this is fantastic!" I could barely speak; the setup was complicated beyond belief and the phantom torso sent a tremor through my entire body.

I did my best to avoid the old mediums who stared derisively from their dour photographs on the walls.

"I'm beat," Polly said. "We've been here since five this morning."

George told her, "Go back to the motel and cool off. I'll sit here on the porch and make sure nothing's disturbed."

"You get some rest, too," I suggested. "I'll take your place. Let Henry stay with me. We still have plenty of time before it'll be dark enough to start the séance. And don't forget the sandwiches and iced tea in the cooler."

George said he'd be back by the time people began to gather. I wondered if he and Polly were upset with me—they seemed sort of distant.

Polly started the car and waited for George with the motor and air-conditioning running. He hung behind and asked how I was doing.

"I'm okay," I shrugged. "Excited, kind of. Scared. I'm glad you're going to be here. What's with Polly?"

"She's scared, too," he said. "She wants this to be just right for you."

Turmoil was mounting inside me—not hunger or panic, not nausea, but definitely the sort of anticipation that something really significant was about to happen. Like Angella's "agonies of stage fright" that she'd confided she had felt upon beginning her blog. It was probably low blood sugar, the effect of not having eaten in quite a long time, but I shuddered with chills and anxiety. I could have used a glass of wine, but alcohol was forbidden at Wocanaga. I got a bottle of cold water from the cooler and swallowed a Valium.

The weather may have been partly to blame for my restlessness. Since childhood I've been known for diving into the basement at the slightest threat of a tornado. In the spring, when warning sirens screamed in Madison, I had headed downstairs after hastily gathering Henry. We stayed there for an hour after the all clear.

I relaxed a little when the Valium kicked in and managed to doze on the porch swing. Henry slept on the floor. The minute I awoke, my stomach was a mess again.

Henry was growling, and Henry never growled. Through the screen door, a man was staring at me. Immediately I recognized the fragrance of Old Spice.

"Eleanora Grendon," Karl Bittner said. "Sorry to wake you."

My sunglasses had fallen off and I awkwardly struggled to put them back on before I realized Bittner already knew who I was.

He was laughing. "Did you really think I never recognized you?"

Despite Henry's vociferous attempts to protect me, Bittner came in and sat down next to me on the slatted swing. He lifted his left arm over my head and hugged me to him as if we were long-lost friends. When he rested his arm behind my shoulder on the back of the swing it made me feel as if I remained inside his embrace. His Hawaiian shirt was unbuttoned halfway down the front, showing off a tan chest and several gold chains. The sickening scent of his cologne was so strong that I stood and moved away.

I really wanted to run off and leave him there on the porch, but I could not have him wandering around the rooms and discovering the complex setup for the hologram.

"So," I said cheerily, standing before him, hands on my hips, "you really think I'm Eleanora Grendon? Who the heck is she?"

Bittner laughed, centering himself on the swing with both arms now spread across the back. He pushed with his feet and I had to move out of his way when he swung forward so he wouldn't accidentally kick the dog or me.

"Nice try, kiddo," he grinned, swinging backward again. "I have to admit, at that message service you had me fooled—last year, at Inspiration Point. But when we met in Chicago? Hey, I may be older now and grayer, but I'd never forget little Nellie Grendon and my years at Little Wolf."

"I didn't want to distract you from the seriousness of Spiritualism," I lied. "You know, just in case being familiar with the medium would affect the message."

"Your messages, Miss Grendon, now have me betting on a best-selling book."

He ran a hand through the gleaming white wave on his forehead and patted it back in place. "I don't give a damn who *you* are, but your Angella Wing is a real winner and I hope to hell we two, we *three*—you, me and Angella—can pull a manuscript together out of this."

He stopped swinging, pulled a handkerchief from his back pocket, and began dabbing his nose and his neck. "Do you suppose she could elaborate on some of the more sordid parts of her past? I have a feeling there's a lot of raw sensuality in Angella that hasn't been tapped."

I exhaled rather loudly. "I don't know about that . . ."

"Can you believe this fucking heat?" He stood up. "Feels like tornado weather. You suppose this place has a cellar?"

He was about to wander inside the séance room when I stopped him.

"Let's walk up and check on Grace Waverly. She's expecting me."

I left a note on the porch door asking that no one disturb the setting for the séance until they were invited inside. Henry lagged behind, panting, as Bittner and I took the path. Late afternoon light had assumed a freaky greenish yellow stain that made everything look like I felt inside. I hated that kind of weather and I hated it happening on the night of my special séance. I had a definite suspicion that something awful was going to happen. I needed to check the latest weather forecast. I wanted to see a Doppler radar for Wisconsin. Were we directly in the path of inevitable disaster?

I should have told George and Polly to turn on the car radio and see if a tornado warning had been declared for this part of the state. The motel rooms didn't have TVs. After all our exhaustive preparations I wouldn't cancel the séance even if there were a threat of bad weather . . . and yet. And yet . . .

"So, do you think Angella Wing will have something to say tonight?"

Bittner was doing his best to have a normal conversation. I gave him credit for that.

"I hope so," I said. "I haven't heard from her in a while."

"Maybe she'll talk to me," he said. "Since you don't seem to give a damn about her anymore."

We came into the cottage and found Grace still awake. As Bittner greeted Grace with a kiss on the cheek, she held out her hands. They were dripping with liquid. Grace was pale and visibly upset. She had not rested at all.

"What's this?" Bittner asked Grace.

"Where did you get this?" she asked, ignoring him, grimly offering me the watery scapular.

"It belonged to a friend," I said.

"A friend who passed over," she said as a matter of fact.

"Yes."

"She drowned."

I nodded.

"She fell through the ice."

"No, it was in August," I said gently.

"She was very cold," Grace suggested. "Cold as ice."

"Maybe it's because she was in the water for a long time?" Bittner said.

He glanced at me quizzically, expecting me to concur. Which I did.

I took the scapular from Grace—it was, indeed, soggy. Grace wiped her hands on her dress and then took Bittner's hand and began to visit with him.

I offered Henry a bowl of cool water. There was *no* way I was going to tell Polly about the scapular before our big production; she'd really get upset. What she had ahead of her was complicated due to the primitive location for her lights and mirrors and lenses and it *had* to go perfectly. Besides, I had no idea how to explain the damp results of Grace's psychometry. Very weird, indeed.

The momentary arrival of Spence and his wife, Barbara, turned out to be excellent timing. Grace stopped conversing with Bittner, so after a few minutes he and I took our leave. Spence said he'd see that Grace was brought down to Assembly Hall on time.

"That was Sharon Gallagher's scapular, wasn't it?" Bittner asked as we left the cottage.

"I've had it for a long time," I said. "I wondered if Grace could tell me more about the circumstances of Sharon's death."

"Long time ago," he mused as if talking to himself. "A long time.

She was a lovely girl. Devastating loss. I never quite recovered from it. Don't suppose you kids did, either. Beautiful child."

I remained silent.

"When we met in Chicago, Nellie, you said Sharon hadn't forgotten me. Were you serious about that? Is that actually what her spirit said—or were you putting me on?"

"I wouldn't *ever* do that," I swore in all seriousness. "Of *course* Sharon said she had not forgotten you!"

Bittner smiled at that and muttered something under his breath. "What?"

"I said I hope they were pleasant memories," Bittner replied. "Once I had to give her an 'F' in history."

"But she was good in math," I said.

"Good enough for you to copy her homework," he grinned and spanked my butt with a playful swat. "You still have a nice little ass, you know . . ."

We parted. I was fuming. The cocky bastard hadn't changed one bit.

The wind was picking up. Bittner walked down to the assembly hall where, according to my watch, I knew George and Polly would be in charge but out of sight. I went over to the motel, changed my clothes, and dabbed the wet scapular with a towel before placing it in the pocket of my linen skirt. I hoped it would not continue to weep or whatever it was doing, but I felt I shouldn't leave it behind in my room. I don't know why. I was really nervous now. Not just because of Bittner being such a jerk or the iffy weather.

The sickly overcast sky possessed a dark green tinge by the time I left the motel, and strong gusts of wind seemed to be trying to keep me back. Tall oaks bent and swayed with a mad rhythm. I could smell rain in the air and the heady scent of pine boughs bent almost to breaking. There was something else, an odor I could not place. Like smoke after fireworks. Or wet ashes. Ozone, maybe? It was foreboding. I felt feverishly warm, but I began to tremble and started to run down the path from the motel toward Assembly Hall.

"A shiver and a shake does not a medium make." Grace had told me that a year ago. It didn't matter now. I didn't need to be a real medium, so I could shiver and shake, jiggle and fake, all I wished. And I was shaking like crazy.

Since darkness was nearly complete, all the participants were gathering. But it was never totally dark that night. Now sheets of lightning flashed in the west along with an ominous rumble—distant but unremitting.

Grace was directing the seating by the time I entered the candlelit Assembly Hall. I'd managed to spend a minute with George and Polly in the adjacent room to fix my hair, catch my breath, and wish them well. Then George came into the next room with me to the séance.

In arranging the chairs, we knew we would of course end up with one extra person. George volunteered that his girlfriend would stay in the next room so we would have an even number. This way, Bittner would not recognize Polly, and Polly could monitor her equipment and carry out my plan. So far, so good. Everything was working nicely.

At first it seemed no one wanted to sit down. The group milled around, looked out the windows, checked their watches, engaged in small talk.

"They're nervous," I muttered to George.

"Tell me *you're* not." He gave me a brief hug. "Don't worry, it's going to be great."

I traced the scar on his left hand, then brought it to my cheek. "Promise me if we have a storm that you won't get all worked up and tear off your clothes and run around in the rain!"

Eventually, eight of us sat around the table in Assembly Hall, in this order: Grace Waverly at the head, then Karl Bittner, Irene (of the bra stone), the little man in black from my workshop, Barbara (Spence's wife) at the other end, George Stafford, me, and Spence. Spence completed the circle and was seated next to Grace. Four men and four women, evenly dispersed.

Polly was able to listen in by way of the baby monitor I held on my lap. It was like the Pope's Nose all over again.

Grace directed us to join hands, right over left. After we began the spirit-circle, she said, if we wished, we could place our hands on the table, palms down. One candle would burn, so we would offer near obscurity for the spirits.

The candle, a hologram, flickered inside a large glass box in the center of the table. It seemed absolutely real.

In this Assembly Hall setting where I'd sat in her class less than a year ago, Grace's poor health was even more evident. I should have waited with the scapular. Or I could have chosen to conduct this make-believe séance without her, somewhere else. Who knew the weather would be so threatening?

On the other hand, we'd experienced a thunderstorm the day Angella first appeared.

"If a clear and decisive character is contacted," Grace continued, fighting to raise her voice over the racket of the growing wind, "questions may be put to ascertain whether the spirit is related to any person present. And, if so, to whom, or with whom, the spirit wishes to speak. The person indicated may then ask questions of the spirit. And the spirit will respond by speaking aloud."

I found myself distracted by menacing shadows the candle image was casting on the walls. Distorted shapes danced recklessly upon the photographs of former mediums with their stern expressions.

"We will achieve, to a very great extent, what we make conditions for," Grace advised our group. "We will observe the manifestations first and draw conclusions afterward. Therefore, we wish, now, to open the doors of the heavens by love and purity."

Grace closed her eyes, and hands on either side of me clutched mine: Spence held my left hand and George was on my right. Having George's hand in mine was almost enough for me to forget where I was.

Thunder in the distance rolled like the sound of timpani rising and falling as a heavenly musician tuned his drums. Beyond the lace-curtained windows I could see an occasional bolt of lightning. A more suitably foreboding atmosphere could not have been designed.

I attempted to quiet my fear of heavy weather and concentrate on this evening that had been exhaustively planned. For this to seem real, I must appear passive and composed. I took a deep, shuddering breath and tried desperately to calm down. George tightened his grasp. I knew he was telling me again it would be okay.

We were a circle, complete, and around me I felt a rising level of anticipation. My clairsentience? Or everyone listening to thunder and worrying about the impending storm?

"HO!" said Spence, reconnecting with his Red Indian guide. He spoke for several minutes, ordering us to observe stricter conservation measures and protect his streams and rivers. Spence's guide apparently belonged to the Sierra Club.

Silence, again. Then Irene began to tick.

"The clock. Will mock," she said. And a bunch of other stuff I paid no attention to; Irene just took up time. But that was all right.

Silence.

As if it had been planned in concert with the thunder growing ever nearer, the candle in the glass box slowly dissolved away. In its place, a phosphorescent green light began to shimmer as Polly's hologram achieved complete luminescence.

There were gasps around the table and even I had to marvel at the thrill I felt with this deception. The image was an awesome sight.

Disorienting in its three-dimensionality, it was as if an actual woman's head and the top half of her body had coalesced, out of nothing, within the glass box. I was stunned with the representation Polly had managed to achieve; it was more than an illusion, it was scientific magic. The likeness was so powerful, so apparently tangible, that my mind could not take in all its implications at once.

I could see the image and *through* the image to the person opposite me at the table . . . Irene. But the transparent woman in the center of the table seemed even more real and believable than Irene did.

The disembodied torso slowly began to revolve. Each of us viewing it could now observe her from various angles. During the revolution the ghostlike woman wiped her eyes, seemingly imploring each of us to share her sorrow at leaving our realm. It was a totally breath-taking, stunningly wonderful effect. I wanted Polly to be in the room to witness it! There was no way for my glance to meet George's because he was at my side. Anyway, if I could have, I'd have begun smiling broadly, most inappropriate for Merrill Chase. He still held my right hand, though, and I could feel his astonishment and pride just as strongly as I felt my own.

The greenish glow reflected in Karl Bittner's eyes and from his gold necklaces. Bittner no longer held hands with Grace or Irene; his hands rested on the tabletop.

"On the wings of a snow white dove . . . ," I sang. My voice trembled as I replicated the lines that began my first Angella Wing channel in Grace's workshop. "I am Angella Wing and I bring my love and gratitude to all. In particular, I have a personal message for Merrill Chase and for Karl Bittner."

"Welcome, Miss Wing," Grace said in a faint whisper. I knew she was blown away by the hologram, too, and I hoped it would not prove too much of a shock.

"I am speaking even though I have been forbidden to enter Merrill Chase's realm of thought. This is due to my wish to express my desire to 'go out,' as they say, in my own way. A bravura perform-ance, as I informed Merrill earlier. You see evidence of that before you. Strange powers are at work, and I am pleased to be received for my final bow."

I continued with such nonsense in my "Angella" voice, informing Bittner that Angella had reconsidered the possibility of having her memoirs published.

There was a pause—a long pause—while thunder drowned my thoughts. I was not certain how to continue; the image on the table was still mesmerizing us. I wasn't certain that anyone was even ab-sorbing "Angella's" words.

"My final curtain can be delayed," Angella declared with a fresh air of triumph, "only with the intercession of another. If he will have me, I shall redirect my powers to Karl Bittner, the new agent of my desires."

Everyone's concentration was still focused hypnotically on the hologram, but where was Polly? She was supposed to be helping me out. Then I saw her enter the darkened room beneath a black silk shroud. No one else (except maybe George) was able to observe her as she placed an envelope containing Angella's film in front of Bittner. His name was written on the envelope in Polly's best spidery script. I hoped it would appear to him as if it had floated there; an old-fashioned mediumship trick. Angella continued to speak without interruption to continue the subterfuge.

"As a medium, Karl Bittner will reveal the tragedies and triumphs that distinguished Angella Wing, Woman of a Thousand Voices. My story is my gift to him, to be channeled day and night. With study and perseverance, the power shall be . . ."

All was proceeding as intended when a sharp crack of lightning and thunder split the air in two. This was followed by the shattering of a nearby tree and then a deep thump as it hit the ground.

Through it all, we remained seated around the table.

"In closing, I have this warning. The Shadow used to say in the old days of radio, 'The seed of crime bears bitter fruit.'"

Angella had actually told that to me in a message only a short time ago, so I felt it was entirely appropriate to repeat in front of Bittner and give him something more to ponder.

Silence. More wind gusts. Thunder rocked the room.

"On the wings of a snow white dove . . ."

The glowing torso continued to revolve. But it was no longer me singing in Angella's voice.

Unaided by anything I could manage to utter, it was *Bittner* singing as Angella. Karl Bittner was singing Angella's song and *speaking in her voice!*

The effect was so dramatic, everyone turned to look at him.

Okay, so that was that. Bittner really was infested with Angella. I was totally spooked, but apparently the transfer was complete. Holy shit. It worked! Imagine that!

Bittner continued as Angella, but I paid little attention to what he/she said.

Hail began a tattoo upon the roof and against the windows. A damp rush of fresh air seemed as cold as ice.

The power went off—Polly's hologram faded from sight.

Angella/Bittner ceased to speak.

Lightning's staccato flash lit our modest group like strobes. But there was very little movement; everyone remained unusually still.

Then I noticed something else had begun to illuminate the room. A small white plume was forming on the table in front of Grace.

Then Grace began to speak. This time it was a poem.

> As the moon from some dark gate or cloud
> Throws o'er the sea a floating bridge of light
> Across whose trembling planks our memories crowd
> Into the realm of mystery and light—
> So far from the world of spirits there descends
> A bridge of light, connecting it with this,
> O'er whose unsteady floor, that sways and bends,
> Wander our thoughts above the dark abyss.

Immediately I thought of the holy cards distributed at Sharon's funeral, the guardian angel with outstretched hands who was guiding the little girl across the worn planks of the perilous bridge from her previous life to the mystery of the next. Certainly that was the *floating bridge of light* and the *realm of mystery.*

"Longfellow," Grace acknowledged, her voice only a sigh. "Henry Wadsworth Longfellow. We studied him in eighth grade. Do you remember, Nell?"

The small cloud, resembling white smoke, was gathering into a shape much like Polly's hologram, but outside the glass box. I didn't think it possible, but this new phenomenon was even more astonishing! I was spellbound, completely unable to move as the transparent substance turned into a gossamer substance that slowly swirled and pulsed to form a reticent outline, then the distinct likeness of a beautiful girl. It was so similar to the wraithlike apparition of Sharon at Inspiration Point that my heartbeat faltered, before it began to chase. This was another torso, but of translucent white. And the young girl had long hair that wound down around her shoulders like wet seaweed that clung to her diaphanous white dress.

I wanted to remove my glasses and rub my eyes, but I was still holding on to George and Spence as if they were the only things anchoring me to earth.

The only explanation was that Grace Waverly was creating an astonishing ectoplasmic representation of Sharon. This was physical mediumship at its most powerful and complete! I barely breathed, afraid the slightest puff of my breath would disintegrate the manifestation.

"May I come to you, Nellie?"

Grace's whisper sounded exactly like Sharon. It *was* her voice!

I fought every symptom of panic. I bit my lips until I could taste blood. My hands would not be still but twitched with energy. Electric sparks filled my veins and charged my body with static. I felt faint. I was afraid I'd be sick.

The spectacle—I don't know what else to call it—floated closer, connected to Grace by a thin thread that ran up to her lips. It paused in front of me.

There was no way I could say anything.

Sharon teased, "Cat got your tongue?"

My mouth was dry with fear. I tried to swallow but could not.

"You must confess . . ."

Was everyone else at the table a witness? I could not withdraw my gaze from Sharon's to look around but in my peripheral vision it seemed they were all frozen like zombies, unable to move.

"You told me sorrow and death were in my future. You wanted me to die!"

I formed the word "no" but did not say it aloud. Was it supposed to happen like this?

"You told everybody Bittner got me pregnant and threw me in Bear Lake and left me there. Go ahead and ask him! Clear your queer friend Polly! Say she isn't guilty of choking me to death with ice. Or are you chicken?"

What was Bittner's reaction? Could he hear Sharon speaking? I had a fleeting moment of wonder but could not see him clearly beyond the white specter floating between us and her familiar taunting persisted.

"Nellie is a chicken! Nellie is a chicken! Cluck, cluck, cluck . . ."

"I didn't kill her," Bittner muttered in his own voice. "Sharon always had a big mouth. You never knew what she was going to say . . ."

"Cock a doodle doo. . . ."

"Polly," I began, then felt George's hand clasp mine hard, as if in warning.

Bittner pleaded, "I didn't kill her! Fine . . . I was there. She was wearing my shirt. But Polly pushed her in the lake. After Polly left, I ran over to help—"

"A lot of help you were," Sharon interrupted.

"Little bitch," Bittner spat, his gaze transfixed on the apparition. "That little bitch smacked her head on the pier and puked on my shoes when I tried to pull her out of the water. Then I grabbed her by the shirt collar. Tried to pull her up again. But she slid out of the shirt and slipped back into the lake. *I didn't kill her.* I just let her go."

"You let me go," Sharon's voice stated flatly. "You let go and ran away."

"Shut up," Bittner rasped.

"Well, I'm not going to let go of *you,*" Sharon threatened. "I'm going to hang on to you for the rest of your goddamned life. You finally fucked your little virgin and let me drown, you son of a bitch!"

"SHUT UP!" Bittner screamed. He reached across the table into the amorphous substance and pushed it aside.

It dispersed like smoke.

Immediately, there was a moan, and Grace Waverly slumped over.

Except for the lightning, it was dark in the room. No one moved but there were whispers.

Spence, seated between Grace and me, reported, "I think she's dead."

Bittner's impulsive action had broken the thread of her ectoplasm. He had caused Grace Waverly to collapse.

310

I went to her side and felt for Grace's pulse. There was none.

"Oh, Grace," I murmured, bending over her crumpled form and rocking her gently in my arms. She had given all she had, even knowing how dangerous the odds were.

"I DIDN'T KILL HER!" Bittner repeated. "I JUST DIDN'T SAVE HER!"

He pushed his chair back so swiftly that it crashed to the floor, and then he ran out of the room onto the porch. When we heard the screen door bang we knew he'd fled into the storm.

The envelope Polly had placed on the table was gone. Bittner had taken Angella's film along with him.

"Wait here," George said, but of course I followed and Polly joined us.

We could barely make out the figure of Bittner in the driving rain. Why would he have turned to the right, I wondered, when I knew his car was in the parking lot up near the gate? Why would he be heading through the woods toward Inspiration Point and the dark abyss beyond?

20

This was the year I didn't have a summer.

The Wocanaga EMT squad arrived at the camp with the ambulance as promptly as possible. A tornado had struck north of the village and broken branches, flooded streets, and downed trees impeded their progress.

Grace was, indeed, dead, and the cause of death was later given as a heart attack. The coroner was satisfied that Grace's age and health problems were to blame. No one mentioned the ectoplasm she had been emanating when she died.

Power was still not restored but even after Grace's body had been removed by the paramedics our séance group was reluctant to leave the room. Everyone (except for George, Polly, and I) totally believed the phosphorescent disembodied torso *was* Angella Wing. And the burden of channeling her spirit had now passed to Karl Bittner.

Polly joined us in the séance room and I returned Sharon's scapular.

"It's wet," she said.

"I've been sweating," I explained.

"Where did Bittner go, by the way?" Spence asked. "Where's Karl?"

"He got, like, crazy and grabbed something. Then he shoved me out of the way and took off," Irene sputtered from under the table. She was searching in the darkness on her hands and knees. "Lost my stone . . ."

George said we had last seen Bittner running through the downpour toward Inspiration Point.

Many of us had flashlights, because we knew how dark the grounds became at night, and together, in the rain, we searched the camp.

Around midnight, Bittner's body was found on a craggy layer of sharp rocks at the base of the limestone shelf.

Polly thought he'd deliberately leaped to his death after "seeing" and speaking with Sharon. Polly's reaction to the ectoplasm was a lot milder than I would have predicted.

George thought the ectoplasm was "interesting" and wanted to know more about it. I told him it was a first for me, too; I had never seen it before. As for Bittner, George said the man may have become disturbed by the events of the séance and ran off just to get out of there, accidentally tumbling over the edge of the limestone shelf.

I privately wondered if it was part of Angella's grand design. Or maybe even Sharon's! Angela's film was not on Bittner's body. I will never search for it. Perhaps it no longer exists.

❧

A week went by, I think. I lost track of days. I did not leave the house, answer the phone, or fire up my computer. Polly brought in groceries and George fixed meals, but mostly I stayed in bed. Not because I was ill, but because it seemed the safest place to be. Henry stayed there, too.

One morning George was lying by my side instead of Henry. He was leaning on his elbow, watching me as I awoke.

"Where's Breeze?" I asked, rubbing the sleep from my eyes.

"Gone with the wind," he whispered.

"You're kidding," I muttered.

"No, I'm not," he said. "She's seeing a guy from Sun Prairie. Owns Leonard's Fine Jewelry and Gems."

"I don't believe it!" I hooted. "Screw you!"

"Frankly my dear, I don't give a damn."

I swiftly plunked a pillow over my head while I declared, "Get out of my bedroom! Go away! I have fur on my teeth. I need a bath!"

After a few nearly suffocating minutes, I could hear water running. George had fixed a soothing bath with an entire envelope of Breeze's leftover European Bath Therapy.

"Eucalyptus and citrus," he read, "to invigorate and relieve the exhausted body, motivate and enliven the spirit."

"Enliven the spirit?" I muttered. "That's just what I need. Another fucking lively spirit."

During my therapeutic immersion, he changed the sheets on my bed.

Sarah Vaughan's husky voice drifted into the bedroom, singing: *"I'm Glad There Is You."*

"Too loud?" George asked.

It was just right. Everything was absolutely perfect.

I sat on the side of the bed, wrapped in my thick terry cloth robe. I noticed it, too, had been freshly laundered.

I shook out my wet hair and took a deep, restorative breath.

"You are one of the bravest women I've ever known," George said, sitting down beside me. "You, Nellie Grendon, are what I'd call downright plucky."

"Oh, wow! That's just what I've been waiting to hear," I chortled, pretending to wring his neck. "Plucky. What does that mean, exactly? That I possess a lot of *pluck?* Remind me to Google *pluck.*"

"Already did," he said, "but the dictionary definition is better." He produced a piece of paper. "In addition to the usual definitions, like pluck a flower, pluck a duck, pluck the strings of an instrument, pluck also means 'Resourceful courage and daring in the face of difficulties; spirit.'"

"So, you're saying I have *spirit*. Thanks. Right now that's just what I want to hear. *Spirit!* And thanks to the bath salts it's an *enlivened spirit*." I made a screechy, banshee cry and fell back on the mattress.

"Quiet," he said. "*Pluck* also means the heart, liver, windpipe, and lungs of a slaughtered animal . . ."

I began hitting him with my pillow.

"It's from the Middle English *plukken,*" he shouted, ducking my blows.

"Plukken?" I struck him again. *"Plukken?"*

"Wait a minute! Wait."

I stopped fighting.

"*Plucky* means 'Having or showing courage or spirited resourcefulness in trying circumstances.' If that's not you, Nellie Grendon, then I'm not a *Chakra Master.*"

I hugged the pillow to my chest and hooted. "Okay, I'll bite. What the hell is that?"

"It's someone who has mastered the understanding of chakras. You know what a chakra is, right?"

"George . . ."

"While you've been malingering, I've been getting familiar with chakras." He proudly revealed a handful of New Age books. "Breeze left her reading material in my apartment. According to my humble estimation, I've determined that your chakras are out of balance."

"This is the estimation of the Chakra Master . . . ?"

"Right. The Chakra Master. At your service. Turn over."

"What?"

"I'm about to give you a chakra massage and meditation. Take off your robe while I get into my Chakra Master uniform."

The hot bath and Sarah Vaughn's music had obviously relaxed my inhibitions. Besides, this was a playful side of George that I'd seldom seen before. It was nice. I lay down on my stomach and pulled the sheet over my body. George wore a pair of blue cotton boxer shorts, a white T-shirt, and a crooked smile.

"There are various essential oils for the individual chakras," he said. "Sandalwood, patchouli, ylang ylang. Today we are going with the house oil, extra virgin olive. I hope this is acceptable."

"Certainly."

"Okay, your seventh chakra is located right here at the top of your head." He sat on the mattress beside me and massaged my damp scalp. "This violet chakra is often referred to as the 'crown chakra,' and it is where your cosmic energy connects you to the All That Is."

George buried his face in my hair. "Right now, you are all that exists for me," he whispered. His words stirred my heart so much that tears seeped out of the corners of my closed eyes.

"Thank you," I said. "I'm already feeling your healing energy."

"Okay," he said, clearing his throat because he, too, had apparently been moved by the uncustomary closeness we'd just experienced. "The sixth chakra is in the center of your forehead. I'm going to have to turn you over to contact that."

I flopped over, limp, still clinging to the sheet. My tension was drained but all my sensory nerves were excited by his touch. I was tranquil, glowing. Relaxed. I couldn't wait to see what he would do when he got to chakra numbers two and one.

"Your sixth chakra is what many refer to as the 'third eye.' It is indigo. Through this third eye, your mental pictures can become reality." His lips brushed my forehead. It was a teasing kiss, leaving me wanting more.

"Imagine this," he said, as he lightly kissed my lips.

"The fifth chakra—"

"Wait a minute," I interrupted. "I didn't quite get that last bit, about the sixth. What I'm supposed to imagine. Could you repeat that part?"

And he did.

"Okay, now the fifth chakra is the one that I judge to be the most developed, in your case. It is located here at your throat and involves all kinds of self-expression, especially the kind that reflects your inner voice. This chakra is blue." He kissed my throat. He tickled it with his tongue. He nibbled my collarbones until my body began to

316

twitch, and Henry jumped on the bed to burrow around until the sheets were pulled down to my toes.

"Henry, get off the bed!"

But, of course, Henry didn't want to leave.

"Your heart chakra is number four. It's right here, in the center of your chest . . . Woops, I got a little distracted there. Forgive me."

I'd felt his soft lips upon my nipples. It made me squirm.

"Back to the heart chakra. This is your soul's residence. The heart is green. Think of your heart as green. I know; it's novel. But it's a peaceful color, green."

He got distracted again.

Then George moved on to chakra number three.

"Here in your solar plexus is the site of your personal power and creativity." Apparently that didn't evoke any passion because he blew a big raspberry on my belly that made Henry yip and hide under the bed.

"But now I want to turn my attention to chakra number two," George insisted. "In my estimation, as a Chakra Master . . ." I whooped at that again and he tried hard to maintain his solemnity. "I notice that you have experienced a definite lack of activity in this region. This is . . . ahem . . . located a couple of inches below your navel and some associate it with the color orange and with sex and sympathy." He placed his hand there. "I can see we are going to have to give this chakra some remedial attention."

"And chakra one," I asked, "what about that?"

"The first chakra is located at the base of your spine. It's red, representing blood and vitality. With this chakra you become grounded in physical reality."

"Physical," I said. "Let's have some of that sex and sympathy and physical stuff. Reality can wait."

We made love with soft jazz in the background. It was more beautiful than anything I could have imagined.

Henry was very confused and whimpered.

It was really hard to tell them both good-bye.

My visa is good for six months. I'm only just now beginning to think about what I'll do when I go home, where George and Henry are waiting. Right now I'm seated in a comfortable chair by the fire at the residence of my daughter, Odessa, and her husband, in Tauranga, New Zealand. Cassia, my granddaughter, wants me to read to her again but I've already read to her for an hour and sleepy Nana needs a nap.

It's winter here and it rains much of the time. I'm learning to knit.

George and Polly are caring for my house. Frydeswyde Quimby's house. George says plans for the veranda have been approved by the National Register of Historic Places, and construction will begin in autumn. Autumn in Madison, spring in New Zealand. Henry sends his regards. I miss them a lot.

My seasons are in disarray. I'm all turned around.

Polly, in touch daily by e-mail, insists that I write a book about the past year. "You have such a great story to tell," she pleads. "You owe it to yourself, and you owe it to me, too. Maybe even Bittner. I suppose you could include Sharon if the equation doesn't cause alarm."

Polly's suggestion has caused me to reflect on my brief life as a spirit-medium. I suppose it would be helpful and even therapeutic if I'd make an attempt to sort it out.

Not long ago, Spirit told me, "Our lives are bound in an inextricable way."

I know how I'll begin, if I do manage the initiative to write. My book will open with these words that Grace taught me, to ask permission:

"May I come to you?"

Author's Note

When my daughter was living in Buffalo, New York, she introduced me to the Lily Dale Assembly in Cassadaga because she suspected I'd find it appealing. Of course I was entranced and owe the genesis of this book to Laura Rath Beausire. Jay Rath, my son and author of several books on unexplained phenomena, also shares my belief of things unseen.

Following my Lily Dale introduction in 1995, I arranged to sit in on a few workshops there and take notes for this book. British medium and clairvoyant Rose Clifford taught a week of "Personal Development of Mediumship" and insisted that everyone in the room participate because "I can see all of your spirit guides standing behind you!" Many of the lessons attributed to Grace Waverly in this novel were offered by Rose, who—at the close of the workshop in which I'd unwittingly participated—told me I had strong psychic powers that she hoped I'd pursue. "I'm surprised you did not channel," she said, "because your throat chakra is so strong."

The following summer Cynthia Pearson Turich and I shared a hotel room at Lily Dale's Leolyn Hotel. Cynthia loaned me her books on channeling and we sought daily messages at Forest Temple and Inspiration Stump. Later, I consulted John Buescher's website, spirithistory.com, for further insight. There I discovered an abundance of data and developed a prized friendship that has endured for over a decade via Internet. John's vast and varied knowledge and his detailed manuscript critiques have proven invaluable to me.

I became familiar with the Morris Pratt Institute in Wauwatosa, Wisconsin, while living only a few miles away in Elm Grove. I

...ast library of Spiritualism materials and the wis-
...ediums. When we moved to Spring Green, I discov-
...ely Wonewoc Spiritualist Camp only forty-three miles
...onewoc became the fictional setting for "Wocanaga" and in-
...orates some of the more arcane Lily Dale attributes.

The "Little Wolf" dimension of this book shares many auto-biographical elements from my childhood in Manawa, Wisconsin. Kathy Jansen contributed her memories of Sister School. I could depend on other reminiscences from Mary Ann Craig, Dick Kaphingst, Betty Groholski, and my brother, Art Lindsay.

I am indebted to my stepdaughter, Nancy McMahon, for her nursing expertise and to Dr. Ron Schmidt, my dentist in Menomonee Falls, who one day during a root canal suggested his ice cube theory of murder.

Dorinda Hartmann at the Wisconsin Center for Film and Theater Research was most helpful with her suggestions, and I hope Ruth Perrott (1899–1996), once known as the "Woman of a Thousand Voices," is pleased with her final starring role as Angella Wing.

Wil B. Roeder, a Llewellyn Setter, served as my model for Henry but he is a much better hunter.

I also extend my gratitude to Ludmilla Bollow, my dependable friend and essential critic of my work; Jill Dean, James Gollata, Eileen Roeder, Gail Peterson, Betty Irwin, Sarah Day, Judy Swartz Marcus, Linda and Ben Bolton, Jack Rath, Judi Rees Alvarado, Carol Anderson and her Spring Green Library staff, my editors Raphael Kadushin and Sheila Moermond, and all my friends at the University of Wisconsin Press.

One of my first short stories in a genre much like this appeared in *The Arkham Collector,* edited by August Derleth. He was an early mentor and taught me to appreciate that reality is not always as it seems.

And finally, my patient husband, Del Lamont, has been an incredible gift in my life. He makes it possible for me to sit at my desk and write all day. When I need to hear it most, he tells me everything will be all right. And it always is.